# DIXIE
## *Hearts*

# ANDREA BOESHAAR
## KAY CORNELIUS DEBRA ULLRICK

BARBOUR
PUBLISHING

Cover model photography: Jim Celuch, Celuch Creative Imaging

Published by Barbour Publishing, Inc., P.O. Box 719, Uhrichsville, Ohio 44683, www.barbourbooks.com

*Our mission is to publish and distribute inspirational products offering exceptional value and biblical encouragement to the masses.*

Member of the
Evangelical Christian
Publishers Association

Printed in the United States of America.

# SOUTHERN SYMPATHIES

by Andrea Boeshaar

# Dedication

This story was originally published almost ten years ago. Back then, my youngest son, Brian, was in high school and *Southern Sympathies* was his favorite out of all my stories. Today, Brian is a grown man, married, and a member of the U.S. Army National Guard. Just recently he learned that he and his wife will deploy to Iraq early in 2009. This will be his second tour of duty.

So this story is dedicated, again, to my son Brian, of whom I am so very proud!

# Chapter 1

*S*ixty-five degrees and sunny! With a smile, Alec Corbett gazed up at the clear blue Alabama sky. *Sure wouldn't see this kind of weather in Wisconsin on the last weekend of January. Then, again, you never know. Wisconsin weather is about as fickle as a woman!*

Walking toward the house he'd just purchased, Alec tried not to let his thoughts stray. No use dwelling on the past—a past that included an engagement gone bad and one whimsical woman named Denise Lisinski.

*Don't think about her,* he admonished himself, pulling the keys from his blue jeans pocket. *Too nice a day to think about Denise.*

Standing on the small front porch, Alec could hear the wind rustling through the treetops of the quiet neighborhood. There weren't any sidewalks such as those he was accustomed to after years of big-city living. Only a simple asphalt road that meandered down the block.

Alec glanced across the narrow strip of lawn that served as a dividing line between his property and his neighbor's. And, although he was quite content with his own place—a low-maintenance ranch-styled home encased in a combination of brown brick and tan aluminum—he had to admit an aesthetic appreciation of the older, two-story red brick house next door. White shutters framed the home's windows facing the street, while the front entrance was graced with a huge cement porch, complete with massive white pillars.

*Well, look at that,* he thought, spying the wooden swing hanging at the end of the portico. He could suddenly envision two lovers sitting there together, talking, sharing their most intimate thoughts.

*Whoa, I gotta quit thinking like some heartsick schoolboy,* he berated himself. *I'm not engaged to Denise anymore. I'm not getting married. I'm moving into this house today, in a different town, a different state—*

"Hey, Alec! Should we start unloading the truck now? I backed it into the driveway."

He turned at the sound of his friend's voice. Tim Parker and four other men from church had volunteered to help him move today. "Yeah, sure. I'll open up and we can start hauling furniture."

Alec unlocked the door and walked in. The air in the living room felt cool and still—the calm before the moving-in storm. Quickly roaming from room to room, he mentally placed all his belongings in various sites. His bedroom set in here, the extra double bed in a guest room there, and an office where he could set up his computer in the smallest of the three bedrooms. He chuckled, thinking that in a matter of minutes this one-story ranch home would be a whirlwind of activity.

"Okay, where do you want 'em?" Tim carried in two matching lamps while his glasses slid slightly down his nose.

Alec strode purposely to the front door. "Those can stay here in the living room."

"Hey, Alec," dark-headed Larry Matthews asked, holding one end of a dresser while Rick Stevens held the other, "where do you want this?"

"Master bedroom. Go down the hallway. . .to the right. That's it."

Alec sighed. It was going to be a long, but very exciting day. Moving into this house meant the start of a new life for him!

🌺

"Boy, he's sure gotta lotta junk!" Eight-year-old Tyler Boswick watched his new neighbor move in. He peered down at his younger sister, Brooke, who stood on the fence beside him. "I hope he's got some kids."

"Me, too. And I hope he's got a girl my age." Her brown eyes grew wide. "Here he comes again, Ty, ask him."

"Okay. . . Hey, mister," he called. The man headed for the moving truck stopped and looked over at them expectantly. "Are you the one moving in?"

"Yep, that's me."

Tyler considered him, straw-colored hair and the kind of face he'd seen on a fighting army man on TV. Tough—but nice to the good guys and kids. His interest shifted to the man's clothing—faded blue T-shirt and dirty jeans. They were hard-working clothes, by the looks of them. *Yeah*, Ty decided, *he just might be a dad.*

"Well, I was just wondering, do you have any kids our age?"

"Nope. Sorry."

Dashing all of Tyler's hopes in a mere fraction of a second, the man continued on his way.

"Do you have any kids at all?" Brooke asked hopefully. "A little girl like me, maybe?"

Pausing and turning toward them again, the man shook his head and grinned. Tyler thought he appeared a lot friendlier when he smiled. "No, I don't have any kids. I'm not married."

Brooke frowned. "That's too bad."

He chuckled. "Depends on how you look at it."

Tyler exchanged puzzled glances with his sister. Then they both shrugged simultaneously and watched the man walk up the ramp into the moving truck and come back out.

"He sure is strong," Brooke remarked.

"Aw, that's nothing." Tyler didn't want to admit that carrying four kitchen chairs, two looped through each arm, was fairly impressive. "Men can carry lots of heavy things at once."

"Not Grampa," Brook countered. "He only carries his Bible."

"That's cuz he's a preacher of a whole big church, dodo bird. He gets other people to carry all his heavy stuff."

Brooke narrowed her eyes at him. "Don't call me 'dodo' or I'm telling Mama."

"Go ahead," Tyler replied, lifting his chin stubbornly. "But if you tell, we'll have to go in."

Brooke clamped her mouth shut. Neither of them wanted to go inside for the night and he knew it. And if little tattletale Brooke told their mother, they'd have to go in early for their Saturday night baths.

Both children looked on curiously as two other men emerged, walked into the truck, then reappeared, wheeling a refrigerator toward the house. Next, their new neighbor carried in a stove, aided by another of his friends. But minutes later, he showed up again with nothing more than a can of cola in one hand. Much to Tyler's surprise, he sauntered over to them.

"Are you gonna holler at us for standing on the fence?" Brooke inquired, her voice quivering slightly. "Mr. Smith used to holler at us."

"Naw, I'm not going to holler." The man sat on the corner of the picnic table that a couple of men had put in the wide backyard hours before. "I don't care if you stand on it. I think that fence has seen better days, anyway." He eyed them speculatively. "What are your names?"

"I'm Tyler Michael Boswick. And this is my sister, Brooke Elizabeth Boswick."

The man grinned. "Glad to meet you, Tyler. . .Brooke. I'm Alec."

"Mr. Alec?" Brooke asked uncertainly.

"No. Alec Corbett. But you can call me by my first name."

"Oh no, sir, we can't!" Brooke shook her blond head vigorously. "Mama says it's *dispectful* to call a grown-up by his first name."

"She means 'disrespectful,'" Tyler said informatively. "She's only five."

"Almost six," Brooke corrected him.

Tyler shrugged, unimpressed. "I'm almost nine."

Mr. Alec smiled. "Have you two lived here a long time?"

"All our lives," Tyler replied. "What about you?"

"I'm from Milwaukee, Wisconsin, but now Woodruff, Alabama, is my home."

"Hmm. Well, my best friend, Matt Smith, used to live in your house, but he moved."

"Where to?"

"Far from here. His dad got another job. . .all the way in Columbus."

"That's not so far away."

"Oh, yes it is." Memories of his friend's moving day resurfaced. That had been the saddest day in all of Tyler's life—next to his dad dying, that is."

"Georgia is just the next state over. Columbus is on the border."

"Georgia?" Tyler felt confused.

"Aren't you talking about Columbus, Georgia?"

Tyler shook his head. "I'm talking about Columbus, Tennessee."

Mr. Alec threw his head back and laughed. It was such a happy sound that it made Tyler smile. "Well, Tennessee isn't all that far, but it's farther away than Georgia. I'll give you that much."

Tyler blew out a sad sigh. Deep inside he knew he'd never see Matt again. Tennessee might as well be on the other side of the world. He wasn't sure what had happened, but something had—something bad. And that was why Mr. Smith got another job and moved away. Far away.

"So where does your dad work?" Mr. Alec wanted to know.

"We don't have a daddy," Brooke informed him with a sad expression. "He died when I was three."

"I'm sorry to hear that."

"But he's in heaven, so it's okay," Tyler quickly added. "And Mama doesn't cry so much anymore. Hardly at all, even."

"That's good. . .I guess."

Tyler watched as Mr. Alec took a gulp of his cola. He wondered what his grandfather would think of this man. Grampa Boswick always said that it was rude to drink straight out of a can. Gentlemen used a drinking glass.

"So, do you guys go to church?"

"Uh-huh," Brooke said, nodding. "Mama says we all but live at church."

"Is that right?" Mr. Alec chuckled again, and Tyler got the feeling his new neighbor liked kids a whole lot more than he let on.

"Mama works at church," Brooke said. "She's a secatary."

"Secretary?" Mr. Alec grinned.

"Yep. And our grampa is the pastor."

"Which church?"

"Southern Pride Community Church," Tyler replied. "We call it SPCC for short."

"Hmm. . ." Their new neighbor got a thoughtful look on his face. "Is that the big church off the highway between here and Montgomery Regional Airport?"

"I think so." Tyler wasn't sure. He'd have to ask Mama later.

"It is," Brooke piped in.

"Aw, you don't know."

"Uh-huh. I see the sign that says *airport* every day on the way to school." She turned to Mr. Alec with a sweet expression—the very one that always made their mama go easier on her when they both got in trouble. "Our school is in the same place as our church."

"I think I know the church and school you mean."

Tyler didn't reply, but it irritated him that his little sister seemed to know something he didn't. Maybe he'd have to pay more attention on the way to church tomorrow.

"Tyler! Brooke!" Their mother's soft voice floated over to them from where she stood on the back porch. "Time to come in now."

"Rats!" Tyler grumbled.

"Comin', Mama," Brooke replied, jumping down off the fence. She was acting like a goody-two-shoes and it annoyed Tyler to no end!

Mr. Alec stood up and stretched. "Well, I guess my break is over, too. Nice meeting you, Tyler."

"Thanks, but you can call me Ty. All my friends do."

The man chuckled. "Okay, *Ty*. I guess we'll be seeing each other around."

"I reckon so." Tyler hopped off the fence and walked as slowly as he could toward the door, where his mother still stood waiting for him. He even stopped to pick up an old, worn-out penny from the driveway, but, much to Tyler's dismay, she didn't go on inside ahead of him.

"Come on, Ty, hurry up. Your bath is getting cold."

He grimaced. "Can't Brooke go first?"

His mother raised her eyebrow in reply and he knew he'd better not fuss—when Mama raised her brow, she meant business!

He trudged up the back steps. "Yes, ma'am," he muttered, walking past her into the house.

"Who were you and Brooke talking to?"

"Mr. Alec Corbett." Tyler perked up. Maybe if he talked about the new neighbor, his mother would forget about the bath. "He's real nice, Mama, and he told Brooke and me to call him Mr. Alec for short."

"So he's the one who bought the Smiths' house. I'd been wondering who was moving in all day."

"Yep, it's him." Tyler watched as his mother threw one last glance out the back door before closing it tightly. "He's certainly a tall fellow, isn't he?"

"Sure is," Brooke piped in. "He's really strong, too."

"Oh?"

"Yes, but he talks kinda funny." She wrinkled her nose just like she did whenever Mama made something different for supper.

"Where's he from?"

"Milwaukee, Wisconsin," Tyler replied with a puzzled frown. "Where is that, anyhow?"

Mama smiled, making her blue gray eyes shine. "I'll show you on the map hanging on your bedroom wall right before bedtime—*after* your bath."

Tyler groaned, ignoring the amused expression on his mother's face. Why did she have to remember *everything*?

"Does Mr. Alec have a family?" she asked, steering him toward the bathroom.

"Nope. Just him." Tyler paused, wishing the knot in his throat would go away. "No kids. . ."

"Oh, I'm so sorry, honey. I know how disappointed you must be."

Mama captured him in an embrace, drawing him to her slim body, which always smelled as good as the summer flower garden she planted every year behind the house. Then she kissed his cheek. "At least you'll always have Jesus," she whispered near his ear. "Jesus will never leave you."

Suddenly Tyler felt like crying. He wiggled out of his mother's arms since he didn't want her to see. "I better go take my bath."

Grabbing hold of the bottom of his T-shirt, he pulled it up over his head as he entered the bathroom. He shut the door, and while he finished undressing, he tried not to think of how Matt Smith had moved away forever and how a grown-up had taken over his best friend's house next door.

# Chapter 2

Lydia Boswick peered out her kitchen window as she finished cleaning up the supper dishes. Lights glowed from the house next door, and seeing them caused her heart to ache for her dear friend Sherry Smith. They'd been close for years, chatting over cups of coffee and helping each other out with their kids. When Michael died, Sherry had been such a comfort to Lydia. But then the Smiths abandoned their faith, according to Lydia's father-in-law, and they'd all but turned their backs on their brothers and sisters in Christ at Southern Pride Community Church. Sherry stopped talking to Lydia right after Christmas; and, though it had been the death of a friendship as opposed to a husband, it hurt almost as much as losing Michael. And losing her mother, even though Mama wasn't dead—physically, anyway.

*Don't think about her now,* she chastened herself. *Mama made her decisions. Now she has to live with them. . .and so do I.*

Pushing aside her tumultuous thoughts, Lydia chanced one last look through the blue-and-white-checked curtains adorning the little window above her kitchen sink. She could see the backyard next door and the five men who sat around a picnic table. Weren't they freezing? Since sundown, the temperatures had fallen into the fifties. Lydia wondered if they were drinking alcoholic beverages and, therefore, had become numb to the cold. Adding soap, closing the dishwasher, and turning on the machine, she silently dreaded being a neighbor to a single man who had nothing better to do than party with his friends all night long.

"Mama, it's eight o'clock," Tyler hollered from upstairs. "Are you coming to hear our prayers?"

"I'm on my way."

Lydia glanced around her kitchen to be sure she hadn't left some task undone. *Now to get those kids to bed.*

"Mama, come hear my prayers first," Brooke insisted.

The girl grabbed Lydia's hand just as she reached the upper hallway, pulling her mother toward her bedroom. Brooke's bright blond hair shone from its scrubbing earlier that evening. She was dressed for bed in her pink nightie, and Lydia thought her daughter resembled a life-sized, huggable, kissable doll. She could hardly refuse the request. Besides, Tyler wouldn't mind if Brooke said her prayers first. Glancing across the hall and into his bedroom, Lydia spied him playing on the computer his grampa Boswick purchased for him a couple of months ago as a Christmas gift.

Lydia followed Brooke into her room. Tucking her in, she sat on the edge of the twin bed that was draped in a pink lacy comforter and heaped with stuffed animals. "There's hardly room for you in this bed," Lydia remarked with a smile.

"That's cuz Grampa keeps buying me all these aminals." Brooke grabbed a sweet-faced lion and hugged it tightly. "I love 'em."

"Animals," she gently corrected, " and I know how much they mean to you."

"And I named every one. . .just like Adam got to name all the aminals that God gave him. This one's name is Mr. Lion."

"That's very original," Lydia said teasingly, although the humor was lost on the five-year-old.

"We're learning about Adam and Eve in Sunday school."

"That's right." Kissing her daughter's forehead, Lydia was suddenly reminded of the lesson she had to prepare for the ladies' Bible study she taught right before the Sunday morning service the next day. "All right, say your prayers now."

Brooke squeezed her eyes closed and then folded her hands over Mr. Lion. "God bless Grampa Boswick and Gramma Boswick, Gramma Reimer—" She paused. "What's her new name again? I forgot."

"Jackson." Another little piece of her heart crumbled. "She's Gramma Jackson now."

Brooke nodded. "And God bless Gramma Jackson, Mama, Tyler. . .and me."

She peeked at Lydia, who raised a questioning brow. "That's not much of a prayer."

"I know, 'cept it's all I can think of right now."

"Very well." Lydia bestowed one last kiss on Brooke's cheek and wished her a good night's sleep. "You can talk to Jesus any time, not just when I'm listening to your bedtime prayers."

The little girl nodded once more.

Smiling, Lydia shut off the lamp beside Brooke's bed and left the room, closing the door behind her.

"Tyler, time to turn off that computer," she announced, crossing the hallway.

"Aw, do I have to?"

"Yes."

"But I'm trying to see if Matt's e-mail still works."

"It probably doesn't."

"I'm almost done typing the letter. . . ."

"Okay. Finish up, but make it quick. You can type a longer message once you find out if Matt has the same online address."

The boy smiled, turned back to the computer screen, and continued his "hunt-and-peck" method of typing out a message to his friend.

Sitting down on the end of Tyler's bed, Lydia surveyed her son's room. Blue and green plaid walls surrounded the heavy mahogany furniture that had once belonged to Michael when he was a child.

Michael. Oddly enough, thinking about him didn't hurt nearly as badly as it once did. She could even talk about him now and his freak heart attack without choking on her emotions and tears. Dead at the age of thirty-four. Who would have ever guessed it? Not Michael's parents, who'd never known about their only son's rare heart condition, one that had gone undetected until the autopsy. Not Lydia, who was crazy in love with the tall, blond, handsome young man whom she'd met right after she and her mother joined Southern Pride Community Church.

She'd been just sixteen years old at the time. He was twenty, refined, educated, and mature. They were immediately and obviously attracted to each other, and they fell hopelessly in love. While the Boswicks encouraged Michael to marry a slew of other young ladies—those closer to his age—Michael had waited determinedly for Lydia, even though they'd been separated while he went to college and law school. Then finally they were married the day after her twenty-first birthday. Tyler arrived three years later and Brooke, three years after him. Life had been perfectly blissful. . .until Michael died.

"Okay, I'm done," Tyler said, causing Lydia to snap out of her reminiscing.

He jumped into bed and dove under the sheets, ruffling the light blue comforter. Smiling, Lydia tousled his hair. Both children had inherited their father's coloring, blond hair with deep brown eyes. Her heart used to ache just looking at them, remembering her beloved husband each and every time she did so. But time was a healer of wounds, and though Lydia once thought she'd never get over the pain of losing Michael, it had dulled to the point of being tolerable. She'd even been able to counsel a new widow at church, another sign that she was healing.

"Thank You, God, for bringing me and my family through another day," Tyler began. "Please bless Grampa and Gramma Boswick. . . ."

As her son continued to say his routine bedtime prayers, Lydia's thoughts strayed, and time after time she had to force herself to concentrate on what he was saying. She still had much to do before she could call it a night.

"And please, God, give me a new bike."

That got her attention. "Tyler. . . ?"

"Well, my birthday is coming up on May first. I just wanna make sure God has plenty of time to get it."

Lydia made a *tsk* sound with her tongue. "You have a bike."

"I know. But I want a mountain bike—like the one Matt got at Christmas."

Shaking her head, Lydia thought her son had more toys than he could possibly ever need—and then some! "Tyler, we should pray for people who don't have all the nice things we do. There are children right here in the United States who don't have a place to sleep tonight. They're poor and homeless. But look at you. . .you're very blessed, all snuggled in a warm, cozy bed with lots of toys around you. It's selfish to ask for more."

Tyler looked quite contrite. "Oh, all right." He closed his eyes and resumed his prayers. "God, if you get me that new bike, I promise I'll give my old one to a poor child."

Lydia shook her head at him, but Tyler kept praying. "And please make that bike a red and black one." Peeking at his mother, he added, "I also ask for all the poor, homeless children in the world—please find them homes, Lord. I'll even share my bedroom with another boy if You want me to."

The offer touched Lydia's heart, reminding her that Tyler could be very benevolent most of the time.

At last, her son finished his prayers and Lydia gave him a good-night kiss on the cheek. "Sweet dreams," she murmured as he turned onto his side sleepily.

"Sweet dreams. . ." Then suddenly he sat upright, his forehead nearly colliding with Lydia's chin.

"Now what?"

"I forgot to ask God something else."

She sighed impatiently, thinking this was one of Ty's many ploys of bedtime procrastination. "All right. Be quick about it."

He closed his eyes. "Dear God, please send me and Brooke a new daddy."

Lydia stifled a gasp of surprise. He'd never prayed for *that* before. Moreover, his voice rang with sincerity.

"He'd have to be a special daddy," Tyler continued, "to take the place of our real daddy who's in heaven. But I know You can do it, God. Amen!" Flopping back against his pillows, the eight-year-old grinned up at her. "Okay, now I can go to sleep."

Startled out of a reply, Lydia could only nod. She walked out of the room and closed the door softly. Taking the stairs slowly, she wondered why her son would ask God for a new daddy. Surely it wasn't because he felt a particular fondness for any certain man. Lydia didn't date, although lately her father-in-law, Gerald Boswick, had been trying to coax her into going out with his attorney, who was also the church's treasurer, Simeon Crenshaw. The only trouble was, Lydia didn't feel interested, and since Gerald wasn't pushing too hard, she politely refused Sim, ignoring the fall bouquet of flowers he'd sent her last Thanksgiving Day and the long-stemmed red roses accompanied by a box of expensive chocolates at Christmas.

*I'll have to make a point to question Ty about this new daddy thing tomorrow,* she thought, picking up the manila folder off the desk in the living room. Opening it, she pulled out her Bible study notes. She crossed the room and, making herself comfortable in the brightly upholstered, wingback armchair, she began to plan her lesson.

🌺

Sunday afternoon shone with promise as Alec drove his sleek black Chevy pickup back home after the worship service and the potluck luncheon that followed. He had visited the small community of Woodruff, Alabama, several times before actually making the move from Wisconsin, and he'd liked what he'd seen—still did. Life moved at a slower pace down here. Even the fast-food places were slow. But people seemed friendlier and more innocent, to the point that Alec considered them backwards, but in a complimentary way. Who needed big-city sophistication with its high crime rate? Not him. Not anymore. This little town, not far from the Florida panhandle and gulf coast, suited him just fine.

Turning into his driveway, Alec sent up a prayer of thanks that he'd so easily found a local church to attend. It was perfect for him, quaint and simple—a reflection of his own personality. And Mark Spencer, the pastor of Berean Baptist Church, was a man with whom Alec's spirit identified. He was a down-to-earth African-American whose heart and enthusiasm for people of all races were contagious. A soft-spoken man, Pastor Spencer wasn't flamboyant. His services were filled with practical teachings from God's Word. Even the church building wasn't anything to speak of, with its gray aluminum siding and modest chapel inside, housing metal folding chairs instead of pews. But Alec had learned firsthand that appearances could be deceiving. He refused to judge the congregation solely on its dwelling. He wasn't disappointed, either. Berean's church members turned out to be warm and personable, and just as they'd received him with open arms weeks ago, during his last "just making sure" visit to Woodruff, they'd welcomed him today. Alec appreciated that.

Parking his truck outside the garage, he suddenly thought about his boss, Greg Nivens. Ever since Alec started working at the national firm of Heritage Craft Furniture and Cabinetry, where he labored as a carpenter, Greg had been doing his best to talk Alec into attending his church, Southern Pride Community Church. It was nearer to Montgomery, the large city in which he worked, so right away he wasn't interested. He'd rather stick closer to home. Then the kids next door had mentioned the very same body of believers yesterday. Alec had begun to wonder if maybe the Lord really wanted him there—as if God were giving him hints, leading his thoughts toward SPCC for a special reason. However, Alec got divine assurance this morning. He was most definitely attending the right church.

Getting out of the garage, he spied the bicycle he'd bought for Denise before she'd broken their engagement. Why had he brought it down here? He should have given it to charity before moving from Wisconsin. Then again, he hadn't been thinking straight since Thanksgiving. Heartbreak did that to a guy, he reasoned. But still, to haul a lousy bike across the country. . .

Alec shook his head and continued making his way toward the house. Childish giggles wafted across the yard, causing him to pause in his tracks. The boy, Ty, waved from his perch on the large wooden gym set, and his little sister repeated the greeting. Alec waved back, smiling and walking the rest of the way to the house. Those kids sure were cute. He fished in his trouser pocket for his keys and then thought of Denise's bike. He couldn't use it—the frame was too small for him. Why not give it to Tyler? The boy would probably appreciate it, and Alex wouldn't have to look at it every time he passed the garage.

"Hey, kid," he called from his small back porch. "Tyler, come over to the fence. I want to ask you something."

The boy immediately complied. "Yes, Mr. Alec?"

"Could you use a bike?"

He shrugged.

"Here, let me show it to you. It's brand new." Alec fetched it from the garage, and the boy's brown eyes grew as big as dessert plates.

"Wow! A red-and-black mountain bike! Just what I prayed for! Mama, Mama," he yelled, turning toward the house and cupping his mouth with his hands, "come see how God answered my prayer. Mama, come out here!"

His mother, a petite brunette, stepped out of the back door. "Tyler, you stop that hollering. It's rude."

She gave Alec an apologetic look and he smiled. How could he help but smile? She was lovely, dressed in a long, bluish gray dress and matching heels. He watched as she gracefully stepped to the fence. Her gaze met his and Alec noticed her eyes were a dusky color—the same hue as her outfit.

"I'm Lydia Boswick," she said in a Southern velvet tone, offering her right hand. "I see you've met my children."

Alec took her hand, keenly aware of how small and cool it felt in his. "Yes. . ." It was the most intelligent reply he could think of.

"Mama, Mr. Alec is giving me this bike. Look!"

Alec released her hand and gave the woman an embarrassed grin. "Bought it for someone who didn't want it. I thought maybe your son would have some use for it."

"Oh, I'm sure he would." She assessed the bicycle with a dubious expression.

"It's what I prayed for, right, Mama?"

"Yes," she answered slowly, "it seems to fit your exact description."

"I prayed for a red-and-black mountain bike," Tyler told Alec, fairly gyrating in all his excitement.

"Well, here you go." Alec lifted the thing over the fence. "It's all yours."

"We can't accept such a gift—"

"Really, you'd be doing me a favor. It's way too small a bike for me anyway.

I'd just have to find another way to get rid of it. And after all, it is the answer to the boy's prayer."

Lydia smiled. "That's very generous of you, Mr. . . ?"

"Corbett. Alec Corbett. Call me Alec." His tongue suddenly felt six inches thick.

She smiled. "Well. . .Alec. . .you're very generous. Thank you."

"Aw, it's nothing. Like I said, I bought it for someone who didn't want it."

Tyler straddled the bike. It looked a little big for him, although he managed to reach the pedals from the seat. He took a quick but shaky spin around the wide end of the driveway.

"Let me grab my tools and then you bring that bike over here," Alec told the boy. "Maybe I can lower the seat a notch—the handlebars, too."

"Thanks!" Tyler beamed, while Brooke had gone back to her swing. He glanced at his mother. "Can I?"

She hesitated, then nodded. "Yes, but don't make a pest of yourself. I'm sure our new neighbor has a lot of other things to accomplish today."

"Naw, nothing's going on. It's okay," Alec heard himself say before he winced inwardly. He had a kazillion things to do! Something about this modern-day Southern belle caused him to act as though he didn't have a brain in his head!

"Now God just has to answer my other prayer. . .for a new daddy. I don't suppose you can help Him out with that one, too, Mr. Alec."

"Tyler!" his mother declared, a crimson blush running up her neck and cheeks.

Alec grinned sardonically, his senses returning in full force. "Sorry, pal." He gazed at Tyler's innocent countenance. "God's on His own there."

He glanced at Lydia, who wore an expression of chagrin. She seemed sincere, but then Denise had seemed sincere, too—at first. Was it a mask? Maybe Lydia Boswick coaxed her kids to "break the ice" with eligible men. Maybe she played the same kind of games that all women played. Well, he wouldn't fall for it again. Praying for a husband, was she? Well, it wouldn't be him!

"Nice meeting you," he said curtly, adding a stiff nod before turning and striding toward his house. No way was he going to get sucked in by another female's wiles. Not even if she was a pretty little thing with kitten gray eyes who looked as though she'd welcome the strength of a man.

*Right.*

He unlocked his back door and walked into the hallway. Women like Lydia Boswick could appeal to a male's ego, that's for sure! But he wasn't going to be swayed by her Southern charm. No sir. Not him!

# Chapter 3

"Tyler, you shouldn't have said that!"

"Said what?"

Lydia gazed into her eight-year-old's face, noting his dark brown eyes were veiled with naiveté. "Oh, never mind," she replied gently, unable to reprimand her son right there and then. They'd have to discuss proper social etiquette another time. "Just make sure you don't go inside the neighbor's house, all right?"

"Why, Mama?"

"Because we don't know Mr. Corbett very well, now do we? Besides, I'm sure he has plenty to do since he just moved in yesterday."

"Okay. . ."

Lydia turned toward the house as Tyler led his new bicycle down the driveway. She entered the kitchen and spotted her straight-backed mother-in-law, standing at the sink, cleaning up lunch dishes.

"Who's that man you were conversing with, Lydia?" she asked over one narrow shoulder.

"My new neighbor. He just moved in yesterday and would you believe he gave Tyler a bicycle? Why, it looks brand new!"

Elberta Boswick turned off the faucet and swung around. "He gave that boy a bicycle?" Her face was heavily lined with age and even more so now that she was frowning. "And you allowed it?"

Lydia shifted uncomfortably. "Yes, Mother Boswick. I mean, I didn't see a reason to reject the kind offer. And Tyler so wanted a bike just exactly like it. . . ."

"We Boswicks take care of our own, Lydia," she stated sharply. "You know that. If Tyler had a need, you should have let Gerald know about it."

Lydia opened her mouth to explain herself but thought better of it. Elberta was a proud woman and often looked at gifts as charity—something the Boswicks would never stoop to accept. Why, they'd starve to death first! Hadn't their ancestors done much the same during the Civil War? Ah, yes, Lydia had heard all about it, and generally she felt privileged to have a part in such a wealth of heritage. Unfortunately, her mother-in-law had never treated her with the same kindnesses as a *real* member of the Boswick family. It used to anger Michael, but it hurt Lydia. Still did.

"What's going on here?" Gerald Boswick asked curiously, entering the kitchen, a cup and saucer in his right hand. A tall man, pushing sixty years old, he remained a handsome and imposing figure. Lydia had always thought he resembled the Hollywood actor Kirk Douglas, right down to the cleft in his chin.

"Lydia has allowed Tyler to accept a bicycle from a perfect stranger." After another disproving frown, Mother Boswick turned back to the dishes in the sink.

Gerald glanced at Lydia, sending her an affectionate wink—one that said he'd handle his wife just as he always did.

"Well now, dear, I won't have you fretting over a bike. I'll take care of everything. Lydia and I will have a talk later."

"Good."

Lydia exchanged a glance with her father-in-law, knowing he'd allow Tyler to keep the bike. Gerald denied the children and her nothing. In fact, Lydia didn't know what she would have done if her father-in-law hadn't stepped in after Michael died. She'd been so frightened, worried, and dazed—with Michael gone, Lydia had felt helpless.

That was when Gerald efficiently took over, handling everything from funeral and burial arrangements to insurance policies and bank statements. Then he'd suggested she become his secretary at SPCC. He promised her flexible hours so Tyler and Brooke would never have to be in daycare. He said it would keep her mind off her grief, and he'd been right. Moreover, he took on the role of her agent, paying her monthly bills and mortgage payment, drawing out of the funds from Michael's life insurance policy, and Lydia felt indebted to Gerald Boswick for his unfailing care and protection.

"How about some more coffee, dear?" he asked now with a winning smile that caused his dark eyes to dance.

"Yes, of course. . ."

She crossed the room, took his cup, then strode to the counter by the sink, where the pot of flavored brew sat warming in its automatic maker. As she reached for the carafe, she glanced out the window and spied Tyler watching Mr. Alec Corbett at work on the bicycle. She poured the coffee, eyeing her new neighbor speculatively. He'd removed his tie and navy suit jacket, revealing a white dress shirt tucked into dark blue pants. *He is quite a handsome man*, she admitted inwardly, taking another note of his full head of sandy blond hair. He had an athletic look about him, and she guessed him to be an inch or two taller than her father-in-law, who stood over six feet. And such broad shoulders, muscular arms—

"Lydia!"

At Mother Boswick's shriek, she stopped pouring the coffee, realizing she'd overfilled the cup and now the steaming liquid was spilling onto the counter.

"Good heavens, what's the matter with you?" Elberta asked, rag in hand ready to wipe up the mess.

Lydia felt a blush warming her cheeks. "I was. . .um. . .just watching Tyler," she fibbed. Then, silently, she had to ask herself the same question: What *was* the matter with her? She wasn't one to gawk at strange men.

Cleaning off the saucer, she turned to Gerald and handed him his coffee. "I'm so sorry," she murmured, feeling oddly nervous. "Forgive me."

He narrowed his gaze suspiciously. "Quite all right, my dear. No harm done."

❧

Alec attended church that evening and afterward grabbed a quick hamburger with a couple of new friends. He got home near nine o'clock.

Inside his house, he pulled off his tie, tossed his jacket onto the nearest chair, and gazed around the living room at the myriad of cardboard boxes waiting to be unpacked. Why had he played around with a bike and an eight-year-old this afternoon instead of setting up housekeeping?

He collapsed into his burgundy leather-upholstered couch, recalling the conversation he'd had with Tyler.

"Do you think my mama is pretty?" the boy had asked, throwing Alec momentarily off guard.

"Well," he hedged, not wanting to lie, but careful to show his disinterest, "she is, as far as women go, I guess."

"She is. . .pretty?"

"I guess."

Tyler had grinned broadly. "So, you think my mama is pretty, huh?"

Alec straightened. "Get on that bike, kid," he'd said gruffly, "and let me see if it fits you better."

"Yes, sir."

The lowered handlebars and seat seemed to make things easier for Tyler, and Alec had watched the boy ride down his driveway, into the street, and around to his own backyard.

That was when Tyler's grandfather emerged from the house.

"Welcome to Woodruff," the older man said, striding confidently to the fence.

Alec met him, regarding his expensive, smartly tailored dark suit. They shook hands, and Alec introduced himself.

"And I'm Gerald Boswick, the pastor at Southern Pride Community Church in nearby Montgomery."

"Good to meet you."

The older man puffed out his chest and stuck his hands in his pants pockets. "So, what line of work are you in, Alex?"

"Alec," he'd corrected, although he got the distinct impression Pastor Boswick had purposely mispronounced his name. "I'm a carpenter."

"You don't say? Well, that's interesting. . .hammering furniture together, eh? Prefab stuff, I imagine. Everything is prefab these days."

The pastor was wrong. Alec was a craftsman, but he held his tongue. He'd lived long enough to know some people really didn't care what a guy did for a living. They were either just trying to start conversation or they liked to hear themselves talk. The latter, Alec guessed, was probably the case in this situation.

"So, how'd you get into that line of work?"

"Always liked woodworking in high school." Alec shrugged. "After I graduated, I attended a tech school and went on for my apprenticeship, and. . . ," Alec rolled his shoulders once more, "here I am."

"And here you are," Pastor Boswick drawled in repetition as his mouth curved upward in a wry grin. "Tyler tells me you're from up North."

"Yep." Alec smiled. "I'm a Yankee and proud of it."

"Well," Pastor Boswick had replied with a curt but amused chuckle, "I wouldn't go advertising that fact, if I were you. There're still folks here in Woodruff who haven't quite gotten over their bad feelings for Northerners. Handed down from generation to generation."

"A one-hundred-and-forty-year grudge, huh?"

"Guess you could say that."

"And are you one of those 'folks' with a chip on your shoulder?" Alec had asked, unable to keep the challenge out of his voice.

"Of course not. Everyone's equal in the sight of God. But you'd be wise to heed my warning, son, just the same. . . ."

*His warning*, Alec thought cynically, rising from the couch now. There was something about the good pastor that really bothered him. Perhaps it was his air of superiority. Nevertheless, Alec hadn't encountered any trouble in town. So far he'd been well-received, despite the fact he was a *Northerner*.

Walking down the beige-carpeted hallway of his single-story home, Alec entered his bedroom and changed clothes. Unable to help himself, he pulled on his favorite Wisconsin Badgers sweatshirt, thinking, *You can take the Yankee out of the North, but you can't take the North out of the Yankee. . . . Just what am I doing in Alabama anyway?*

Regardless of the momentary doubt, Alec knew the answer to that question. He'd moved here to start a new life, and so far, so good. New job, new house. . .

The doorbell chimed and he peered out the front door's half-moon-shaped window before answering it. "And a new neighbor," he muttered, before greeting Lydia with a stiff smile.

"Well, Mrs. Boswick, what a surprise," Alec said, flicking on the porch light.

"Sorry to bother you," she stated sweetly. Alec wondered if her amiable demeanor was part of her act—her scheme to get a husband. "Our bathroom sink is clogged something awful and I wondered if you might have a pliers so I can take off the pipe."

"A pliers?" Alec tried not to smirk. "Personally, I'd use a wrench to take off a pipe."

"Oh. . .well, that's what I meant. Excuse me." Lydia smiled. "I'm not very familiar with tools. I usually call my father-in-law when I need help, but I can't locate either of my in-laws right now. And my neighbors on the other side, Connie and Terrence Wilberson. . .well, they're out of town, visiting one of Connie's relatives, and—"

"Look, I've got a wrench, and you can borrow it," Alec interrupted, "but, um. . ." He raised a brow. "Are you sure you'd know what to do with it?"

She lifted her chin defiantly. "Yes. I'm quite capable, thank you."

"Okay. I'll go get it for you. Want to come in?" He opened the screen door, bidding her enter.

"No," she replied, shaking her head. "I don't believe that'd be proper. I'll wait right here. Besides, I don't like to leave my children unattended, and they're both standing right up there in that window." Turning slightly, she pointed toward her red brick home. "There they are. . .right where I can see them."

She waved and Alec stepped onto the porch so he could see if what she said was true. Sure enough, Tyler and Brooke stood at the window where the white mini blinds had been pulled up. When the children saw him, they smiled and waved vigorously.

Alec grinned and glanced at Lydia. "Be right back with the wrench."

"Thank you."

As he walked through the living room, dining area, and into the kitchen where his tools lay already unpacked but awaiting their permanent place in his home, Alec felt a pang of obligation. He supposed he should help the lady, seeing as he knew a little something about plumbing while it didn't sound like she was even sure how to use a wrench. Besides, if she really meant to work her female wiles on him, she'd have accepted his invitation and entered his house, yet she preferred to wait outside where the temperatures had plummeted into the forties—for propriety's sake, she'd said. Somehow, her decision gave Alec pause. Maybe he'd been wrong about her, but he still wasn't entirely convinced.

Toolbox in hand, he strode back through the house, stepping out onto the porch. Lydia took one look at the large red metal container he carried and cast him a nervous smile.

"You know, I was just thinking maybe I'd call one of those emergency plumbing places."

"On a Sunday? At this hour?" Alec shook his head. "They'll charge you a fortune."

"But, I'm not sure if I can—"

"Carry this heavy toolbox over to your place, much less use a wrench?" He chuckled softly. "Yeah, I figured. How 'bout I come over and see what I can do instead?"

An expression of relief flittered across her delicate features, softly illuminated by the porch light. "That's very kind of you. . .thanks."

Lydia led the way down the steps, over the lawn, and to her house. Alec had admired the structure from afar yesterday while he moved in, and it was every bit as impressive on the inside as he'd imagined—perhaps even more so.

He gazed appreciatively at the mahogany woodwork in her living room, noting the built-in bookcases on either side of the fireplace on the far wall. Next he marveled at the beautiful banister and railing as he walked up the polished wooden stairs.

"This is some house you've got here."

"Why, thank you. I'm partial to it." Lydia paused on the first landing. "When my husband, Michael, and I first looked at this house, he said it was haunted because of its poor condition. And I must say, it appeared that way, broken shutters outside banging against the house in the wind, peeling paint, rotting wood and spider webs galore inside! The kitchen was a ghastly sight, terribly outdated. The two bathrooms, one downstairs and this one up here, were equally as obsolete. But I managed to talk Michael into buying it anyway. I just imagined what this house would look like once it had been restored." She gave him a bittersweet smile. "I'm glad my husband shared my vision. We had a lot of good times fixing up this old place."

Alec merely nodded, feeling fascinated. "Did you do the refurbishing yourself?"

"Yes, most of it anyway."

She turned and he followed her the rest of the way upstairs, where the kids met them in the hallway. After a grand welcome, Lydia instructed Tyler and Brooke to go to their bedrooms and read until she and "Mr. Alec" finished up with the clogged sink.

"So you can remodel a home but can't use a wrench, eh?" he asked half-teasingly.

"I can paint and I can wallpaper, if that's what you mean. But when it comes to nuts and bolts, I'm lost. And plumbing. . . ? Forget it, although I was willing to give it a try tonight."

Assessing the situation, Alec concluded that the sink had overflowed, judging by the water still in its basin and the heap of wet towels in the bathtub.

Lydia stepped back and watched him expertly take the pipes apart.

"Would you mind stopping the drain so I don't get soaked?"

She did as he asked, having to step over his long, horizontal form in the process. Minutes later, Alec had disconnected the U-shaped pipe from the drain.

"Got a wire hanger?"

"Yes." Lydia ran to fetch the object, and when she returned, he straightened it out and stuck it into the pipe, producing a glob of unsightly hair and unidentifiable muck. Then he poked and prodded and, much to Lydia's surprise, a small, die-cast metal car fell into his outstretched palm.

"I think this has been in here for a while," he said amusedly, inspecting the rusty thing. "You might ask Ty about it."

Alec chuckled and tossed the slimy toy at her. Lydia grimaced but caught it while he began replacing the piping. Once it was secure again, he stood and pulled the sink's stopper. The water went down easily.

"Thank you," Lydia said gratefully.

"No sweat. That was an easy one."

He washed his hands, dried them, picked up his tools, and then strode into the hallway, where Lydia was waiting. "G'night, you two," he called toward Tyler and Brooke's bedrooms.

They rushed out to say good-bye and marveled at how fast he'd fixed the clogged drain. Lydia rolled her eyes, somewhat embarrassed that her children were treating the man like a superhero.

"All right, back to bed," she ordered. "I'm going to see Mr. Alec out and then I'll be up to hear your prayers."

"You got some polite kids there, Mrs. Boswick, I'll grant you that much."

"Why, thank you." It wasn't the first time she'd heard the compliment, and Lydia felt very proud of her children.

"But let me say this," Alec began, pivoting just before he reached the front door. "I was just being neighborly tonight. Doing the Christian thing, nothing else. Got it?"

"You're saying that because of what Tyler said earlier today, aren't you?" Lydia asked perceptively. "Well, to be honest, I'm not shopping for a daddy for my children, if that's what you think." Her voice was calm and steady. "I surely can't blame you for being put off, but, you see, children often speak their minds without thinking first. I am truly sorry if you were offended."

"Yeah, well, I—"

"The truth is, I don't want to remarry. I loved my husband so much and. . . well, I just don't think I could ever feel that way about anyone ever again."

She yanked on the heavy, polished front door and it opened. Alec stepped out of the house and onto her two-story covered front porch.

"Thank you for your help tonight."

"Sure thing."

"Good night, Mr. Corbett."

"Alec," he reminded her as the large front door closed in his face.

Slowly, he made his way back to his house. When he arrived, he cast one last glance at the Boswick place across the way. Why did he suddenly feel as though that woman with her sweet, Southern manner was a challenge he'd like to accept?

*Forget her, you fool*, he groused inwardly. *She's not looking for a romantic relationship and neither are you. So just forget her!*

# Chapter 4

Once his wife entered the bathroom and busied herself with her nightly routine, Gerald Boswick lifted the phone, dialing the number he'd come to know so well. With the receiver to his ear, he listened as it rang while he tapped the toe of his shoe impatiently. After a few moments, he seated himself on the wide bed covered with a pale blue satin comforter and allowed his gaze to take in the opulent splendor of the rest of the room. Elberta had hired just the right decorator—a darling little thing from Birmingham. What was her name again?

The phone suddenly stopped ringing. "It's me," he said, announcing himself.

"What can I do for you on this late Sunday night?"

"I think you'd better step up the romance," Gerald advised.

"I thought you told me to take it slow."

"Things have changed."

A pause. "What things?"

"She's got a new neighbor. I met him this afternoon and if we're not careful, he could ruin everything."

"What do you suggest?"

"I'll make some arrangements; you just do your part. Woo and coo her as though your life depends on it." Gerald paused for effect, the way he'd been taught back in seminary training. "Because it does."

❀

On Monday morning Lydia deposited Tyler and Brooke in their respective classrooms at Southern Pride Christian School before making her way around the large building to where the church office suites were located. They consisted of three offices: her father-in-law's, the assistant pastor's, and the youth pastor's. Lydia's desk was centered between them, as she did some secretarial work for all three men. However, the majority of her time was spent answering calls and scheduling appointments for Gerald, as well as tending to minor bookkeeping responsibilities. Once inside her warm, violet-carpeted work space, she made a pot of coffee and set it in the reception area. As usual, her father-in-law had one appointment after another today.

As she walked to her desk, adjacent to the small lobby, Lydia noticed the Do Not Disturb sign on Gerald's office door and heard voices coming from within. A female's—and her father-in-law's. She glanced at her wristwatch. Odd, she thought. It was only eight o'clock. Lydia did all the scheduling and she never penciled anything in before nine. But perhaps a crisis arose, so he'd created the slot himself.

She sat down and momentarily glanced at the row of pictures on the back of her desktop. Tyler, Brooke, Michael, and herself. Her family, minus one, and in spite of what she'd told her neighbor last night, the loss of her husband had left a chasm in her heart that ached to be filled. Except she seriously doubted she'd ever love again, that she could find the kind of soul mate she'd found in Michael.

The outer door suddenly opened, bringing Lydia out of her lonesome reverie, and a lovely African-American woman stepped into the reception area. She wore a tan rain-or-shine coat and had a large leather satchel draped over her left shoulder. In her other arm she carried a day planner.

"May I help you?" Lydia asked politely, rising slowly from her chair.

"Yes." The woman came forward and set her planner on the desk. "I'm Michelle Marx from the *Montgomery Observer*."

"A reporter?" Lydia asked, surprised.

"That's right. I wanted to know if I could speak with Pastor Boswick regarding allegations that were made by some of his former church members. Is he in?"

"Allegations?"

"Yes. You're not aware of them?"

"Um, no. . ."

At that very moment, the door to Gerald's office swung open and he stepped out, followed by an attractive blond named Cindy Tanner. Lydia knew Cindy and her husband were having awful marital problems. The man had left her and their two young children, and Cindy was heartbroken, so she consulted with Gerald frequently.

"Thank you, Pastor," she murmured with a grateful expression. "I don't know what I'd do without you."

"There, now, Cindy, you're going to be fine. A good shepherd always takes care of his flock, and as I said, I will take care of you."

Lydia felt a moment's pride at how chivalrous her father-in-law sounded in front of the reporter wanting to investigate him. But the way Cindy gazed up adoringly at him caused Lydia a good measure of discomfort. Was that a come-hither look? Lydia glanced at Gerald. Was he looking back? Lydia checked herself. Of course he wasn't flirting. How could she have even thought such a thing?

She cleared her throat. Both the pastor and Cindy turned toward her.

"Pastor Boswick," Lydia began formally since they were in the workplace, "this is Michelle Marx. She's a reporter."

"How do you do, Pastor," Michelle replied with a tight smile.

He nodded curtly, then whispered something to Cindy, who turned and left the office. After watching her go, he wheeled his gaze back to the journalist and assessed her in two sweeping glances. "I don't have time for reporters," he stated at last. "Have a good day." With that, he turned and headed for his office.

"But. . ." Lydia's argument was lost on the oak-paneled door that closed soundly behind him.

"Not very friendly for a pastor," Michelle remarked.

Lydia fingered her phone and thought about buzzing him but noticed his line was lit; he was already on his extension. She glanced at the visitor. "I'm sorry, Ms. Marx."

The woman shrugged. "I'll just have to print the story with what I've got. But I can promise you, it won't be pretty."

Lydia felt a moment's panic. "Perhaps I should try to talk him into speaking with you. Just a moment." She made for Gerald's office, but Michelle halted her.

"Don't bother. I think I've seen and heard enough."

"No, wait. . ."

Lydia glanced at her father-in-law's door, wondering why he was behaving so brusquely this morning. That wasn't like him. Turning, she followed Michelle into the outer hallway, unable to abide the thought of the woman slandering the Boswick name.

"Perhaps I can help," she called after the reporter who stopped in midstride. "Please, come back into the office. I'll get you some coffee and we can talk."

Pivoting, the woman eyed her speculatively.

"I'm Lydia Boswick, the pastor's daughter-in-law, and. . . well, since I work here, I might be able to answer some of your questions."

One well-sculptured eyebrow went up. "His daughter-in-law, huh? Yes, all right. . ."

Back inside the reception area, Lydia poured coffee and then sat down in one of the lilac-printed upholstered armchairs. "Now, what allegations were you referring to, Ms. Marx?"

She flipped open her planner. "Do you know Jordan and Sherry Smith?"

"Why, yes," Lydia replied with a curious frown. Sherry had once been Lydia's best friend.

"Mr. Smith was the treasurer here, wasn't he?"

"Yes."

"Hmm. . .well, according to Mr. Smith, Pastor Boswick uses some unethical, if not illegal, practices to ensure the church's financial stability as well as his own. He says that was why he left Southern Pride Community Church. Is that true?"

Lydia tried to hide her surprise. Unethical? Her father-in-law? "Not to my knowledge. I understood the Smiths left SPCC for entirely different reasons."

"I see. And what about Mrs. Belva Applegate and Miss Marion Campbell? Their families plan to file lawsuits, but the district attorney's office states that it plans to file its own charges of extortion against the pastor sometime this week.

Can you tell me about this?"

"Extortion?" This time Lydia couldn't conceal her shock.

"You don't know? The families claim Pastor Boswick used undue influence to convince the two elderly women to purchase expensive term life insurance policies, naming him as beneficiary instead of paying for necessary medical treatments. The result, the families allege, was the premature deaths of their loved ones."

"I don't believe that's the case at all," Lydia replied, raising her chin defensively. "Both Mrs. Applegate and Miss Campbell were elderly women who were quite sickly much of the time."

"So you don't believe medical care from a licensed provider might have forestalled their deaths?"

"Neither woman wanted to go into a nursing home, so many of us here at church took turns preparing meals, cleaning, writing letters—"

"You, personally, helped care for the women?"

"I took my turn, yes. Once a month. And they were lovely gentlewomen who were grateful to be in their own homes at the end of their lives."

"Hmm. . ." The reporter nodded thoughtfully. "Well, is it true that many more women are accepted into the fold here at Southern Pride Community Church than are men?"

"I beg your pardon?"

"Especially widows and single women?"

Lydia frowned. "I don't know. I guess I never noticed anything like that." She shifted uncomfortably, recalling that her own mother had been a widow when they had first come to SPCC, back when Lydia was sixteen years old. But so what?

"Is it true that scores of men are turned away from this church every year because Pastor Boswick will not abide anyone disagreeing with his theology?"

"No, that's not true," Lydia answered confidently. "Many of our members are high-profile men in the community."

She smiled weakly, but Michelle's expression remained stony. "Do they agree with your father-in-law on every issue?"

"Probably not."

"But you're not sure?"

Lydia swallowed hard, thinking that the woman missed her calling as a lawyer. Why, she was as good at interrogating a subject as Michael had been!

Then suddenly her smile broadened. "Yes, I'm sure. My husband didn't agree with his father on every issue. He was very opinionated and they debated quite often." Lydia sat back in the chair. "So you see, that's a misconception."

"I noticed that you speak of your husband in the past tense."

"He died two and a half years ago."

"How unfortunate. I'm sorry."

Glancing down at her hands folded neatly in her lap, Lydia merely nodded.
"And what about Patricia Reimer Jackson. Do you know her?"

Lydia raised her head quickly. "Yes." She swallowed the fact that Patricia Jackson was her mother.

"Is it true Mrs. Jackson was church disciplined for rebellion simply because she was a widow who wanted to marry a man who was not a member of Southern Pride Community Church?"

"There's a little more to it than that."

"Oh? What more?" Michelle took up her pen, ready to write down anything Lydia might say.

But she didn't utter a sound. How could she? It'd been a horrible, shameful situation.

"Was Mrs. Jackson openly rebellious?"

"Yes," Lydia forced herself to reply.

"She was rebellious because she wanted to remarry and Pastor Boswick was against the match?"

"Yes."

"So, going against Pastor Boswick's will is open rebellion and grounds for church discipline here at Southern Pride Community Church. Is that correct?"

"That's a blanket statement and I can't possibly answer a simple 'yes' or 'no.'"

"I see. . ."

"Are you insinuating my father-in-law is a legalistic man?"

"Isn't he? From the reports I've heard—"

"No!" Lydia raised her chin. "He maintains high standards, but he's not legalistic."

Michelle put the capped end of the pen against her lower lip thoughtfully. "Back to Mrs. Jackson. . .she stated she discovered after she was disciplined by the church that Pastor Boswick had years ago coerced her into signing over her late husband's life insurance funds while she'd been under the impression he was merely managing them for her. Do you know anything about that?"

"It wasn't coercion. My. . .Mrs. Jackson," she said, catching herself, "donated those funds to SPCC."

Lydia still remembered the night her mother had signed the documents. Michael had come along and they'd sat together on the sofa, where they talked and he comforted her in her grief over losing her dad. That was really when it all began—they fell in love while business matters were being settled in the dining room.

"So, Mrs. Jackson donated the funds and Pastor Boswick promised her security and safety within the arms of Southern Pride Community Church. But once she was no longer a member, she no longer had that protection—or her money. Is that right?"

"Well, sort of. . .Pastor Boswick can only offer protection to his flock."

"But he can keep the flock's money regardless."

"It was a donation," Lydia maintained. She stood, suddenly desiring to end the cross-examination. "I have work to do, Ms. Marx, and I think you should be on your way."

"I understand, but answer me one more question," Michelle said, standing and looping her bag over her shoulder. "Is it true that Southern Pride Community Church's membership is all white? No African-Americans? No Hispanics? No Hmong or Native Americans?"

"Um. . ." Lydia had to think. Weren't there other races represented here? SPCC was a large church and drew people from within a thirty-mile radius around Woodruff—surely it was racially blended. "I'm afraid I honestly don't know the answer to your question, Ms. Marx," she replied lamely.

"Well," she said, throwing Lydia a disappointed look, "thanks for your time, anyway."

"You're not still going to print the article about those allegations against my father-in-law, are you?"

"You better believe I am!" The journalist turned and strode toward the door. "My readers deserve to know the truth, and I hope to bring it to light. Have a nice day, Mrs. Boswick."

Lydia stared in horror after the woman. The truth? She couldn't possibly know the truth! Her father-in-law was the kindest, most caring man on earth, not some criminal!

The phone rang, and Lydia snapped to her senses, walked back to her desk, and answered it. It was the assistant pastor's wife, Eileen Camden.

"I haven't seen him this morning, but I can put you through to his voice mail."

"Sure, that would be fine. Thanks."

She took care of the call just as Gerald reappeared from his office. "That woman," she said with jangled nerves, "that reporter—"

"I hope you got rid of her."

Lydia swallowed. "She left. But she promised to print some awful lies about you."

Her father-in-law puffed out his chest and grinned wryly. "Lydia, my dear, the Lord said there would be persecution from the world when we try to further God's kingdom. I'm not afraid of anything the newspapers might disclose. Such things have happened to me before. Every intelligent person knows those daily newspapers are filled with gossip and sensationalism."

"Yes, of course. Everyone knows that—"

"Don't let it upset you. Now, what about my coffee?"

Lydia managed a smile. "Coming right up."

❀

As much as Lydia tried to take Gerald's advice, she felt anxious for the rest of the day. The questions Michelle Marx had asked troubled her and put doubts into her head, causing her to feel confused. But, as her father-in-law often said from the pulpit, questions were the workings of the devil. After all, Satan had questioned Eve in the garden, causing her to doubt God's word. . . .

By early afternoon, Lydia determined to push aside her worry and concentrate on her work. The hours ticked by. Soon it was three thirty and Tyler and Brooke burst into the church offices.

"Hi, Mama. Ready to go home?" Tyler asked in his usual exuberant tone.

"Lower your voice, Ty," Lydia lightly scolded him. "And I'm just about done."

"Well, well, two of my favorite people," Gerald said, strolling out from his quarters. "I thought I heard you come in, Tyler."

Lydia grinned. Tyler with his boisterous ways could be heard for a mile. Gerald liked to say he was "a preacher in the making."

"And, little Brooke. . .you just get prettier every day."

"Thank you, Grampa," she said, beaming.

While the children chattered amicably with their grandfather, Lydia cleared her desk and prepared to leave. Then Gerald scooted them into the outer hallway, motioning with his head for Lydia to join him in his office.

"What is it?" Lydia asked, trailing him. She felt certain he'd bring up the reporter. But to her surprise, such was not the case.

"Simeon Crenshaw phoned earlier, saying he needs an escort to a dinner meeting this evening. He asked my permission to take you, and I told him you'd be delighted to go along."

Lydia frowned. "But—"

"Elberta and I will take the children overnight. I'll follow you home, you can pack their things and still have plenty of time to pretty yourself up for your date."

"Gerald, I don't want to go out with Sim Crenshaw. I'm not interested in him."

"Now, Lydia, Sim is a brother in Christ, an upstanding member here at SPCC, and he's my attorney. Furthermore, you and I agreed that I'd have the say on whom you dated. That way, you won't feel pressured to accept or turn away a possible suitor. I've suggested Sim before, but this time you'll go out with him, all right?"

Gerald gave her an indulgent smile. "Women are so emotional, as you well know. And so vulnerable. The weaker vessel."

Lydia managed a nod. That was what the Bible said: the weaker vessel. And since Michael died, she'd been emotionally shipwrecked. She had come to depend on her father-in-law's guidance and protection. She needed him.

"You need me. Am I right?" he asked as if divining her thoughts.

"Yes."

"Good. Then you're willing to continue with our arrangement. I'd like to see you remarry. . .go on with your life."

"I'm trying," she insisted.

"You need a husband," Gerald maintained. "Someone who can take a firm hand to Tyler and set a good example for him. That boy is the apple of my eye, you know." A faraway look entered his swarthy gaze. "He's all I have left, since Michael died. . . ."

Lydia sensed that Gerald still missed his son deeply, just as she did at times. Nevertheless, she just couldn't enter into a marital relationship that was not of her choosing. "Gerald, Simeon Crenshaw is not the man for me, nor is he the kind of father I'd want for my children."

"You say that now, dear, but that's because you haven't gotten to know Sim. He can really be quite charming. You'll see."

"But, I—"

"Lydia, dear, won't you please go out with him tonight as a special favor to me? I'm going to require Sim's help in the next few months, what with all these horrible accusations stacked against me." Lowering his voice, he smiled. "Couldn't you just help me get on his good side?"

"You're already on his good side," she assured him.

Gerald's gaze hardened in a way that caused Lydia to retreat from further debate. She didn't want to go out with Sim, but more than anything, she wanted to please her father-in-law. Her own father had died when she was seven years old, and Gerald Boswick was the only father figure she'd ever known. He'd been generous and compassionate to her, despite his wife's subtle animosity—and in spite of her mother's rebellion—and he'd helped Lydia over the most difficult time in her life when Michael died. How, then, could she let Gerald down after all he'd done for her over the years?

"Yes, I'll go out with Simeon Crenshaw tonight," she forced herself to reply, albeit reluctantly.

"Wonderful. He'll be delighted." Pulling her into a quick embrace, her father-in-law kissed her cheek. "That's my girl. Chin up. Smile. That's it. Now, let me get my car keys, and we'll call it a day."

Nodding, Lydia fetched her purse and coat. *Oh, Lord,* she silently pleaded, *help me make it through this night.*

# Chapter 5

Settling himself into a white plastic lawn chair on the front porch, Alec stretched out lazily. The weather had been mild today—another seventy-degree day. Some of the guys at work said the annual spring rain showers would begin soon and suggested Alec enjoy the sun while he could. So now, as the fiery red ball began its descent in the western sky, he reveled in its fading glory.

After a few minutes passed, he glanced next door, thinking it had been awfully quiet over at the Boswick house this evening. He guessed they were home, since the family minivan was parked in the driveway. He shrugged and lifted his newspaper. Maybe the kids had to stay inside and do their homework. In any case, it wasn't any of his concern.

Leafing through the newspaper, Alec scanned the headlines until one in particular caught his attention. *Local Pastor to Face Extortion Charges.* Interested, he read on, nearly choking on the first sentence. *Gerald Boswick, pastor of Southern Pride Community Church, is likely to be formally charged with extortion later this week, according to the district attorney's office.*

Alec let out a long, slow whistle, casting another glance next door. Perhaps that was why it had been so quiet over there.

As soon as he'd completed the thought, a silver Lincoln Continental pulled into Lydia's driveway. Alec watched curiously as a short, stocky man with dark brown woolly hair climbed out of the driver's side and walked up to the front door. Within moments, Lydia emerged from the house, wearing a black silk dress with burgundy trim and a matching jacket. Her chestnut brown hair was swept up, regally, emphasizing her delicate features, and even from his distance, Alec noticed her wide but nicely shaped lips, painted the same color as the trim of her dress.

Alec felt his jaw drop in awe, but quickly snapped it shut. But there was no doubt about it: Lydia Boswick was gorgeous! Was she going on a date with that fuzzy little elf in the navy pinstriped suit?

*Good thing she's got better taste in homes than in men,* Alec thought dryly, *or else I'd be living next door to a major eyesore!*

Watching her gracefully stroll toward the Lincoln, Alec folded his newspaper, catching her attention. Lydia smiled a brief greeting, but something in her gaze told him she wasn't very happy. Either the nasty business surrounding her father-in-law troubled her, or she wasn't very excited about going on this date, he decided. And as the car backed out of the Boswicks' driveway, Alec found himself wishing the latter were the cause of her discontent.

*Knucklehead*, he chided himself, reopening the newspaper. *There could be a million reasons why Lydia doesn't seem happy. Maybe she's not even going on a date. Maybe she's going to a funeral. That'd make anyone look somber!*

In any case, Alec found himself having a difficult time dismissing his pretty neighbor from his thoughts.

❁

Alec dozed, only to awaken suddenly to the sound of a car door slamming. Then another. He roused himself, feeling a stiffness in his back, and lifting his feet from the wide brick porch rail, he wriggled his toes, trying to get the circulation back into them. He'd fallen asleep right there in the lawn chair! At that very moment Lydia and her date walked up the driveway.

"How about I come in for a while and make us both some cappuccino?" her escort suggested. "Chocolate? French vanilla?"

Lydia stopped short. "Not tonight. I'm very tired."

Alec grinned. Yeah, he'd heard that excuse before.

He sat very still in the darkness, waiting for Lydia to move again so he could get up and go into the house undetected. As it was, he felt as though he were watching a play since the spotlight from Lydia's porch streamed down on her and the fuzzy-haired guy trying to persuade her not to end their date. But Alec didn't want to appear the spying neighbor, and if he stood right then, they'd know he'd been there and likely be embarrassed—and so would he.

"Well, then, how about a good-night kiss, Lydia?"

Alec groaned inwardly. This was getting worse by the moment.

"Why, Sim," Lydia drawled politely, "I'm flattered you asked, but I never kiss on the first date."

Alec held his breath, trying not to laugh out loud. Sim? What kind of name was that for a human being? And get a load of that expression; he obviously didn't appreciate being turned down.

Lydia turned to climb the steps of her porch, but Sim caught her arm.

"Just a little kiss? Please?"

She jerked out of his grasp, looking surprised. "No."

"But I've waited all night to kiss you. I've waited months to kiss you…years, even!"

"Sim!" She stepped backwards, and he grabbed her shoulders.

"Just one kiss…"

"No! Stop it!"

Although her voice wasn't loud, Alec could hear the note of desperation, and something inside him snapped into action. He stood and found himself over on

Lydia's driveway before he even realized what he was doing there. Taking hold of the husky elf by the back of his shirt collar, Alec yanked him away from Lydia.

"I believe the lady wants you to back off."

Astonishment flashed across the shorter man's face, but it quickly turned to contempt. "Who are you? Mind your own business!"

Alec didn't reply but turned to Lydia as he released the man from his grasp. She appeared shaken but unharmed. "You're free to go inside if you like," he said calmly.

She nodded and, after tossing the other man a look of mild disdain, she hurried up the steps to the porch, unlocked her front door, and disappeared into the house.

When Alec glanced back at Sim, he was already heading toward his Lincoln, muttering under his breath. He got in, closed the door, and peeled out of the driveway.

"Hey, little man," Alec said as if the guy could hear him, "you're doing it all wrong. You've got to sweet talk a woman into a good-night kiss, not act like an ogre."

Shaking his head, Alec watched the car take off down the dimly lit street, wondering if he'd be able to get a good-night kiss out of Lydia Boswick on a first date.

*Except, there ain't gonna be a first date,* he mused resolutely. *I'm through with dating and good-night kisses forever!*

"Thank you, Mr. Corbett," he heard Lydia say as her airy Southern voice wafted down from her porch.

He pivoted, facing her. "Alec, remember? My friends call me Alec."

"That's right." She smiled. "Thanks again, *Alec.*"

"Don't mention it. Only next time I'll remember my cape."

She momentarily frowned, obviously not understanding the joke. But suddenly she got it and burst into laughter so light-sounding and contagious it caused Alec to grin broadly.

"All right, *Superman*," she quipped.

He chuckled and then couldn't resist asking the question on his mind ever since he saw the Lincoln pull into her driveway.

"Tell me something," he began, slowly striding toward her. "Why would a woman like you go out with a guy like. . .*Sim?*"

"A woman like me?" A puzzled frown marred her nicely shaped brows.

"Yeah. You seem like you're reasonably intelligent."

"Oh, thank you very much," she replied sarcastically.

Alec laughed at her reaction.

"If you must know, I went out with Simeon Crenshaw as a favor to my father-in-law. It was not of my own doing."

"Ah. I knew there had to be an explanation." He eyed her speculatively. "Can I ask you something else?"

Lydia nodded, albeit hesitantly.

"Speaking of your father-in-law, I read about him in tonight's newspaper. Is he really facing extortion charges?"

She sighed wearily. "I'm afraid so. This morning a reporter came to the office asking all sorts of questions and I really didn't get a chance to talk to Gerald about the whole situation until he came here tonight to pick up the children. That's when he told me about the district attorney's office threatening him with this awful business."

"Any truth to it?"

"Of course not. And my father-in-law has his attorneys working on the case already. In fact, Sim is one of his lawyers."

Alec mulled over the information, then smirked. "Well, he seems pushy enough to be a lawyer. Maybe he'll get your father-in-law off the hook."

"I have my doubts. And not all lawyers have to be 'pushy' to be successful. My late husband, Michael, for instance, was an attorney and he'd been thoughtful, caring, and respectful—nothing like Sim! In fact, I wish Gerald would consult with the firm my husband had worked for, but he refuses."

"Hmm. . ." Alec observed that it was the second time she'd brought up her deceased husband in conversation, causing him to question his husband-seeker theory about her again. "Well, Lydia—is it okay if I call you Lydia?"

"Of course."

"Well, Lydia," he began again, "I think I'll call it a night."

"Me, too."

After a parting smile, she reentered her house, and Alec, feeling more curious than ever about his neighbor, made his way back home.

❀

Tyler stood on the fence the next day after supper and watched Mr. Alec play basketball. "Now you let me do the talking, Brooke, you hear?"

She lifted her little nose as if to say she wouldn't listen.

"Brooke," he said in warning, "you'd better. . .else I'll tell Mama you threw away your green beans tonight when she wasn't looking."

"Okay," she replied with a pout.

"Hey, Mr. Alec," Tyler called across the yard, "can I ask you something?"

"Sure." Picking up his basketball and holding it against his hip with one arm, he walked to the fence. "What's up, kid?"

"Well," he hedged, "I just wondered. . .well, my grampa Boswick is a preacher, you know. . . ."

"Yeah, what about him?"

"Well, he says folks are gonna go either to heaven or hell after they die and, see, me and Brooke know we're goin' to heaven cuz we asked Jesus to save us. I was six and a half and she was—"

"Last summer," Brooke interrupted proudly. "I was just four and a half."

Tyler elbowed her to keep quiet. This was important! Mama wouldn't marry a man who wasn't a Christian, so Mr. Alec had to get saved.

"Anyway, me and Brooke want you to go to heaven after you die. Want to? I can tell you how to get born again. It's easy." Tyler nodded persuasively.

"Just ask Jesus into your heart to live forever," Brooke said. "But then you gotta read your Bible and pray every day so you grow, grow, grow."

Tyler gave his sister a scowl for reciting the words to that dumb song she learned in the kindergarten choir at church, but Mr. Alec started to laugh. Puzzled, he looked back at their neighbor.

"You kids are too much." He smiled. "But I appreciate the fact that you're concerned about my soul. That's good. Real good. Lots of people need the Lord, but I'm a Christian already. I got saved about five years ago."

Tyler widened his wondering gaze. "You did?"

Mr. Alec nodded.

"Awesome!"

"But I didn't see you at church on Sunday," Brooke told him.

"That's because I attend a different church."

Tyler frowned. A different church? That could mean trouble. Grampa wouldn't like it. He says other churches are "steeped in rebellion and pride." And Mama wouldn't leave SPCC. So Mr. Alec would have to make the switch. And maybe he would. . .once he and Mama got married. Oh, well, better leave that problem to the grown-ups.

Tipping his head, Tyler studied the man before him. He wore blue jeans and a green sweatshirt with yellow letters across the front that read GREEN BAY PACKERS.

Mr. Alec caught him looking at it and grinned. "You like football, Ty?"

"Sure do."

"Yeah, me, too."

"I don't like football," Brooke announced, shaking her blond head.

"That's cuz you're just a dumb girl."

She gasped. "I'm tellin' Mama!" She jumped off the fence and ran for the back door before Tyler could stop her.

"I hate sisters," he groused.

"Aw, now, Jesus wouldn't want you to hate her." Mr. Alec tousled his hair and chuckled. "But I know how you feel. I grew up with two *older* sisters. See, things could be worse."

"Tyler," Mama called from the back door. "Time to come in."

He sighed, knowing he was doomed. But he saw Mr. Alec wave in his mother's direction—and Tyler noticed that he kind of smiled, too. *He likes her!* Tyler thought, brightening.

"Tyler. . .right now, son."

"Yes, ma'am," he called back. He gazed up at his tall, strong-looking new friend. "See ya later. . .I hope."

As Tyler walked slowly toward his awaiting mother, he heard Mr. Alec call, "Go easy on the kid, Lydia. He's one man in a house full of women. Outnumbered. That'd be tough on any guy."

Mama gave him one of her looks—the one that meant she thought something was funny except she wasn't going to laugh. But she smiled in a way that made her cheeks pink.

*She likes him, too. She does! She really does!*

The back door closed and Tyler swung around to face his mother. "Upstairs to your room, young man," she commanded sternly. "And you may not use the computer tonight."

"But aren't you gonna go easy on me like Mr. Alec said?"

Mama's eyes narrowed slightly, and Tyler knew the answer before she even voiced it. "No."

Shoulders slumped, he turned and marched upstairs. *If Mr. Alec were my daddy,* he mused grumpily, *I'd be able to use my computer tonight.* In his room, he lay down on top of his bed, hands behind his head as he stared at the ceiling. *I gotta think of something. . . .*

He thought and thought, then suddenly he remembered a movie he'd seen at Matt's house once. It was about twin girls who were trying to get their mother and father back together again. He grinned, recalling some of their antics, and decided it wouldn't hurt to create a few of his own. Maybe if the sink got clogged again. . .or maybe. . .maybe. . .

He smiled broadly. *Yeah, that's it!*

# Chapter 6

Things were going from bad to worse—at least in Lydia's estimation. Standing by the counter in her kitchen, she continued grating the cheddar cheese for tonight's supper and rehashing the day's events in her mind.

Gerald had been charged with three counts of extortion. He'd been finger-printed and photographed like a common criminal, and if all that weren't bad enough, the media seemed delighted to broadcast the scandal. Reporters from both the local newspaper and television stations descended on the church that afternoon. It had gotten so hectic, the Christian day school let out early so the children wouldn't be exposed to any of the malicious reports. Lydia had to admit that Sim Crenshaw handled the press with tact and dignity, promising "his client" would fight the slanderous lawsuit. But Lydia wondered if the damage to Gerald's ministry hadn't already been done.

She glanced over her shoulder at the telephone, wondering if she should call her mother. Her own mother...one of Gerald's accusers. Unthinkable. But hadn't it been Mama's new husband's fault? Pete Jackson? He was the kind of man Gerald summed up from 2 Timothy 3: "For of this sort are they which creep into houses, and lead captive silly women laden with sins, led away with divers lusts, ever learning, and never able to come to the knowledge of the truth." It had been difficult for Lydia to accept, but she guessed Gerald was right. Her mother was one of those "silly women."

Nevertheless, Lydia missed her terribly.

"Mama?" Brooke's sweet, childish voice broke into her troubled thoughts. "Can Tyler and me have candles for supper?"

"Candles?" Lydia grinned. "You mean candlelight while you eat?"

Brooke nodded her blond head, wearing a wide smile.

It was a game they played sometimes, eating at the "restaurant" with candle-light, and Lydia hoped it taught her children good manners for when they'd experience the real thing.

"Sure, you can have candles for dinner," Lydia said. "In fact that might be the very thing to cheer me up, too."

Brooke ran outside and, watching through the kitchen window, Lydia saw her tell Tyler the news. He smiled triumphantly, whispered back to his little sister, and suddenly Lydia suspected those two were up to something. She glanced into Alec's backyard and didn't see him. *Good. At least they're not pestering him.*

She shrugged it off, thinking her children were planning some kind of cute little "surprise" as they often did.

Turning her attention back to making supper, Lydia sprinkled the grated cheese over the partially boiled macaroni, added butter, milk, mixed the ingredients well, and topped it off with bread crumbs. Finally, she slid the casserole into the oven.

Then she proceeded to set the table for two. Lydia just wasn't hungry tonight—she'd barely eaten all day, with all the commotion in her life. But she wanted to make the evening meal atmosphere pleasant and family-oriented tonight. They needed some semblance of normalcy in their lives. So she'd at least sit with Tyler and Brooke while they dined.

With her immediate tasks completed, at least for the next half hour while the casserole baked, Lydia returned her thoughts to whether she should phone her mother. More than ever, she felt stuck in the ugly crossfire between church and family.

"God wants us to be happy, Lydia," her mother had said when they'd last spoken—just before she'd been excommunicated. "Pete makes me happy. He's fun to be around, and he loves the Lord Jesus just as much as Gerald does. Why shouldn't I marry him? God's body of believers is not restricted to Southern Pride Community Church. I've realized what an ostrich I've been all these years. There are so many other Christians out there just as zealous and fervent as anyone at SPCC. Just remember that, Lydia. Remember that. . . ."

She shook herself from her musings in time to see Alec in her driveway with his toolbox in hand, heading for her back door. She frowned, wondering at his visit.

"Lydia?" he called through the screen before knocking loudly.

She walked to the door. "Hi. What's up?"

"I'm here to fix your sink." He opened the door and entered.

She frowned in confusion. "My sink?"

"Yeah. Didn't you send Tyler over to tell me that drain's giving you problems again?"

"No, I. . ." She watched him glance over at the table where two tapers stood in silver holders, awaiting a light. A Victorian rose-printed cloth covered the round table and places were set for two. Lydia felt herself blanch with embarrassment as the realization set in. "I think my son has outdone himself this time."

Alec looked back at her, a baffled expression on his face.

"I hate to tell you this, but, um, we've been set up. By an eight-year-old, who had some help from his little sister," Lydia said.

Alec set down his tools. "Oh, yeah?" By the glower on his face, Lydia could tell he didn't believe her. Most likely her neighbor thought *she* had arranged this little tête-à-tête.

"Look, I'm so sorry about this. My sink is not stopped up, and I'll see to it that Tyler is properly disciplined for his shenanigans. Brooke, too, for her part in it. Please, take your wrenches and pliers back home. I just feel terrible for bothering you, and on a Friday evening, too. I'm sure you've got plans." She stooped to lift the metal tool chest and hand it to him, but Alec quickly scooped it up.

"You know, Lydia," he said, wagging a long finger at her, "that kid of yours..."

He suddenly burst into chuckles and Lydia nearly fainted with relief. *He's not angry. Thank You, Lord.*

"Lydia," he began again, "that kid's precocious now, but just wait till he's a teenager. Then what are you going to do?"

She shrugged helplessly. "Lock him in his room till he's twenty-one? I don't know."

"Good luck."

Lydia managed a weak smile. "I'm sorry, Alec."

"No harm done, I guess." He raised a brow as if in afterthought. "But it was Tyler who concocted this and not you, right? I mean, this isn't some kind of plot to lure me into your house for an impromptu romantic dinner, using your kids' little prank as the bait...is it?"

Stunned by the accusation, Lydia was rendered momentarily speechless. "I'd never devise a plan to entice a man into my home. If I wanted a dinner guest, I'd just send an invitation."

Alec nodded, while eyeing her speculatively. "And this wasn't your way of 'sending' out the invite, huh?"

"No, this wasn't it." Indignation quickly set in. "And for your information, I have more integrity than to use my children for anything sneaky and underhanded. I'm only sorry you have such a dark opinion of my character."

"Look, Lydia, I didn't mean to insult you, but I wasn't sure. I've been the recipient of this kind of thing far too often. I dislike being set up and I hate blind dates."

"Ditto." She placed her hand on his upper arm and gave him a push toward the door, though it didn't even budge him. "Good night," she said tersely, "and, again, I apologize for the inconvenience."

He turned and left peaceably without another word, and after soundly closing the door behind him, Lydia sagged against it. She squeezed her eyes together, forestalling the urge to break down and sob. How could Alec have insinuated she was some kind of Jezebel? She felt humiliated to the depth of her being.

"Mama?"

Glancing across the room, she saw Tyler and Brooke standing in the hallway near the kitchen entrance. Their small faces had worry lines creasing their brows.

"That was not nice, you two."

The children had the good grace to look contrite.

"Go wash up and I'll serve supper," she instructed. "And while you eat, you're both going to have a lesson on proper manners concerning next-door neighbors."

"Yes, ma'am," they replied as one before heading to the bathroom.

"And, Tyler?"

He paused. "Yes?"

"You are not to speak to that man again, do you understand? Furthermore, tomorrow morning you're going to give that bicycle back."

"But, Mama—"

"Don't you argue with me. My mind's made up."

The boy's face fell. "Yes, ma'am."

❧

As Alec put dishes away in the kitchen cupboards, he spied Lydia through his window above the sink. It faced directly into her kitchen, and although there was a good deal of distance between them, Alec had a clear view as long as she didn't close her blinds.

Curious, he stood there watching. She sat across the table from her kids, whose backs were to him, and she appeared to be in serious discussion. As far as he could tell, she wasn't raising her voice as some mothers were known to do, but at the same time, Alec instinctively knew Tyler and Brooke were getting a thorough reprimand.

He'd like to laugh off the whole incident, but his conscience sorely pricked him. He shouldn't have confronted Lydia the way he did. She had looked as though she were going to cry. And he might have been tempted to think tears were part of the ploy, except something in her dusky eyes said otherwise.

*Women. Go figure.* His thoughts floated back.

When he'd met Denise shortly after becoming a Christian, he'd known immediately she was the one for him. Denise with her stunning long blond hair and big baby blues. He would have lassoed the moon for her—he'd been that captivated by the woman—and he had thought she felt the same. So when she broke their engagement, saying she'd "changed her mind," Alec thought she was kidding. But she wasn't, and within a week of their breakup, Denise had found someone new from their singles group at church. Unable to bear watching the romance unfold before his eyes, Alec decided to leave—first the church, then Milwaukee, and finally the whole state of Wisconsin. He'd left family behind, but they had never been closely knit. His parents divorced when Alec and his sisters were young; they'd been shuffled from mother to father and back to their mother again. No, there hadn't been anything or anybody standing in Alec's way once he'd made up his mind to leave.

But now that he was here, he didn't quite know how to deal with his pretty new neighbor. Oh, he felt attracted to her, no doubt about it, except he sure wished he didn't. Besides, he'd learned beauty was only skin deep and he wasn't about to make another mistake and fall headlong in love with some fickle-minded woman, like Denise, who'd break his heart again.

*It's best Lydia thinks I'm a jerk*, he decided, turning away from the window and resuming his task of unpacking his kitchen. *Then she'll hate me, and she'll stay away. Good. That's just fine by me.*

The next morning Alec awoke to the sun streaming through his bedroom window. Another glorious day in the South. He dressed and straightened up a bit, reminding himself the singles group from church was meeting at his house tonight for a Bible study. Around noon he ambled outside into his backyard, deciding to cut the lawn. He'd just pulled the mower out of the garage when he spotted Lydia and Tyler walking up his driveway wheeling along the new bike he'd given the kid last week.

"Good morning," he called, still feeling a bit sheepish for his bad behavior yesterday.

Lydia smiled a taut greeting as he strode across the grass to meet them.

"Hi, Tyler."

"Hi." The boy glanced down at his tennis shoes.

"We came to give the bicycle back to you," his mother began. She wore a short-sleeved denim dress with little pink flowers sewn onto its bodice, and Alec noticed its color made her eyes look bluer. . .or was that anger darkening her gaze? "Tyler really has all the toys he needs," she drawled, "and he has a bicycle. We decided this should go to somebody who doesn't own one already."

"Hmm. . ." Alec looked at the boy, still studying the pavement.

"But we appreciate your generosity all the same. . .don't we, Ty?"

"Yeah," he replied, sounding less than enthused.

"Look, Lydia, if this is about last night—"

"Take the bike," she said curtly, pushing it toward him. "We don't want it." She put an arm around her son's drooping shoulders. "Come along, Ty."

As they retreated down the driveway, Alec stood there holding onto the handlebars, watching them go. Lydia had put her thick chestnut mane in some sort of clip at the back of her head, and her hair bobbed with each irritated step she took. "Aren't you making a little too much of this?" he couldn't help but call after her.

She stopped short. Turning to Tyler, she sent him on his way before spinning on her heel and marching back toward him.

Alec wanted to chuckle, except he knew from the determined expression on her face that he was about to get a good tongue-lashing. However, when she reached him, she seemed to swallow whatever she really wanted to say and, instead, smiled up at him kindly.

"I know you can't help it, Mr. Corbett."

He arched a brow. "Help what?"

"Your rude behavior. Your bitter attitude. Since I am surrounded by Christians at work all week long, and seeing as my friends are believers, I forget what the world is really like. But the Lord Jesus Christ can make a difference in your life. He made a difference in mine."

Alec smirked. "I'm a believer. You're preaching to the choir, honey."

"Yes, well," she glanced down momentarily before meeting his gaze once more. "Tyler told me you said you were a Christian, but just going to a church doesn't make you a born-again child of God. It's not about a religion, it's about a relationship with the Savior."

"Lydia, I am a born-again believer. I got saved five years ago."

Confusion crossed her pretty face. "But you don't act like it, and Jesus said we would know fellow believers by their fruit."

"Listen, don't you dare stand in judgment of me," he stated harshly. "You don't even know me."

"But you stand in judgment of me and you don't know me, either."

Alec brought his chin up sharply as her comment met its mark.

"Now, as you're aware, we're having a little trouble at our church," she said in that sweet Southern voice of hers. "Some resentful former members are out to get my father-in-law, but he is a good preacher and I'd like to invite you to come out and hear him tomorrow morning."

"I attend another church, but thanks," Alec replied dryly.

Lydia just nodded before walking away. Again, Alec watched her go, but this time he didn't feel as remorseful about having offended her as he did about having offended the Lord Himself.

# *Chapter 7*

B oy, Alec, some neighbor you are. I'm glad you don't live next door to me!"
He looked over at the woman with short, light brown hair, sitting sideways in a chair, her jean-encased legs dangling over its arm.
"Thanks, Debbie," he replied sarcastically. "I knew I could count on you for some encouragement."

The young woman laughed, as did several of his other friends. Since they began tonight's Bible study with prayer requests, Alec mentioned Lydia, the situation with her father-in-law, and then before he knew it, he'd spilled the whole story—how he'd fixed her sink, come to her rescue last Monday night, and finally how he had insulted her character and she, in return, had doubted his faith.

He sighed heavily. "I feel doubly bad," he added, "because Lydia has told her kids they can't speak to me. Poor Tyler. . . you should have seen him out in his yard this afternoon. He seemed miserable. He's just dying for some male companionship, not to mention the fact that he's mourning the loss of a new bike."

"Well, there's a reason why God moved you in next door," dark-headed Larry said, lifting another slice of pizza out of the box sitting on the coffee table. "Maybe He wants you to be a father figure to the boy."

"Too late now," Alec replied. "I blew it."

"Did you try apologizing?" Debbie asked sarcastically.

Alec clenched his jaw, but he had to confess—he hadn't.

"Why don't you go over right now and tell your neighbor you're sorry?" Judy suggested, folding her leg beneath her as she sat on the floor near Debbie. She flipped a portion of her long hair over her shoulder.

"Yeah. . .wouldn't want the sun to go down on your anger," Tim said from his place on the sofa next to Alec. "Or hers."

Alec shook his head. "If I go over there, Lydia will most likely slam the door in my face. And I'd deserve it."

"Regardless of her reaction," Debbie stated bluntly, "you still have an obligation to do what's right."

"Hey, who invited you tonight, anyway?" Alec teased, grinning all the while.

"Go on, Alec," Judy prodded. "And after you make amends, invite her to our Bible study."

"She won't come. Her kids are probably asleep and Lydia told me she doesn't like to leave them unattended, even to walk next door."

"Well, if she's Gerald Boswick's daughter-in-law," Larry put in, "she most likely won't come just because we're not a part of Southern Pride Community Church. They think they're the only ones going to heaven."

"Hmm. . ." Alec mulled over the remark, wondering if that was the real reason Lydia had doubted his faith.

"Hold on, you guys," Debbie said, "we're getting off track. The problem isn't Lydia, it's Alec. He did wrong and he's got to apologize." She gave him a pointed stare. "So, go on. Git."

"You know," Alec said, rising from the sofa, "I think you need to practice some of that meek and quiet spirit stuff."

"Which is in the sight of God of great price," Tim added, pushing his wire-rim glasses higher up on his nose. He was always the one to quote scripture.

Debbie threw her empty Styrofoam cup at the both of them and everyone laughed again.

❧

Lydia sat on the couch with the cordless phone in her lap. Beside her was her address book, containing her mother's new phone number. Should she call? What would she say?

*Lord, I feel like a little girl who's missing her mama.* She picked up the receiver, but then set it down again. She couldn't decide.

The front doorbell rang, causing Lydia to jump. Slowly, she rose from the immaculate cream upholstered sofa and padded in her stocking feet to the living room window. She peeked out through the lacy sheers. *Alec. What does he want?*

Reluctantly, she went to the door and pulled hard on the knob, simultaneously donning her best hostess expression. "Well, Mr. Corbett," she greeted. "What a surprise."

"Can the 'Mr. Corbett' stuff, Lydia. I came here to apologize."

She took a deep breath, bracing herself. This man, while handsome enough, possessed an abrasive demeanor, and his presence threatened her fragile composure at the moment. She could scarcely believe she'd had the courage to stand up to him this morning.

"I shouldn't have said what I did last night," he began, his voice sounding softer. Lydia noticed his eyes. She had thought they were plain brown, a lighter shade than her children's dark gazes, but she'd been mistaken. They were the color of topaz, and beneath her porch light they shone with sincerity. "I guess I'm one of those guys once bitten, twice shy, as the old cliché goes. And you were right. I've been standing in judgment of you, using the same measuring stick I hold to the woman who hurt me. That wasn't fair. I'm sorry."

Unsure of her emotions, Lydia merely nodded. On one hand, she felt taken aback by his humility, on the other, she was grateful for his candidness.

"How 'bout we call a truce, okay?" Alec stuck out his right hand.

She smiled. How could she help it? When he put his mind to it, this man could be downright charming. "All right. Truce." She slipped her hand into his much larger one.

Alec gave it a gentle squeeze and grinned. "Truce." Then, much to her surprise, he didn't let it go. "Say, listen, some friends from church and I are having a Bible study. Want to join us?"

"I can't," she replied, feeling oddly disappointed. "Tyler and Brooke are sleeping."

At last, he released her hand. "Yeah, I figured, but I thought I'd invite you anyhow."

Lydia managed a weak smile as Alec sharpened his gaze and searched her face.

"You weren't. . .crying, were you?"

"No. I think I'm catching a cold," she fibbed. In truth, she'd been sobbing on and off all day—whenever she thought the kids wouldn't see. But she hadn't expected her new neighbor to be so perceptive and now she felt embarrassed. Were her eyes still red? Her face puffy? Good night! Why had she even answered the door?

"Yeah, well, I heard there's a flu bug going around."

Lydia nodded. "And you'd better put on a coat," she advised in her strongest voice, "or you're liable to catch pneumonia."

"Are you kidding?" Alec chuckled, and she thought it had a nice, happy sound to it. He didn't appear quite so formidable when he smiled, either. "It's fifty-five degrees out here. That's practically summer to me."

She folded her arms, feeling chilled to the bone. "Then you'll positively melt when it's July and one hundred degrees in the shade."

"You're probably right. But I'd rather melt than freeze to death." He smiled at her again. "Well, I'd better get back. See ya, Lydia."

She smiled back. "See ya."

She watched him walk away—Alec in his purple-and-green long-sleeved shirt with THE MILWAUKEE BUCKS printed across the front. *At least it's neatly tucked into his blue jeans*, she thought, closing the door. He might be a casual dresser, but he never looked like a slob. Walking farther into the living room, she allowed her gaze to fall on the telephone. *You'd like him, Mama. You'd like Alec Corbett. In a way, he reminds me of Michael.*

# Chapter 8

Alec reentered his house and all eyes turned on him.

"So?" Debbie asked. "What happened?"

"I apologized and everything's fine." His friends cheered and Alec couldn't help a grin, although inside he felt sorry for Lydia. She'd been crying, all right. He could tell. He'd grown up with sisters and he knew the signs. What's more, she looked like she might have enjoyed some company tonight.

"Did you invite her to the Bible study?" Judy asked.

"Yeah, but just like I told you, her kids are sleeping."

"And it's probably too late to get a baby-sitter," Debbie remarked. She lifted a contemplative brow. "But we could take our Bible study over to her place. You think she'd be interested, Alec?"

"Yeah, I think Lydia might be interested."

"No kidding?" Larry feigned a shocked expression. "A Boswick wants to attend a Bible study outside of SPCC? I'm about to have heart failure!"

Alec shot him a quelling look. "She didn't exactly say she wanted to attend. It's just a hunch."

"Judy, let's you and me go over and ask," Debbie suggested, getting up from the armchair.

"Maybe I'd better go along," Alec said.

"Why don't we all just go over, and if she says no, we'll come back here," Tim proposed.

"You don't think we'll scare her, do you?" Judy asked seriously. "I mean, if a group of strangers knocked on my door and asked to come in for a Bible study, I'd feel a little nervous."

"Well, Alec will be there," Debbie reasoned, picking up her Bible. "She knows him, right?"

"Sort of," he said. "We've only been neighbors for a week."

"Good enough. Larry, you take the pizza. Tim, you bring the pop. Everyone got their Bibles? Okay. Come on, gang," Debbie ordered, "let's go."

Out she marched, leading the way, and Alec shook his head as he followed. *Bossy woman. . .*

❧

Lydia ditched her ideas about phoning her mother and started turning off lights, beginning in the den. Glancing around the room and making sure everything was in its place, Lydia switched off the lamp. The darkness of the room increased her loneliness, and for a brief moment she thought it might consume her. She felt disconnected from the total universe. Friends had become scarce over the years since many people seemed intimidated by the fact that she was a Boswick. She spent most of her life at church, surrounded by its members. And the women there were cordial, but distant. Men, in general, were polite, and those who were single voiced their desire to date her, although none of them piqued Lydia's interest. The only man who caused her head to turn lately was her new neighbor. But she scarcely knew him, other than that he came from up North and had an intense aversion to blind dates. What had he said? He'd been hurt?

Mulling over his apology, Lydia walked into the living room as the doorbell rang again, but this time when she peeked out the curtains, she saw more than just Alec standing on her porch. Intuitively, she knew he was accompanied by the "friends" he'd mentioned when he invited her to the Bible study. But what did they want with her? More than curious, she walked to the door and opened it.

"Hi," said a short-haired woman wearing jeans and a T-shirt. "I'm Debbie Thompson and this is Judy Landers, Larry Matthews, Tim Parker. . .and you know Alec."

Lydia managed a polite smile, nodding at everyone. "Hello."

"Alec had an inkling you might like to join our Bible study tonight, and since you don't have a baby-sitter, we figured we'd come on over to your place. That is, if you really want to participate. We'd love it if you would, but we don't want to intrude if you're busy."

"Well, I. . ." Surprised by the offer, Lydia didn't know what to say. She glanced at Alec, who stood off to the side.

He smiled easily. "Just thought maybe you'd appreciate some Christian fellowship tonight."

"We're not part of a cult or anything, looking for converts," Tim told her, "so don't get scared. All of us are from Berean Baptist Church. Ever heard of it?"

"Yes, as a matter of fact, I know your pastor." Lydia recalled an evening long ago when Mark Spencer and his wife, Jerrica Dawn, attended a dinner party right here at her house. Lydia remembered the pastor as a man with an easy smile and a solid faith.

"Well, what's it gonna be? Pizza's getting cold," Larry said, prompting her decision.

Lydia laughed softly in spite of herself. "Sure. Come on in. Alec's right," she said, casting a glance his way. "I'm in the mood for some company."

The group of five filed into the foyer, ooh-ing and aah-ing over her awesome house.

"Please, come in and make yourselves comfortable." Lydia showed them into the living room.

"It looks so perfect in here that I'm afraid to sit down on the furniture," said Judy. She was a plump woman, but nice looking, and Lydia found herself impressed by her hair. It hung in dark blond waves that fell past her hips.

"Nonsense," she replied. "My children are known for jumping all over it."

She heard Alec's deep chuckle as he walked into the room, and she felt immensely relieved that the animosity between them had dissipated. Watching him settle into the couch, she tried to imagine why and how he'd been hurt before. Once bitten, twice shy—wasn't that what he'd said? Lydia suddenly found herself longing to prove the old "love of a good woman" theory true—except she couldn't understand her feelings. They barely knew each other. Still, there was just something about him. . .

"Oh, wow," Debbie exclaimed, drawing Lydia's attention away from Alec, "look at this fireplace." She whirled around. "Let's make a fire. I live in an apartment. I never get to enjoy such a luxury. But don't worry," she stated hastily, "I'll start it. You just sit down and relax, Lydia. I'll take care of everything."

"I'd better do it," Alec remarked, standing. "I don't want you burning this whole house down."

"Oh, quiet. I know what I'm doing," Debbie insisted.

"Lydia," Alec asked, turning toward her, "is it all right with you?"

Lydia nodded, relishing the thought of a cozy fire as they studied God's Word.

He leaned forward. "Listen, don't mind Debbie," he whispered. "She could make a marine cower."

"I heard that, Alec," the short-haired woman stated over her shoulder while hunkering in front of the stone hearth.

Everyone chuckled at the exchange, including Lydia. "Well," she managed at last, "I'll go get some plates for the pizza and glasses and ice for the pop." Turning, she headed for the kitchen.

"Allow me to help you," Larry called from behind her.

"Well, thank you," she replied gratefully.

In the kitchen, she pulled out a large serving tray before collecting the necessary items and handing them to Larry, who carried everything back into the living room.

"Maybe we should all introduce ourselves for Lydia's sake," Judy suggested from her place in one of the swivel rockers. Larry took the other matching rocker, and Debbie sat on the floor by the now-glowing hearth. Tim and Alec were seated at opposite ends of the couch, leaving the middle cushion vacant, so Lydia politely settled herself in between the two men.

"Ladies first," Tim said, "and since you came up with the idea, why don't you begin, Judy?"

"Okeydokey."

Judy gave a brief autobiography, including her salvation testimony.

"Lydia, you're our hostess, so you go next."

"All right. But there's not much to tell. I've lived in Alabama all my life. I became a Christian at nine years old and met my husband when I was sixteen. We dated until I was twenty-one, and then we had eight blissful years of marriage before God took Michael home. I'm a widow now, but I'm thankful that I've got two precious children, ages eight and five."

"Do you work outside the home?" Larry asked.

"Yes. I'm a secretary at Southern Pride Community Church."

"And your father-in-law is *the* Gerald Boswick," Tim added. "Didn't he write a book awhile ago? He's pretty well known, especially around here."

"Yes, he's authored several books." Lydia turned toward the man with the strawberry blond hair and glasses, sitting to her right.

"Hey, is all that true about him? His fall from grace, so to speak? Boy, there's an example of how power and money'll lead a man down the path of destruction." Larry sat forward in his chair, reaching for a slice of pizza. He was a fairly nice-looking man, in Lydia's opinion, with his slim build, dark brown hair, and hazel eyes. But his comment caused her to bristle.

"The allegations against my father-in-law are vicious lies!" She heard the terseness in her own voice. The room grew uncomfortably quiet and Larry had the good grace to look chagrined. Then Alec stretched his arm across the back of the couch just behind her in a reassuring gesture. Lydia suddenly felt foolish for her display of emotion. "I apologize for my outburst." She examined her folded hands. "It's just all very upsetting."

"Nothing for you to be sorry about," Alec stated. "Larry was out of line."

"I was," he admitted. "Forgive me. Guess I wasn't thinking."

Lydia managed a tight smile, willing herself not to burst into tears.

Alec's arm came down around her, his hand briefly touching her shoulder consolingly before he stood. "Want some pop? Hey, Debbie, pour some pop into that glass and hand it to me."

"Yes, sir, Mr. Drill Sergeant," she quipped, although she readily complied.

Laughing, Judy turned to Lydia. "Since the day these two met, they've been on each other's case."

"Yeah, the last two Saturday nights, they've sort of been our entertainment," Tim added, wearing a wide grin.

"I pity you, living next door to him," Debbie told Lydia. "I'll pray for you daily."

Lydia couldn't help feeling amused as Alec handed her the glass. "Hey, don't smile at her wisecracks," he said with an indignant expression. Just when Lydia was about to apologize, he sent her a wink.

She sipped her soda while Alec sat back down beside her.

Debbie introduced herself next. She was born and raised in New York City and got transferred to Montgomery eighteen months ago. "It's been quite an adjustment for me," she confessed. "But I'm really beginning to like it down here."

Then came Larry's turn, followed by Tim's, and as Lydia heard their testimonies, she felt impressed by them. Somehow she sensed they were committed Christians. Other than their pastor, she hadn't met people with such a strong faith outside of her own church in a long while. She wondered why Gerald was so adamant about not fellowshipping with those from other churches, and she also found herself recalling Michelle Marx's questions. *Is it true that many more women are accepted into the fold here at Southern Pride Community Church than are men? Is it true that scores of men are turned away from this church every year because Pastor Boswick will not abide anyone disagreeing with his theology? Is it true? Is it true?*

*Of course not,* Lydia thought, shifting slightly on the couch, and yet she tumultuously wondered if the three men sitting in her living room tonight would be "accepted into the fold." She had a feeling they would not. They didn't seem the SPCC type. Then again, neither had Michael, and that "perfect man syndrome," as he called it, had always irked him. He often said some of the men at SPCC were nothing more than "plastic people." Until now, however, Lydia hadn't paid much attention to his remarks, thinking he'd made them in jest. *And hadn't he?*

"I'm from Milwaukee, Wisconsin," Alec began, pulling Lydia from her reverie. "I was engaged to be married, but it busted up and I felt like starting over someplace new. So I put in for a transfer at work and wound up here. My first week in Woodruff has been. . .interesting. Guess I didn't make a great first impression on my neighbor." He gave Lydia a hooded glance and she felt herself blush. "But my job's going well. I think I'll stick around awhile."

"What's your occupation?" Lydia asked curiously.

"I'm a carpenter and I'm employed by a national firm that does a lot of cabinetry work—especially in new homes."

"A carpenter? Really?" Lydia smiled. "We sure could have used your help around here when we first bought this place."

He chuckled. "Yeah, I imagine."

"A carpenter," she repeated somewhat reverently. "After fixing up this house, I certainly have a great respect for men who work with wood. Besides, it's quite likely that Jesus was a carpenter before He began His ministry."

"Oh, why'd you have to say that?" Debbie groaned. "I can see Alec's ego inflating before my very eyes."

"You're just jealous," he shot back, wearing a wry grin.

"Of you? Hardly."

"Children, children," Larry said exaggeratedly with uplifted hands. "We're here to have a Bible study, remember? What will Miss Lydia think?"

"A good thing she's used to kids," Tim muttered glibly.

And on and on it went. Soon Lydia found herself giggling until her eyes teared. She couldn't remember the last time she'd had such a good laugh.

Finally, they got down to the whole purpose of the evening. Alec offered to share his Bible with Lydia so she wouldn't have to get up and fetch hers. Tim led the study of Isaiah 40:28–31. Tying it in with the theme of singleness, he concluded, "If we trust the Lord to bring the right person into our lives, He'll give us His strength and we won't 'faint' while we wait—in other words, we won't be discouraged while we wait on Him."

"What if He never does bring someone into your life?" Lydia asked sincerely.

"Weeks ago, we did a study of Psalm 37," Judy explained, "and determined that if God has placed a desire in our hearts to marry, He will make it happen. We just need to trust Him for the right timing—and the right one."

"And in the case of my broken engagement," Alec added candidly, "I realized tonight I need to trust that God made the right decision there. I know He never makes mistakes, but it's taken me all these months to accept the fact that He *allowed* it to happen. . .for my own good."

"That's right," Larry said.

"And what about your husband's death, Lydia?" Debbie asked. "Have you been able to accept it?"

"Oh yes. I accepted it long ago. I know Michael is in a place so wonderful he wouldn't come back here to me and the children for anything. Besides, the Bible says a day with the Lord is like a thousand on earth. Michael will meet the Savior and then look over his shoulder and there we'll be."

"But what about you?" Judy asked, looking concerned.

"Me? Oh, I'm all right." Despite her guests' ability to wear their hearts on their sleeves, Lydia couldn't get herself to admit to the loneliness that frequently haunted her.

"I'm sure you get plenty of support from your church, huh?" Larry asked.

"Yes, that's right," Lydia replied. "I'm most grateful to my father-in-law for all his care of Tyler, Brooke, and me."

There was a moment's pause and then Tim began speaking about a young woman with whom he worked. He was interested in her, but she didn't know the Lord. . .yet. Next Debbie talked about a man she'd met through the Internet. Was it safe for singles to meet each other on the Web? Was it of God?

It was nearly midnight when they wrapped up their topics and closed in prayer. Lydia felt as though she'd gotten more out of this casual Bible study and its following discussion than she got out of a month's worth of Sunday morning sermons.

"I'm glad y'all came over tonight," she drawled, seeing them to the door.

"Well, how 'bout next Saturday night, too?" Debbie asked. "Can you get a sitter?"

"Perhaps. I'll do my best."

"It's at my apartment," Debbie said. "Alec will give you my address and phone number if you want to come."

"Bossy," Alec muttered. Looking at Lydia, he said, "But, yes, I will give you the information."

"Thank you."

Bidding her new friends farewell, Lydia closed the front door after they left. She proceeded to clear the dishes and empty boxes of pizza, thinking how much she'd enjoyed their company tonight. And Alec. . .she had certainly seen a different side of him. Beneath that gruff exterior beat a tender heart.

With everything cleaned up, she sat back down in the living room and watched the last of the embers in the fireplace die out. Maybe she wouldn't mind remarrying after all—if the Lord brought along the right one. But Alec Corbett? He couldn't possibly be a running candidate for her husband. Gerald would never approve of him. He wasn't a member of SPCC, for one thing. Besides, what on earth was she thinking? She barely knew the man!

"Mama?"

Lydia snapped from her musings. "Tyler. What are you doing awake at this hour?"

"I've been awake a long time," he said, coming down the stairs slowly. "Who were all those people?"

"Just some friends. We had a Bible study tonight."

"Oh." Tyler paused, looking confused. "Mama, I saw you sitting next to Mr. Alec and smiling. You're not mad at him anymore, huh?"

"No. I'm not mad at him anymore."

He immediately beamed. "Cool!"

"Shh. . .you're going to wake up Brooke."

The boy broke into a whisper. "Sorry, Mama, but I've been praying and praying that you wouldn't be angry with Mr. Alec anymore."

"Seems God answered your prayers," she said, turning off the living room light. She slipped her arm around Tyler's shoulders as she walked him upstairs.

"Does that mean I can still talk to him?"

"Yes. But, Ty, you mustn't try to create situations to get Mr. Alec and me together."

"Like last night?"

"Yes. That was wrong of you and Brooke, just like we talked about at the supper table. If the Lord wants Mr. Alec. . .or anyone else to have a part of our lives, then we need to let Him work everything out."

Tyler searched her face as they stood at his bedroom door. "You like him, don't you, Mama?"

She tried not to grin at the direct question that caught her somewhat off guard. Still, she had a hard time hiding her feelings.

"You do! I knew it!"

"Shh. . .lower your voice."

He ran into his room, leaping into his bed. "I knew it!"

Lydia suddenly felt nervous—she didn't want her in-laws privy to this new, unexpected turn of her heart, and she certainly didn't want Alec to know. He'd most likely decide his initial suspicions of her were correct.

"Tyler," she said, padding across the carpeted floor and sitting on the edge of his bed, "let's just keep this a secret between you and me, all right?"

"Why?"

"Because God has to work in Mr. Alec's heart first. Right now all we can do is pray. . .and not say a word to *anyone*. Then, if something happens, we'll know for sure it's the Lord's will."

"Okay. I promise."

She smiled at his exuberance.

"God likes to answer my prayers."

"Yes, He sure does," Lydia admitted, standing and making her way out of the room.

"Grampa says God's gonna use me in a big way."

"I believe that." She blew him a kiss. "Good night. I love you."

"Love you, too."

Walking toward her own bedroom, Lydia couldn't suppress the chuckle bubbling up inside her. The future suddenly seemed to sparkle again. For the first time in two and a half years, she felt alive. Had she really been only existing for the sake of her children and others? No wonder Gerald had been concerned, telling her she should remarry. She'd been lifeless.

She strolled to the window and pulled back the blinds. *But everything changed in a week*, she thought incredulously, peering down at Alec's house. *All because a neighbor moved in next door.* Shaking her head, she added silently, *Alec Corbett, why do you make me feel like I'm a hopeful sixteen-year-old again?*

# Chapter 9

Days passed and the rain began. The cold dampness had a way of creeping into the bones, not to mention the mind and spirit. For the first time in twelve years, Lydia felt sorry for her mother-in-law. The scandal surrounding Gerald leveled her to a mere shadow of the strong-willed, opinionated woman Lydia had known. She hadn't even fallen apart like this after losing her only son. But by the mid-week worship service on Thursday evening, Elberta had had more than she could bear and packed her bags and flew off to Tallahassee to stay indefinitely with her daughter, Mary. At church there were murmurs of Gerald's resignation—at least temporarily, until the talk quieted, Elberta returned, and the charges against him were dismissed. Gerald stubbornly refused to give in, saying he'd "raised this church up from the ground," but he acknowledged his need for some time away. On Friday morning Sim obtained permission from the DA, and Gerald left at noon for his posh condo on the gulf coast. After he'd gone, Lydia wished there were something she could do for her in-laws. Things at SPCC seemed to be unraveling like a cheap sweater, and that afternoon as she drove home with Tyler and Brooke, she felt as bleak as the gloomy winter weather.

"Hey, Lydia," Alec called out his back door as she began to run for the house in the freezing downpour, "I want to talk to you. Can I come over? Won't take long."

"Sure." She reached the back door and fished in her purse for her keys.

"Hurry," Brooke whined, "I'm getting wet."

Lydia unlocked the door and the three of them spilled into the house. "What a day," she said with a long sigh.

Removing their wet things, the children agreed.

"Maybe we'll order a pizza for supper tonight."

"Yeah! And maybe Mr. Alec will stay and eat with us."

"Tyler, don't start. We talked about this, remember?"

He nodded grimly and followed his sister into the den. Still in the kitchen, Lydia heard the television go on. She rolled her head in a circle, stretching her tense neck muscles. This hadn't been a good day, and she wondered what Alec wanted. She hadn't seen him all week.

As if on cue, the doorbell rang and Tyler ran to answer it. "Hi, Mr. Alec," she heard him say. "Come on in."

"Hey, kid, how you doing?"

"Okay."

"Got your ark built yet?" Meeting him in the foyer, Lydia saw Alec chuckle while confusion flittered across Tyler's face. "Ark, get it?" he explained. "Like Noah and all the rain. . ."

"Oh!" The boy laughed.

Smiling, Alec looked over at Lydia. Clad in blue jeans and a striped, long-sleeve, button-down shirt, he made an impressive sight there in her hallway. Just seeing him again caused her a small measure of happiness after enduring the last seven hours at work.

"How are you?"

"Good," she fibbed. "And yourself?"

"Fine. I had a short day. Got off at noon." He scratched his jaw and shifted his stance uncomfortably.

Lydia glanced at Tyler, who watched the exchange with interest. Brooke, sitting on one of the sofas in the den, seemed to care less that their neighbor had stopped by and looked completely absorbed by the cartoon sing-along video on TV.

"Alec, why don't you and I talk in the kitchen," she said, realizing he wanted to speak with her privately. "Tyler, you go back in the den."

"But, Mama—"

"Tyler." She gave him a direct look and he didn't argue.

"Yes, ma'am."

Alec grinned. "Kitchen's fine."

Turning, Lydia led the way. "I think I'll make some herbal tea. Would you like a cup?"

"Naw. Thanks anyway. This really won't take long. I just wondered if. . . um. . ." They reached the kitchen, and Lydia stopped by the counter, giving him her full attention. "Well, tomorrow is February thirteenth and the company I work for is throwing a Valentine's Day party. I normally wouldn't go, but being the new guy, I sort of feel obligated and I, um, need a date. If I show up without one, Norm Whitehall says he'll fix me up with his sister and if she resembles Norm even a little. . . Lydia, this isn't funny. Quit laughing."

"I'm sorry," she said, doing her best to swallow her giggles. "It's been a long day and I guess I'm punchy." In truth, she felt a bit giddy that Alec was asking her out—even if it was in order to escape a blind date.

"Lydia, I wondered if maybe you'd go to the party with me," he asked, looking stone faced but very vulnerable.

"I would be honored," she said.

He relaxed visibly. "Thanks."

"What time will you pick me up?"

"How's seven sound?"

"Fine." She smiled and then remembered their previous plans. "What about the Bible study?"

"Would you mind skipping it with me this week?"

Lydia shook her head.

"Sorry this is such short notice, but it took me four days to work up the courage to ask you."

"Oh, Alec. . ." She waved a hand at him. "I don't bite. Honest."

He laughed curtly. "Well, if you bit me, you'd have every good reason, considering the things I've said to you."

"I forgot all about them."

"Oh, yeah?" Pursing his lips, Alec scrutinized her in a way that caused Lydia's cheeks to warm.

She turned away. "Are you sure you don't want some tea?"

"Yeah. I'd better go." He walked back through the house to the foyer, then stopped short. "On second thought. . ." He spun around.

Right behind him, Lydia halted midstride and arched questioning brows.

"I might be pushing my luck here, but would you and the kids want to go out for pizza tonight?"

Tyler whooped from the den. "Say yes, Mama!"

Lydia rolled her eyes at her son's response, but inside, her heart beat with as much enthusiasm. "Sure," she said at last, "we'd love to."

❈

It was ten o'clock that night when Alec finally arrived back home. He tossed his truck keys onto his kitchen counter and stared at them as though they might come to life and turn somersaults. *I'm doing it again*, he thought almost miserably. *I'm falling head over heels in love with a woman—the very thing I vowed I wouldn't do.* He sighed, glancing at the ceiling. "Two weeks, Lord," he muttered in prayer. "Do you see what I've done in two short weeks? Got myself in another fine mess."

He sauntered through the house and into the living room, feeling a surge of disbelief shoot through him. Lydia Boswick—he didn't even know her middle name. He didn't know much about her at all, other than she owned and refurbished the house next door, was a widow, a Christian. . .and liked pizza. And she sure could talk, but that was all right with him. Tyler and Brook had been well-mannered at the table, and they obviously liked him—and, better yet, so did their mother.

Alec sat down on the couch and turned on the television set, mindlessly watching in muted silence whatever happened to be on. That Lydia shared his romantic interest, well, that made things easier. Wouldn't be hard to win her heart. But did he want to? In his experience, romances always started off all warm and fuzzy only to become complicated matters that messed with his mind and tore at his emotions. But there was always the chance this time could be different.

This time. . .

Pointing the remote control at the TV, Alec flipped it off. He hadn't kissed Lydia tonight, but he'd sure wanted to. They'd spent a long time gazing into each other's eyes at her front door before he took his leave, and now he felt like some lovesick schoolboy. It'd happened just this way with Denise, too. He'd fallen fast, and he'd fallen hard. And now Lydia.

*Lord, You're going to have to take over here, 'cause I'm scared. Real scared. And Lydia and I have another date tomorrow night—except I just might die if I have to wait that long to see her again.*

Standing, Alec turned off the lamp on the end table beside the sofa and walked into his bedroom. Maybe if he had a good night's sleep he'd wake up thinking straight in the morning.

Yeah, that's it. A good night's sleep.

# Chapter 10

Alec made it until eleven o'clock before he couldn't stand it anymore and decided to trek over to Lydia's house. Thinking he needed an excuse, he wheeled the bike he'd given Tyler alongside him. The day was damp and gloomy, but the rain had stopped, and Alec thought if the kid played his cards right, his mother might even allow him to take back his new bike.

Walking up the driveway, he paused outside the back door and knocked loudly. Tyler answered.

"Hi, Mr. Alec."

"Hi. Is your mom busy?"

"No. I'll get her."

He turned and Alec watched through the screen door as the boy ran back into the kitchen, calling for her. Within minutes, Lydia strode toward him, wearing a pink wool sweater with an off-white turtleneck underneath it, a denim split skirt, and thick ivory socks tucked snugly into brown leather ankle boots.

"Hi." She opened the door and beckoned him into the hallway.

He smiled. "Expecting the temperature to fall to fifty below?"

She frowned, feeling puzzled, and Alec chuckled.

"Your outfit, Lydia. You look like someone who lives in the North Pole."

"Excuse me," she said in feigned haughtiness, "but I'm freezing."

"It's warm out here."

"Oh, it is not. You're just a thick-blooded Northerner."

Throwing his head back, Alec hooted.

Lydia gave him a quelling look, smiling all the while, and then Alec spotted Tyler standing a short distance away, watching them curiously.

"I, um, brought the bike back," he said earnestly now. "That is, if it's okay with you."

Lydia turned and eyed her son before bringing her gaze back to his, and Alec realized for the first time just what a petite little thing she really was, standing no taller than his shoulders.

"Tyler has a bike," she began. "He doesn't really need another. I've been trying to teach both my children the difference between wanting something and needing it."

"That's a good lesson," Alec replied carefully, trying to ignore the way the boy's face fell with disappointment. "But he'll probably outgrow the bike he's got soon enough and then he'll *need* a new one. Might as well keep this one. It's free."

"Yeah, Mama. Otherwise, it'll cost you money."

Lydia glanced at her son before her dusky blue eyes swung back around, searching Alec's face. The tiny tug at the corner of her mouth let him know she found his and Tyler's persuasiveness somewhat comical.

He grinned back at her. "Come on, Lydia," he said softly, "it's just a bike." Then, before he could think better of it, he reached out and brushed a strand of chestnut-colored hair from her cheek. A moment's look of surprise and something else—something unidentifiable—flittered across her lovely features before she blinked, obviously regaining her composure.

"That's right. It's just a bike," she repeated.

"Say yes, Mama," Tyler begged. "Please, say yes."

"Oh, well, I guess it can't hurt," Lydia agreed at last.

"Yippee!"

"But there's one condition," Alec declared above Tyler's cheering. He narrowed his gaze at Lydia. "You can't give the thing back—even if you get mad at me again."

She blushed, her cheeks matching the color of her sweater, and Alec felt thoroughly charmed.

"Can I go outside and ride it for a while?" Tyler asked.

Lydia nodded. "Yes, but put on a jacket."

"Aw, do I hafta? Mr. Alec said it's warm."

"Not warm enough for you. Jacket on."

Alec regarded her with interest as she gave her son one of those expressions only a mother could impart. He laughed softly under his breath.

"Yes, ma'am," Tyler muttered.

Lydia turned back to Alec. "Would you like to come in for a cup of coffee?"

"Sure."

As Tyler rushed out the back door, Alec followed Lydia into the kitchen. She invited him to sit down at the table and he recognized the fancy rose tablecloth that he'd first seen last week. Then Brooke entered the kitchen, asking if she could go outside and play, too.

"Yes, but stay in the backyard."

The little girl nodded.

"How do you like your coffee, Alec?"

"Black."

Lydia fixed up two cups before claiming a seat beside him at the table.

"So did you say you've lived in Alabama all your life?" Alec asked, taking a swallow of his brew.

"Yes. I was born in a small city near the coast, but after my father died, my mother moved us to Montgomery."

"Brothers? Sisters?"

"Neither. Just me. What about you?"

"Two older sisters. I'm the baby of the family."

Lydia grinned. "You're an awfully big baby," she drawled teasingly.

"Yeah, well, what can I say?" Alec chuckled and a few moments of silence passed. "So, does your mother still live around here?"

"Yes. She's in Greenville, but now lives with her new husband. She and Pete were married about nine months ago."

"Interesting." Alec took another drink. "My folks are divorced, but neither remarried. I guess the first time around was enough for both of them."

"What about you?" Lydia asked. "You talked about a broken engagement at the Bible study. . . ."

"Yep. And there's not much to tell, other than Denise—that was her name—up and changed her mind about marrying me."

"I'm so sorry."

Alec shrugged. "Nothing to be sorry about, really. Can I ask you something personal?"

"I suppose. . .but how personal?"

Alec laughed. "What's your middle name?"

Lydia paused, as if momentarily taken aback. "My middle name? It's Rose. Why do you ask?"

"Just wondering. I've been trying to imagine what it'd be. I thought maybe Ann or Marie. But Rose fits you just perfect. Lydia Rose, Southern belle."

"Oh, hush," she quipped, blushing profusely. "And what's your middle name?"

"Guess."

Lydia rolled her eyes but sat thinking it over. Alec watched her pretty mouth trying different names on her tongue. Finally she picked one. "James."

"Right."

"Really? And here I'm not very good at guessing games." Laughing softly, she stood and walked to the counter with her cup. "Would you care for more coffee?"

"Sure would."

Lydia refilled his cup once, then again, and finally three times before their coffee klatch came to an end two hours later. After Alec left the house, she took the cups to the sink. Pulling out the bread and the peanut butter and jelly jars, she made sandwiches for Tyler and Brooke, who were no doubt ready to dash inside any minute for lunch. Before she finished, the door banged shut behind her predictable pair.

"Mama, you like him more and more, don't you?" Ty sat down, scraping the chair closer to the table.

"Yes, I do."

"And he likes you, too."

"I think he does."

"Oh, he does," Brooke said adamantly, nodding her blond head as though she were an expert on such matters.

Lydia just smiled and began wiping off the counter. Yes, they liked each other—enough to pursue this relationship further. The thought sent a stream of delight mingled with apprehension through her veins. Gerald wouldn't like him—somehow she just knew it.

She and Alec had discussed a wide gamut of subjects this morning, and Lydia ended up divulging the details surrounding her mother and the church discipline issue. Alec had said the disciplinary action didn't sound right to him, since Pete professed to be a Christian. "Sounds to me like your father-in-law was standing in judgment of the guy. But, Lydia, I'm no authority on the subject. I'd have to research the topic of church discipline in the Bible."

Lydia nibbled her lower lip in contemplation. *It didn't sound right to Alec.* He'd given her his objective opinion, putting the question in her own heart. And now more than ever, Lydia wanted to phone her mother. Glancing out the window, she realized it had started raining again.

"Can me 'n' Brooke watch a movie?" Tyler asked. "What about the one Gramma bought us?"

"Yes, that's fine."

The children left the table and headed for the den. Standing with her back to the kitchen sink, Lydia watched them go before she eyed the phone on the wall. *Should I call?*

*Lord, if I'm wrong to do this, then I deserve to be found out. If going against Gerald's wishes is going against Your will, I'll suffer the consequences.* She collected her address book from the drawer at the end of the counter where she kept the phone books. *But if my mother's church discipline wasn't fair—if it wasn't right—I trust You will protect me from suffering a similar reproof.* Picking up the phone, Lydia dialed her mother's number.

# Chapter 11

Mesmerized, Alec watched Lydia gracefully move around her living room in a winter white tea-length jacket-dress accented with red satin embroidery on the bodice and along the skirt's hem. He thought the outfit hugged her form, but in a modest way, and in a fashion that offered Lydia a certain elegance and grace. He felt like the luckiest guy in the world, taking her out tonight.

"All right now, you two behave yourselves," she drawled, kissing Brooke then Tyler before giving the baby-sitter a final word of instruction. The sitter, an older woman with a grandmotherly disposition, had been introduced to Alec as Lydia's next-door neighbor on the other side—Mrs. Connie Wilberson.

"We'll be just fine, honey," the matronly woman insisted, her stocky frame perched on one end of the sofa. "You and Mr. Alec have a nice time." She grinned like a cat, looking from one to the other. "Did Pastor Boswick set up this match?"

"No, he didn't," Lydia replied vaguely.

"Oh?" The gray-haired woman's round face contorted with concern.

"Not to fret, Mrs. Wilberson, my father-in-law has met Alec." Lydia turned toward him. "Isn't that right? You two met the Sunday after you moved in."

"That's true." Alec thought Lydia looked a bit nervous, and he wondered, again, if they were making a mistake. Maybe they should put a stop to this relationship before it went any further. Maybe—

*No, I prayed about this and decided to trust the Lord to guide my steps,* Alec reminded himself. *I'm not going to wimp out now.*

"Alec, I think we'd best go before we're late."

He snapped to attention. "Right."

Lydia snatched her coat and purse and they headed for the door.

"Bye, Mr. Alec!" Ty called.

"Bye, kid."

Brooke waved shyly and smiled. Mrs. Wilberson appeared glued to her post, unanswered questions pooling in her eyes.

Outside, Alec helped Lydia into his truck. Before closing the door, he propped a palm against the frame and peered at her. "You're not obligated to come with me tonight, Lydia. I mean, if you don't think it's a good idea or that your father-in-law might not approve. . ."

"But I want to go out with you tonight," she replied softly, causing Alec's heart to flip inside his chest. "And for the record, my father-in-law does not make my decisions."

Alec grinned. "Okay, lady. I gave you one last chance to back out." Closing the door, he laughingly walked around to the driver's side and climbed in. *So, Lydia has some spunk after all.* He strapped on his seatbelt and glanced at her. "By the way, you look like a million bucks tonight."

"Only a million?" Lydia retorted.

Starting the engine, he chuckled and backed out of the driveway. The night definitely held promise. "I can tell we're going to have a good time."

She returned his smile.

"Except," Alec added, shifting gears as he drove down the street, "I never imagined a Southern belle like you would have even an ounce of gumption in your veins. I thought you were a docile little thing."

"Disappointed?" she asked carefully.

"No. Just surprised."

"I imagine it's my mother's fault," she drawled. "I called her this afternoon and obviously some of her *rebellion* rubbed off on me."

"I sincerely hope you're kidding, Lydia," Alec said, seriously now. "I mean, following your heart and marrying a Christian man, like you said your mom did, isn't rebellion in my book—God's either, as far as I know."

"And it's not as though my mother is a teenager who thwarted parental authority."

"That's right." He momentarily looked her way. "So, were you kidding just now or what?"

"Yes, I was being sarcastic. I apologize."

"No need. But I guess I never saw your sense of humor in action before either. And, no, I'm not disappointed. I like it."

Lydia glanced his way, wearing a slip of a grin. "May I share something very personal with you?"

"Sure, as long as it's not going to get me arrested or anything."

She laughed. "Hardly."

"Okay, go for it."

Her voice quickly became soft and solemn. "I'm realizing that after Michael died, part of me went dormant. But now I feel like I'm awakening to life again."

"Oh, yeah?" Alec saw her nod.

"And I think it all began when you moved in next door."

"Hmm. . ." He wasn't sure how to respond. He felt flattered, more than flattered. He was both glad and relieved she felt the same way he did, but this thing between them was happening too fast. Wasn't it? "Look, Lydia—"

"I know. Don't say it."

"Say what?"

"That you're not ready for a commitment, we barely know each other, that we're only on our first date. I'm aware of the facts. And the last thing I want to do is push you in any one direction. But, just the same, what I told you is the truth. I can't help it."

"Aw, I'll bet you say that to all the guys," he teased her, suddenly uncomfortable with the perilous turn to their conversation.

Lydia rapped him in the arm with her purse and Alec chuckled. But she didn't say another word about their relationship during the remainder of the trip to the restaurant. Oddly, he couldn't figure out if that made him feel better or worse.

When at last they arrived, he walked around his vehicle to assist Lydia. "I never rode in a pickup truck before," she told him when her feet touched the pavement.

"Used to Lincolns, eh?"

"Oh, please, don't remind me about that ill-fated night with Sim." She clucked her tongue.

Smiling, Alec threw caution to the wind and took her hand as they walked through the parking lot. The Valentine's Day dinner party was held in one of the banquet rooms of the Southern Cross Restaurant, which overflowed with a laughing, chatting throng of people. They squeezed their way through the queue of smartly dressed men and women, waiting for vacant tables, and found the Heritage Craft Furniture group standing around, mingling.

"Don't look now, Lydia," Alec leaned over and whispered loudly, "but Greg Nivens is about to drop his teeth."

"What?" Lydia frowned in confusion.

"Greg Nivens," he explained, his hand still enveloping hers, "is my supervisor. He also attends your church, and I think he's surprised to see you here. No, make that *shocked*. The guy is definitely shocked."

"Greg Nivens?" Lydia repeated the name. "I don't believe I know him. But then again, ours is such a large church. It's impossible to know everybody."

"Well, here he comes, so you'll get a chance to meet him now. And I think that's his wife with him."

Lydia followed the direction of Alec's gaze and spotted the attractive pair heading their way. Having faces to put with the name, she recognized them at once. Still, when the Nivenses reached them, introductions were made.

"We know Mrs. Boswick," Greg said, rocking on his heels. "Doesn't everyone at SPCC?"

Lydia gave the man a polite smile. He was the proverbial tall, dark, and handsome type right down to the dimple in his left cheek, and suddenly she recalled Michael's term for men at SPCC—*plastic people*.

Alec released Lydia's hand, turning her way. "Want a pop or something? I'll go get you one."

"Mineral water would be nice."

"Coming right up."

Lydia watched him walk away before giving her attention back to the Nivenses.

"Small world, isn't it?" Greg said curiously.

"Yes, sir, it is."

"How'd you meet up with Alec, anyway? He just moved to town."

"He's my next-door neighbor."

"Ahh. . . ," the couple said simultaneously, as though they'd just figured out one of the great mysteries of the world.

"Guess he works fast, too, eh?" Greg replied slyly, laughing at his own comment.

Lydia forced a smile.

"Okay, now, be honest," he said amusedly as he leaned slightly forward. "Does the pastor know you're out with my newest employee?"

"Why do you ask?"

"Well, it's just that Pastor Boswick seems awful particular about who his family associates with."

"He is, but Alec is a fine man."

"I agree. And he's a hard worker. I just meant. . .well, he's not one of *us*."

"A member of SPCC?"

"That's right."

"Well, now, perhaps Mrs. Boswick will be the one to persuade him to apply for membership," Greg's wife suggested, patting the side of her French twist. "You know how convincing those Boswicks are." She smiled indulgently.

Greg agreed. "But I don't need convincing when it comes to our pastor's innocence, and I want you to know that my wife and I are behind your family all the way."

"Why, thank you." When Greg looked like he might enjoy continuing their discussion about the scandal, Lydia sought a quick escape. "I'd better go see if Alec needs some help. Excuse me." She hurried toward Alec, just as he finished getting their mineral water.

"People are really putting away the booze here tonight," Alec remarked, handing Lydia one of the glasses in his hands. "But I shouldn't be surprised. Before I knew the Lord, I drank like a fish myself."

She smiled. "You have the funniest sayings. 'Dropped his teeth.' 'Drank like a fish. . .'"

"I'm glad you find me so entertaining."

Several of Alec's buddies approached them, and Lydia was introduced to more people. The evening progressed and dinner was served. She discreetly observed Alec's table manners and felt mildly impressed—he selected the correct fork for his salad, even going so far as to pick up his knife and cut some of the larger leafy greens on his plate. He didn't talk with his mouth full, and he made good use of his napkin. Lydia wondered if perhaps his mother played "restaurant" with him like she did with her children. Regardless, he'd picked up proper social etiquette somewhere along the line.

In between dinner and dessert, Alec sat back and stretched his arm over the top of her chair. At the same time, she caught sight of the Nivenses sitting two tables away, staring in her direction. No doubt they disapproved of her being there with Alec. Gerald wouldn't approve of her dating him, either, especially without his permission; however, Lydia hoped to get around him somehow. How exactly, she wasn't sure. But she planned to be firm about her decision to see Alec—even if it meant standing up to Gerald, something she wanted to avoid. He'd done so much for her in the past, but did she owe him her life in return? According to her mother, yes. Gerald would expect that and nothing less.

"I had always thought Southern Pride Community Church was a wonderful place to worship God and fellowship with other believers," her mother had stated during their conversation that afternoon. "I had the utmost respect for Gerald, but he'd been using me—and my money—all along. He's using you, too, honey."

Although the statement worried her, Lydia wanted to shrug off what her mother said as sheer ridiculousness. Using her? Hardly. Gerald had been a bulwark in Lydia's life since Michael died. And yet, in her heart of hearts rang a warning knell. Could the extortion allegations be true? And if such problems were really rippling through SPCC, why hadn't she taken notice of them? Were they that imperceptible as her mother claimed, or had she been totally blind to the facts? It was true—while in her hibernation of grief, Lydia hadn't been able to see beyond her everyday duties, caring for her children, working at her job. Now, however, it seemed she was awakening to a veritable nightmare!

※

"I don't know why I'm telling you all this," Alec said much later as they sat in his truck, parked in Lydia's driveway. "Your baby-sitter is probably anxious to get home."

Lydia shook her head. "Mrs. Wilberson always falls asleep. It's all right. Besides, I'm glad you told me about Denise. It helps me get to know you. Except. . ." She paused and, under the glow of the full moon, Alec saw her thoughtful expression. "I can't understand why that woman up and changed her mind."

"Me, neither."

"Does it still hurt?"

Lydia's velvet drawl was like a soothing salve, but he'd be a liar if he said the pain of being dumped had completely gone. "A little," he finally replied. "It still hurts a little."

A long paused settled between them.

"Well, we should get you inside before you catch a night chill," Alec announced facetiously. "You Southern belles aren't used to these frigid temperatures."

"Ooh! You can say that again!" As if to emphasize it, she shivered.

Unable to contain his laughter, he climbed out of his truck and walked around to the other side. Lydia hadn't budged but waited for him to open the door and help her down. And a good thing he noticed, too, or he'd look pretty stupid walking to the porch all by himself. *Denise usually beat me out of the truck. I never held the door for her.*

Together he and Lydia walked to her front door, and Alec recalled her conversation with Sim about kissing on the first date. Whether it was pure arrogance or a good case of male ego, Alec couldn't be sure, but he knew he was going to get a kiss out of Lydia tonight or die trying.

"Thanks a lot for coming to the party with me," he began.

She smiled. "It was fun—and I mean it."

He grinned and watched her dig in her purse for her house keys. Clasping them in her palm, she looked back at him.

"Good night."

" 'Night, Lydia."

In two smooth, practiced moves, Alec stepped forward and gathered her into his arms, pausing only briefly to view her reaction. When she didn't protest, he lowered his mouth to hers. But the moment their lips met, Alec knew he'd made a grave error.

He cut the kiss short. "I better go."

Lydia nodded. Was that disappointment he saw in her eyes?

"See ya," he said hastily.

"Good night," she replied once more.

Back in his truck and leaving her driveway, Alec berated himself for being such a fool. Oh, he'd won the challenge and gotten the prize, but he hadn't considered the consequences, and they were steep. Having tasted Lydia's sweet kiss tonight cost him plenty.

It had just cost Alec Corbett his very heart.

# Chapter 12

As Lydia fed her children a snack the following evening, she threw a glance next door. She hadn't seen Alec all day, even though she'd hoped to run into him after church that morning and invite him over for lunch—since it was Valentine's Day. But then as now, his house looked dark and deserted.

"Mama?" Tyler's voice penetrated her thoughts and Lydia gave him her full attention. "Matt's e-mail address doesn't work."

"Yes, I figured."

"Could I call him? I won't talk long."

"I don't know. . . ."

"I got his phone number from his aunt Rita. I saw her at church tonight."

Lydia hesitated, but only because she wasn't sure how welcomed Ty's call would be. Then again, he and Matt had stayed true-blue companions even though her and Sherry's friendship had come to an abrupt halt. "All right," she acquiesced. "I suppose you can phone Matt."

His mouth full of cheese and crackers, Tyler jumped off his chair and ran for the phone hanging on the wall on the other side of the kitchen.

"Chew your food before placing the call."

The boy swallowed. "Okay." He pulled a slip of paper from his pants pocket, picked up the receiver, and dialed the number. After a few moments, he smiled. "Hello, this is Tyler. Can Matt talk?"

Lydia listened quietly as she straightened up the kitchen.

"Mama?" Brooke asked, still sitting at the table. "Could I have a friend from school come over and play?"

"I think so," Lydia replied, sensing that her daughter missed the Smiths' little girl, Pamela, even though she was a year older than Brooke. "Maybe next weekend."

"Goodie!" Brooke exclaimed before nibbling on another cracker.

"Yeah, and a man moved next door named Mr. Alec," Tyler was saying. "He's really big, and he doesn't even care if me 'n' Brooke stand on the fence. And guess what else? He and my mom went on a date last night!"

"Oh, Ty, I don't think Matt cares about that," Lydia remarked softly, feeling oddly embarrassed.

"I think they're gonna get married."

"Tyler!" This time Lydia's voice carried throughout the entire room.

"It's true, Mama," the boy replied with the receiver under his chin and an earnest expression on his face. "I knew it from the first day I saw Mr. Alec moving in. Isn't that right, Brooke?"

She nodded. "We thought you'd like him, Mama."

Lydia sighed. "My two children, Woodruff's own matchmakers!" After rolling her eyes, she tapered her gaze at Tyler. "Hurry up and finish your call, now. Long distance is expensive."

"Yes, ma'am. What did you say, Matt? Oh, yeah."

Tyler began disclosing various events at school while Lydia instructed Brooke to go upstairs and change into her nightie.

"Mama? Mrs. Smith wants to talk to you now," Tyler announced, following several minutes of idle chitchat with Matt.

Lydia was taken aback. Sherry? Wanted to talk to *her*? Slowly, she stepped to the phone and took the proffered receiver.

"Hello?" she said cautiously.

"Lydia? I know you probably loathe and despise me, but—"

"What are you talking about?"

A pause.

"I'm talking about Jordan and me and our public statement about Gerald."

"Oh, that." With one hand holding the phone to her ear, Lydia rubbed a troubled hand across her forehead. Why would Sherry even care what she thought? They hadn't spoken in months! And although Lydia still felt hurt and mourned the loss of their friendship, she wasn't angry, and she certainly didn't "despise" Sherry.

"May I explain?" Sherry asked.

"You don't have to. . . ."

"Yes, I do. I want you to understand. I want to. . .apologize. There's so much you don't know."

Lydia stretched the phone cord out and grabbed a kitchen chair. Lowering herself into it, she waved Tyler upstairs so he couldn't eavesdrop.

"It started last November," Sherry began softly. "Jordan, being the treasurer at SPCC, noticed some things about the books that made him uncomfortable. For instance, Gerald had withdrawn an awful lot of money for that new car he drives. Now, while SPCC agreed to furnish its pastor with an automobile, Jordan never expected him to choose a BMW 750iL—the thing cost nearly seventy thousand dollars! I mean, really!" Sherry declared. "What's wrong with a twenty-thousand-dollar Ford or Chevrolet?"

"I didn't realize the church paid for Gerald's car," Lydia stated lamely.

"His car *and* his house," Sherry added emphatically. "When the congregation agreed to purchase a home for SPCC's pastor, they weren't thinking of the half-a-million-dollar mansion he chose. What does an older couple nearing retirement need with seven bedrooms, a swimming pool, Jacuzzi, and tennis courts when there are needy families at SPCC?"

Sherry paused and Lydia sensed she was gathering steam. "When Jordan suspected a misuse of funds, he approached Gerald with his concerns and that's when your father-in-law threw a fit. He called Jordan a backslider for having the audacity to question his motives. Next, Gerald removed him from his treasurer's position, only to replace him with Sim Crenshaw."

"Oh, Sherry, I don't know what to think anymore," Lydia lamented. "I'm so confused over all of this."

"I'm sure you are. When Jordan told me everything, I had a hard time coming to grips with the truth myself."

Lydia shook her head, trying to clear it. Her thoughts were as boggled as this whole ordeal. "Why didn't you say something to me sooner? Why did you end our friendship?"

"I didn't want to," she replied, sounding contrite. "But Jordan and I were scared Gerald would retaliate somehow, so we laid low for a while until Jordan got his new managerial position here in Tennessee. Then we moved. But now we see how wrong we were to run away from the situation instead of braving it out and trusting the Lord to see us through. That's why I need to apologize to you." She paused, her voice breaking slightly. "I'm so sorry and I've missed you so much!"

Lydia was trying to swallow her own onslaught of emotion. "I've missed you, too."

Sherry sniffed. "And I've been so worried about you. Gerald's been planning a match between you and Sim. Are you even aware of it?"

"Yes, I've gotten that impression."

"Honestly, Lyd," Sherry continued, using the pet name she'd coined for her years ago, "the very idea nauseates me. I know you trust Gerald completely, but don't be persuaded to marry Sim no matter how wonderful the promises sound. Simeon Crenshaw cannot be trusted."

"Don't worry. I'm not interested in Sim."

"Good. You put my mind at ease. Well, I have more to say to you, but we've talked plenty long on your bill. Let me call you right back and we can chat some more."

"I'd like that. . .but wait about a half hour so I can get Ty and Brooke into bed. Okay?"

Sherry agreed, they hung up, and Lydia took to the stairs, climbing them two at a time. She felt a bit of remorse for making such quick work of tucking her children in for the night, but she didn't want to miss Sherry's call. So many questions suddenly had answers, although Lydia couldn't say she cared for any of them. And it seemed she was caught in some sort of double bind, for if she chose to believe her mother and Sherry, then she'd have to conclude Gerald wasn't the godly, benevolent pastor she'd thought.

*Oh, Lord, I'm so confused right now.*

Walking into the den, Lydia grabbed the cordless phone and made her way into the living room. She sat down on the couch just as it rang. *Sherry always had uncanny timing.* Chuckling softly, she pressed the TALK button.

"My, but you're prompt," she answered.

"Lydia?" a male voice said.

She swallowed her amusement. "Gerald. Hello."

"Hello. Obviously you weren't expecting my call."

"No, I. . .I thought you were someone else. But how are you? Have you talked to Elberta?"

"I'm fine and I spoke with Elberta not long ago. She's decided to spend the rest of the winter in Florida with Mary."

"I see." Lydia felt troubled by the news. Was this some kind of separation, the first step toward divorce?

"Now I have a question for you. What's this I hear about you carrying on with your next-door neighbor?"

Lydia almost choked on her reply. "Who told you that? Mrs. Wilberson?"

"It doesn't matter. I want the truth, Lydia."

"I'm hardly 'carrying on' with him. We had a date and he kissed me goodnight. That's all."

"Hmm. . .that's more than Sim got, from what I understand."

"That's because I don't like Sim." Lydia wished she'd realized sooner that her father-in-law had been bent on a match between them. It just wasn't going to happen.

"Am I to assume you *like* your neighbor? What's his name? Alex?"

"Alec. Alec Corbett. And, yes. . . ," she paused, sending up a quick arrow of a prayer for understanding, "yes, I like him. Very much."

"Very much?" he repeated as if he couldn't quite grasp the concept. Then a long pause passed between them before Gerald spoke up again. "Lydia, I thought we had an agreement. I was to screen prospective suitors for you."

"Yes, but I only went along with it because I wasn't capable of such a decision on my own so soon after Michael died. I couldn't think of dating. But it's different now."

"And why's that?"

She shrugged, forgetting her father-in-law couldn't see the gesture. "I don't know. It's as if the fog that hung over me has finally lifted."

"And we have *Alex* to thank for this, eh?"

"Alec." Lydia bristled under the condescension, but she fought to keep her temper in check. She'd known Gerald wouldn't approve of her seeing him, and yet this was the moment she'd hoped for—her shot at changing his mind. "Won't you please give him a chance? I think you'll like him. In some ways, Alec reminds me of Michael."

Gerald seemed to ignore the comment. "Is he a believer?"

"Yes."

"You're sure?"

"Positive."

"Where is he attending church?"

"At Berean Baptist."

"Oh, Lydia," her father-in-law ground out, sounding frustrated, "that's a milquetoast church. If this man is a Christian—and I do mean *if*—he's probably a very weak one with no godly standards to speak of."

"On the contrary, I think he's a strong Christian. Please don't pass judgment on him before getting to know him first. I think you'll be surprised."

Another pause. "Very well. I didn't call to argue. I'm only looking after your welfare. . .and that of the children."

"Thank you, but there's no need to be concerned."

"Well, of course there is! I'm Tyler and Brooke's grandfather. I have a vested interest in your love life."

The front doorbell suddenly chimed, startling Lydia from her thoughts. Standing, she padded to the hallway, where she flipped on the porch light. Peeking out the side window, she saw Alec.

"Lydia? Are you still there?"

"Yes, but I have to go. I'll talk to you soon. Bye." She clicked off the phone before setting it on the adjacent table. Then she pulled open the door and smiled.

"Happy Valentine's Day." Alec set a green tissue-wrapped bouquet in her arms. "Roses for Lydia Rose."

She felt her cheeks warm with a blush. "How thoughtful of you. . ."

He looked beyond her. "Am I disturbing anything?"

"No. Would you care to come in?"

Alec shook his blond head. "Better not. After last night, I don't trust myself."

"What do you mean?"

A frown furrowed his thick, sandy-colored brows. "Lydia, at the risk of you freezing to death there in the doorway. . ." He grinned good-naturedly. "Want to go put on your winter coat, cap, and mittens? It's about fifty degrees out here and what I want to say might take awhile."

"I think I'll survive the frigid temperatures, Alec." She smiled in spite of herself. "What's on your mind?"

He leaned against the doorjamb. "Well, I've got to confess that in all the months I was engaged to Denise, I never kissed her. Do you believe that? It's true. You see, shortly after my conversion to Christ, I committed myself to the principles of courtship—no kissing, hugging, hand holding. . .any intimate physical contact, no matter how accepted it might be as far as worldly dating."

"I see."

"Are you sure?" Alec looked amused. "Most Christians haven't even heard of this sort of courtship."

"Well, I've heard of it. I just thought it went out with the antebellum South."

He hung his head back and hooted. "That's a good one, Lydia."

She smiled, although she had to admit, she wasn't sure where Alec was going with all of this.

Then he pulled out several pamphlets from his inside jacket pocket and gave them to her. With the flowers cradled in one arm, Lydia accepted them with her other hand.

"I talked to Pastor Spencer tonight after church. He promotes a conservative-styled courtship, and he managed to dig up some literature on the subject. I'd like you to read those brochures. They'll explain everything a lot better than I can."

"I'll read them tonight."

"Great. I wrote down my cell phone and home phone numbers. Call me if you have any questions. And I apologize for kissing you last night. I violated my own code of ethics."

Lydia nodded, but inside, her heart was breaking. "Alec, I think you're politely trying to tell me you don't want to see me anymore."

His topaz-colored eyes widened in shock. "No way, quite the opposite. But you're the one who said you weren't interested in remarrying. See, Lydia, that's a problem since courtship is a forerunner to marriage. For myself, I don't consider it another word for dating. It's completely different." He gave her a sympathetic smile. "Will you just read those brochures?"

"Yes. . .yes, I will. Now I'm curious."

"Good. And, um, just one more thing. . ."

Lydia raised her brows expectantly.

"I want you to know this is no light matter with me. I left Wisconsin determined not to get involved with another woman as long as I lived. After we met, I wanted to stay as far away from you, Lydia, as I could get. . .because I felt an immediate attraction to you. And, honestly, I'm not a man who's easily swayed by a pretty face. I've seen enough of them to know better. I became a Christian when I was thirty years old and I didn't exactly live a priestly existence. But, praise the Lord, He saved me before I could really mess up my life."

Lydia smiled, touched that Alec would share something so personal. His sensitivity was showing again, his vulnerability on display, and she could see why he was hurt so deeply over his broken engagement. Once more, that particular feeling came over her, the one that caused her to want to be the woman who changed Alec Corbett's heart about love and marriage.

"Lydia, at the risk of sounding like a complete lunatic, I want to—well, that is, if you agree—I mean, I know we've only known each other a couple of weeks and everything, but. . ."

She sucked her lower lip between her teeth to keep from smiling. He looked so cute standing there, rambling on nervously.

"What I'm trying to say is, I'd like to court you."

"I'm flattered, and I—"

He tapped the literature in her hand. "Read the pamphlets before you answer, okay? But if you have reservations or doubts of any kind, I understand. Like I said, we've only known each other a short time. It's just that. . .well, I could fall in love with you real easy. . .if I haven't already."

"Oh, Alec. . ." Lydia was touched to the heart.

"You go on in the house now, before you turn into an icicle."

She nodded and, watching him go, she felt more impressed with Alec than ever. In her mind, he was a gentleman among gentlemen.

The phone rang again, and she reentered the hallway, closing the door and latching it securely behind her. Picking up the cordless, she smiled, hearing Sherry's voice.

"Okay, Lyd, kids are asleep and we can catch up. . .it's about time, wouldn't you say?"

"Oh, I'd say, all right. And, Sherry, I've got to tell you about my new next-door neighbor. You're not going to believe this. . .I think I'm falling in love with him!"

❧

"You fool. He's done in two short weeks what you've been trying to do for over a year!" Gerald paced the hardwood floor of his condo while Sim sat comfortably in a nearby armchair.

"It's not over yet. I've still got a couple of tricks up my sleeve."

"There's no time for tricks. Lydia is positively smitten."

"She won't be for long." Sim grinned conspiratorially, rose from the chair, and walked to his briefcase, lifting out a folded document. "I hired an investigator who ran a check on our friend, Mr. Alec Corbett. Take a look."

Gerald felt hopeful for the first time in days.

"He's got a past a mile long."

Reading over the report, Gerald smiled. "Very good. Very good." He glanced up at Sim. "You've done a fine job. When Lydia sees this, she'll be appalled." He pursed his lips in thought. "I'll return home tomorrow and confront her."

"No. Wait a week or so."

"What? And give Mr. Corbett another week at romancing Lydia?"

Sim nodded. "Another week and she'll be all the more hurt when you spring the news of his jaded past on her. Emphasize the women, Gerald. Don't be afraid to break her heart. And then I'll come along, and—"

"And dry her tears," Gerald finished incisively. He mulled over the idea. "Yes, I think that'll work just fine."

"Let's hope so," Sim said crisply. "SPCC's future is depending on it."

# *Chapter 13*

Alec lay awake in bed, unable to sleep. He glanced at the digital alarm clock/radio on his headboard. It read 1:00.

*Man, I've got to get some shut-eye!*

He thought ahead to the busy day he had planned at work, starting in just several short hours, and groaned. Turning over, he plumped his pillow. If he could quit thinking about Lydia, a good night's rest might still be achieved.

It had been at Pastor Spencer's suggestion that Alec decided to share his heart with her, and now he couldn't help wondering if he'd turned her off completely. He thought she would have called, but she hadn't. What did that mean? She wasn't interested in him and his courtship convictions?

*Well, better to alienate her now than have her change her mind later,* he tried to convince himself.

He began to reflect on how different they were—Lydia, a pretty little Southern belle, and he, a "Yankee." She seemed so dignified compared to him, and yet Alec never felt inferior with her—she didn't allow it. In fact, Lydia Boswick, with her sweet ways, made him feel more like a man than any other woman he'd ever known.

Rolling over once more, he closed his eyes and, out of sheer will, finally slept.

❀

All of Monday, Alec stayed busy. He'd been assigned to work on a kitchen remodeling project and spent a majority of his day tearing out the old cabinetry and preparing to install the new cupboards. When he arrived back at home, it was dark outside. Lights glowed from Lydia's house as he walked from the garage, and he debated whether to call her, but decided not to push. She had a decision to make, and if she was waiting on the Lord, praying for His direction, Alec didn't want to intrude.

He showered and thought he heard the phone ring. But after he was out and dressed, he checked his voice mail and since there weren't any messages, he figured he'd imagined it.

He watched a football game, read his Bible, and went to sleep, too exhausted to fret over his lovely next-door neighbor another whole night long.

❀

Tuesday morning found Lydia sitting at her desk, flipping through the literature

Alec had given her Sunday night. She'd read and reread each pamphlet and, again, saw the wisdom behind this particular theory on courtship. Its principles actually mirrored her own beliefs.

Glancing at her wristwatch, Lydia realized it was past noon. She wondered if Alec got a lunch break. Should she try calling him? Deciding to chance it, she picked up the receiver of her desk phone and dialed the cellular number he'd written down on one of the brochures. The adjacent offices around her were silent. The assistant pastor and youth pastor were attending seminars in Raleigh and her father-in-law was still out of town. With the moment's privacy, Lydia hoped to get to talk to Alec.

His phone rang for the third time and she was tempted to hang up when suddenly it stopped.

"Yeah, Corbett here."

She brought her chin back in surprise at the brusque greeting. "Alec? It's me. Lydia."

A pause. "Hang on a sec." She heard muffled voices and the whir of a drill or electric saw in the background. Then Alec came back on the line. "Sorry about that. I had to tell the guys I was taking a break."

"Is this a bad time?"

"Nope."

"Good." She felt oddly nervous. "I just wanted to tell you I read the information you gave me."

"And?"

"And, I agree with it. . .them. . .I mean, the courtship idea."

"Are you okay? You sound upset or something."

"Yes, I'm fine. I just feel like. . .like I'm an awkward sixteen-year-old again," Lydia admitted, twirling the phone cord around her index finger.

Alec laughed. "You, too, huh?"

She smiled.

"Well, maybe we can talk some more tonight. It's a nice day. How 'bout if I try to get off at a reasonable hour and we take the kids for ice cream?"

"I'm sure they'd love that, although I don't know how much of a discussion we'll be able to have with Ty along."

"Guess we'll have to take our chances."

As much as Lydia loved her children, she felt a tad disappointed she couldn't have Alec's company all to herself. But the fact remained: If he was serious about pursuing her, he would have to make a commitment to Tyler and Brooke also. It might be a good thing if he discovered just what he was in for at this early stage of their relationship.

"See you tonight, Lydia."

"Yes, see you tonight. . . ."

The evening wind felt like a cold slap against Lydia's face as she sat in the park bleachers and watched Alec and Tyler throwing the football to each other. Having just indulged in a scoop of Death by Chocolate ice cream, she felt all the more chilled.

"Yea! Touchdown!" Brooke cheered beside her.

Lydia grinned. She didn't think her daughter even knew what a touchdown was, but she seemed to be having a fun time clapping her hands and rooting for Tyler first and then "Mr. Alec." And Tyler was in his glory. Lydia hadn't seen her son so happy since last Christmas, when he got that computer from Gerald.

"Yea! Tyler caught the ball!" Brooke jumped up and down, applauding loudly, while Lydia shivered beneath her winter jacket.

At long last, Alec and Tyler walked off the field.

"Nice warm night for a football game, eh, Lydia?" Alec razzed with a mischievous gleam in his eyes.

"Very nice," she replied dryly, attempting to keep her teeth from chattering.

He chuckled as they all walked toward his pickup truck. Reaching it, Alec unlocked the door and Tyler and Brooke climbed into the backseat of the cab. Lydia slid into the passenger seat, glad to be out of the chilling wind.

"That was awesome!" Tyler exclaimed.

"You're a good football player," Brooke drawled, complimenting her brother. "And I was a good cheerleader. Right, Mama?"

"That's right."

Alec opened the driver's door and seated himself behind the wheel. Turning the key in the ignition, the engine came to life and soon they were on their way home. Once they arrived, Lydia gave in and let the kids watch one of their favorite videos before bedtime.

"And I think I need some hot tea," she declared, rubbing her frozen hands together.

"I think I need an ice cold cola," Alec said, opening the fridge. "Mind if I help myself?"

"Sure, go ahead. But all I've got in there is apple juice."

"You're kidding?" He closed the door, looking disappointed. "I think I'll go home."

"Oh, don't do that," Lydia said, feigning a pout.

He winked. "Okay, guess I'll come back after I grab a soft drink."

She chuckled lightly at Alec's retreating form, and in his absence, she set the kettle to boiling and steeped her tea. Pulling on a cozy sweater, she sat down at the kitchen table, listening to Tyler and Brooke giggling in the den. Minutes later, Alec walked through the back door.

"You know, your boy is starving for some male companionship," he announced, taking a seat opposite from Lydia's at the table. "I don't mean that as an insult. I know you're doing the best you can."

"But you're right. Ty needs a good male friend. He used to have Matt next door until the Smiths moved to Tennessee."

"Yeah, he told me about that." Alec took a few swallows from his can of cola. "He said something 'bad' happened."

"It did. And it involves my father-in-law and the extortion charges he's facing."

"Uh-oh." Alec twirled his pop can between his hands, studying it thoughtfully. "How are you coping with all of that?" he finally asked, bringing his gaze back to hers. "It's got to be stressful."

"It is and I'm a baffled mess," she admitted. "Sherry Smith was my very best friend, and even though Gerald wouldn't like it if he knew, I've had contact with her. We spoke on Sunday night. Hearing her version of why she and her husband left the church and ultimately Alabama answered many of my questions. But it also raised some more." Lydia shook her head sadly. "I don't want to think badly of my father-in-law. He's been good to me and the children."

"Does he ever do anything special with Tyler? Man-to-man stuff, like taking him to a basketball game?"

Lydia shook her head. "He's too busy."

"Well, would you mind if I spent a little extra time with him? He can tag along with me when I shoot hoops with some of the guys from church. We try to get together a couple of times a month."

"Courting my son, too, are you?" Lydia teased.

Alec gave her a furtive glance. "Courting trouble's more like it."

"Who me?" she asked, batting her lashes innocently.

He smirked in reply and took another drink. "Speaking of trouble, I can foresee some obstacles ahead of us." His tone took on a serious note. "And your father-in-law is one of them."

"I talked to him on Sunday night, too, and I told him we went out the night before. . .well, actually he'd heard about it from someone at church." Lydia lifted the corners of her mouth in a slight grin. "News travels fast among SPCC's congregation."

"I guess. So did the good pastor blow a gasket?" Alec chuckled. "I mean, I am a *Northerner*, you know, and he was very quick to point that out when we were introduced."

"He's willing to give you a chance," Lydia said, praying it was so.

"And what if he doesn't approve?" he asked, wearing a hardened expression. "Then it's off between you and me regardless of what we might feel the Lord is doing?"

When Lydia hesitated, he scooted his chair back and stood. "Look, I think you need to get that matter settled first. Who are you listening to? God or your father-in-law?"

"God, of course," she replied, standing as well.

He gave her a skeptical look.

"Please, be patient with me," she whispered.

"I don't want to get hurt again," Alec said candidly. "So if you're going to change your mind, do it now."

"I'm not changing my mind. But at the same time, we need to stay open to the Lord's leading. What if He closes the door on this relationship?"

"If He does, it won't be for a political reason."

"I agree." She gazed at Alec, silently pleading with him for understanding.

"Obstacle number two," he touted in spite of her efforts. "Money. I'm a lowly carpenter, Lydia, and don't exactly make a fortune. Judging by this house and your lifestyle, you're accustomed to wealth."

"I didn't grow up with it. Mama wanted to save the insurance money Daddy left her for my college education and her retirement. I worked a part-time job all through high school while Mama cleaned houses for a living. We lived in a one-bedroom apartment and. . .we were very happy. As for my present situation, I know Michael left me some money, but my father-in-law is my agent. He takes care of everything. I get a monthly allotment, but I suspect the church is supporting me for the most part."

"You mean you don't know how much your husband left you?"

"I should, shouldn't I? But I'm afraid I was so distraught at the reading of Michael's will that I don't recall the exact figures. And since Gerald so kindly agreed to take care of it all. . . ."

Alec shook his blond head. "This bothers me."

"Why?"

"Because your father-in-law could decide to pull your support if he doesn't approve and we continue to see each other." He tipped his head slightly. "Are you prepared for that, Lydia? What if you lose your financial security because of me?"

"That won't happen."

"Oh? Why won't it?"

"You're forgetting something. My children. Gerald would never allow them—or me—to suffer financial hardship if he could help it."

"Well, I've got news for you. You might suffer financial hardship with me—and I will not have anyone else supporting my family. I'll be the one to take care of my wife and kids." He paused, considering her earnestly. "You may have to choose between living in luxury in this grand house or living with me. And you might as well decide now and save us both a lot of grief."

"Can't I let God decide?" She smiled. "Actually, it's already been determined;

all I have to do is let the Lord lead the way."

"Being less than wealthy doesn't scare you?"

"Not in the least."

"I'm warning you, Lydia, I won't ever accept financial help from your father-in-law or anyone else—not while I'm an able-bodied man and I can work."

She walked toward him. "I think you're wonderful."

"I think I'm crazy. You're out of my league, Lydia Rose Boswick."

"No, I am not 'out of your league,' and don't you ever say that again. You're a child of God and there are not *leagues* among Christians."

"You haven't been paying attention to your father-in-law's sermons, have you?" Alec asked facetiously before chuckling.

Lydia smiled, watching him and thinking his eyes fairly danced when he laughed like that. "I'm falling in love with you," she murmured helplessly.

"Yeah, well, I think I passed that point. So now you know just what kind of fool you're dealing with." He smirked. "And on that note, I'd better say good night."

She watched him go in a mixture of disappointment and admiration. The kitchen had a lonely atmosphere about it after Alec left. Lydia stood there, staring at the closed back door. From the den, she could hear silly music playing on the video, but since Tyler and Brooke weren't laughing as usual, she guessed they'd fallen asleep.

On a long sigh, Lydia made her way into the den, thinking she'd met some kind of hero when Alec Corbett moved in next door.

# Chapter 14

The rain fell in sheets as Alec stood in the doorway of Berean Baptist Church with his friend Larry after the midweek worship service.

"Okay, lemme get this straight," Larry said. "She loves you. You love her. . . ." He tipped his head. "What are you waiting for, stupid? Do you know how hard it is to find somebody to love in this world—somebody who loves you back?"

"Yeah, I know," Alec countered, "but I'd like to get to know her before I pop the question."

"You've got the rest of your lives to get to know each other." Larry seemed momentarily thoughtful—almost remorsefully so. "I entertained ideas of asking Lydia out, after that first night we were in her house for the Bible study."

Alec cut him a furtive glance. "Think again, buddy."

"Oh, I know. She's yours. But, to be honest, the fact that Lydia is a Boswick turned me off from the get-go. You I'd go up against 'cause you'd fight fair. But Gerald Boswick? Forget it."

"The guy's that bad, eh?"

Larry nodded and pulled his jacket collar closer around his neck. "His Holiness has a lot of clout around here. Knows people in high places. If he doesn't like you, he'll make your life miserable."

"Do you know that firsthand?"

"Somewhat. I know a guy who dared to stand up to Pastor Boswick. It was in regards to the good pastor wanting to erect that nice big church building he's got. This happened, oh. . .five years ago or so. There was a dispute between the pastor and SPCC's neighbors who didn't want a huge church on their corner and the crowd it would bring. Bill headed up the city council and he sided with the townsfolk. Suddenly, his dog was found shot to death, and threatening phone calls were made to his wife during the day when Bill wasn't around. When he still refused to back down, Pastor Boswick allegedly called up one of his henchmen and, would you believe, Bill lost his job within a matter of hours? Next, there were a couple of mysterious fires at the homes of the neighboring opponents and so the others quickly shut their mouths. Of course, no one can actually *prove* Gerald Boswick's involvement, although the fire marshal at that time was a member of SPCC."

"Unbelievable." It was all Alec could think to say. And he had to admit, part of him felt leery about courting Lydia because of what he heard about her father-in-law. Except, the alternative didn't suit him either. Besides, God was bigger than Gerald Boswick.

"I have to admit," Larry added, "I still feel bad about getting rejected for membership at SPCC, but not because it was a good church and I wanted to sit under the teaching there. I'd been seeing a lovely, sweet lady named Maria. I sensed she might be the one for me. But when she got accepted into the fold and we no longer were 'equally yoked,' according to what Maria had been told, she broke things off with me. That was what really hurt. Worse, I see her around town sometimes. We had a special thing going, but now she won't even say hello to me."

"That's a bummer, all right." Alec pursed his lips thoughtfully. "Unequally yoked, huh? But that passage of scripture warns believers not to join together with nonbelievers. It's not pegging Christians against each other."

"I know, but that's what they teach over there. If you aren't a member of SPCC, then you're not going to heaven—and those deacons, Pastor Boswick's own henchmen, are the ones deciding who's saved and who isn't."

"That's crazy."

"No kidding."

Alec took a moment to digest the information. "I don't think Lydia subscribes to that philosophy."

"Doesn't sound like it. Makes you wonder, though, how did she, Pastor Boswick's daughter-in-law, make it to this point unscathed?"

"I think a lot of it had to do with her husband. Sounds like he was a pretty balanced guy. In fact, I spoke with our pastor and he said he had a lot of respect for Michael Boswick. Told me he was a 'good man.'"

"What did Mark say about Pastor Boswick? If you don't mind me asking." Larry grinned expectantly.

Alec smirked. "He said the guy scares him as much as the Ku Klux Klan."

"Whew! Well, buddy, I wish you a lot of luck," Larry said, clapping him on the back.

"Forget the luck," Alec retorted, "I need your prayers."

His friend sobered. "You got 'em, man."

❀

Gerald Boswick's office was never one Lydia enjoyed being inside. Oh, it had a pleasant enough decor from the warm blue-and-white scrolled wallpaper to the dark blue carpet covering the floor. The furniture was fashioned after a colonial style and offered adequate comfort. It wasn't the room itself Lydia minded. It was the ever-present sad memories that seemed to linger within its perimeters. How many times had she sat in this exact spot on the settee and wept over losing Michael, the situation with the Smiths, her mother. . .and now Alec.

"Lydia, I forbid you to see that man!" Gerald said, causing her to wish he hadn't come back from his oceanside retreat.

"But you don't understand. I love him."

"That's ridiculous. He came to town three short weeks ago. You can't fall in love with someone in three weeks."

Lydia shrugged. "It happened."

With a derisive snort, he walked around his wide desk and sat on its edge. "What do you know of his background, his past? What kind of family does he come from?"

"I know he's got two older sisters," Lydia began, hating how insipid she sounded. "I know his parents divorced when Alec was young."

"A broken family?" An expression of disdain marred his features.

Lydia swallowed hard. "Many of today's godliest men have come from troubled homes, Gerald. You know that as well as I."

"But it's not been without consequence. Now, what else do you know about this neighbor of yours?"

"I know Alec became a born-again Christian at the age of thirty—he's thirty-five now."

Gerald folded his arms, hardly impressed. "Is that it?"

Was it? She searched her memory, thinking that surely she could come up with another fact or two. Finally, indignant over having to defend the man she loved, Lydia shook her head in aggravation. "He's a good man," she argued. "He wants to court me. When was the last time you heard of a man wanting to court a woman? Alec Corbett might be from Wisconsin, but he's got a manner about him that reminds me of an old-fashioned Southern gentleman."

"That tells me you know very little about him, my dear." Reaching across the desk, Gerald picked up a piece of paper. "Here's what a private investigator discovered."

Lydia stifled a gasp. "An investigator?"

"That's right." He glanced at the report in his hand. "Let's see…Alec Corbett was arrested not once, but twice. The first time it was for disorderly conduct, the second for driving under the influence."

"That had to be before he was saved."

"Regardless, it's a reflection on his character."

"No, it's the past. The Lord Jesus changed all that."

"Let me finish. Mr. Corbett has had three jobs in the last seven years—which spells instability. Furthermore, he's cohabited with three different women outside the bonds of marriage. The first in 1984, the second in 1987, and the third in 1992."

Lydia began to feel sick.

"That tells me he's unable to commit to a lasting relationship. In fact, he was engaged to be married to a woman named Denise Lisinski. She broke it off just three short months ago."

"I know about Denise," Lydia muttered.

"Then you're aware of why she broke the engagement?"

"Yes. She changed her mind."

"Yes. . .but do you know *why*?"

Lydia looked up into her father-in-law's supremely satisfied face. "I have a feeling you're going to tell me."

He gave her a patient smile. "Miss Lisinski told the investigator that Alec Corbett frightened her with his bad temper. She called him extremely possessive and said he wouldn't allow her to see her friends." Handing the piece of paper to Lydia, he added, "Read it for yourself. It would seem he's got some psychological problems. I've seen the pattern before. Now, while he claims to know the Lord, I do not want him associated with my flock here at SPCC, and I especially do not want him near my family. Think of the children, Lydia! Youngsters can rile even the most patient of men. What would happen if you married this veritable stranger and he lost his temper and hurt either Tyler or Brooke?"

"He'd never do that," she maintained, staring in disbelief at the sheet of paper in her hands. The typewritten words on the page were swimming before her rapidly filling eyes.

"You can do better than a man like Alec Corbett, my dear."

Wounded beyond imagination, she stood and slowly walked to the door, unwilling that Gerald should see her cry.

"I've got an idea," he said, halting her steps. Coming up behind her, he put his hands on her shoulders. "Why don't you and I go to your favorite restaurant this evening. We'll get someone to watch the children. . .my treat."

"No, thank you."

He gently but firmly turned her around and peered into her face. "I know it hurts, dear. But he's not for you. Better to weep now and get him out of your system than marry him and live the rest of your life in utter misery."

"But—"

Gerald put a finger to her lips. "Shh. . .no more argument," he whispered, placing a kiss on her forehead. "Father knows best."

She nodded slightly and returned to her desk, where she fought down her emotions and tried desperately to concentrate on her work. She thought about phoning Alec and questioning him, but she didn't dare under her father-in-law's watchful gaze. Then Sim entered the office just before Tyler and Brooke were dismissed from school.

"Hello, Lydia," he greeted, sounding chipper. He paused at her desk, leaning sideways, one elbow resting on its surface. "You look down in the dumps today. Everything all right?"

"Just a bad day," she said, trying not to cry again.

"I'm sorry to hear that. What can I do to help?"

She shook her head. "Nothing, but thank you anyway."

"Lydia, you must know by now how much I care about you."

"I appreciate that, Sim, but—"

He walked around and entered her small work space. Kneeling by her chair, he took her hand. Lydia pulled away, glancing around the office nervously. She didn't want to be the subject of the latest gossip—especially not with Sim.

"I'm all right, really," she tried to assure him.

"Then I must tell you—I'm in love with you, my darling. I'll do anything to make you mine."

For the first time in hours, Lydia smiled. Sim's declaration sounded so melodramatic, it seemed funny.

She quickly swallowed her amusement, however, in order to be polite. "You're so kind to say that, but, I—"

"Name it and it's yours."

"Alec Corbett," she replied wistfully.

Sim frowned. "What?"

Lydia shook her head. "Never mind. It was a bad joke on my part. Forgive me." She stood and pushed her chair in under her desk. "Please excuse me, my children will be here shortly, and I've got to take them home."

Skirting her way around Sim, she left the office, leaving him there on his knees.

# Chapter 15

With Tyler and Brooke in bed for the night, the house was very quiet. Too quiet. Shivering, more so from stress than from the cold March temperature or the rain outside, Lydia wandered from room to room, straightening this, tidying that, and all the while thinking about Alec and wondering. One glance next door told her he hadn't gotten home yet. He said sometimes he worked twelve- or fourteen-hour days Monday through Thursday and took Friday afternoons off. But obviously today wasn't one of those Fridays. Unless, of course, he had other plans she didn't know about.

Still feeling chilled, Lydia made a fire in the fireplace and sat down before it, watching the flames leaping upward. She felt convinced her father-in-law had told her the truth today, and she longed to ask Alec about the investigator's report, but she was scared. Suppose he was some kind of psychopath? What did she really know about him anyway?

Suddenly spying her Bible on the end table, Lydia felt a sudden longing for God's Word. *Speak to me, Lord. Show me the truth.*

She looked up her reading for the day: 2 Corinthians 5. She'd been too harried this morning for devotions. She began at verse 17. *"Therefore if any man be in Christ, he is a new creature: old things are passed away; behold, all things are become new."* On the lower half of the page, in the commentary portion of her Bible, Lydia continued to read that the apostle Paul literally meant those in Christ were God's new creations. Salvation brought on a changed lifestyle.

Lydia felt like laughing! It was no coincidence that *this* passage was part of her scripture reading for *this* day. Just that small bit of God's Word had renewed her spirit.

She read through the rest of the chapter before reverently setting aside her Bible. She found the cordless phone and Alec's cellular number and placed the call.

"Corbett here."

"Hi, Alec. You must be working late tonight." Her casual air surprised even herself.

"Yep, but I'm just about home. We finished the project, the client is ecstatic, our whole crew gets a bonus. Guess the long hours were worth it." A pause. "Oh, hey. . .I didn't forget, did I? Were we supposed to go out tonight?"

"No." Lydia sighed, hating what had to come next. "Can you stop over? I have to talk to you. It's important."

"Sounds serious."

"It is."

"Hmm. . .can you give me a hint?"

Lydia paused to weigh the pros and cons—should she tell him or not? Finally, she decided to be direct. "My father-in-law hired an investigator who did a background check on you." When no immediate reply came forth, she wondered if they'd lost their connection. "Alec? Are you still there?"

"Yeah. I'm pulling into my driveway. Give me a half hour to clean up, okay?"

"Of course. . . ."

He'd hung up before she'd barely finished the last word.

*Oh, Lord, I'm frightened. What if Alec does, indeed, have a nasty temper? What if he yells? What if he hates me for confronting him about his past?*

As if in reply, she recalled a verse in 1 John 4: *"There is no fear in love; but perfect love casteth out fear."*

" 'For God hath not given us the spirit of fear," she said out loud, quoting one of her favorite promises from 2 Timothy, "but of power, and of love, and of a sound mind.' "

Lydia sat back down in her chair by the fire and prayerfully waited. Almost exactly thirty minutes later, the doorbell chimed. She swallowed nervously but was determined to let him have his say.

"Hi," she said, opening the door and bidding him enter.

"Hi yourself." He walked into the hallway. "Where do you want to talk?"

"Living room?"

With a nod, Alec strode across the room and made himself comfortable on the couch. Clad in a red-checked flannel shirt, he reminded Lydia of a big, blond lumberjack.

"Don't you ever wear a coat?" she couldn't help asking as she made her way toward him.

He seemed momentarily surprised by the question. "Who needs a coat? It's fifty-two degrees outside."

Giving him a hooded glance and a bit of a smile, she took the investigator's report off the coffee table and handed it to him. Then she sat on the opposite end of the couch while he read it over.

After a few minutes, he tossed it onto the cushion between them. He met her gaze, his expression revealing nothing. "What do you want me to say? It's all true."

"Alec, I've prayed about this and God reminded me that everyone in Christ is a new creature. Old things are passed away. But I wondered if you'd mind explaining."

"I don't mind, but it won't exactly be easy. I'm not proud of my past, Lydia.

I try very hard to forget it. And I'm not sure where to start, so why don't you ask me some questions? What do want to know?"

She lifted the sheet of paper. "The disorderly conduct charge?"

"I was twenty-one and stupid. Got into a fight in a tavern over some woman."

"Driving while under the influence. . . ?"

"Yep. I was drunk as a skunk. I'm just glad I didn't kill anyone. I think I was about twenty-five when that happened."

"And the women?" That of all things caused Lydia the most heartache. "Did I read it correctly? There were three listed on that report?"

She nodded.

He scratched his jaw pensively. "I think there were more."

"Oh, Alec. . .you *think*?"

He shifted his weight, facing her directly. "Look, Lydia, I know my past is not pretty, but I'm a miracle of God's grace. Christ died for sinful men—for me! And maybe now you'll understand why I take courtship so seriously. While lost, I defiled myself, but I don't intend on sinning against my Savior."

She nodded. "Yes, I see your point clearly."

"But I can ease your mind by telling you I don't have any social diseases or HIV, and I haven't fathered any children."

"Well," she said, feeling a blush running up her neck, "I guess that's something." She fretted over her lower lip for several moments. "Alec, what about the things Denise said?"

Looking puzzled, he took the report and reread it. "I didn't see this the first time through." Glancing back at her, he added, "But I guess now I know why she broke off our engagement. She never would tell me. If she would have said something, we could have discussed it. And, yeah, I raised my voice with her— plenty of times. She liked to go to a downtown nightclub with her friends after work every Thursday night—Ladies' Night. Being a Christian woman, I didn't think it was right for her to be in such a place, so I gave her a piece of my mind on several occasions, figuring I had the right since I was her fiancé. If that makes me a possessive lunatic, then I guess I am."

"Sounds to me like you were just trying to protect her."

"I planned to marry the woman. Do you think I wanted her in a downtown bar week after week?"

His heated reply caused Lydia to wonder if he wasn't still in love with Denise. She watched as he raked a hand through his hair and stood. He walked to the window and stared out at the dark nighttime sky. Lydia felt like sobbing. Maybe Alec wasn't the one for her. Maybe Gerald was right. Perhaps his jaded past would, indeed, prove to be far too great a contender.

*"With men this is impossible; but with God all things are possible"*—Jesus' words from Matthew 19 rang in her heart in a divine reply, and Lydia knew He

was telling her she *could* handle it. With the Lord's help, she could. . .and she would!

"I guess this is obstacle number three," Alec said in a discouraged voice from his place at the window.

"No, it's not."

He glanced over his shoulder at her, before turning around. "What do you mean, it's not?"

She picked up the report and began tearing it into pieces. "You explained. I believe you. It's over. Done. . .nothing's left." Standing to her feet, she walked to the fireplace and tossed in the slips of paper. "No obstacle." She smiled.

"Are you telling me you're willing to overlook my past?"

"Only if you're willing to overlook mine."

He grinned. "Oh, right. What's the worst thing you ever did?"

"Um, let's see. . .I stole a pack of gum from the grocery store when I was ten. I couldn't even sleep that night because my conscience bothered me so much."

Alec feigned a gasp. "I'm shocked."

He lifted her chin. "It was as much of a sin as anything you ever did."

He just stood there, eyeing her carefully. "Lydia, if you're serious, I don't ever want you to bring up my past again. Not ever. You know things I never told Denise because I felt I wouldn't grow spiritually, that I'd never get past the shame of that sinful life, if I had a wife reminding me of what a loser I used to be."

"I'll never bring it up again," Lydia promised. She tipped her head, considering him. "But. . ."

"But?"

She hesitated. Dare she even ask him the question foremost on her heart? Did she want to hear the answer?

"Do you still love Denise?" she managed at last.

Alec took a moment to consider his reply. "Sort of. . .do you still love Michael?"

It was not the response she'd hoped for. In fact, it was the one she dreaded most. But she answered him in spite of her quivering chin. "That's different. Michael's in heaven. He can't show up one day and take me away from you."

A grin spread across Alec's face. "Denise isn't ever going to take me away from you, either. But I loved her enough to ask her to be my wife, and those feelings don't just disappear in three months."

With a sorrowful, audible sigh, Lydia turned and plopped down on the sofa. "Your past isn't obstacle number three," she stated forlornly. "Denise is."

# Chapter 16

The following morning, Gerald stopped over. He seemed satisfied to find Lydia sufficiently depressed over the situation with Alec, although she didn't divulge last night's events. Then after tousling Tyler's hair and giving Brooke a little hug, he went merrily on his way, causing Lydia to feel even worse. How could he revel in her misery?

Not much later, the doorbell rang and three giggling little girls sprang into the house. It was the day Lydia had promised her daughter she could invite a friend over, and one guest had quickly turned to three.

Outside, it rained off and on while, inside, Lydia conducted a tea party with the girls, set up a board game for them, allowed them to watch a video and finally play with Brooke's dolls. Tyler followed his mother around, grumbling about how stupid girls were, and she quickly decided she wasn't going to please everyone today.

Alec didn't phone, much to her great disappointment. He'd left angry last night—obviously she'd struck a nerve. But Sherry called, and Lydia wound up pouring her heart out while she made supper and waited for the girls' mothers to pick up their children.

"Oh, you poor thing," Sherry cooed sympathetically. She paused, apparently in thought. "Say, why don't y'all come here for a little holiday next weekend? The kids can see each other and we can talk and catch up on everything."

"I'd like that, but. . .I don't know." Lydia wondered how she'd get around her father-in-law. He'd surely discover if she disappeared for a whole weekend, and he wouldn't stand for her visiting with the Smiths.

"Let's ask the Lord to make a way," Sherry suggested. "How 'bout it?"

"If the Lord makes a way," she agreed on a discouraged note, "then, yes, we'll come."

Soon Brooke's friends' parents arrived and took their little girls home. Lydia served dinner and forced herself not to glance next door.

After supper, she cleaned up and the telephone rang. Drying her hands on a dish towel, she answered it, glad to hear Alec's voice.

"Were you planning on coming to the Bible study?" he asked in a somewhat brusque tone.

"I don't have a sitter," she said, wishing she would have remembered and tried to find someone to stay with Tyler and Brooke.

"I guess that's a no, huh?"

"It's a no."

"Okay, then. See ya."

When Alec hung up, Lydia tried not to feel hurt by his abruptness. No doubt he was smarting, too. Was love really supposed to hurt this much? She reflected on her relationship with Michael. They'd had their lovers' quarrels, but at least she'd always felt secure about her future with him.

For the rest of the evening she fell into her usual Saturday night routine, supervising her children's baths, tucking them in, and preparing her lesson for Sunday morning. Oddly, the subject was joy.

*Great,* she thought on a cynical note. *I'll be a first-rate hypocrite teaching this topic in the mood I'm in.* After further speculation, the Lord changed her heart. She realized her happiness couldn't be dependent on another individual. People weren't perfect. They'd always disappoint her, and they'd always let her down. But God never would. And even though she'd known that fact all along, she'd never put it into practice. She built her whole world around Michael and, after the kids were born, she'd made her family the very reason for her being. When he died, she transferred her dependence to Gerald—and now, having met Alec, she was slowly beginning to rely on him to supply her joy. But that wasn't right, either.

*Heavenly Father, forgive me,* she silently pleaded. *My joy needs to come from You.*

She stayed in prayer a few more minutes and then, turning her attention back to her lesson, she felt much more prepared to teach her class.

❦

"Now, while I'm away," Gerald was saying the following afternoon as they dined together at Lydia's house, "I've instructed Sim to check on you."

"I don't need checking." Lydia couldn't hide her irritation as she refilled her father-in-law's coffee cup. "I'll be fine."

"But I'm going to be gone at least two weeks, and—"

"Gerald, I can manage on my own. If anything comes up, I'll phone you in Florida."

He didn't reply but thanked her as he reached for his cup. "In addition to making sure my wife is in good spirits, I hope to convince Mary and her husband to move back to Woodruff," he stated, changing the subject, which, to Lydia, meant he had no intention of heeding her request.

Setting down the coffeepot, she almost groaned aloud, thinking of having to deal with Sim Crenshaw for the next couple of weeks. But at least she'd be free to see Sherry!

"I'm convinced my dear daughter and her husband are attending a weak church," Gerald continued. "Sounds lukewarm, and Mary has adopted some very liberal ideas."

"Like what?" Tyler wanted to know, sitting across from Lydia with Brooke on his right side.

"Young man," Gerald reprimanded, "this is an adult conversation. Children should be seen and not heard. Is that clear?"

"Yes, sir." The boy glanced at his mother before looking down at his plate.

"This is what I mean, Lydia. Tyler needs a father."

"Mr. Alec would make a good one," Tyler piped in. But at Gerald's menacing gaze, he immediately quieted and resumed eating.

Lydia felt taken aback by the exchange. Her father-in-law had never prohibited her children from voicing their opinions or asking questions before. *He must be under a tremendous amount of pressure*, Lydia thought. Nevertheless, she wasn't going to allow him to coerce her into an unwanted relationship with Sim or any other man.

"Gerald, I'm praying about it—about a father for my children, a husband for me, except I'd like God to do the choosing, not you. Please don't be offended," Lydia quickly added. "I'm not trying to sound ungrateful. But the fact is, I do not like Simeon Crenshaw and I want you to stop pushing him on me."

"Grampa?" Brooke asked sweetly.

"What is it, dear?"

"Mama's gonna marry Mr. Alec. Me 'n' Ty already 'cided that."

"That's a fun game, but in real life children can't decide anything. That's why they have a mother and a *father*." With a raised brow, Gerald branded Lydia with a scalding glare before turning his attention back to Brooke. "But your mother can't marry Mr. Alec. He is a bad man."

"Gerald!" Lydia's tone sounded sharp to her own ears.

"Well, it's the truth."

"No, it's not!" Tyler spouted angrily.

"This is getting out of hand," Lydia said, trying to curb the sudden tension. "We're not going to discuss Mr. Alec anymore."

Ignoring her, Gerald continued, "Tyler, Brooke, a trusted friend of mine looked into all the things Mr. Alec has ever done and they are very, very bad."

"Your friend is wrong!" Tyler yelled, pitching his fork. It clanged against his glass of milk, and Brooke gasped. "You're wrong, too, Grampa! Wrong!" He shot up off his chair and ran from the dining room, pounding his feet up the stairs where, at last, he slammed his bedroom door. The echo reverberated through the house.

"That boy needs a firm hand," Gerald muttered through a clenched jaw. "Sim could modify his attitude in a minute."

"Who's Sim?" Brooke wanted to know, looking confused.

"He's someone I went to dinner with when you slept over at Gramma and Grampa's house," Lydia explained. "And you met him. He stopped by one evening—the same day the Smiths moved away. He's got dark hair that's sort of bushy. . ."

"Oh, him," Brooke said, wrinkling her little nose. "He gotsa lotta perfume on!"

Lydia tried not to chuckle at her daughter's remark, but it was true; Sim wore far too much cologne. The night she'd gone out with him, she'd ended up with a terrible headache. That was the night Alec had come to her rescue.

Glancing at her father-in-law, she realized he found nothing amusing about the turn in conversation. He irritably tossed his napkin onto his plate. "I see you've succeeded in brainwashing my grandchildren." He stood.

Lydia did likewise, shocked by the accusation. "I've done no such thing. I've never said a negative word about Sim in front of Tyler or Brooke."

He took a deep breath and his voice softened. "What's happened to you? You've never been an argumentative woman."

"That was always Michael's department, wasn't it?" Tears gathered in the backs of her eyes. She wished Michael were here to handle Tyler and Gerald, but, of course, he wasn't. Then suddenly a vision of Alec, her knight in shining armor, replaced the memory of her late husband. She had no doubt that he would defend her against Gerald's tyranny, and he'd have managed Ty's outburst as well. But the very idea caused her heart to ache all the more since it seemed she'd lost Alec, too.

*My joy is in the Lord Jesus,* she reminded herself, closing her eyes. *He'll take care of me.*

"I'm leaving," Gerald announced. "See you tonight at church."

"Bye, Grampa," Brooke called.

No reply.

🌺

"He's not a bad man," Tyler grumbled, gazing out his bedroom window at Mr. Alec's house. He folded his arms tightly and clenched his jaw.

Suddenly he saw Mr. Alec's truck roll into the driveway. He watched him climb out, look over toward the back door, and for a minute, Tyler wondered if Mr. Alec was going to come over for a visit. He brightened at the thought, but resumed scowling when his new friend just walked into his house instead.

Then he got an idea. He could go ask Mr. Alec about what Grampa said. Yeah! He'd prove Grampa wrong.

Leaving his room, he heard his mother clearing the dining room table. As quietly as he could, he crept downstairs.

"Eat your peas, Brooke," he heard Mama say.

"Tyler didn't eat his peas," she complained.

"Tyler's going to get a spanking for talking back to Grampa. You want one of those, too?"

"No, ma'am, I'll be eating my peas right up. See? I'm eating 'em."

*What a little goodie-goodie,* Tyler thought with a frown. He'd better make his getaway quick or else!

He inched his way to the kitchen and watched as his mother set a stack of dishes in the sink. He waited impatiently until she walked back into the dining room. Then, sneaking to the back door, he made his escape. Outside, he stayed close to the house, feeling like a spy in a movie he and Matt watched on TV. When he reached the front, he ran fast across the lawn and up the cement steps to Mr. Alec's front porch. Ringing the bell, he plastered his body flat against the house in case his mother should happen to glance out the window.

The door creaked open.

"Pssst. Mr. Alec. Over here."

Tyler peered around the corner frame of the screen door.

"Tyler, what are you doing? Hiding?"

"Uh-huh. I can't let my mama see me."

"How come?" Frowning, Mr. Alec came out and sat down on the brick porch rail, blocking the view between his house and Tyler's.

" 'Cause I'm supposed to be getting a lickin' about now."

"Oh, yeah?" Tyler heard the smile in Mr. Alec's voice. "What did you do?"

"Sassed my grampa."

He chuckled. "Well, you can't come over here seeking refuge." Mr. Alec stood and got ready to go back inside.

"No. Wait. I gotta talk to you. That's why I came over."

Slowly, he sat back down. "Okay. What's up, kid?"

Tyler swallowed. "My grampa says you're a bad man, but I don't believe him. I think you're a good man."

Mr. Alec looked a little mad, and Tyler wondered if maybe he shouldn't have told him.

"You know what? I was a bad man," Mr. Alec began. His face seemed much friendlier all of a sudden. "But it was a long time ago. Then I heard about what Jesus did on the cross, and I believe He died for all the rotten things I did. I became a Christian and didn't want to be a bad man anymore—and I'm not. Except I'm not perfect, either."

Tyler nodded. "We're all bad till Jesus saves us."

"Right."

He frowned. "But how come Grampa said that stuff about you?"

Mr. Alec had to think about the question for a while. Finally, he said, "Sometimes we look at how bad a person used to be and forget to see how far Jesus has brought him. Take me, for instance. It seems like your grampa is only looking at all the sin that used to be in my life instead of giving me a chance to show him that God helped me change my ways. But don't be angry at him, kid. He's just trying to protect your mom, you, and Brooke."

"Mama wouldn't care if you sinned before—and I don't, either."

Mr. Alec grinned a little. "Yeah, I know."

"And she can make real good chocolate cake. We were supposed to have it after lunch, but—"

"Hey, you don't have to sell me on your mother, okay?"

"No, I don't want to sell her." Tyler couldn't believe grown-ups could be so dumb. "I just want you to like her."

Mr. Alec put his head back and laughed. "I do like her. I like her a lot. Now, you get yourself home and take your punishment like a man."

"What's that mean?" Tyler asked slowly, not liking the sound of this.

"A man takes his punishment without complaining, and he doesn't cry."

Tyler sighed. "Good thing I'm not a man, 'cause Mama's spankings hurt real bad." His rear end stung just thinking about it.

"Tyler? Tyler. . ." Mama's voice came from the driveway right behind Mr. Alec.

"Uh-oh. Reckoning time." Mr. Alec grinned as if he thought it was funny.

"Couldn't you just talk to her for a while?" Ty whispered pleadingly. "She'll forget about me if you talk to her."

Mr. Alec scratched his jaw, and Tyler guessed he was thinking about it.

"Pleeeeze?" he begged.

"Tyler. . . ," Mama called once more.

"He's right here, Lydia," Mr. Alec replied over his shoulder. Then he gave Tyler a wink.

Tyler sighed with relief.

Mama came up to the porch slowly. "What are you doing here?" she asked with one of those curiously annoyed expressions Tyler had seen plenty of times before.

"Just talkin', Mama," he said innocently.

He turned to their neighbor for help but realized Mr. Alec was staring at Mama hard. . .like it hurt or something. Glancing at his mother, he saw she was staring right back. Was she going to cry?

It seemed like a whole hour before Mr. Alec cleared his throat. "You got any pop over at your house yet, Lydia?"

"What?" Mama seemed confused by the question.

"I thought maybe I could come over and we could talk. Actually, I wanted to share something that happened at the Bible study last night. Oh, by the way, the gang says 'hi.'"

A little smile tugged at the corners of Mama's mouth. "Yes, I'd like to hear all about it. But you'll have to bring your own soft drink. I didn't get to the grocery store yesterday."

"Okay." Mr. Alec stood and walked toward the door.

"And give me a few minutes, would you, Alec?" Mama asked sweetly. "My son and I have unfinished business."

*Rats! She didn't forget!*

Mr. Alec gave Tyler a slug in the arm—the kind friends gave each other. "Sorry, kid, I tried."

"Thanks," Tyler answered glumly as he trudged home behind his mother.

# *Chapter 17*

Lydia wound her way through the Monday morning rush-hour as she drove Gerald to the airport. Even more nerve-wracking than the bumper-to-bumper traffic jams was having to listen to him giving her instructions.

"Make sure the office supply company delivers the four new chairs for the meeting room."

"I will."

"And help Pastor Camden get the flyers created for our Easter program. It'll be here before we know it."

Lydia promised to do her best and then pulled alongside the curb at the terminal.

"Lastly, I want you to let Sim know your whereabouts at all times, what with that madman living next door to you. There's no telling when he might strike."

"Alec is not a madman," Lydia said, desperately trying to keep her temper in check. "Please don't call him that. I'm in love with him."

"Spare me. I don't have time for this now!"

Lydia clamped her mouth shut. How could she have been so wrong about Gerald? He didn't care about her. How could he? He refused to lend a sympathetic ear.

"Stay away from him," her father-in-law warned. He narrowed his dark gaze for emphasis.

Tightening her grip on the minivan's steering wheel, Lydia gazed out the windshield and took a deep, calming breath. "I don't want to stay away from him," she confessed. "I love him and he loves me. Granted, we have a few things to work out, but—"

"Listen to me!" Gerald shouted, grabbing her arm roughly. Lydia gasped in surprise and pain. Suddenly, as if realizing what he'd done, her father-in-law released her. "Forgive me, dear. I have so much on my mind right now. The district attorney is threatening me with all kinds of nasty business—all of it unwarranted, of course. I can't imagine how Sim convinced him to let me leave the state for the next ten days." He gave her an indulgent smile. "In any event, I can't handle any more problems. For your own good, take my advice.

Lydia didn't answer. On one hand, she felt sorry for him, and on the other, she was determined not to allow him to rule her life any longer. But for now, she didn't argue further, fearing Gerald would change his mind and stay home. She had made wonderful plans with Sherry for the upcoming weekend and, having been invited, Alec agreed to go along. They'd had such a special time together yesterday afternoon, sharing things from the Bible and describing how God used His Word to shape their lives. If Lydia ever questioned Alec's faith, she didn't anymore. He loved the Lord with all his heart.

Now if only Gerald would see it.

"Be a good girl while I'm gone," he told her in a voice he would have just as easily used with Brooke.

She bristled and didn't trust herself to reply.

After considering her for a long while, he hopped out of the van, and he hailed a porter to carry his luggage. "I mean it, Lydia, don't cross me." With that, he slammed the door with more force than necessary.

She winced before pulling away from the curb, aware that she was destined for trouble. She fully intended to "cross" her father-in-law, and the consequences frightened her. Not only would she not have Gerald's financial support, Lydia surmised she'd be church disciplined for her disobedience. Just like her mother.

*Mama.* Lydia now had much more compassion for her mother's situation. And as she drove through the city streets, she suddenly longed to see her. Lydia needed to ask her forgiveness—how could she have been so blind? Worse, she hadn't even tried to get to know her stepfather. Lydia had a feeling he was probably a very nice man.

Heeding her heart's desire, she stopped at a gas station and phoned for directions.

She was going to see her mother!

❧

By Thursday, Alec felt dead-dog tired. He'd put in forty-two hours the last three days. What was Greg Nivens's problem, anyway? The guy was moody and short-tempered lately. Couldn't be their latest project. Everything was running smoothly.

"Hey, Corbett, I need to talk to you!"

As Alec pulled out his cup of coffee from the machine in the back of the shop, he turned, hearing Greg's voice. "Yeah, what's up?"

"C'mon into my office."

Grudgingly, Alec complied.

"Have a seat," Greg said.

Alec lowered himself into one of the cracked leather chairs in front of his supervisor's paper-strewn desk.

"I've got a message for you."

"And what's that?"

"Stay away from Lydia Boswick."

Alec couldn't conceal his surprise. "Lydia? What's she got to do with anything?"

"You've been over at her house every night this week."

"So. It's none of your business." Alec tipped his head. "And how'd you know I've been at her house?"

His face flushed crimson. "I just do."

"What, are you tailing me? Get a life!" Alec stood and headed for the door.

"Come back here. We're not done yet."

"Yes, we are. You want to discuss business? Fine. But my personal life is just that. Personal."

"This is about your job, Corbett."

Alec halted in his tracks. Turning slowly, he scrutinized the other man. Greg just stood there, rubbing his chin and looking tense. "I think your involvement with Mrs. Boswick," he stated woodenly, "is affecting the quality of your work."

"Oh, yeah?" Alec stepped back into the office and suddenly Larry's words from last week reverberated in his head. *Pastor Boswick has a lot of clout around here. Knows people in high places. If he doesn't like you, he'll make your life miserable.* "You're a member of SPCC, aren't you? So the message you just gave me is from Gerald Boswick...? How much did he pay you to harass me?" He shook his head disbelievingly. "Man, I thought you served God, not a power-hungry man."

"This has nothing to do with me." Greg shifted uncomfortably. "Your work is...is suffering."

"Right. So much so that you gave me a bonus last week."

"Corbett, I'm warning you. I'll have to write you up if this keeps going."

"Do what you have to. But I'll see Lydia when and where I please. It's a free country—at least it was the last time I heard. But you did your part, Nivens, so you ought to get your blood money. Except, I've got to tell you—" Alec paused for effect. "—don't quit your day job. You're a terrible actor."

Exiting the office, he tossed his coffee into the nearest trash bin. He'd never felt so angry in his life. He had thought Greg was a friend—a brother in Christ. And the disappointment suddenly filling his being overshadowed his fury. *But, Lord, You're bigger than Greg Nivens and Gerald Boswick, and I'm thankful I've got You on my side!*

❧

"Oh, Alec, I'm so sorry," Lydia said that night as they stood in their respective backyards, talking over the fence. She'd just arrived home after being at church for Thursday evening worship service. "Even more than sorry," she added, "I'm embarrassed. I can't believe my father-in-law would go to such lengths to keep us apart. Threatening you with your job?" She shook her head. "I'm shocked."

"I'm not. I hate to tell you, honey, but this seems to be typical behavior for your father-in-law."

She winced, hearing the cynicism in Alec's voice, and yet she could hardly blame him. "Do you want to call it quits?" she asked, her throat tightening with emotion. "I'd understand."

"Would you?"

She shrugged, lowering her gaze. She kicked at a clump of dirt near a fence post. Who was she trying to fool? She'd be heartbroken if they broke up.

"No, I don't want to call it quits," he said at last, causing her to sigh inwardly with relief. "I'm no wimp. Your father-in-law doesn't scare me, but he sure makes me angry." Alec put a booted foot on the fence and leaned forward. He softened his voice. "Do you want to call it quits?"

"No." Lydia nibbled her lower lip in consternation, then glanced at her house. Tyler and Brooke had gone in ahead of her. "Alec, I need to get my children into bed, but I'd like to continue our conversation."

"Go ahead. I'll call you in a while."

Within the hour, Lydia had managed to tuck her two children into bed. They weren't sleeping when Alec phoned, but she had a feeling they were well on their way. They'd never gotten home after school because Lydia had been so busy with office work, so they'd stayed right through until the evening service. Such days made for exhausted children by nine thirty at night.

"So how was your day?" Alec asked.

"Long." Lydia held the cordless handset between her shoulder and chin while changing into her nightgown.

"Hey, don't complain to me about long days. I've already put over fifty hours in this week."

"Yes, but you're a man. You're made to handle such hardships."

"Right. I forgot—the 'hardships' part, that is."

She laughed softly and wondered if he was unaccustomed to women behaving like women. It seemed he was used to females being loud and tough—even competing with men.

"Will you tell me about Denise? I don't mean to pry, Alec, it's just I'm curious about what kind of woman she was, how she won your heart."

There was silence for a long spell and Lydia was about to apologize for getting so personal. But then he spoke up.

"Denise was fun. She liked to go to basketball games, and. . .well, you remember Debbie from the Bible study, right?"

"Of course."

"Denise was a lot like her."

"I didn't think you liked Debbie. You two acted more like enemies than friends."

Alec chuckled. "Yeah, some people said that about me and Denise, too."

"Well, I hope you won't mind my saying so, but that doesn't seem quite right."

"Guess it wasn't quite right in God's eyes, either, because look what happened."

"Hmm. . ." Clad in her nightgown, Lydia felt chilled and crawled into bed where she could finish her conversation with Alec in cozy comfort.

Then suddenly she heard the front door close downstairs. *Odd*, she thought, *Tyler and Brooke are up here in bed.*

Thinking it might be the wind that rattled this old house frequently, she relaxed but then decided she'd better check on the children just in case Tyler had come up with one of his bright ideas. Flipping back the covers, she swung her legs off the bed and padded as far as the doorway when she heard the scuff of a hard-sole shoe against the floor at the bottom of the stairs.

"Hey, Lydia. You're so quiet. Did I say something to offend you?"

"No, but. . ." She retreated a few steps. "Alec," she whispered into the phone, "someone's in my house." Panic ripped through her as she wondered how she'd protect her precious children from an intruder.

"You sure?"

The stairs creaked in protest under the weight of her uninvited guest's foot-falls. "Yes, I'm sure."

"Hang up and call the cops. I'm on my way over."

With shaky hands, Lydia did as Alec instructed, simultaneously pulling on her robe. She crept into Brooke's room, the closest of the three, and hid behind the door, whispering her address to the 911 operator.

"Please hurry!"

"A squad is on the way, ma'am."

In the darkened hallway, Lydia saw the shadowy figure walk across the landing before climbing the last four stairs.

"Mama?"

"Shh. . . ," she silenced her daughter, but only too late. The intruder had heard. He turned toward the sound of Brooke's voice, and the soft light from Lydia's bedroom illuminated his features. "Sim!" she gasped, feeling both alarmed and indignant. "What are you doing here?"

He stepped closer, and she wrapped her robe more tightly around her. "I just came to check on you." His tone had an eerie sound to it.

"Ch–check on me? You nearly gave me heart failure. How did you get into my house?"

He dangled a single gold key just above her head. As she looked up at it, he brought his mouth down in a vampire-like swoop and kissed her neck. Lydia shrieked in shock and disgust, and pushing him away, she brought her palm hard against his cheek in a sound slap.

"You'll pay for that," he promised maliciously.

"Mama!" Brooke screamed from her bed.

"It's all right. Don't be afraid," Lydia tried to assure her daughter as her own heart hammered wildly.

Lydia could hear Alec pounding on the door as Sim grabbed her, pulling her toward her bedroom. Brooke began to wail. The phone clunked to the floor as Lydia fought her aggressor with all her might.

Then Tyler emerged from his room. "Mama?"

Before she could utter a word, Sim's rough hand clamped over her mouth. But thankfully Ty drew his own conclusions and ran down the steps. It seemed to take forever before Lydia heard Alec coming. By then, Sim, crazed with evil intent, had her cornered.

"Don't do this, Sim. Stop!"

In a flash he was yanked away, and Lydia watched in a mixture of horror and relief as Alec's powerful fists delivered several well-directed blows. Sim suddenly resembled a life-size rag doll being pushed and pummeled across the room.

"No, Alec, don't kill him!"

Sim's burly body collided with her mirrored bureau, sending pictures, her jewelry box, and perfume bottles crashing to the floor. At last he lay in a heap near her closet.

"Mama! Mr. Alec! The police are here! I let 'em in!" Tyler shouted above the din of Brooke's hysteria.

As the two officers entered the room, Alec breathlessly explained what had happened, and Lydia gathered Brooke into her arms, trying to soothe her. It was then Lydia realized she'd been sobbing, too.

# Chapter 18

Brooke lay fast asleep on Lydia's lap in a rocking chair in the far corner of the living room. Thankfully, Lydia had been able to dress before giving her statement to police. Then Sim was transported to the hospital, where he regained consciousness and appeared fine for the most part. The authorities said he'd be arraigned later. Unfortunately, the sirens brought folks from their homes all up and down the street, and Lydia felt so ashamed and embarrassed. She was only too grateful for Alec, who stepped in and answered questions.

"What a lousy way to meet the neighbors," he remarked facetiously after he saw the last of them out the door. The police had just left as well. Walking through the hallway to the living room, he paused beneath the threshold and gave Lydia a troubled stare. "You sure you're okay?"

Hearing the note of concern in his voice, she felt like sobbing all over again, but managed a weak nod.

Alec strode toward her and, reaching the chair, hunkered beside it and took her hand, holding it tight between both of his. "First thing in the morning, I want you to call a locksmith and get him to come and change the locks."

"I thought about it," Lydia replied. "But Ron Zimmerman is the only locksmith in Woodruff, and since he's a member of SPCC, I'm afraid he'll give my father-in-law a key."

Alec looked momentarily thoughtful. "Well, I could do it, but I have to work a half day, so I won't get to it till the afternoon. Is that all right?"

"Fine. I'm taking the day off tomorrow anyway. I have every intention of phoning Gerald in Florida and reporting this awful incident." Lydia sniffed back a fresh onslaught of tears.

"I just hope he's not the one behind it."

"Oh, Alec, I wondered the same thing." Lydia shook her head ruefully. "But it's incomprehensible—my own father-in-law, a man whom I have trusted completely for almost three years, the person I counted on to care for and protect the children and me. . . . How could he be even remotely involved with tonight's episode? And yet, with everything that's happened lately, I can't help but think it's possible."

After giving her hand a gentle squeeze, Alec stood to his feet. He ran a hand through his blond hair. "Even so, it's doubtful we'll ever prove it." He pursed his lips, inclining his head slightly. "Okay, what about this weekend? Still want to go visit your friends?"

"Most definitely. I need to get away for a while."

"Good. I was hoping you'd say that."

Lydia suddenly glanced around the side of him. "Where's Tyler?"

"Oh. . ." Alec chuckled and motioned toward the front door with his thumb. "He walked out with one of the officers to see the inside of a police car. I didn't think it'd hurt anything. In fact, I thought it might even get his mind off what happened tonight."

As if on cue, the door opened and slammed shut—Tyler style. "That was awesome!" he declared, bouncing into the living room. "Mr. Alec, you shoulda seen the stuff they all got in there. Radios, and—"

Alec put a finger to his lips to shush him, but too late.

"Mama," Brooke whimpered.

Lydia frowned at her son for being so noisy. On the other hand, she felt relieved that he wasn't traumatized like Brooke.

Rousing the sleepy girl on her lap, Lydia sat forward. "Y'all had better get to bed. It's very late."

The little girl suddenly began crying again. "No, Mama, I don't want to go to bed. That bad man will come back."

"No, he won't," Lydia said soothingly. "Shh. . ." She stroked her silky blond hair comfortingly.

"He can't come back, Brooke," Tyler told her, "the police got him."

"That's right," Alec added, lowering himself to her eye level and cupping the side of her small face. "He won't hurt you or your mom anymore. It's okay to go to bed now."

"I don't wanna!" With that she buried her face in Lydia's sweater.

"She's overtired," Lydia softly explained. "She can sleep in my bed tonight."

Alec straightened his tall frame. "All right. Guess I'll let you do your mother-thing and I'll get myself home."

Nodding, Lydia got up from the rocker, holding Brooke in her arms. "I can't thank you enough for your help tonight. I don't know what I would have done if you hadn't—"

"Don't even think about the what-ifs. It's over. Try to forget it, all right?" Alec turned. "G'night, kid," he said to Tyler. He gave him a sort of sideways hug with one arm slung around his shoulders. "Help your mom out, and I'll see you tomorrow."

"Sure."

"Come and lock the door after me."

"Okay. . .I know how to lock it real tight."

"I know you do."

With a little smile, Lydia bid Alec good night and climbed the stairs. She felt Brooke's small arms encircle her neck in a death grip as the little girl began to cry, and Lydia tried not to hate Simeon Crenshaw for terrorizing her family—and her!

🏵

On Friday Alec expertly changed Lydia's locks, and then, under a clear, sunny sky, Lydia and Alec packed up her minivan and drove off toward Tennessee. Tyler chatted incessantly for the first part of the journey. He asked Alec, who sat behind the wheel, every kind of question his eight-year-old mind could imagine. Did he like dogs? How about cats?

"I like dogs and cats, too," Ty said.

The conversation continued for a while longer, and then Ty grew bored and sat back to play one of his handheld electronic games while Brooke watched curiously.

"Brooke seems to be calmer today," Alec remarked to Lydia in a hushed tone so Brooke wouldn't overhear.

"Yes. In the daylight, everything that happened last night seems like a nightmare instead of real life. I just hope she'll be able to forget it easily enough."

Alec nodded reflectively. "Know what I realized last night?"

"What?"

"I realized how much I've really come to care about you and the kids. I wanted to kill that guy—not a very Christian-like response, is it?"

"Oh, I don't know. You were protecting us, and Sim wasn't exactly in the right state of mind for a discussion."

"I'll say." Alec momentarily took his eyes off the road and glanced her way. "Know what I also realized?"

"Hmm?"

"I don't love Denise—maybe I never did. It's weird, but I can't ever recall feeling the way I did when I saw Sim with his hands on you. I felt scared and angry all at once. Oh, I've been jealous before. Denise was good at making me feel jealous. But this was different. Much different. And I guess I can't explain it any better than I just tried."

Lydia looked down at her hands, folded neatly in her lap, and smiled. She couldn't care less that Alec wasn't eloquent when it came to sharing his feelings. He was honest and that was what mattered most to her. Besides, he'd just said the very words she longed to hear. He didn't love Denise!

"Alec, if it took something like last night to cause you to realize your true feelings, then I'll count it no small blessing." Her smile broadened. "You know what I've decided? I've decided God sent you here to rescue me. You're my knight in shining armor."

"Right." He laughed, obviously to cover his sudden embarrassment. "Oh, and speaking of rescuing. . .you never did tell me what your father-in-law had to say this morning."

"He didn't say much—I did most of the talking. I told him how disappointed I felt with him for threatening you and causing you to lose your job. He claimed he didn't know what I was talking about. Then I informed him about what happened last night with Sim, and he got very quiet. Perhaps he felt angry or maybe he felt guilty. I don't know. I couldn't bring myself to ask."

Alec changed lanes, passing a long truck carrying a large piece of machinery. Tyler and Brooke began to chatter excitedly over it.

"Lydia, I'm wondering. . .would you tell me what kind of relationship your husband had with his father?"

"Sure. They were a lot alike in many ways, and keep in mind that Michael was an attorney so he loved a good debate." Lydia couldn't help a smile. "He and Gerald had plenty of them."

"About anything specific?"

"Not that I can recall. I know Michael didn't approve of his father involving himself so heavily with the church's finances as well as those of some of the congregation—like my mother, for instance. But I remember Gerald claiming to be a sharp accountant, and he argued that he had a personal interest in the financial success of SPCC and its members." She sighed regretfully. "But Michael would never tell me details. He said he didn't want me worrying over anything. Of course, Elberta never allowed either of us to sit in on the men's conversations and, frankly, I didn't care to. But now I wished I would have paid more attention and asked more questions."

"Your father-in-law drives an awful fancy car—not that I begrudge pastors any luxuries. It's just that when I saw him pulling into your driveway last weekend, it made me all the more suspicious, considering the allegations against him."

"Yes, I know. . . ." Lydia mentally pictured the grand house in which her in-laws resided. She had always thought they deserved the "blessing" for being such servants of God, but now she, too, felt suspicious—and it troubled her deeply.

It was almost nine o'clock when Alec found his way to the Smiths' new house. After they'd parked, Sherry was the first to greet them. Tall and shapely, she had curly honey blond hair that hung slightly past her shoulders.

"Lydia, you sweet thing!" she cried, with outstretched arms.

They embraced before Sherry pulled back, and Lydia found herself looking up into her dear friend's freckled face.

"I'm so sorry, Lyd; will you ever forgive me for shunning you? I swear I hurt myself more than I hurt you."

Tears gathered in Lydia's eyes. "I already forgave you." She sniffed.

Sherry's gaze grew misty as well. "I'm so glad to see you."

"I'm so glad to see you, too."

They embraced again as Jordan Smith walked out of the house. "With these two blubbering over each other," he said to Alec, "I guess we're on our own." He stuck out his right hand and introduced himself just before his three children bounded out the door. All at once there were five little ones squealing happily in the driveway.

"C'mon, Ty, I'll show you my room," Matt said. He was dark-headed like his father, and beneath the yard light, Lydia smiled at the excitement in his brown eyes. "Tomorrow I'll show you the tree house Daddy built. No girls allowed."

"Cool!" Tyler replied.

The boys took off in a flash with the girls laughingly chasing after them.

"Why don't y'all come on inside?" Jordan invited. "And, Alec, let me help you with the luggage."

With her arm around Lydia's shoulders, Sherry ushered her into the living room.

"So what do you think about Alec?" Lydia whispered. "I want your first impression."

"He's quite tall."

Lydia tossed a maroon throw pillow at her friend. "You're so observant."

Sherry laughed and tossed it back.

"And here they are," Jordan said facetiously, "taking out the living room already." He shook his dark head and walked in with Alec right behind him. "You two are worse than the kids."

Lydia glanced at Alec, who sent her an affectionate wink before lowering himself into a mauve swivel rocker. Lydia remembered when the Smiths bought this living room ensemble, couch and two chairs, glass-top coffee table and matching end tables. And she recalled vividly just how excited Sherry had been the day it arrived. It was just before Michael died.

She gazed at Sherry, then Jordan, and back to Sherry once more. "You two are a sight for sore eyes, do you know that?" Her throat constricted with unshed emotion.

"So are you."

"Oh, will you two knock it off," Jordan muttered irritably.

"I see he hasn't changed a bit," Lydia told Sherry.

Sherry, in turn, looked at Alec. "My husband has no patience for female sensibilities," she explained. "But I hope you do. Lydia and I can cry at the drop of a hat, can't we, honey?"

Jordan's expression was oblique as he faced Alec. "Do you like a good game of Ping-Pong? I've got a table set up in the rec room."

"You're on." Alec seemed relieved. Standing, he crossed the room, trailing Jordan.

"Oh, Sherry, you scared him off," Lydia said in mild rebuff. "We've only known each other a month."

"If he scares that easily," she drawled in reply, "then he ain't a man worth having. Besides, if Tyler hasn't spooked him by now, chances are he's a keeper."

They laughed together.

"You've changed," Sherry said at last.

"I have?"

"Uh-huh. You look. . .happy again."

"I feel happy again," Lydia admitted.

"I'm so glad. Come on," she said, holding out her hand. "I'll show you around the rest of the house. I just love it here!"

Lydia stood, and as she toured her good friend's nicely decorated home, she recognized objects that had once hung on the walls of a different house, in a different state. So familiar and yet strange in their new environment that they might as well have been brand new, and suddenly Lydia was reminded of herself. Things around her had changed dramatically. She looked the same on the outside, but she could hardly claim to be the person she'd been a month ago. She was finally back among the living.

And it was all because the Lord had brought Alec Corbett into her life.

# Chapter 19

"You're awfully quiet," Alec remarked during the drive homeward late Sunday night.

"Just thinking."

"Did you have a nice weekend?"

Lydia smiled. "Very nice." From the passenger seat, she glanced over her shoulder into the back, where Tyler and Brooke slept peacefully. "How about you? Did you enjoy meeting the Smiths?"

"Yeah. Nice people."

"And you really didn't mind bunking down in the family room with two rambunctious boys?" Lydia couldn't suppress a giggle. "Did you get any sleep at all?"

"Some." The lights from the highway illuminated his rugged features, and Lydia saw the smirk on his face. "Tyler and Matt sure like to talk."

"You've been a good sport, Alec. And you're very patient with children."

"Kids never bothered me. But it seemed Jordan got a little hot under the collar a few times."

"Yes, he has a habit of raising his voice when the children play too loudly. It used to really upset Tyler, but I think in time he grew accustomed to it."

"I remember the first day I met your kids. They asked if I was going to holler at them for standing on the fence." Alec chuckled. "Must have been what Jordan used to do."

"It was."

Alec laughed again. "But the highlight of the weekend was hearing all about you from Sherry."

"I already told you, she exaggerates," Lydia stated with a bit of a huff. She'd like to get even with her longtime friend for sharing those silly stories—like the time they were both expecting babies and Lydia locked herself out of the house after grocery shopping. Sherry came up with the brilliant notion to climb through the window, but in their conditions neither fit. Nevertheless, Sherry had to try and managed to get herself good and stuck. That was when the Woodruff police were called. . . .

"The tales I heard," Alec said amusedly, "sounded more like *I Love Lucy* reruns."

"Oh, hush," Lydia replied in mild rebuff, but she laughed softly in spite of herself.

She thought this weekend had been a wonderful blessing. She and Alec had gotten to know more about each other. And he had been a perfect gentleman the whole time—even Sherry commented on it. Somehow her friend's approval affirmed in her heart that God truly had His hand on her relationship with Alec.

"Did the dinner conversation tonight upset you?" he asked, drawing her from her reverie.

Lydia thought it over. The topic had been her father-in-law. "Yes, it upset me," she admitted. "I feel betrayed."

"So you believe the Smiths and your mother?"

Lydia nodded as a vision of her father-in-law handling her roughly in the minivan last Monday flittered through her mind. "I'm convinced Gerald enjoys controlling others, and for so long, I was content to be controlled by him."

"Hmm..."

"I am scared though, Alec. When I stand up to him, my father-in-law could very well pull the rug of security right out from under me."

"I warned you that could happen."

"Yes, you did...but I'm not turning back. I can't! I believe the Lord has opened my eyes and allowed me to learn the things I have for a reason. He now expects me to act upon my knowledge even if it means I have to find another job...another church."

"I hope you're planning to contact your husband's attorney and find out the specifics regarding any money Michael left you. I'd hate to see what happened to your mother happen to you, too."

"Oh yes, that's another area of my life I intend to take back from Gerald."

Alec chuckled. "You know, for a sweet little Southern thing, you sure are brave. I admire you for that, especially since I've got a feeling many men cower around your father-in-law."

"I'm not so brave. My insides feel like jelly right now." Glancing over at him, Lydia glimpsed his smile. "But, you know, Alec, I think Jordan was right—about us worshiping together."

"I was going to bring up the subject myself." He momentarily took his eyes off the road and looked over at her. "What do you suggest?"

"From what I recall, I liked Pastor Spencer. I wouldn't mind giving his church a try. Of course, Gerald believes Berean Baptist is inferior to SPCC. But I think that might have been an issue Michael would have gone toe-to-toe with his father on."

"Mark's a strong preacher and I think you'll be blessed, but ours is a small church. We're lucky if fifty people show up on Sunday morning. That'll be different for you."

"Yes. SPCC runs about two thousand attendees on any given Sunday morning."

Alec was silent for several miles. At last, Lydia heard him expel a long breath before he spoke again. "You sure about this, Lydia? You sure about me. . .us?"

She smiled, sensing his insecurity. "Don't worry. I won't change my mind no matter what." She paused in earnest. "I just hope you don't."

"Not me."

They continued to chat amicably the rest of the way into Woodruff. Then, as Alec was about to make the turn into Lydia's driveway, she caught sight of Gerald's BMW parked out front.

"Oh no," she murmured. "I thought he was in Florida!"

"Your father-in-law?"

"Yes. But it's nearly midnight. What's he doing here at this hour?"

Gerald's stern countenance suddenly flashed before the headlights as he stepped down from the front porch.

"Judgment day." Alec brought the van to a halt near the garage.

"Please don't make jokes. I feel like I might be sick."

"Listen," he stated earnestly, "neither of us has done anything wrong."

Her heart hammering anxiously in her chest, Lydia didn't trust herself to reply. But Gerald would discover their plans eventually; it may as well be now.

Sending up a tiny prayer, she opened the door, climbed out, then pulled on the back door, rousing Tyler and Brooke.

Gerald happened upon her fast. "Where have you been?" Beneath the yard light, Lydia could barely make out his features, although she heard the controlled anger in his voice. "And why doesn't my key work in the lock?"

"Which question would you like me to answer first?" Lydia countered firmly but politely.

Alec came around, popped the hatch, and began removing luggage from the minivan. Seeing him, Gerald's jaw dropped slightly.

"What in the world have you done? Taking off with a strange man for the weekend? And in front of the children. . ."

"It was all very proper, I assure you," Lydia stated, feeling insulted. She lifted Brooke out of the vehicle, then moved aside so Tyler could jump down.

"Hi, Grampa. Guess what? I got to see Matt this weekend. His dad made him a tree house and it's pretty cool, but Mr. Alec had to finish off the side of it 'cuz Mr. Smith isn't as good at building stuff as Mr. Alec."

"Well, well, isn't that. . .nice," came Gerald's barbed reply while he pierced Lydia with his dark gaze. "The Smiths. You visited the Smiths."

Alec closed the hatch and then tossed Tyler the house keys. "Go open the back door, will you?"

"Sure. I caught those keys good, didn't I?"

"Yep."

Lydia set Brooke down, instructing her to follow her brother into the house.

"But it's dark in there." Her small voice trembled.

"Ty will turn on the lights," Lydia promised, hating the way Brooke was suddenly so afraid of the nighttime. For the past two nights, Lydia had had to sleep with Brooke so she wouldn't cry.

Once the children were out of earshot, Lydia turned to her father-in-law. "Sherry's my friend and I've missed her."

"I see."

"And just so you know, I visited my mother last Monday."

"Mm..."

"Furthermore, Alec and I are still seeing each other."

"So I gathered." He stuck his hands in the pockets of his beige London Fog trench coat. "You've thwarted my every word of warning."

Lydia could only nod.

Gerald grunted. "You certainly know how to hurt an old man. I only wanted the best for you—for my grandchildren—and to have my efforts tossed back in my face is quite distressing."

Experiencing a sudden wave of shame, Lydia chanced a look at Alec and saw him smirk. She wondered what he found amusing. Then leaning casually against the minivan, he met her gaze and mouthed, "Guilt trip."

She nodded back knowingly before facing Gerald again.

Just then Tyler burst out the back door. "Mama, Brooke is screaming her head off and I turned on the lights upstairs. But it didn't help."

"Want me to go in?" Alec asked.

"Would you mind?"

"Nope."

"Wait a moment," Gerald demanded. He turned to Alec, then returned his gaze to Lydia. "Since when does a stranger see after Brooke's welfare?"

"Alec is hardly a stranger." She gave him the go-ahead to proceed to the house before continuing. "And since Sim terrorized all of us last week, Alec is something of a hero in our eyes—especially Brooke's. She feels safe with him. So do Tyler and I for that matter."

"Now there's an oxymoron for you," he stated sarcastically. "You feel safe with a man who's been convicted of offenses such as disorderly conduct and drunk driving? Where's your head, Lydia? In addition, I think you misunderstood Sim's intentions."

"There was no misunderstanding."

"He only came to see after your well-being."

"He attacked me!" Lydia couldn't believe her father-in-law was taking Sim's side against hers. And yet, she told herself she shouldn't be surprised.

"Sim never meant to cause you any harm. He merely wanted a kiss. He's crazy about you."

"He's crazy. I'll grant you that much."

"Now, listen," her father-in-law said, gently taking hold of her upper arm, "we will discuss your relationship with your, um, *neighbor* another time. But for now, there's a more urgent matter to address. Let's go in the house, send your friend home, and make some coffee while we talk, shall we?"

"Thank you, but no. Whatever you have to say to me, Gerald, you can say out here. I'm tired and I don't feel much like having coffee." She'd never dared to speak to her father-in-law that way, and she felt a bit amazed at herself. Next, she pulled her arm from his grasp.

"Very well." He inhaled deeply, audibly. "I must insist you drop any litigation against Sim. He's not even going to sue your *hero* for assault and battery. Isn't that a relief?"

"He doesn't have a case. Why would he sue Alec?"

"Lydia, two men were fighting in your bedroom—one had the key to your house, the other has a criminal record. This could get very ugly and my point is this—with all the bad publicity out there, we cannot afford any more. Sim is my attorney. I need him right now. Everything is running smoothly and he expects to have the case against me dismissed by the end of the week. Then Elberta will return and things will fall back into place." He paused, his dark gaze boring down at her. "You wouldn't want to ruin the Boswick family's good name just to get back at Sim, now would you? Vengeance is mine, saith the Lord. I will repay." The threat lingered in the air.

Lydia was tempted to succumb to his persuasion, but soon recognized it as another manipulative ploy. "I'll consider what you've said," she promised, despising the fragility in her own voice. But squaring her shoulders in spite of her trembling emotions, she made her way toward the house.

❧

"I cannot begin to fathom what went through your head last Thursday night!" Gerald glared at Sim's bruised face and swollen eyes. "She hates you. I just left her place and I'm convinced of it. What's more, Lydia seems more determined than ever to continue her little liaison with Alec Corbett."

"So that's what brought you back from Florida so early." Sim's puffy lips twisted into a cynical grin. "And here I thought you were worried about me."

Gerald snorted in disgust. "You've likely ruined everything."

"Not so fast. Not so fast. I've come up with a plan."

"Oh? And what might that be?"

"We'll get rid of that big ox of Lydia's." He rubbed his jaw gingerly and hardened his gaze.

Gerald shook his head. "Murder is out of the question. I do have some scruples left, you know."

"I'm not talking about killing the man. We'll just make his life so miserable that he won't want anything more to do with Lydia or the entire Boswick family. We'll get him to leave town."

"Intimidation won't work on him. He'll keep coming back for more. I know his type. And this whole ordeal has already gotten out of control. Such a shame. I almost had Lydia in the palm of my hand. We removed her nosy mother, but managed to keep her funds—that was a plus. You did a splendid job, altering those financial documents."

"Thank you." Sim took a little bow.

"Next we sent those meddlesome Smiths packing. Lydia trusted me. Believed in me. I know I could have convinced her to marry you." He swung a look of contempt Sim's way. "But you blew it. And when Lydia finds out about her trust account, she'll never speak to me again and I'll be denied the privilege of seeing my grandchildren."

"She's not going to find out. Sit down, Gerry," Sim said loosely. "I've got it all planned. You're still going to be the most acclaimed preacher in the United States—perhaps even the world. When we're through, Billy Graham won't be able to hold a candle to you. Your legacy will last for generations to come."

A satisfied warmth coursed through Gerald's veins as he lowered himself into an armchair. He allowed his gaze to wander around Sim's posh, high-rise apartment. Yes, Gerald preferred riches to rags any day. "I gave my life to Christ, sacrificed in those early years, but what has God ever done for me in return? Nothing. He even took my son! Everything I possess now, I've acquired on my own."

"God helps those who help themselves," Sim said. "And after we pull off this little caper, you'll be rich enough to obtain the power you've longed for—worked for." He smiled, a sinister light flickering in his eyes. "And after two years of watching and waiting, I'll finally have half a million dollars. . .and Lydia."

# Chapter 20

Lydia threw open the drapes and peered outside as the Monday morning sunshine flooded her bedroom. "Tyler, Brooke. . .time to wake up," she called, walking into the hallway.

Soon nothing short of mayhem broke loose as Brooke tried to find her favorite dress to wear to school and Tyler searched for his gym shoes. Lydia directed their steps from the kitchen while preparing breakfast, then rushed to get herself ready. At last they were all dressed and on their way.

After depositing her children in their respective classrooms, Lydia entered the church offices. To her relief, Gerald behaved as though nothing was amiss and it was business as usual for most of the day. Around two in the afternoon, Lydia managed to discreetly place a call to Michael's one-time partner and attorney. His secretary stated that Brian was out of town, but she penciled Lydia in for an appointment late Friday at four o'clock. With that taken care of, Lydia sat back and continued working until Tyler and Brooke were dismissed from school. But later, as she pulled into her driveway and spotted Alec's truck next door, she had an inkling something was wrong. Alec never got home early on Monday.

As soon as she could, she phoned him, only to hear him knocking on her back door. With an amused grin, she answered it. "Great minds think alike," she greeted. "I was just trying to get a hold of you."

Alec stepped into the house, a dour expression clouding his face. "I lost my job today," he stated abruptly.

Lydia inhaled sharply. "Oh no. . .I wondered what was up when I saw you were home."

"Greg Nivens wouldn't come out and admit I was getting canned because you and I are still seeing each other," Alec continued as he shut the back door behind him. "He just kept saying the quality in my work hasn't been up to company standards and that's a bald-faced lie. But I have a call in to the company's national headquarters, and I e-mailed my old supervisor. I'm planning to appeal."

Lydia didn't know what to say.

"Did you buy any pop yet?" Alec asked, entering the kitchen.

"I'm afraid not," she replied weakly. "I haven't had a chance to go to the grocery store."

"That's a downer."

She followed him in and watched as he collapsed his large frame into a chair near the table. She felt so incredibly responsible for Alec losing his job that hot tears sprang into her eyes. "Oh, Alec, I'm so sorry."

"Forget it. I really didn't want a soft drink anyhow."

"No, not that. . .your job."

He frowned curiously. "It's not your fault the axe fell today."

"Yes, it is."

Alec shook his head. "No, it isn't. And, like I said, I plan to fight this thing. In the meantime, there are plenty of other jobs around. I'm not worried. Besides, I've been employed with Heritage Craft Furniture for a long time. If I don't find employment right away, I'll get some compensation until a hearing takes place."

Lydia didn't feel assuaged in the least.

"Listen." He stood and strode toward her. Then he took her hand in his. "I'm angry. I'll admit it. But not with you. You mean more to me than a lousy job." He raised his shoulders like it was no big deal. "I'll get another one."

She swallowed a sob. It certainly was a "big deal" and to think Gerald was the motivation behind it all caused her an enormous amount of grief.

Alec cupped her face, urging her gaze to his. "But whatever you do, don't let your father-in-law know my getting fired has upset you. That's what he wants, except we've got God on our side. What can Gerald or anyone else do to us?"

❀

It was a challenge for Lydia to keep quiet the next couple of days—especially when she sensed that her father-in-law enjoyed goading her.

"How's Alec?" he asked on Wednesday afternoon as he thumbed through the mail that had been deposited on her desk.

"He's fine," she replied, trying to sound nonchalant even though her nerves were utterly jangled.

"You know, Elberta has been talking about doing some remodeling. Maybe Alec would like to give me an estimate—since he is a carpenter. I'm sure he'd appreciate the extra money. After all, carpenters don't exactly make a fortune."

Lydia forced a subtle shrug, while inside she was seething with indignation. "You'd have to ask him," she replied offhandedly.

Hours later she left work, still fuming.

But that evening she attended Berean Baptist's midweek service with Alec, and Pastor Spencer's message lifted her spirits. Afterward, she chatted for several minutes with Debbie and Judy before Alec reintroduced her to the pastor and his wife. Lydia couldn't recall a nicer exchange, and she decided there was something very quaint, personal, even intimate about worshiping the Lord with a smaller body of believers.

"So what did you think?" Alec asked as they walked through the parking lot.

"I liked children's church with Mrs. Spencer," Tyler piped in. "Grampa doesn't have anything like that at SPCC cuz he says us kids should sit still and be quiet in regular church."

"It wasn't quiet in children's church tonight," Brooke said, shaking her head. "We played a game, sang songs, learned a Bible verse, and even heard a story."

"It's kind of a neat ministry," Alec explained to Lydia. "Some students from the local Christian college volunteer their time and help Mrs. Spencer." Placing a hand under her elbow, he assisted her into his truck.

"Mama," Tyler asked once Alec closed the door and began walking around to the other side, "is Grampa gonna be mad that we came here tonight?"

"Probably," Lydia replied carefully. "But, even so, he'd never be angry with either you or Brooke."

A sudden burst of cold March wind blew into the truck as Alec opened the door and slid behind the wheel. "Who wants ice cream?"

Cheers hailed from the backseat while Lydia shook her head in amazement. "It's winter and y'all want ice cream?"

"Ice cream's good any time," Tyler said, and his little sister quickly agreed.

"You're outnumbered, Lydia," Alec told her as he started up the truck. "Ice cream it is."

It was nearly ten o'clock when Alec finally headed for home. From the silence filling the backseat, Lydia could tell her children were tired. She glanced at them and found that both sat staring dazedly out the window, watching streetlights go by.

"Want to hear my latest wild idea?"

Turning her attention to Alec, Lydia smiled. "Sure."

He paused, turning a corner. "I think I want to start my own business."

"Wonderful."

"Really think so?"

"Certainly. I think working for yourself is much better than doling out weeks, months, and years to a company that doesn't appreciate you."

"My thoughts exactly. Listen to the name I thought up. Yankee Doodle Dandy's Carpentry."

A laugh erupted before Lydia could forestall it. "In Woodruff, Alabama? I don't think so."

"No?"

"No!"

Alec chuckled. "I was just kidding anyway."

"I'm relieved to hear that."

His smile widened as he turned the truck onto their street until a horrific sight greeted them. Red lights glowed from several fire engines, voices echoed from two-way radios, and adding to the pandemonium were shouts from firemen and neighbors.

"Wow! What's happening?" Tyler asked.

Alec pulled the truck to a halt where a policeman had barricaded the entrance to the street. "Major house fire near the end of the block," he said as Lydia's insides did a nervous flip. Was it her place? Had an appliance been left on and ignited somehow? She strained her vision, trying to see.

Alec seemed to be doing the same thing. "That's my house," he finally said. All at once, he killed the engine, climbed out of the truck, and began jogging toward all the commotion.

"Oh, dear Lord, no. . .please don't let it be true." But even as Lydia sent up the plea, a heavy dread settled over her.

"Mama, is Mr. Alec's house really on fire?"

"I hope not."

"Maybe it's really Mrs. Cavendish's. She's old and smokes a pipe on her back porch all the time. Matt said so. . ."

Slowly, Lydia climbed from the truck. She began shivering, not so much from the cold, but from the realization that Alec's house was indeed on fire!

🌺

Alec picked his way through the rubble of what had once been his home, thinking he might have believed last night was a nightmare if, when the first pinks of dawn streaked the eastern sky, he'd awakened. But he hadn't, largely because he'd been up all night. And all day.

Despite a valiant effort by firefighters, his house was a total loss.

Neighbors claimed they heard some sort of blast before flames could be seen jutting from the windows. Many had feared he perished in the blaze until he showed up. Their concern had touched him despite the tumult in his heart.

"Lydia's house has some damage," Larry remarked, crossing the driveway. "But nothing major. . .hey, is she still at her mother's place? She seemed pretty upset last night."

"She wasn't the only one." Alec darted a gaze at his friend, glad he had thought to call Larry on the cell phone. Larry had been a great source of encouragement. "But, in answer to your question, yeah, Lydia's still at her mom's. . .as far as I know." He hesitated briefly. "Thanks for dropping her and the kids off last night."

"No problem. She was in no condition to drive—even if she'd been able to access her van back there in the garage."

Alec blew out a long breath, turning his gaze to the burned-out remains of the chimney.

"Are you thinking it's arson?" Larry asked, stepping over the charred wreckage and coming to stand beside him.

"It has to be—and that guy from the insurance company who was here earlier seemed to agree. Of course, no one's going to know for sure until the police do their own investigation. But I have a feeling they'll never find the person who's responsible." He faced Larry again. "You know, if I would have come home right after church, I could very easily be dead now—or worse."

"Man, that's God's hand of protection for you!"

"Sure is." Alec swung around and, again, surveyed the incredible scene before him, praising the Lord for sparing his life. Even so, he'd lost everything he owned, except for some of his tools over in the garage. It had suffered minimal damage but would hardly provide him adequate shelter. Worse, he didn't even have a change of clothes.

"Listen, Alec, you're welcome to stay at my place for as long as you want."

"Thanks," he muttered, discouragement quickly settling in. "I appreciate the offer and everything else you've done. But I think I'll leave town instead."

"What? Why?"

Pivoting, Alec considered his buddy. "He won. Don't you get it? Pastor Boswick got what he wanted—he destroyed me. I mean, I've got two hundred bucks in the bank, fifty dollars in my wallet, along with some credit cards that are almost maxed out. The only clothes I own are on my back. I've got no job, no house. . .even after the insurance comes through—*if* they come through, considering it could be arson—it's going to take me years to gain back my losses. What can I possibly offer Lydia now?"

Larry chuckled lightly and shrugged. "I have a feeling she'd take you as is."

Alec shook his head. "I'd never ask her to."

"Aw, c'mon, don't give up now. God will work it out. In the meantime, I think you'd better stay at my place. Take a shower, get some sleep. . ." Larry glanced at his watch. "I hate to do this to you, but I've got to get to work. My boss stuck me on second shift for the next two weeks. Here are the keys. I'll talk at you later."

Alec turned the house keys in his palm. "Thanks."

"You bet." Larry gave him a parting salute before walking to the street and climbing into his car.

Exhausted to the bone and utterly spent in spirit, Alec climbed into his truck and drove to Larry's place, where he managed to sleep the afternoon away.

# Chapter 21

Lydia hadn't seen Alec since the fire Wednesday night and here it was Friday afternoon. She feared the worst—that Gerald had succeeded in dissuading Alec from ever wanting to see her again. Perhaps Alec had decided she wasn't worth the trouble. The fact that she couldn't reach Alec on his cell phone and that he hadn't returned any of her voice mail messages only increased her anxiety. Did he blame her after all?

On a long sigh, she glanced at the white contemporary-styled wall clock above the secretaries' station of Josephson, Hamill, and Bosh Law Offices. Four o'clock exactly.

"Lydia?"

At the sound of a man's deep voice, she stood and smiled a greeting. "Hello, Brian."

"How nice to see you again," he said with a genuine inflection. "Come on back to my office and let's talk."

She followed him down a narrow hallway and couldn't help a glance to the left—where Michael's office had been. A man she'd never seen before sat behind a large oak desk, talking on the phone.

"Have a seat," Brian said as she entered his office. "Make yourself comfortable." He lowered himself into a chair across from hers. "How've you been?"

"Good." Lydia managed to smile in spite of the nastiness incurred by her father-in-law.

"So, what can I do for you?" He ran a hand through his short brownish blond hair.

Lydia slowly began to explain. "I guess I was just in too much shock to really hear what you told me at the reading of Michael's will. I wondered if you'd kindly explain things to me again."

"Sure, but your father-in-law is your agent, and he ought to be able to inform you as well as I can."

She hedged, expelling a weary breath. "There's a bit of a problem between Gerald and me. . .unfortunately."

Brian didn't seem surprised. "Forgive me, Lydia, but I never did trust that man. I often wondered why Michael didn't attend church elsewhere since he obviously had very little faith in his own father's ethical stance. But Michael felt convinced he could make a difference with his dad—and perhaps for a time he did. But from what I've been hearing, Gerald Boswick has finally crossed the line."

Standing, Brian walked to his file cabinet and retrieved a folder. He opened it and scanned the terms of Lydia's trust account before defining them for her one by one. When he was through, she stared back at Brian in mild shock.

Suddenly everything made sense, sickening as it was.

"A one-million-dollar trust?"

Brian nodded. "Because you haven't been eligible to draw from its principal yet, you've only received quarterly dividend checks, generated by the interest."

"And to be *eligible*, I have to. . .remarry?"

"That's right. Michael feared Southern Pride Community Church would somehow end up absorbing your bequest," Brian stated more cynically than emphatically, "and he took great pains to be sure such a thing wouldn't happen while ensuring that you were well taken care of in the meantime. He wanted there to be a two-year interim, which expired over six months ago, so now if you remarry, the money is yours in full."

*That's why Gerald wanted me to marry Sim,* Lydia silently concluded. *They're in this together. Neither loves nor cares about me. They just want my money!* Tears pooled in her eyes at the realization. "I feel so betrayed," she murmured. "All this time, I trusted him."

Brian frowned. "Has something happened?"

"Oh yes." Lydia spilled the entire story—about Alec and how she loved him, but how Gerald forbade her to see him, pushing Sim on her instead. She detailed the break-in, Alec losing his job, and finally the fire that destroyed his house. By the time she finished, she was weeping openly, and Brian handed her a box of tissues.

"Lydia," he said solemnly, sitting forward with his elbows braced on his knees, "we've got to call the police. Right now. They need to hear everything you just told me."

He didn't have to convince her. She readily agreed.

※

By the glow of his large flashlight, Alec loaded his arms with tools from his garage. Since Lydia's house was dark next door, he figured now would be a good time to gather up his stuff and get out of here—before she came home. Alec had no intention of talking to her, much less telling her good-bye. But good-bye it was. He'd had a good forty-eight hours to work himself into an emotional black hole, and he'd concluded that he would make her one unfit spouse. What had he been thinking? He'd lived a veritable fairy tale the past six weeks. But reality had delivered its staggering blow. His future seemed as bleak as his present-day situation, not to mention his sorry past.

Walking to his truck, Alec deposited the tools into the backseat beside his duffle bag containing the new jeans, underwear, and a few sweatshirts he'd managed to purchase. Now, with a full tank of gas, he planned on driving until his pickup ran out of fuel. Wherever he found himself, he'd stay. Maybe he'd find work. So what if he lived the rest of his life alone? He ought to be used to it by now.

"Alec?"

He froze at the sound of Lydia's soft voice coming from behind him. Then he inwardly cursed his misfortune. Why did she have to show up now?

Straightening slowly, he expelled a breath.

"I've been looking everywhere for you."

Without a glance in her direction, he turned and walked back into the garage. "Ever think maybe I was avoiding you on purpose?" The barbed reply pricked his conscience, but he continued with his task and picked up another box, carrying it back to his truck.

"I. . .I just wanted to know if we could talk."

"Nothing to talk about."

"Well, I've got a few things on my mind. Would you hear me out?"

Alec threw the box into his truck with more force than necessary, startling Lydia. So she'd been right. Gerald had succeeded in tearing them apart. Obviously, Alec had changed his mind about her. . .about them.

"As you can see, I'm kinda busy," he said tersely. "But if it'll make you feel better, then by all means, vent. I'll try to pay attention." He walked back into the garage.

Lydia felt tempted to just walk away and not say another word; however, she somehow sensed that Alec's gruff demeanor was a mask to cover his pain. But could she get through to him—past that steel armor of his?

*Lord, I've got one shot here,* she quickly prayed. *Please give me wisdom.*

Alec set more items into his truck and then it suddenly occurred to Lydia that he was boxing up the remainder of his belongings.

"Are you going somewhere?"

"Yep." He walked away again.

This time she pursued him into the garage.

He glanced over his shoulder. "I'm leaving Woodruff. In fact, I'm leaving Alabama."

"I see." Lydia fought the onslaught of tears that threatened. She lifted her chin. "Weren't you even going to say good-bye?"

Alec turned slowly, his expression a mask of remorse.

Lydia pressed on. "You're content with letting Gerald win?"

"Yeah, he won. Look at me!" He stretched his arms out wide. "He's taken everything!"

"You still have the Lord." Lydia paused. "And you still have me."

He swung back around, but not before she saw his eyes fill with an indescribable sadness.

She stepped forward and touched his shoulder. "As for your job, you said it didn't mean more to you than I do. And your house. . .well, the homeowners insurance should cover the loss. Don't you see, Alec, you lost things. Temporal things. They can be replaced."

"Easy for you to say." He moved away from her and strode to his truck.

Again, she trailed him. "So this is really it? You're leaving? It doesn't matter to you that we love each other?"

"Lydia, get real, will you?" He faced her. "I love you as much as I could love any human being, but it won't work. I've got nothing to offer you. I can't support myself, let alone a family, and it'll take me years to get back on my feet again. That's too long for me to ask you to wait."

"I'm willing."

He swallowed hard.

"We're meant to be together."

"Didn't you hear what I said?" His voice held no conviction. "It's. . .over between us. Now, get out of here."

"You don't mean that. I know you don't. And we could fight back. . .if you'd only stop feeling sorry for yourself long enough to hear my idea. But, then again, if your mind is made up, there's nothing more I can say."

She wheeled around and walked away, only to pause several strides later. "Alec Corbett, I would have never believed you could be such a. . .*wimp!*"

Spinning on her heel, she continued down his driveway. She heard him slam the door of his truck forcefully, and she couldn't help the satisfied little smile that curled her lips. "Yellow-belly coward!" she called over her shoulder.

That did it. From the corner of her eye, she saw him round his pickup and come after her. She almost laughed out loud. Nothing like insulting a guy's ego to get his attention! But she nonchalantly kept walking to her car and had almost reached it when Alec grabbed hold of her elbow and whirled her to face him. His hold was surprisingly gentle considering the ferocious expression contorting his handsome features.

"Where's your brain, Lydia? You can't marry a guy like me no matter how much we love each other."

"Are you asking me to marry you?"

"No, because it's out of the question. Can't you see?"

"Well, then, could I ask you? Will you marry me, Alec?"

Beneath the street lamp, she saw a flicker of amusement cross his face. "Sorry, honey, I'm the man and I do the asking."

"In that case, could I interest you in a business proposition?"

Releasing her, Alec folded his arms, looking curious. "What kind of business proposition?"

She set her hands on his thick forearms. "It'll solve everything and we can be together. . .forever." She tipped her head. "Buy me a cup of coffee and let's discuss it."

❁

"It's a tempting offer," Alec said, sipping his coffee at the Calico Junction restaurant in town. The place had closed at nine, but the owner had been one of Michael's clients and graciously allowed them to sit and talk while he cleaned up the kitchen. Thus, they had the place to themselves. "But I'm not marrying you for your money."

"No, you're marrying me because you love me. And I love you. The money is an added blessing."

He blew out a weary-sounding sigh.

"Alec, if you don't marry me," she pressed, "just think of the precarious position I'll be in. Word will get out that I've got this trust hanging over my head and awful men like Sim will start crawling out of the woodwork, trying to entice me. Of course, I'll never marry anyone except you, so their efforts will be in vain. . .but what a nuisance. Furthermore, that million dollars will go to waste. I can't touch it unless I remarry."

Alec eyed her speculatively. "You Boswicks sure know how to get to a guy."

"Does that mean yes?" Lydia asked hopefully, drawing comfort from the lightness of his expression.

"I'll think about it," he said tersely, downing the rest of his coffee.

"Don't think too long. Brian feels my life could be in danger, but I don't really believe it. Nevertheless, the idea upset Mama and Pete enough that they took Tyler and Brooke to the Smiths' in Tennessee. Pete was afraid Gerald might hire someone to kidnap the children and, as a ransom of sorts, I'd have to marry Sim."

Alec paled visibly. "I never thought of that. I guess I've been so focused on myself, I failed to think about you and the kids." A look of regret washed over his face. "I'm so sorry, Lydia."

She set her hand on top of his. "You have nothing to apologize for."

He looked over at her, his eyes searching her face in uncertainty. "You're too good for me, know that?"

With a smile, she leaned toward him. "You're my hero, Alec. My knight in shining armor."

"Yeah, and you're my damsel in distress." He grinned but slowly sobered once again. "I'd like to laugh off the abduction idea, but the fact is, I wouldn't put it past your father-in-law. I mean, if he was desperate enough to firebomb my house, why wouldn't he resort to kidnapping his grandchildren?"

"That's exactly what Pete said."

"And if that's really the case, Tyler and Brooke aren't safe anywhere."

"There's only one solution."

He met her gaze, then took her hand and squeezed it affectionately as they stood. "Come on, let's go talk to Mark Spencer."

While Alec fairly tugged her toward the door of the restaurant, elation filled Lydia's heart. Everything was going to be all right.

# *Epilogue*

B oy, you sure gotta lotta junk!"
     Standing on the fence beside his best friend, Matt Smith, Tyler nodded as he watched the movers unloading several pieces of furniture. "We filled up the whole truck and my new dad's pickup was bursting with stuff."

"Wow. Good thing you bought the Maxwells' house. It's gotta lotta rooms."

"And the best thing is, we get to live next door to each other again!"

"Yeah!"

A few minutes passed and then Tyler looked at his buddy. "What's humble pie?"

Matt shrugged. "I'm not sure, but I think it's got spinach in it and tastes nasty."

"Oh." Tyler mulled over the explanation. "My dad said he had to eat a lot of it before marrying Mama."

"I wonder why."

Tyler shrugged. He'd never understand grown-ups. Except, maybe once he became one, things would make more sense. All he knew was that Mama looked happy all the time, and Mr. Alec was now his dad. In fact, Mr. Alec looked happy all the time, too. And Tyler had been practicing calling him "Daddy," and the name seemed to fit just right. The only bad thing was Daddy's business kept him gone a lot, but Mama promised things would change once they all moved to Tennessee.

After Mama and Mr. Alec got married, he'd gone ahead to Tennessee to "scope things out," only returning home on weekends. Daddy started his own company, building all kinds of furniture and cabinets, and he told Mama, "Business is booming." Daddy said he wanted to start over somewhere new and not long after, he found this house right next to Matt's, bought it, and here they were!

"Hey, Ty," Matt began, "I heard my daddy say your grampa Boswick is going to jail."

Tyler nodded sadly. "Yep, he did some pretty bad things, but I don't know what exactly."

"Are you gonna visit him ever?"

"Beats me."

"That'd be cool to see the inside of a real jail."

Tyler let the comment go. He wasn't sure if it'd be cool or not. He'd just decided he would rather feel happy that Mama married Mr. Alec—that is, *Daddy*—than feel sad that his grampa messed up. But Daddy said everybody messed up sometimes, and now he and Brooke and Mama all had to forgive and forget.

Suddenly Tyler's parents walked out the back door of their new house with Brooke running after them. Daddy whispered something to Mama and then kissed her long and slow, like he did all the time.

"Yuck," Matt grumbled, his face scrunched up in distaste.

Daddy looked over. "Ty, you want to come to the hardware store with me? Maybe we'll pick up a pizza on the way home."

"Sure!" He never missed a chance to go someplace with his new dad—even if it meant not hanging out with his best friend. "See ya, Matt."

"Yeah, see ya."

Climbing over the fence rail, Tyler jumped down and ran across the lawn. Then he and Daddy made their way to the pickup with Mama and Brooke waving after them. A surge of utter happiness filled Tyler's being. Nothing beat having Matt as his next-door neighbor again, except maybe getting the daddy he'd prayed for. That was awesome!

And just like his best friend, Tyler now had a real family of his own!

ANDREA BOESHAAR

Andrea and her husband Daniel have three adult sons, two of whom are married. Andrea attended college, first at the University of Wisconsin—Milwaukee, where she studied English, and then at Alverno College where she studied Professional Communications and Business Management.

Andrea has been writing stories and poems since she was a little girl; however, it wasn't until 1991, after she became a Christian, that she answered God's call to write exclusively for the Christian market. Since then, Andrea has written articles, devotionals, novels, and novellas—many of which have made the CBA Bestseller lists. For more on Andrea and a list of her published works, visit her Web site at www.andreaboeshaar.com.

# A MATTER
# OF SECURITY

by Kay Cornelius

# *Dedication*

I proudly dedicate this book to Don, who represents the founding of the United States Space Program, and to Kyle, who is its future. And as always, to God be any glory.

# Chapter 1

Leslie Christopher pulled her blue Toyota into the parking lot of ArrowSpace/South, turned off the ignition, and stared at the imposing red brick building before her.

It was still hard for Leslie to realize that she was about to become a project manager, a position that few women—and certainly none who had barely turned thirty—had ever held in the history of the huge ArrowSpace company.

Everything had moved so quickly that it still seemed somehow unreal. Leslie had been looking forward to a few days off after working as deputy on a project at Vandenburg Air Force Base when David Douglass, their division director, had told her she had been selected to fill an opening at ArrowSpace/South. Leslie had applied for it almost automatically, without any idea that she would get it and without any inkling what Huntsville, Alabama, the location of ArrowSpace/South, would be like. But once she had been offered the job, Leslie hadn't hesitated to take it. She had no personal ties to Los Angeles, no one to beg her to stay there. And for her career, it was definitely the right move.

Leslie reached for the new burgundy leather briefcase that her co-workers had given her for a farewell party and hoped she looked more confident than she felt. Her initial excitement over winning the management position had faded, leaving her to consider sober reality. Suppose she couldn't handle the pressure? Leslie imagined the possible consequences of failure—demotion and returning to Los Angeles in disgrace at best, dismissal from the company at worst—and shuddered.

"No!" she exclaimed, shaking her head as if to clear it. She wouldn't allow herself such thoughts. This would be a tough job, but she could handle it. Over the last nine years, Arrow had invested a great deal in Leslie, paying for her master's degree and moving her into positions of ever-increasing responsibility. They would never have sent her here if they didn't think she could do the job.

Leslie squared her shoulders, took a deep breath, and all but marched up the long walkway to the ArrowSpace/South main entrance.

❧

Sitting in the ArrowSpace waiting room, Hampton Travis was bored. For the tenth time that morning he looked at his watch. It gave the time in any part of the world, computed the elapsed time between any two events, and performed arithmetic and algebraic calculations. But it couldn't tell him when he would be summoned by ArrowSpace's frosty receptionist. Hampton opened his briefcase and removed a slender file folder containing his resume and Arrow's most recent advertisement for engineers and physicists. Dozens of such notices appeared in newspapers all over the country. Most of them, like the one to which he was responding, were placed by companies that planned to bid on lucrative contracts. The winning company would have good jobs to offer for the duration of the project, often many years. Losing companies threw the resumes away, so engineers usually applied to many firms.

Hampton glanced over his resume, satisfied that it would impress any Arrow project manager. As an ex-astronaut, he had all the right credentials. And if all else failed, there were strings to be pulled to get him into the job he had to do. But for now, he knew he was simply one of many applicants seeking an interesting position.

Hampton had just closed his briefcase when he heard the receptionist speak. He half rose, assuming that she was summoning him, only to see her talking to a trim young woman in a periwinkle blue suit. She had honey blond hair, worn just below her shoulders in the back and short around her oval face. He noted with approval that the skirt of her strictly business suit was modestly long, and that she was, indeed, an attractive young woman. She smiled at the receptionist and said something that Hampton was too far away to hear, but he liked the sound of her voice. *A new executive secretary, perhaps,* he thought; he doubted that she was an engineer.

The receptionist pointed toward the elevators, and the young woman moved toward them with an easy, unaffected stride. Then Hampton noticed that she had left a briefcase on the floor by the desk. Picking it up, Hampton hurried after her.

"I believe this may belong to you," he said.

Leslie turned to see a man with very dark hair and startling blue eyes holding out her briefcase. His smile appeared genuine—he didn't seem to be making fun of her forgetfulness—and Leslie smiled back and thanked him.

"I would have wondered where it was," she said, realizing even as she spoke that it wasn't a particularly brilliant remark.

"Now you won't have to."

Before Leslie could think of anything else to say, the elevator arrived and Leslie entered it. As the doors closed, the man lifted his hand in a lazy salute.

*I must be more nervous than I thought to leave my briefcase like that,* Leslie thought. She wanted to make a good first impression, but she feared she hadn't made a very good start.

"I'm Leslie Christopher from the Los Angeles office," she told the Special Projects administrative aide a few moments later, when she finally located the office.

"Sally Hanover," the woman said, offering her hand in a firm shake. Leslie judged her to be in her early forties, perhaps, with frosted blond hair and tasteful, understated makeup. Her charm bracelet jangled as she spoke into the phone, then turned back to Leslie. "Mr. Meredith wants you to report to Personnel and get badged. I'll take you there." Sally added, seeing Leslie's hesitation, "This building can be rather confusing."

As they walked to the elevator, Sally began telling Leslie where the cafeteria was—"not that anyone can eat the food"—and where the best parking spots were—"you have to ask, they won't assign you one unless you do." Leslie knew she had found someone who knew the really important things about ArrowSpace/ South, Huntsville Division.

"Are you married?" Sally asked unexpectedly, and Leslie shook her head. "Well, watch out for the guys around here," she said. A young mail clerk riding the elevator with them grinned at Leslie.

"Don't pay her no nevermind," he said. "She couldn't catch herself a man with a rope."

"There, see what I mean?" Sally punched the boy on his arm as the elevator doors opened and he pushed his mail cart down the hall. "Actually, I caught the only man I ever wanted when I was eighteen. . .Jeff. But he died several years ago," Sally said more seriously. "Of course, he wasn't an engineer—as a lot, they make poor husbands."

"So I hear," Leslie said, thinking of some of the engineers she had known in Los Angeles, men so wrapped up in their own work that they hardly knew other people existed, much less how to deal with them.

"Here you are," Sally said at the door to Personnel. "I'll leave you in Mrs. Garrett's clutches. Oh. I almost forgot—welcome to Arrow."

"Thank you," Leslie said. Sally walked away, her heels clicking on the waxed tiles in time with the clink of her bracelet.

"That one's a real card," Mrs. Garrett said dryly. "Transfer or new hire?"

"Transfer," Leslie replied, somewhat deflated that she hadn't been expected. "I have my file with me."

"Give it to me and fill out these papers." Mrs. Garrett handed Leslie a clipboard bearing a sheaf of pages. "You can sit over there," she added, waving to a table to the right of the receptionist's desk.

Leslie wanted to tell the woman that all the information the forms requested, except for her local address and telephone, was already in the file, but she knew the bureaucratic drill well enough to realize she would only be wasting her breath.

Leslie had just written "deceased" in the blanks that asked about her parents when she heard a pleasant male voice and looked up to see the man who had returned her briefcase talking to Mrs. Garrett. He wore a visitor's badge and held a black briefcase. Her first impression—that he was a very handsome man and knew it—was reinforced as he smiled at Mrs. Garrett, who smiled back almost as if against her will. Leslie watched to see if he would also be given papers to fill out, but apparently he was there on other business, for after a brief conversation that Leslie could not hear, he walked away. The man never looked her way, and she certainly had no reason to think that he would speak to her if he had. But Leslie was curious and asked about him when she returned her papers.

"He looks familiar," Leslie added as Mrs. Garrett regarded her coolly.

"His name is Hampton Travis. He's not currently working here."

"Oh, I see. I don't suppose I know him, after all. What next?"

Mrs. Garrett handed Leslie a slip of paper. "Take this to the second door on the left. They'll make you an ID badge."

To Leslie's relief the young, crew-cut photographer was much more pleasant than Mrs. Garrett had been.

"You can smile for this, you know," he told her when she stood before the camera. "You may not feel much like smiling after you get to know this place."

Like most people she had met so far, including the manager of her apartment complex, the photographer spoke with a distinct Southern inflection, and she smiled in spite of herself as he snapped the shutter.

"Is working here really that bad?"

"It beats unemployment, but you have to look out for yourself."

Leslie would have asked what he meant, but the clerk who would make the badge motioned for Leslie to follow her into another room where the photo was laminated. *I look like a simpering half-wit,* Leslie thought when she saw the shot. Deftly the girl attached a clip and handed it to Leslie.

"This is a temporary badge. When you get security clearance, you'll get a permanent one. Any questions?"

Leslie shook her head. When she made no move to put on the badge, the clerk prompted her to do so in the tone of a mother to a backward child. "Security's very strict here," she added sternly.

With her badge safely in place, Leslie was allowed to return to the fifth floor. Sally Hanover's smile was friendly as she welcomed Leslie back, but her news was disappointing.

"Mr. Meredith has been called to a meeting upstairs. He sends his apologies and suggests that you take a long coffee break."

"When can he see me?"

Sally shrugged. "Sometimes these front-office sessions last through lunch, or he could be back in fifteen or twenty minutes. You might as well have coffee while you wait. Take the elevator down to the basement and follow your nose. But watch those sweet rolls—they're lethal."

None of the several dozen people in the cafeteria paid Leslie any attention as she took her coffee to an empty table. She felt uncomfortable as she had so many times throughout her childhood, always the new girl sitting down herself as her father followed elusive job leads from town to town.

*But this is different,* Leslie told herself; even though she knew no one, she belonged here. The dining area was decorated with huge murals of the Saturn V moon rocket, the Space Shuttle *Endeavour*, and the Space Station, three of the many NASA projects in which ArrowSpace had played a major role. She felt a quiet pride that she was about to join such a prestigious team.

Leslie hadn't been in the cafeteria very long when she again saw the briefcase man, as she thought of him—Hampton Travis, Mrs. Garrett had called him. *His name is familiar,* Leslie thought, but she couldn't make a connection. He stood in the door and looked around as if searching for someone. He glanced at Leslie, then looked again in a classic doubletake. She lowered her head, not wanting him to see her staring at him, and when she looked up again, he was talking to a woman who wore her almost-black hair in a shoulder-length page-boy cut. The woman took his arm in a familiar way, as if she was accustomed to walking with him, and they left the cafeteria. Had he really noticed her? Or had she so expected that he would that she had imagined his interest?

*Don't be stupid, Leslie,* she lectured herself sternly. She hadn't come to Arrow to ogle men, but to take a responsible job that would require her full attention. Whoever Hampton Travis was, she couldn't allow him—or anyone else—to distract her.

❧

Thirty minutes later, Leslie was being ushered into Mr. Meredith's office, and Hampton Travis was leaving Personnel with a last smile for Mrs. Garrett.

"Don't look at me like that, Barbara," Hampton admonished the brunette who almost matched his five-feet, ten-inch height and who walked with him toward the main entrance. "The Personnel woman may be a real dragon, but I want her on my side."

Barbara looked annoyed. "You don't really have to go through channels at all. A word in the right place, and. . ."

"You know that wouldn't do," Hampton said. "Everything has to be open and above board, or it won't work."

"But suppose you aren't hired?" Barbara asked.

They reached the door and stopped. Hampton glanced over at the bored security guard, then back to Barbara.

"I won't worry about that yet. You have your job. Do it, and let me worry about mine."

"But—" she began.

"No, Barbara. This is my show, remember? I'll be in touch."

Hampton returned his visitor's badge to the security guard and left the building before she could reply. Outside, the warmth of the sun reminded him that it would be another hot Alabama day. Hampton sighed and wished that he didn't have to deal with Barbara—she could be difficult.

As he got in his Thunderbird, Hampton thought briefly of the pretty blond he had seen that morning and wished, not for the first time, that he had never agreed to undertake this particular assignment.

❧

Mr. Meredith stood as Leslie entered his office. A large-framed man whose loose clothing suggested a recent weight loss, he extended his hand for a firm handshake and motioned her to be seated.

"I'm sorry you had to wait, Miss Christopher, but one of the first things you learn around here is that when the top floor calls, you answer."

Leslie nodded. "I took your advice and went to the cafeteria, which is probably the only part of the building I could find again."

"Yes, these windowless wonders are difficult, but you'll soon find the short-cuts. Have you found a place to live yet?'

"Yes, I've taken an apartment at the Willows. I'll be at the Guest Inn until my furniture arrives."

"If there is anything I can do to help you get settled, please let me know."

"Thank you, but so far everything has gone very well."

*That's enough small talk. Now tell me about my job,* Leslie thought.

He was silent for a moment, then he leaned back in his chair and picked up a Shuttle-shaped letter opener, turning it in his hands as he spoke. "I know you're curious about the project you'll be working with. I wish you could begin right away, but we must wait for your security clearance."

Leslie looked surprised. "I have clearance—I'm sure that must be on my record."

"Indeed, yes," Mr. Meredith agreed, "but that was obtained when you first went to work for Arrow. You'll need the highest clearance here. Until it comes through, you can rotate through every office you'll interface and meet some of the people you'll be dealing with. Then you'll be in a better position to manage your project."

Leslie wet her lips and leaned forward. "Can you tell me something about it now? Mr. Douglass said it was important, but that's all he told me."

"He knew a little, but I asked him not to discuss it with you, and this is not the time to go into details. But as you know, this is different from our usual work."

"Mr. Douglas said it concerned a joint Pentagon and NASA project."

"That's partly correct—" Mr. Meredith started to speak, then frowned as if he had just thought of something unpleasant.

Leslie sensed the new boss wished that Arrow had chosen someone else—someone older, more experienced, and, above all, male—to fill her position.

"There's one thing you should probably know from the start." Mr. Meredith chose his words with care. "You weren't the only person considered for this job. In fact, many might argue that you weren't even the most qualified candidate. Some of our local people resent being passed over. I hope no one will give you a hard time, but I think you should be aware of the situation from the start."

Leslie nodded, feeling a chill at his words. Perhaps unspoken was Mr. Meredith's own reluctance to have her instead of someone he already knew. It was common knowledge that Arrow had been sued by a woman in their Long Island facility who claimed that qualified women were not being considered for enough management positions. The case had been settled out of court, but Leslie had no doubt that it had some influence on her rapid advancement to Los Angeles. It could also explain why she had been chosen to fill this job as well. The thought was not comforting.

"Thank you for telling me," Leslie said.

Mr. Meredith nodded curtly and reached for the telephone. "I'll ask Sally to show you around a bit. You can begin meeting the people in Design tomorrow."

"How long will it be before I can start to work?" Leslie asked, disappointment clear in her tone.

"That depends on the FBI, but it shouldn't take more than a few days or so—and in the meantime, you'll be learning things that will help you do the job."

"I understand that, and I'm looking forward to meeting everyone. But I had expected to go to work right away."

"Exactly the way I'd feel in your place," Mr. Meredith said as he escorted her to the door of his office.

❧

Leslie thought that no work she could ever do in her life would be as hard as the days she spent at Arrow *not* working. In spite of Mr. Meredith's wish for her to rotate through other offices, everyone seemed to be busy, and once she had met them, no one knew quite what to do with her. Her chief accomplishment was learning the layout of the building, much of which would remain off-limits until she got the proper clearance. She met many people, few very impressive. All in all, it was such a waste of time that Leslie was glad when her furniture arrived and she had an excuse to take a few days off to get moved into her apartment.

"Go ahead," Mr. Meredith said, seeming to be equally relieved that she had something else to occupy her mind. "I'll call if we need you."

On the way out, Leslie stopped to tell Sally that she was leaving.

"Do you have any plans for Sunday?" Sally asked. "I'd like to come by for you and take you to my church."

"Your church?" Leslie repeated, as if surprised to think of Sally in connection with any churches she had noted around Huntsville.

"Yes, Glenview. The singles group there has been my lifesaver."

Leslie hadn't been to a church in years, and the thought of joining a widow Sally's age in a singles group wasn't at all appealing. "Thanks for the invitation, but I really do need to work all weekend to get my apartment in shape."

Sally looked disappointed. "I'll give you a rain check, then," she said.

Leslie nodded. "Maybe some day," she murmured. *But most likely never. I'm not ready to go looking for a man just yet,* Leslie thought. She had never gone to a singles bar in California, but she supposed that if a woman had to have male companionship, a church might be as good a place as any to find it.

Grateful to have something to do, Leslie attacked the business of settling into her apartment. She bought a telephone and had it hooked up, and on impulse she dialed her old office.

"Leslie! How's the South? You taken your shoes off yet?" teased Alice Morrison, who had been Leslie's best friend at Arrow/West.

"The South is fine, and everyone I've seen so far has shoes—even a few Gucci loafers," Leslie replied.

"Your old job hasn't been filled yet, and we miss you. Want to come back?"

Leslie pictured Alice sprawled at her desk, muttering under her breath every time her computer beeped at a command it didn't like, and smiled. "No, thanks. I think my California bridges are pretty well burned."

They talked for a few more minutes, then Leslie hung up. She was glad she'd made the call, but despite the frustration she had encountered in her new job, Leslie was still not sorry she'd left Los Angeles.

Leslie had just replaced the receiver when the doorbell rang. She opened the door to a man of medium height with graying hair and wire-rimmed spectacles.

"Miss Christopher? I'm Special Agent Jack Taylor, with the FBI," he said, displaying a badge. "I need to ask you a few questions, if this is a convenient time."

"Of course—come in." Leslie moved a stack of towels so he could sit down.

"I understand that you work for ArrowSpace/South, Huntsville Division?"

Leslie nodded. "I can't imagine what else the FBI would need to know about me. I had clearance in Los Angeles."

"Yes, I know. We just need to update your file."

He wrote in a notebook as Leslie answered several routine questions, then when she thought he had finished, he had one more. "Is there anyone who works for the federal government or its contractors on secret matters with whom you have a personal relationship?"

"No," Leslie said quickly. *I had no personal relationships in Los Angeles at all,* she thought. It was one reason that leaving it had been so easy.

He nodded and closed his notebook. "That's all we need. Thank you for your time."

"When will I have my clearance?" Leslie asked at the door.

"By the first of next week, if everything checks out."

"Thanks. I'll look forward to that."

Feeling somewhat cheered that at least a start had been made on her clearance, Leslie returned to her unpacking, humming under her breath. When the doorbell rang again late that afternoon, Leslie's first thought was that the FBI agent must have thought of something else and returned, and she opened the door without first looking through the peephole.

Leslie was startled to see Hampton Travis—and a little surprised that she hadn't forgotten his name—at the door. Leslie was suddenly and painfully aware that her hair needed combing and that her nose was probably shiny and that she didn't want him to see her when she was in such a mess. But it was too late—there he stood on her doorstep, his blue eyes opened wide and his mouth an O of surprise as she opened the door.

"Is your husband at home?" he asked.

"My husband?" Leslie repeated.

"Yes, Leslie Christopher, who works for ArrowSpace."

"Leslie Christopher is not my husband," she said.

Hampton rubbed his chin, which had a charming cleft right in the middle, and looked embarrassed. "I'm sorry to disturb you, but I wanted to see Leslie Christopher about a work-related matter, and I was given this address. I suppose I got some incorrect information."

Leslie had momentarily relished his discomfort, but now she felt guilty and hastened to end the misunderstanding. "My name is Leslie Christopher, and I do work at Arrow. Did they give you my address?"

"Well, not exactly. I asked someone who works there to find out who would manage a project I'm interested in, and your name turned up. Directory assistance did the rest."

"And told you I was a man?"

"No. I did that on my own," he said with such an engaging smile that Leslie had no choice but to return it.

"So here you are, Mr. Travis," she said.

His face registered surprise, then a dawning recognition. "I saw you at Arrow, didn't I?"

"Yes. You rescued a briefcase I left behind the first day I was there."

"So that's why your face is so familiar," he said. "I came here to ask Mr. Christopher to discuss the new project with me over dinner. Since he doesn't seem to live here, will Miss Christopher dine with me in his place?"

The logical, sensible part of her mind told Leslie she ought to refuse his invitation, but the part that had found him attractive from the first urged her to accept. Without letting herself think through all the possible consequences, Leslie found herself agreeing.

"But I can't go anywhere like this," she added, glancing down at her well-worn jeans and ancient UCLA sweatshirt.

"I'll come back in an hour, then," he offered.

"I'll be ready," Leslie said, but for what, she wasn't so sure.

As she showered, Leslie tried to imagine what it would be like to work with Hampton Travis. At the moment, he seemed to know more about her job than she did—and it intrigued her to think that he might give her information that her own boss wouldn't.

*I cannot become interested in him personally,* Leslie told herself. She had vowed to succeed as a project manager, and succeed she would, with no frivolous romantic involvements to get in her way. Hampton Travis would be a good business contact, period.

But Leslie had to admit that it certainly didn't hurt that he was also one of the most attractive men she had ever met.

# Chapter 2

Leslie wasn't sure what she should wear for a business dinner. After standing before her closet for some time, she chose a simple black skirt and an oversized silk shirt and topped it with a single gold chain. Understated and safe.

When she opened the door to Hampton again, the admiration in his eyes told Leslie that she had chosen well. As he held the car door for her—*a nice gentlemanly touch,* she thought—she deliberated telling him that she probably shouldn't have agreed to have dinner with him.

"If you think I can talk anything that is going on at Arrow, you're wrong. I don't even know what I'm going to be doing. On the other hand, I'll be glad to hear anything you might know about it."

Hampton glanced at her and narrowed his blue eyes as if he doubted her. "That would be quite a switch, wouldn't it? The thing is, we ought to be acquainted, anyway—someone should welcome you to Huntsville. Just think of this evening in that light and enjoy yourself."

"Where are we going?" Leslie asked. They had passed the gaudy restaurant row on University Drive and were heading west to an area Leslie had never seen.

"Trust me," he said. "One of my main areas of expertise is knowing where to find good food."

"You're not from around here, are you?" Leslie asked as he turned off the main highway onto a narrow asphalt road.

"What makes you think that?"

"The way you talk—definitely no Southern drawl."

"What is the idear of this inquisition?" Hampton said, adopting a broad Southern accent. "Ahr you makin' fun of the way Ah speak?"

"No, just trying to place it. I've lived a lot of different places, and I can usually guess what section of the country people are from. But you're a real challenge."

"Let's leave it that way for now. Here we are."

Hampton turned the car into a long driveway edged with huge, ancient boxwoods, pungently fragrant in the cool evening air. An old house, with white columns shining in the dusk, stood at the end of the driveway. A few automobiles were parked to one side, and a small sign identified the place as the Stagecoach Inn, ca. 1855.

"It's lovely!" Leslie exclaimed as Hampton opened her door. A white jack-eted maitre d' bowed to them at the entrance and smiled broadly at Hampton.

"I wondered when we'd see you again. You have been away a long time, Mist Travis."

"Yes, I was out of town for a while, Joseph. This is Miss Christopher, who is new to Alabama. She's from—" He stopped, and Leslie realized she hadn't told him.

"I'm from the South, too—Southern California," she said.

"Believe me, it's not the same South," Hampton said.

"Joseph, shall we show the lady some real Southern hospitality?"

"Oh yes, sir, we'll have to do that." Joseph looked at Leslie as if he pitied her unfortunate origins. "Right this way."

Two large rooms of the inn had been refurbished, forming the dining area. The very formal room was accented with antique buffets and sideboards, and every table was covered with the finest damask and set with sparkling crystal and translucent porcelain. Although there were empty tables in the dining room, Joseph led them through it and seated them on the veranda at the rear, overlooking a small lake. With a pale moon rising in the darkening sky, it could have been a movie set. Leslie had never seen anything remotely like the place.

"It's almost like traveling back in time," she said.

"Wait until you taste the food. I didn't call ahead to see what they're serving tonight, but it's always good."

A waiter appeared to fill their water glasses, and another brought in bowls of cold soup. Just as they were finishing, a young girl wearing an old-South hoop-skirted gown came onto the porch, camera in hand.

"Smile, y'all," she said, pointing the camera at them.

To Leslie's surprise, Hampton spoke sharply to the girl. "We don't want a pic-ture." He rose as if he might escort her from the room or seize the camera, or both.

"As you like, sir," the girl said as she backed away in haste.

"What was that all about?" Leslie asked when the girl had left.

"Oh, it's just a silly thing they do to make a few dollars. When I'm eating, I want to be left alone," he added, as if he feared that Leslie might think him a penny-pinching old grouch.

"Like an old dog with a bone?" Leslie suggested, trying for a light touch.

Hampton look relieved. "Exactly," he said, and smiled again. "I've had all the publicity I ever want."

Before Leslie could ask him what he meant, their entrees arrived with a great deal of ceremony, and Leslie was content to enjoy the food in silence, occa-sionally asking Hampton about the dishes they were served.

"The sauce on the chicken was wonderful," she told the waiter as he cleared away their dinner plates. "What gives it such a distinct flavor?"

"I don't know, ma'am. The cook don't allow nobody to see what-all goes in it."

"There seems to be all kinds of things around here that are top secret," Leslie said when the waiter left.

"It's the nature of the place. Around Huntsville, if you don't have a few secrets, you're not very important."

"I'll have to remember that," Leslie said.

The rising moon traced a silver path across the water. Joseph had brought a hurricane lamp to their table as the daylight faded, and now the candlelight cast wavering shadows around them.

*What a setting for romance,* Leslie thought, tempted for a moment to forget that ArrowSpace existed and give her attraction to Hampton free rein, letting it lead where it would. But then she remembered that she hadn't come here for personal reasons. *This is strictly business,* Leslie reminded herself.

"This has been a most unusual business dinner," she declared as they sipped coffee from delicate cups. "The question is, when will we get around to discussing business?"

"Why spoil a lovely evening?"

"I don't consider talking about my work spoiling anything," Leslie said. "I'm really curious to find out what I'll be doing here. If you know, I wish you'd tell me."

"There's something I have to know first," he said, and even though he was leaning back in his chair, she had the eerie feeling that he had moved closer.

"What is that?"

"How did you happen to know my name?"

"That's easy—the day you returned my briefcase, I saw you again at Personnel. I asked Mrs. Garrett who you were."

"You were there when I was talking to her?" he asked. "And later—that was you in the cafeteria, wasn't it?"

Leslie nodded. "It's your turn now. What do you know about my job?"

"You make me sound like a fortune teller," he said. "I don't believe in such things." Nevertheless, Hampton took her left hand and turned it palm up, as if studying its lines. "This is the hand of an attractive young woman who is about to begin an interesting association with a new technology. She will meet many hazards, but the rewards will be great."

"That's too general," Leslie said. "Tell me something specific."

"I'm afraid that's all for now," Hampton said, but he continued to hold her hand until Leslie withdrew it.

"Because you can't? Or because you won't?"

"Let's just say that this is neither the time nor the place for such a discussion."

"That's not fair! You said this would be a business dinner."

"And it has been. This is the way things work around here. You might as well get used to it."

"I seem to have a lot to learn," Leslie said.

"You'll be all right." Hampton studied her face closely for a moment before he signaled the waiter for the check.

"I still expect to hear what you know," Leslie said, trying to salvage some faint command of the situation.

"In due time. In the meantime, I should get you home."

"Thank you for the dinner," Leslie said as he came around to pull out her chair. "Everything was wonderful."

"The pleasure is mine, Miss Christopher. I had planned to take Mr. Christopher to the Steak House, but I'm glad he wasn't there."

Leslie stood and took Hampton's arm as they left the restaurant. The evening had turned chilly, and the sky blazed with stars as they walked slowly to the car.

"Look at that beautiful sight," Hampton said, pointing to the heavens. "I always think of Psalm 19 when I see so many stars—'The heavens declare the glory of God.' People have been wondering about those stars for years, and we're the first generation that's going to be able to find out what's really going on out there. It's almost mind boggling, isn't it?"

"Yes, I suppose it is," replied Leslie, surprised that a technically minded man like Hampton Travis could quote from a Psalm and be so enthusiastic about the beauty of the skies. "Do you know much about astronomy?" she asked as he helped her into the car and closed the door.

"A little," he said, and Leslie thought he sounded amused.

"Just what do you do?" Leslie asked. "Are you an engineer?"

Hampton started the car and backed out of the parking space before replying. "I've done a little bit of everything," he said. "I spent some time in the Air Force and I've worked for NASA and on several contracts."

"And now you're with Arrow?" she asked.

"Not exactly. When your project gets revved up, I hope to be a part of it. That is, if the program manager decides to hire me."

Leslie made no effort to hide her surprise. "In Los Angeles, project staffing isn't done by mid-level managers."

"In case you haven't noticed, you're not in LA anymore."

"I noticed," Leslie said stiffly, her curiosity piqued. How could Hampton Travis know so much more than she did about the project that she was supposed to be managing? A new thought struck her, and she turned to Hampton. "Did you apply for the job they gave me?"

Hampton laughed. "No, Miss Christopher, I'm no manager. See those?" He had taken the interstate spur that led into the city and now pointed to the Space and Rocket Center, where the space shuttle and a display of rockets gleamed ghostly white in the moonlight. "That's my background. These show where we've been. And over there is where space exploration is continuing," he added as they passed the research park where ArrowSpace/South, Huntsville Division, occupied a sprawling complex.

"It's really an exciting place to work, isn't it?" Leslie said softly. Sometimes it was easy to lose sight of what she was doing in the midst of the multitude of tiny details that made up the big picture, much as the thousands of pieces of a mosaic seem totally unrelated until they are joined. But every piece was important, even the most seemingly insignificant—and she was here to become part of it.

"Yes, it is," Hampton agreed, "and Huntsville is a good place to live as well."

"How long have you lived here?" Leslie asked.

Hampton didn't look at her. "I don't actually live in Huntsville permanently," he said.

"Surely you don't live in California!" she exclaimed, thinking that would be the crowning irony.

"Not really. I suppose you might say I'm one of those aerospace gypsies. We travel by airplane now instead of in caravans, but we're a pretty rootless bunch. We work a job, move on to another, finish it, and move on again."

"That sort of life is awfully insecure, isn't it?" Leslie said, reminded of the way she had felt as a child with the constant moves.

"My security doesn't come from this earth," he said.

"That sounds ominous," Leslie said. *Was he teasing her?*

They had left the interstate spur and were passing under a series of bright yellow lights, and Leslie could see from Hampton's expression that he was serious. "It isn't at all ominous," he said. "My faith is the anchor of my life."

*Why is this man so enigmatic?* Leslie asked herself. Hampton Travis had taken her out for a wonderful meal, but he hadn't told her anything about her job or even about himself. *Either he has something to hide, he's trying to confuse me, or he's a very private person.*

"I don't suppose you'll tell me what that means, either," Leslie said. Hampton laughed at the resigned tone of her voice.

"I'll be glad to—but not now. I can see that you're tired. I'd like to show you some of the sights by day." Hampton pulled into the Willows apartment complex and shut off the engine. "How about taking a picnic lunch to the top of the mountain on Saturday if the nice weather holds?"

"Strictly business, of course?" Leslie asked, and he nodded solemnly.

"Of course. How about it?"

Leslie hesitated, not wanting to seem too eager to see him again. "Can I let you know?"

"Sure—I'll call you."

Hampton came around to open her door and they walked in silence from the parking lot, past the deserted pool, and up a single flight of stairs to Leslie's apartment

"Thank you again for the evening," Leslie said as she fitted her key into the lock. As Hampton pushed the door open, Leslie thought for a split second that he was going to follow her inside, but he merely waited on the threshold until she turned on a light. Leslie felt a little angry with herself for wishing that he had.

*Hampton Travis might turn out to be a useful business associate, but for now, I mustn't let him be anything else.*

Then another thought struck Leslie. Why, for all I know, he might even be married! He didn't wear a wedding ring, but then, neither did many men she knew. It hadn't occurred to her to ask. Maybe that was why he hadn't kissed her. Most of the men she had dated would have taken a friendly kiss for granted after taking someone out for such a sumptuous evening.

"Well, as long as I keep this strictly business, it won't matter," Leslie told the mirror as she brushed her teeth. At any rate, she was too tired to worry about it any more that evening.

Leslie quickly got ready for bed and was asleep almost as soon as her head touched the pillow. Along toward dawn she dreamed that she was on an airplane, about to sit down beside Hampton Travis, when a tall, faceless woman with long black hair materialized and beckoned to him. Without a glance at Leslie, Hampton got up and went to the woman, and they floated out of the plane in some sort of murky gray cloud. Leslie wanted to follow them, but her legs felt like lead, and when she tried to call out, no sound came out of her tight throat.

Leslie awoke, her mouth dry and her heart beating wildly. Gray light filtered in through the miniblinds at her bedroom window, and her luminous clock dial showed just past six. She climbed out of bed, went into the bathroom, and splashed cold water on her face. Then she went to the kitchen and started the coffee.

The morning paper lay on her doorstep, and Leslie picked it up and turned the pages idly as she ate breakfast. Then suddenly a photograph all but leaped at her. It was of a couple she remembered seeing the night before at the Stagecoach Inn, no doubt taken by the girl who had attempted to snap their picture. Under the heading "Dining Out in Huntsville," the caption said that Mr. and Mrs. Morgan Gilruth had celebrated their tenth wedding anniversary at the Stagecoach Inn. Leslie had recalled how upset Hampton had seemed when the girl had pointed her camera at them. Was it because he didn't want his picture taken with her for business reasons? That seemed unlikely. But if Hampton had a personal reason— like having a wife, a fiancée, or a girl friend who might question that his business dinner had been with a woman and at a romantic place. . .That could be a very good reason for him to avoid the camera.

The rest of the morning, as Leslie hung the few pictures she owned and finished stocking her cabinets, she alternated between feeling foolish for suspecting him of deviousness and thinking that it would be even more foolish to see him again, even if he weren't married. By the time she stopped working long enough to eat a quick lunch, Leslie had decided to tell Hampton she couldn't go on Saturday, and just leave it at that.

When he called her that afternoon, the sound of his voice shook her resolve so much that she almost changed her mind, but she held firm. "I'm sorry, Hampton, but I can't make it on Saturday. Thanks for the invitation, though."

"Mind telling me why?" he asked, and Leslie thought he sounded genuinely disappointed. "I'll even provide the lunch."

"I've been thinking of what you said about possibly working with me at Arrow. I don't know my way around the Huntsville office yet, but in Los Angeles, I wouldn't see someone socially that I might be working with unless it was related to our business. It just doesn't look right."

"This isn't Los Angeles, and I can assure you that things aren't all that cut and dried here. It's perfectly all right for you to have a private life, you know."

*Who would care if I did go out with Hampton Travis?* Leslie asked herself. *Who would even know about it?* But it was no use.

"Not this weekend—maybe later," she said with what she hoped was the right mixture of firmness and regret.

"All right, but don't think you've heard the last of me, Miss Christopher."

"Is that a threat?" Leslie asked, knowing that it wasn't.

"More like a promise. Look, I'll probably see you around Arrow. But if you ever decide to go up on top of the mountain alone, be careful. People are always falling over the edge. The rocks are sharp, and it's a long way down."

"I'll remember that," Leslie said, and heard the click as he hung up the phone.

Leslie sat with the receiver in her hand for a long time before she replaced it. A lonely weekend stretched ahead, and for a moment she remembered Sally's invitation to attend her church. Then she thought of the strain involved with meeting so many new people and decided she wasn't that desperate to make new friends. And with any luck at all, she would be at work—really at work this time—on Monday. Maybe she would find out what she was up against—and more about the mysterious Hampton Travis, as well.

# *Chapter 3*

S ally looked up in surprise when Leslie came in just before eight o'clock on Monday morning. "We didn't really expect to see you today. You must have gotten settled in record time."

"I'm not completely finished, but I had no real reason to stay away any longer."

"I'm glad you came back today," Mr. Meredith said when she entered his office.

"The FBI paid me a visit last week," Leslie said.

Mr. Meredith nodded. "I know—I told the chief of the local office that you needed to be brought on board right away. Your clearance might even come in today. In the meantime, Sally will show you your office."

Her office was not what Leslie expected. At ArrowSpace/West a project manager rated a rather large office with a carpeted floor and upscale furnishings. Her office at ArrowSpace/South had been hastily made by partitioning a larger office into two rooms, the other vacant for the moment—"For your lead technical staff person," Sally had said. Its sparse furnishings included a desk, two metal chairs, an oversized filing cabinet, a metal bookcase, and a coat rack. A computer terminal sat on the desk, flanked by a tall stack of manuals. All Arrow offices made heavy use of software programs, so Leslie wasn't surprised to see it. She switched on the computer, which immediately beeped and asked for a password she hadn't been given. She turned it off and flipped through some of the manuals and was relieved to see that the system was similar to the one she had been using.

Leslie had just finished stowing the manuals in her bookcase when Mr. Meredith summoned her to his office.

"Jack Taylor just called to confirm your clearance," Mr. Meredith said. "That means I can now tell you you'll be working on Arrow's proposal for NASA's VIRCO project. I'm sure you must have heard something about it."

*You can't be serious.* Leslie's first thought was almost expressed aloud, but she managed to nod her head as if she had known it all along. There had been rumors for months that something really big was in the works, something that would bring lucrative contracts to the successful bidders. "It has something to do with unmanned space exploration, doesn't it?"

Mr. Meredith nodded. "That's a bit of an understatement. It calls for a completely new technology involving orbiting advanced virtual reality computers and robotics." He pointed to a formidable stack of documents. "Here's the outline of NASA's preliminary request for proposals. Read it carefully and you'll have an idea of the overt project."

Leslie reached for the bundle of papers and looked up questioningly at Mr. Meredith's use of the word "overt."

"I say that because the technology involved in this thing has many military applications as well—and that's why every company bidding on this contract and any foreign country who wants cheap space capability will be falling all over themselves to get a system together. Because Arrow already had a considerable base of expertise in these matters, we think we have the inside edge. But we must move fast, because so many others also want this award—and they may have done more on it than we have."

Leslie looked again at the Request for Proposal, the "RFP" in the shorthand of the space business, and the words seemed to swim on the paper as she tried to make out the stated scope of the project. "It appears that NASA wants something very complex."

"Yes, and something that goes far beyond what we now think of as 'state of the art.' It will take an interdisciplinary team of the very best scientists to win this bid."

"And it's our job to see that Arrow puts together such a team," Leslie said, understanding at least that much.

"Yes, and also to make sure that no one else knows the details of our proposal. Security is your top priority from now on."

Leslie was silent, feeling mingled excitement and fright that she would be playing a key role in such an important undertaking.

"I know you'll have questions after you review the material," Mr. Meredith said. "It's pretty overwhelming at first glance."

*And the second and third glance, too,* Leslie thought. "I have never worked on anything this complex. I'm surprised that I got the job."

Mr. Meredith looked as if he wished she hadn't mentioned her inexperience. "That decision was made by others," he said, confirming Leslie's earlier suspicions. "Mr. Douglas assured me that you are a quick learner. I hope he's right."

"Thank you for your frankness," Leslie said with what she hoped was the right tone. "I'll do my very best."

Mr. Meredith's nod was curt. "That's all anyone can ask. Now go back to your office and start reading every word of that RFP. And get Sally to help you with the computer system. You need to be up to speed with it as soon as possible."

"Is it still Monday?" Leslie asked as she and Sally shared an elevator at the end of the day.

"I'm afraid so. I see you don't waste any time taking work home."

Leslie glanced at the proposal in her arms, too large to fit into her briefcase, and sighed. "I have a feeling taking work home might get to be a habit."

"You deserve a little fun," Sally said as the elevator reached the ground floor. "I can introduce you to some people from my singles group at church."

*Fun with people from church?* Leslie doubted it. "Thanks, but my life's complicated enough for just now." Not wanting to hurt Sally's feelings, she added, "Later, maybe."

That night Leslie's mind replayed her interview with Mr. Meredith. *Security is your top priority from now on,* he told her, and Leslie knew that he meant seeing to it that nothing about their proposal ever got into anyone else's hands. But in a way, she reflected, "security" had always been her top priority, although she had never really managed to attain it. She'd thought that a good education and a stable job would make her feel secure, and for a while they had. But now, starting this formidable new task in a strange place, Leslie had never felt less secure.

*I'll feel better when I've been here longer and am really accepted by everyone,* she told herself.

After only a few days Leslie felt that she had been working on the VIRCO proposal for months. She came home each night too exhausted to do more than have a quick supper before wading through more reading and then falling into bed. She wouldn't have felt like going out, even if she had been asked, but Hampton Travis hadn't called nor had she seen him around Arrow. Looking at her staffing charts, Leslie was reminded that he had told her he had applied for a job at Arrow.

*What would it be like to work with him?* Leslie briefly wondered, envisioning him working in the office next to hers each day, taking care of the technical aspects of the proposal. She quickly dismissed the thought as idle speculation for which she had no time.

Still, when Leslie found Hampton waiting for her outside Arrow after work late one Monday evening, her heart began to beat a bit faster.

"I'd hoped I'd catch you." He took her briefcase and fell into step beside her like a schoolboy carrying his girl's books home.

"What brings you to Arrow? I haven't seen you lately."

"Just checking. I have to go out of town for a few days, and I wanted to make sure that you and Arrow don't forget me."

"Never!" Leslie exclaimed, matching his smile despite her intention not to.

"Will you join me in a farewell dinner tonight?"

"I'm afraid I would be very bad company. I have so much work to do—"

"Hey, you're not in school anymore, remember? Tell the truth, now—have you done anything for fun since you got here?"

"I had dinner with you," Leslie said before she had time to think how it might sound. "Learning my new job is fun enough for now," she added, then despaired. What must he think of her! Every time Leslie saw Hampton, she seemed to produce idiotic babble.

"You still have to eat, though."

"I'd have to be home early," Leslie said, weakening.

"I promise. My car is over here." He took her arm as they reached the curb and then seated her ceremoniously.

*He knows a woman would have to be made of stone not to enjoy such attention,* Leslie realized.

"We should go somewhere nearby," she said as they left the almost-empty Arrow parking lot.

"That's a project manager for you, always telling everyone what to do," Hampton said lightly.

"I'm very good at that," she agreed.

"We'll go to the Steak House, where I had intended to take Mr. Christopher. It's quite close."

When they arrived, Leslie was relieved to see that the atmosphere of the brightly lit Steak House was much more utilitarian than romantic. Leslie noted that a large number of the diners were business-suited men.

"This place is a favorite of men who come here on TDY," Hampton said.

"Women never travel on temporary duty?"

He smiled. "Touché, Miss Executive. What would you like to have to eat?" he added as a waiter appeared to take their orders.

"What's good?"

"Beef, of course—the specialty of the house. Shall I order for both of us?"

"By all means." Leslie folded her menu without looking at it. After a long day of making decisions, having someone else to do the thinking was a pleasant change.

"Tell me—what do you think of your new job, and how do you like Huntsville?"

"You've asked two completely different questions," Leslie said. "Huntsville seems to be a good place to live so far, although I haven't seen much of it. The work is the hardest I've ever had—and the most interesting."

"I thought you'd like it. But you're going to need some good help to get your proposal in on deadline."

*Oh, no—here comes the job pitch,* Leslie thought. "I am quite aware of that fact," she said stiffly.

"I wondered if you'd had a chance to look at my resume yet?"

"Your resume?" Leslie repeated.

"I left it at Arrow the same day we met. I thought perhaps you had come across it by now."

His tone had changed only slightly, but Leslie picked up on it immediately.

Now Hampton Travis was a man wanting a job that he thought she had the power to give him.

"I haven't seen any resumes yet," Leslie said truthfully enough; she had not really started staffing yet.

"Ask Personnel for it, then. Sometimes they can move with glacial slowness."

"I can't promise anything," Leslie said in her best professional voice. She avoided looking at him directly, not wanting him to see the disappointment in her eyes.

"I'm not asking for special treatment, but you won't find anyone more experienced in preparing the kind of bid that Arrow will need to make on this project."

Their salads arrived, and Leslie was grateful that Hampton seemed ready to concentrate on eating and drop the subject of his employment.

They had almost finished their steaks when Leslie noticed a tall, striking brunette enter the restaurant. She glanced over at them, then quickly looked away.

"Don't you know her?" Leslie asked, but by the time Hampton turned around to look, she was gone.

"What did she look like?"

"Tall, slender. I've seen her at Arrow."

Hampton looked amused. "I'm sorry to disappoint you, but I'm not acquainted with Arrow's entire female work force."

*Is he telling the truth?* Looking at him closely, Leslie decided that either Hampton was being honest or he should take up acting professionally.

"That was the first steak I've had in ages," Leslie said as their plates were removed.

"Admit it—you've let this job keep you from eating properly."

"That's my concern, not yours," Leslie said with an edge of irritation. *The man can't have it both ways,* she thought. He was Hampton the job-seeker, or he was Hampton the charmer. She couldn't keep them straight in her own mind, much less know how to deal with them.

"Quite right it is," he said, sounding properly chastened. "Shall we go?"

Hampton said little on the short drive back to Arrow. He parked next to her car and turned off the engine. "It may be awhile before I see you again," he said when he came around to open her door. "I have to go out of town again."

Foolishly Leslie wished she could see his eyes, but the darkness masked his expression. "When will you be back?"

"I don't know. Be careful, Leslie."

He had said the same thing to her before, she recalled. "I can take care of myself, thank you," Leslie said, then immediately regretted the prissy way it had sounded.

*What is the matter with me?* Leslie asked herself. She had held her own with some of the top scientists at Arrow/West, but Leslie seemed incapable of carrying on an even halfway intelligent conversation with Hampton Travis.

"I hope so," he said. "Well, I'll see you around."

Leslie had buckled her seat belt and started her motor before she realized she didn't have her briefcase. Quickly she rolled down her car window and called to him, "My briefcase is still in your car."

He stopped and nodded. "Oh—so it is." Hampton returned with it and handed it to her with a mock bow. "You can't afford to get careless with Arrow's papers," he said, then turned away before she could reply.

*Strange,* Leslie thought. Why had he felt the need to remind her of security considerations? She was quite aware she must be careful of the VIRCO material. She didn't need to be reminded of that—and most especially not by Hampton Travis.

🌸

The phone was ringing as Hampton Travis let himself into his apartment some fifteen minutes after leaving Leslie in the Arrow parking lot. He was not surprised to hear Barbara's voice at the other end of the line.

"What on earth do you think you're doing?" she asked as soon as he answered.

"Minding my own business, which is more than I can say for you."

"Someone needs to mind it for you, apparently. You took Leslie Christopher out to dinner again—you can't deny it, because I saw you. What's more, she saw me, too."

"What's so bad about that? She asked me if I knew who you were, but by the time I turned around, you were gone.

"Great! I suppose I should have barged right in and joined you."

"I don't see why you're so upset. My strategy might change, but the aim is still the same."

"Just be sure you have the right target!"

Hampton winced, then shook his head as Barbara slammed down the receiver.

*Women!* Would he ever understand them? What had made a pro like Barbara Redmond behave like a jealous schoolgirl? And Leslie—

Well, she was a different matter. He thought he was making some progress with her. At least he hoped so. He would have to be very careful.

🌸

"Guess what's waiting in your office," Sally said when Leslie came in on Thursday morning.

"I'm not up to games this early. Is it animate of inanimate?"

"Never mind—just enjoy it."

"I may not have time to enjoy anything today. Is my staff meeting still on for ten this morning?"

"Yes, and the material you asked me to copy is on your desk."

Leslie went down the hall and opened her office door to find a vase filled with a dozen red long-stemmed roses sitting on her desk. The attached note, written in a bold, masculine hand, was brief: "Good luck with your new project—Hampton."

Leslie sat down hard in her desk chair and closed her eyes, half-believing that when she opened them, the roses would be gone. But they were not, and apparently, neither was Hampton Travis.

Flustered, Leslie threw the card into the wastebasket. What did he think he was doing, sending her flowers? Did he think he'd have the inside track for a job if he romanced her a little? Leslie was certain that if the VIRCO project manager were a man, Hampton wouldn't be sending him flowers.

"Men!" she said aloud. Then she set about getting ready for her first staff meeting, determined not to allow Hampton and his roses to rattle her composure.

"You've been holding out on me," Sally said later as she helped Leslie set up the conference room. "You must have met someone pretty special to be getting flowers like that."

"They don't mean what you think. I wish he hadn't sent them, as a matter of fact."

"You don't care for roses?"

"They overpower that small room. Would you like to put them on your desk, take them home with you tonight?"

Sally looked shocked. "I should say not! Listen, even if they came from Attila the Hun you ought to enjoy every whiff."

"I won't enjoy anything until after this meeting is over. I'm afraid Mr. Meredith already thinks that Arrow sent him an idiot."

"You'll do fine," Sally assured her.

Mr. Meredith entered the conference promptly at ten, looking a bit drawn. He nodded to Leslie and took a seat at the end of the table. A personnel specialist arrive to sit in on the meeting, along with the cost analyst and a systems engineer on loan from another Special Projects office.

After calling on the systems engineer to comment on VIRCO's complex engineering requirements, Leslie turned to the cost analyst. "Mr. Garner, what about the VIRCO budget?"

"Nothing's been worked up yet," the man said somewhat defensively.

"I know it's early yet—" Leslie began.

Mr. Meredith interrupted her. "Have you looked at what has been prepared so far?" The analyst nodded. "Then you should definitely have some figures on what each of the approaches will cost based on our previous experience with similar projects."

Mr. Meredith had not raised his voice, but there was no doubt that his displeasure had registered. Sam Garner made a few notes and promised to have some figures ready by the end of the week.

"Thank you," Leslie said. Embarrassed that Mr. Meredith had had to intervene, she hurried on to the next agenda item. "Concerning staffing, I've asked Mr. Birch to prepare a list of technical personnel already working here who might be able to help us ready the proposal. As you can see," she added, holding up the report, "the list is rather short. Is there anything else you can tell us today?"

Lowell Birch handed Leslie a folder containing several pages of information about engineers and consultants who had previously applied for work at Arrow. "This is all the computer search gave me. One problem is that we have no local pool of computer scientists. Ours are all busy, so we must look elsewhere."

"What about it, Mr. Meredith? Can we give the go ahead?" Leslie asked.

"We'll discuss it later," Mr. Meredith said, and once more Leslie had the distinct feeling that she had made a terrible mistake.

"Does anyone have anything else to bring up now?" Leslie asked. When no one responded, Leslie thanked them for coming and adjourned her first staff meeting.

"Let's go into my office." Mr. Meredith nodded toward the hall. Leslie gathered up her briefcase and followed her boss. She noticed that he seemed a bit less energetic than usual. He put an antacid mint in his mouth as he sat down at his desk.

"I didn't do very well, did I?" Leslie asked. "I thought I was ready, but it doesn't seem that much was accomplished."

"Everyone has to start somewhere," he said, not unkindly. "Next time make sure that you have a reason to meet. Have all material submitted to you in advance—staff meetings are no place for surprises."

"I know I have a lot to learn," Leslie said. "I'll be better prepared next time."

"I'm sure you will," he said, unsmiling. "Miss Christopher, I hadn't realized you need to be reminded that if there's a slot on the chart for a job, it must be filled as soon as possible. Funds are available for immediate hiring."

"Then I can tell Mr. Birch to start looking for computer geniuses?"

"You should have already been doing that. I assumed that you were. . ."

Leslie sighed. "What else should I be doing that I haven't been?"

"The main thing is to get your staff together while the preliminary design team is working. And one more thing—"

"Yes?" The doubts she felt about her job performance were clear in both her face and her tone.

"Don't look so glum," Mr. Meredith said. "I know we don't do things the way you did them in Los Angeles, but you're trying, and I think you are willing to learn. But you absolutely must learn to be wary of everyone."

"Except for the people of Arrow, I know hardly anyone in Huntsville," Leslie said, not quite sure what Mr. Meredith meant.

"I'm sure as time passes that will change, as it should. Our business is very complicated, and it involves a great many people. We ought to be able to trust another, but sometimes—well, it doesn't always work out that way. You must always be on guard."

Leslie waited for him to elaborate on the statement, but instead he stood, concluding their conversation. "Your first presentation is now history. Do your homework, and I can guarantee that the next one will be much easier."

"I hope so," Leslie said, but as she returned to her office, she doubted it. When she opened her door and the scent of roses engulfed her, Leslie felt a momentary pang of regret over what might have possibly developed between them on a personal level.

That night Leslie had an early supper, then curled up with the folder from Personnel on her lap and a note pad nearby, determined to make some progress in staffing. As Lowell Birch had mentioned, the few astrophysicists who already worked for Arrow were engaged in other projects. But there was one name listed—

"Hampton Travis," she said aloud, imagining his blue eyes smiling at her as his name all but leaped off the page. The information was quite sketchy; he had a bachelor's and master's degrees in physics and a PhD in computer science.

"He never told me he was a doctor," Leslie said aloud accusingly. Reading on, she saw that he had last worked for Arrow two years ago. His current occupation was "consultant," and his current address was a post office box. But there was a local telephone number.

"Okay, Dr. Travis," Leslie said, putting a checkmark by his name. "You're now on my official list."

Arrow needed a computer scientist, and he wanted a job. He had said he was going out of town, but perhaps he might be back. Dialing his number, Leslie felt strangely jittery. She recalled an incident in high school when she had worked up the nerve to call a boy she liked to invite him to a "backwards" party. She'd been so nervous she had hung up when she heard his voice, and she had never tried again. But things were different now. Leslie was an adult and this was a business call. She would be quite cool and professional.

Then a female voice answered, and at once Leslie felt a blind panic, imagining the tall brunette—probably his wife—on the other end of the line. Then reason returned, and Leslie asked to speak to Dr. Travis.

"This is his answering service," the voice said, and Leslie felt an absurd surge of relief. "Dr. Travis is unavailable. Is there a message?"

"Please ask him to call Leslie Christopher," she said, and gave her office phone number.

Leslie returned to her list and made a few more calls, arranging for two engineers with appropriate experience to come in for interviews in the week ahead. By the time she had finished, Leslie felt far from confident about what she would say to Hampton Travis.

Only one thing bothered her: if they were to work together, she would never consider going out with Hampton again.

# Chapter 4

Friday began with the normal traffic tie-ups and extra congestion that usually occurred just before each weekend, and everything seemed to be headed downhill in a hurry as the day progressed. The scent of Hampton's roses permeated her office, making Leslie sneeze. She put the vase on Sally's desk and wished she had some way to air out her office.

Aggravation piled on aggravation as the day proceeded. The copying machine quit working, and copy work had to be taken to another floor, slowing down the paper flow and complicating Leslie's tasks. At midmorning came the news that Mr. Meredith would be out yet another day. He told Sally he was taking sick leave, but he didn't say what ailed him.

"I thought he looked pale at the staff meeting," Leslie said as she and Sally had lunch. "Did you notice it, too?"

Sally nodded. "To tell the truth, I've been worried about his health for some time. He's lost a lot of weight lately, and whenever anyone says anything about it, he just makes a joke and says he's not eating as much junk food since Alicia—that's his daughter—went off to college."

"I hope he comes back soon," Leslie said. "I need his advice on so many things."

All day the pace continued to be hectic, and Leslie was out of her office much of the time. When she checked her voice mail at the end of the day, she had nothing from Hampton. Either he hadn't gotten her message, or he was still out of town. Surely he would have returned her call had he known about it.

"You gonna leave your roses here over the weekend?" Sally called after her when Leslie walked past her desk at the end of the day.

"Why don't you take them?" Leslie suggested. "The way I've been sneezing today, I think I may be allergic to roses."

Sally shook her head. "No thanks. But Mr. Meredith might enjoy them. You know, as a get well gesture."

"That's a good idea. I can drop them off tomorrow," Leslie said, wishing she had thought of it herself. "Write down his address for me, please."

Leslie was one of the last ones out of the building as she struggled to see around the masses of opening buds. Bracing the vase on the floor of the passenger's side, she opened the windows to the mild air. Although it was late September and the green mountains rimming the city had begun to hint of fall, the temperature remained pleasantly warm. Leslie still had not seen the city from the top of the mountain, and as she drove home, she made a mental note to do so soon.

Leslie was so engrossed in getting the roses up the stairs to her apartment that she didn't see the man standing near her door until she was almost upon him. She lowered the vase and saw a stocky, red-faced man in a three-piece suit regarding her without much expression.

"Miss Christopher? I hope I didn't startle you." The man briefly displayed a badge in a leather folder. "My name is Andrew Miller. I'm a special agent with the FBI. May I talk with you for a moment?"

"I suppose so," Leslie said, hoping there hadn't been some problem with her clearance.

"Those are nice roses," Mr. Miller said. "Did someone from Arrow send them?"

*What an odd question!* Leslie thought, a bit puzzled that an FBI agent would ask such a personal question. "No. They're just from a friend," she said, then sneezed.

"I see." Andrew Miller stood awkwardly in the middle of the room until Leslie motioned to an upholstered chair. She sat opposite the sofa.

"I hope there's no problem with my clearance. I understood that it had been approved."

"Quite true. I'm here on another matter." He looked at Leslie thoughtfully, then leaned forward slightly and lowered his voice. "Miss Christopher, for some time we have been concerned about a security leak at the ArrowSpace facility here in Huntsville. We've tried to find the source, but so far we haven't been able to get enough evidence to move in on anyone. We think you can help us."

"I don't understand."

"I can't give you the details, of course, but take it from me, there have been some pretty serious consequences as a result of the leaks at Arrow. Your background tells us that you are the right person to help us find the guilty party—or parties, as the case may be—and that your own loyalty is beyond reproach."

He stopped for a moment as if waiting to see the effect his words would have. When Leslie said nothing, he continued in the same steady, measured tones, speaking softly as if he feared he might be overheard.

"We can do very little from the outside—there must be someone working on the inside. And with the VIRCO project coming up, you are ideally placed to help us. Will you do it, Miss Christopher?"

"Why me? I'm new to the Huntsville office and barely know my way around the building. I don't see how I could be at all useful."

"Actually, you're ideal for this assignment because you are new—and you don't have any contacts that are suspect. In addition, VIRCO is sensitive enough to attract attention from many different quarters. You must be aware that our country's defense could even be affected by this technology."

"Mr. Miller," Leslie said finally, "I understand there could be a serious security problem with this project, and certainly anyone who passes on information to unauthorized sources for any reason must be stopped. But why me? A dozen people have already begun work on the project, and every one of them has more experience than I do. Why not ask one of them?"

Mr. Miller leaned back and frowned impatiently. "I don't think you grasp the situation yet. We aren't sure where these leaks are coming from, so anyone at Arrow while the information was being passed on has to be suspect. That includes everyone in your office, from the chief down to the maintenance crew. But we can trust you, and we know you have the best chance to get evidence for us, if you are willing."

"Suppose I'm not? What happens then?

Mr. Miller shrugged. "Either way you can keep on working as you are now. But keep this in mind—your VIRCO bid won't be worth a plug nickel to Arrow if another company steals its technology—and that could also cost our country a great deal if certain foreign powers got it. I don't think you'd want either result on your conscience."

"What would I have to do?" Leslie asked, and for the first time her visitor seemed to relax a little. *He thinks he's got me now,* she realized with a sinking feeling in the pit of her stomach.

"Not a great deal. From time to time you'll be asked to do certain things that might not make much sense to you but could help us find the source of the security leak."

"Such as?" she asked.

He shook his head. "I can't give you the specifics now—it depends on how things seem to be going. We do have some contacts in place around Arrow—I'm sure you'll understand that I can't say who they are—and when they suggest things that might be useful for you to tell us, you'll be asked for the information. But, believe me, this won't interfere in any way with your regular job."

"There must be some strings attached. It can't be as easy as you make it out to be."

"Strings? I wouldn't say that, exactly, but there are a few conditions that we must insist upon. First, no one at Arrow is to ever know that you are cooperating with us. Not your boss or secretary or anyone else. Second, you are to contact me and only me if you come across anything we should know."

He handed Leslie a plain white card bearing a penciled telephone number. "I can be reached through this number, usually within a very short time. Don't hesitate to use it if you need it, but don't leave it lying around where other people might see it. And don't write it or my name down, either."

For the first time, Leslie smiled faintly. *This whole thing is getting quite absurd,* she thought. Aloud she said, "I suppose I should memorize the number and then eat the card. Isn't that what spies do in the movies?"

Mr. Miller's face darkened, and Leslie realized that a sense of humor wasn't necessarily standard issue for FBI agents. "Miss Christopher, we consider this a serious matter," he said sternly.

"I'm sorry," Leslie said quickly. "How will you contact me?" she added, visions of all sorts of complicated plans coming to her mind.

"Usually by telephone, or I might drop by in the evening. However, I'll make sure you're alone first, so you won't have to deal with possible awkward introductions."

"You seem to have thought of everything," Leslie said, and Mr. Miller permitted himself a small smile.

"We try, Miss Christopher. Now, the first thing we need is a list of the names of everyone you hire to work on the VIRCO bid."

"Why?" Leslie asked, surprised.

"There are certain people who have been known to pass information from one company to another—nothing directly related to security as such, but certainly the kind of industrial espionage that Arrow doesn't want."

"I didn't know that," Leslie said and wondered if that was what Mr. Meredith's vague warnings had concerned.

"I know you didn't—that's why I'm here." Mr. Miller rose and walked to the door. "I'm looking forward to working with you, Miss Christopher."

"Good-bye, Mr. Miller." Leslie shook the hand he offered, then firmly closed the door behind him and leaned against it for a moment, considering what she had just done.

*What have I gotten myself into?* she thought, but Leslie didn't see how she could very well have refused to cooperate. The more she turned over the interview in her mind, the more confused she became. It was hard for Leslie to think that anyone she had met could be a security risk, but she had no doubt that the agent knew his business.

*Now,* she thought, *it's up to me to know my business as thoroughly.*

❀

Leslie spent a restless night during which she dreamed she went to work with a huge FBI badge on her blue suit and was promptly fired. When she awoke on Saturday, the agent's visit seemed remote and unreal. If it hadn't happened, she wouldn't have to worry about it. In any case, she reassured herself, nothing was likely to come of it. Intrigue was entertaining in movies, but could it happen in the flesh, here in Alabama? Forget it!

As she sneezed her way through a late breakfast, Leslie regretted leaving Hampton's roses in the kitchen. They definitely had to go, and soon. After trimming the outer petals, Leslie decided they still looked good enough to take to Mr. Meredith. Leslie pulled on jeans and a patterned cotton sweater and readied the roses for the last ride. She decided against calling Mr. Meredith first; if he was at home, she'd give him the roses. If he wasn't, she'd get rid of them somewhere. Then she'd drive up the mountain.

The day was too nice to waste indoors. Sally had told her that September and October were good months in Alabama, and Leslie could see why. The air was cool and crisp this morning, a welcome change from the oppressive heat and humidity that persisted in the first part of the month, and everything seemed outlined in sharp relief. Even traffic moved along more smoothly than usual as Leslie negotiated the route to the older part of town where Mr. Meredith lived.

"It's a pinkish two-story house in the middle of the block," Sally told Leslie. "Of course, it's way too big for him now, but after his wife died he said he'd keep it so his children would have a place to stay when they came to visit."

"Do you think he'll ever marry again?" Leslie had asked Sally, who responded with a shrug.

"Mr. Meredith doesn't seem to have much time for a personal life. He and his wife always lived quietly, and after she became ill, he devoted himself to her. It's been three years since she died, but he still seems to be grieving."

Leslie knew how that was. Her parents, who should have been enjoying retirement after years of constant traveling, had been killed by a drunk driver soon after Leslie had started to work in Los Angeles. Her life had gone on, though, and keeping busy had helped ease her pain. Apparently Mr. Meredith had gotten on with his life too. She gave him credit for keeping his personal problems to himself and suspected that he would prefer his employees to do likewise.

When she pulled her car into the driveway, Leslie noticed a couple of newspapers lying in the front yard, and as she approached the porch, she saw that the mailbox was jammed full. Leslie rang the doorbell and felt awkward when the door opened to reveal the usually well-groomed Richard Meredith unshaven and wearing a wrinkled robe over his pajamas.

"I hope I'm not disturbing you," she said quickly. "I have something for you out in the car. Are you all right?" she added, noting that he held onto the doorframe as if to keep from falling.

"I've felt better, but I'm sure to be up and about more. Won't you come in?" he added, remembering his manners.

"Just a minute—I'll be right back."

Leslie retrieved the flowers, noticing that they looked less lovely in the morning sunlight than they had under the artificial light in her kitchen. She set the vase on the front porch while gathering his mail and newspapers.

"I was just thinking that I should bring those in," Mr. Meredith said when she handed the stack to him. Then he saw the vase and looked surprised. "Red roses! You must have some connections."

"Not really," Leslie said. She set the vase on the coffee table, the only surface in the living room that wasn't already cluttered. "I've enjoyed these for two days, and now it's your turn."

"Thank you for thinking of me. Please sit down."

"Is there anything I can do for you?" Leslie thought he looked quite ill, but he waved away her concern.

"I have a little stomach problem that acts up now and again. In a few days, I'll be good as new."

"We missed you yesterday," Leslie said. Her recital of some of the office "catastrophes" brought a faint smile to Mr. Meredith's pale face.

"Sounds like I picked a good time to stay home. What else happened? Any luck with your staffing?"

"Some." Leslie wanted to tell Mr. Meredith about her visitor from the FBI, but since she had promised not to, she told him about the calls she had made. "I have some interviews set up for early next week, so I hope you have names on those chart slots soon."

"Good," Mr. Meredith said, "Keep working on that lead computer scientist slot—that really is critical."

Leslie nodded. "I'd like to ask you about one of the consultants on the list. Do you know a Dr. Hampton Travis?"

Mr. Meredith looked at Leslie as if he thought she might be making a joke. "Certainly. Hampton Travis was one of the first non-pilot scientists to become an astronaut," he said.

"He was an *astronaut*?" Leslie said, tardily realizing why Hampton's name had seemed so familiar.

Mr. Meredith smiled faintly. "That was a long time ago," he said. "I take it that you have met the gentleman?"

Leslie nodded and felt chagrined at Mr. Meredith's knowing look. *What would he think if I told him the roses came from Hampton?* she asked herself, but she had no intention of telling him.

"Astronauts do seem to have a way with women," Mr. Meredith said dryly. "I don't suppose I need to remind you that mixing business and pleasure isn't a good idea, but Travis knows the ropes. When we get down to the wire on this proposal, that kind of experience can mean a great deal."

"Thanks for the information." Leslie stood. "Are you positive that I can't do something for you?"

"My housekeeper will be in later on today, and I'll be fine until then. But I do appreciate your concern—and if anything comes up at the office that you can't handle, call me. Maybe we can solve it together by telephone."

"Oh, don't worry about us. One way or another, we'll manage to muddle through."

For the first time that day, Mr. Meredith smiled as if he really meant it. "That's what I fear the most!" he exclaimed as Leslie left.

*He's a nice man,* Leslie thought as she backed her car out of his driveway. She hoped she wouldn't disappoint him.

Before she started up the mountain, Leslie stopped to buy a sandwich and soda to take along. The main route up Monte Sano, known locally as Monte Sano Mountain, was a four-lane highway, but near the crest Leslie turned off onto a narrow, twisting road that straightened out as it reached the top of the mountain. She caught an occasional glimpse into the valley as she climbed higher, but trees hid most of the view. Leslie followed the signs to Monte Sano State Park, where Sally had said there were hiking trails.

When she reached the picnic area, Leslie opened her trunk and took out her hiking boots. She had last worn them backpacking in Yosemite with the ArrowSpace/West Hiking Club. Those had been challenging mountains, and more than a thousand feet higher—not smooth and rounded like these at the southern end of the Appalachians.

Leslie looked around as she locked her car. In a meadow to her left was a small playground. Beyond it, a couple of teenage boys were throwing a Frisbee, which a wildly barking black dog kept trying to intercept. To the right and directly in front of her several families had gathered under the shade of the central pavilion. The smoke from hamburgers sizzling on the grill tantalized Leslie as she passed the picnickers and walked down the path to a bulletin board where hiking information was posted. From the several trails that began at that point, Leslie chose a two-mile walk that promised a waterfall and two over-looks in an easy loop.

A sign at the head of the trail gave the usual warnings about staying on the marked path, not disturbing any wildlife or vegetation, or climbing over the overlook fences. Before starting on the hike, Leslie walked over to the bluff at the end of the picnic grounds and looked at the valley spread out below her, then down at the jagged rocks and underbrush on the other side of the low retaining wall. She recalled something Hampton had said about the mountain being dangerous. Certainly people who weren't watching where they were going could lose their footing and fall, but it would be dangerous only to the careless.

Leslie turned into the woods and started down the trail, which was an almost too-easy walk. The promised waterfall was perhaps six feet high, hardly on a par with those in Yosemite. The overlooks offered views similar to the one she had seen at the edge of the picnic grounds, a checkerboard patchwork of fields and pastures bisected by streams and occasional swatches of woods.

After her hike, Leslie returned to the picnic area and sat on the low stone retaining wall. She pulled out the sandwich she had picked up at the deli and began her lunch. She felt a stab of loneliness that she had no one with whom to share the spectacular view.

Hampton Travis had offered to bring her up here, but she had refused his invitation, which hadn't been repeated. Then there was the matter of his roses—

"Nice, isn't it?"

The voice was so sudden and unexpected that Leslie gasped. For a second she had the crazy idea that thinking about Hampton had somehow caused him to materialize. But there he was, sitting down beside her on the ledge, his too-blue eyes regarding her steadily.

"You startled me."

"I'm sorry. I thought you saw me when you came out of the woods—you looked right at me."

"I guess I was thinking of something else."

"Deeply, no doubt."

"I got the roses. I was quite surprised," Leslie said.

"I thought you deserved them," Hampton said. "I know that a job like yours can be overwhelming, especially at first."

"It has been that, all right, but I'm holding my own."

"I never doubted you would."

"I tried to call you. You must be important, having an answering service."

Hampton shrugged. "Not really. I move around a lot, and I hate beepers and car phones and machines that try to talk like humans. The answering service comes in handy."

"Did they tell you I called?"

He looked amused. "They did, but I got in late last night, and you weren't home this morning. I suppose you wanted to let me know you got the roses?"

"Yes, that was it," Leslie said quickly. She couldn't bring herself to tell him she had called to ask him to come in for an interview—in the light of what Mr. Meredith had said, it would effectively end any chance they might have for a more intimate relationship. She might have to do that yet, but on this beautiful day, Leslie wasn't ready to close that door.

"Looking at a view like this, it's easy to see why our ancestors thought that God lived on top of a mountain," Hampton said, waving toward the valley below.

"They did?" Leslie said, then regretted it. Of course she knew that the Greeks thought that the gods lived on Mt. Olympus. *Hampton must think I'm hopeless,* she thought.

He nodded. " 'I will lift up mine eyes unto the hills, from whence cometh my help,' the psalmist said. Of course, we know that God is everywhere, but being here on a mountain always makes me feel closer to heaven."

"I suppose so," said Leslie, who had never thought about it before.

"I was just about to have lunch. Will you join me?" Hampton waved to a picnic table under some pines, and she walked over to it with him.

"They say great minds run in the same channels," Hampton said as he opened his backpack and brought out a sandwich. "I see you stopped at the same deli. Do you have Dijon mustard and bean sprouts, too?"

"Of course."

"Is this the first time you've come up here?" he asked.

"Yes, I had no idea it was so lovely."

"If you like, I'll give you the grand tour—unless, of course, you have other pressing business," he added, seeing her hesitation.

Leslie tried to think of a reason not to go with him but could not. "All right," she said.

"Good—my car is over there by the field."

After they finished eating, Hampton took her to the top of the mountain and another spectacular view. The southern part of the city stretched out before them, and Leslie thought she could make out her apartment complex, or at least part of it. With binoculars, she could probably see into her own living room—a thought that brought with it a mental note to make sure she closed her drapes, especially at night.

Hampton looked back out on the valley below them. "Can you find the Willows?"

"Not without binoculars," she said, noticing that Hampton had a pair slung around his neck.

Immediately he handed them to her. "Here, try these."

As Leslie attempted to focus the lenses, Hampton directed her movements with his hands covering hers. She was keenly aware of his nearness, of the spicy fragrance of his after-shave, of the electricity where their hands touched. After a few moments she lowered the glasses and glanced at the jagged rocks just below. The touch of dizziness she felt wasn't entirely due to the height. When Leslie swayed a little, Hampton put an arm around her waist and drew her back. She quickly pulled away from him.

"We can't have you falling off the side of the mountain," he said.

Leslie returned the glasses and shuddered. "I have no desire to make the evening news that way, thank you."

"Feel like walking more? There are other trails nearby."

"I'm game. The first hike wasn't very much."

"This one is a bit steeper. The last time I took it I saw several deer."

"It's hard to believe we're so close to civilization up here," Leslie said after they had traveled several hundred feet on the trail. There was little underbrush in this area because the tall, canopied hardwood forest didn't admit enough light for anything to grow. From time to time they had to detour around a fallen tree or stump, and except for the occasional cry of a bird and the rustling of the trees' leaves in the pleasant breeze, the trail was silent and deserted.

Hampton took Leslie's hand when they climbed across a large tree limb in the path and continued to hold it as they walked.

"Is that a persimmon?" Leslie asked, pointing to a rough-barked tree.

Hampton shrugged. "I'm not sure. But for the record, if you ever get lost in the woods, don't walk to the left."

"Why not?"

"Lost people tend to do that—that's how they come to walk in circles."

"How interesting," Leslie said, her tone suggesting the opposite.

Hampton laughed. "I just wanted you to know that I'm not a total ignoramus concerning the woods."

Leslie looked levelly at Hampton and decided it was time to make him squirm a bit. "I know you're not an ignoramus, *Doctor* Travis. Why didn't you tell me who you were the first time we met?"

Hampton looked chagrined. "I suppose my ego was a little wounded that you didn't know. Anyway, all that astronaut business happened a long time ago."

"But it's an important part of your life, isn't it?"

Hampton nodded gravely. "Yes, it is. Once you've touched heaven, earth is never the same again."

Leslie shivered unaccountably. "I'd like to hear about it," she said.

"That can be arranged. Will you let me see you again?"

He had half turned to face her, his blue eyes regarding her intently. As she looked into his eyes, Leslie felt her resistance draining away. She has worked hard all week. What harm could there be in getting to know an interesting person better? It had nothing to do with her work, nothing at all.

"I suppose so," she said at last. He nodded in satisfaction.

"You won't be sorry," he said. Hampton's expression brightened, and he pointed down the trail. "Come on. I want to show you a fossil bed just off the path over there."

Leslie followed him, trying to dismiss the nagging thought that by encouraging a personal association with Hampton Travis, she was, indeed, not only mixing business with pleasure but also somehow endangering her career and perhaps even the entire VIRCO project.

# Chapter 5

Hampton appeared promptly at seven, dressed in a navy blazer with matching slacks and a colorful paisley tie against his white shirt. She had chosen a full-skirted blue jersey dress, which she wore with a single strand of pearls and matching pearl earrings.

"Well, at least we're color-coordinated," Hampton said with a smile.

"Now will you tell me where we're going?" Leslie asked on the way to his car.

"Would it make any difference?" he asked. She shook her head.

"There must be two hundred restaurants in this town. So far I've been to about six, not counting the fast-food chains—I'm sure I've hit all of them."

"I doubt that you've been where we're going tonight," Hampton said.

Driving through the deepening twilight into the center of town, he stopped the car in front of an old building with a New Orleans-style courtyard, complete with old brick and elaborate wrought iron. They were greeted by a doorman, and a uniformed parking attendant drove the car away. At the entrance of the courtyard, a brass plate beside double doors read CENTURY CLUB—MEMBERS ONLY.

"Elegant," Leslie said, noting the circular stairway and crystal chandeliers in the marble-floored foyer. A young woman in black seated at a Louis XIV desk greeted Hampton by name, then a maitre d' in tails appeared from the dim recesses to the left and beckoned them to follow him.

After they were seated at a table for two in the rear of a small dining room, Leslie looked at a single yellow rose in a crystal vase, heard the muted notes of a piano playing in the main dining room, and realized that, whatever else the Century Club might be, it was not inexpensive.

"You're a member here?" she asked, making it a question.

Hampton shrugged, a gesture she was coming to expect from him whenever he didn't particularly care for one of her questions.

"Yes and no. I did a favor for a member, a rather important old-cotton type, and he lets me use his membership on occasion."

"I'd think that 'on occasion' would be all one could afford," Leslie remarked, "or maybe once a year, on my salary."

"Good evening, sir, madam. May I bring you a cocktail?"

A white-gloved waiter clad in tails offered a tasseled, many-paged menu to Hampton, then a smaller one, lacking prices, to Leslie. *I wonder what they do when two women come in together?* Leslie thought, faintly annoyed at the assumption that a woman should automatically be sheltered from knowing how much a man was spending on her.

"How about it? Do you want something to drink before dinner?" Hampton asked, and Leslie shook her head.

"I don't drink."

Hampton dismissed the waiter and turned back to Leslie with a smile.

"Do you find it amusing that I don't drink?" Leslie asked somewhat defensively when the waiter left.

"Not at all. In fact, I had a hunch you didn't. It's always nice to know when I'm proven to be right."

Leslie looked closely at him, then took a sip of water from her glass. The moment she put it down, prepared to frame a reply, another waiter appeared from nowhere to refill it. Leslie could scarcely keep from laughing at the over-attentive service that persisted throughout the meal, making private conversation all but impossible.

When it seemed they might finally be left alone for a while, Hampton leaned forward and waved his hand in the direction of Leslie's head. "I like the way you've done your hair tonight."

Leslie had swept it back from her face into a French twist, hoping that it might give her a certain sophistication, but she was surprised that Hampton had commented on it. Most of the men she had known probably wouldn't have noticed her hair unless she dyed it purple or cut it into a Mohawk. "Thank you," she said. *Is he being sincere or merely trying to flatter me?* Leslie privately wondered.

"I mean it," Hampton said, once more showing his uncanny knack of seeming to know what she was thinking. "I thought it needed to be said."

"You don't always say what needs to be said, though, do you?" Leslie countered.

Hampton cocked his head to one side and pursed his lips at her direct gaze. "That's a strange question. I wonder what's behind it?"

"Nothing sinister. I just don't quite know what to make of you."

Hampton looked amused and cocked one eyebrow. "Oh?"

"You've learned a lot about me, yet I hardly know anything at all about you. And every time I ask where you're from or who you work for, it's like trying to grab a handful of fog."

"Apt phrase," he said with admiration. "However, you're wrong about me. I'm really quite substantial."

"You can't deny that you're not very forthcoming," Leslie persisted.

Hampton shook his head. "Let's just say that in my business, performance is all that matters. No one likes a blabbermouth."

"The Sphinx could be considered a blabbermouth compared to you," Leslie said. Once more Hampton smiled.

"You do have a way with words, Miss Christopher."

"Mine, perhaps, not yours."

Hampton sighed. "All right, just what is so important for you to know?"

"For starters, let's talk about where you're from—and where you went earlier this week."

Hampton leaned back in his chair and looked reflective. "I'm really not from anywhere. My father was in the military and we lived all over the world. I never liked any of the places well enough to claim them as a hometown."

"I know how that it is," Leslie said, thinking of her own childhood. "Didn't you feel that you were missing something?"

"Not really. People are more important than places, and my parents were careful to make sure that our quarters, however temporary, were a real home."

Hampton broke off as one waiter appeared to remove their plates and another wheeled in a dessert cart.

"The Viennese torte is especially good tonight," she said.

Leslie shook her head. "I don't care for dessert," she said.

Hampton motioned for the waiter to remove the cart. "Just bring us coffee, please."

"Service is very good here." Leslie observed with a twinkle in her eye.

"Almost too good," Hampton said. Nothing further was said until their coffee had been served with elaborate ceremony and once more they were left alone.

"You were saying that you moved around a lot when you were growing up?" Hampton prompted, and Leslie shook her head.

"We were talking about you," she reminded him.

Hampton shook his head. "I'd rather talk about you. You must have had a lonely childhood." He took her hand with such a look of compassion that Leslie realized she must have sounded more forlorn than she intended.

"My father kept thinking he'd find a pot of gold at the end of the next job. I kept hoping he'd just stop somewhere long enough to put down roots, but he never did."

Leslie withdrew her hand and straightened in her chair. "That's all there is to my story—now it's your turn again."

The persistent waiter appeared without warning. "Do you require anything further, sir and madame?"

"No, thank you. We'll be leaving now."

"Shall I have your car brought around?" the hostess asked when they reached the foyer.

"No, I think we'll take a turn around the park first, if the lady is willing."

Leslie glanced down at her high-heeled shoes. "I certainly can't go very far or very fast in these, but if it's nearby, I'm game."

"It is. I'll be back for the car in half an hour," Hampton told the hostess.

As they went outside, Leslie noticed that the clock on the bank across the street indicated it was already past nine. "Is it safe to be out walking at this time of night?"

"We're practically next door to the police station, and everything is well lighted. See, the park is full of people," he added as they reached the end of the block and crossed the street to the Big Spring Park, built around the city's first source of water.

Several bicyclists and walkers passed them, and they saw a family eating ice cream cones, despite the autumn chill. Hampton took Leslie's arm as they walked around the little lagoon to sit in a gazebo where, Hampton said, there were summer concerts.

"You make a good tour guide," Leslie said.

"I'm good at a lot of things. You'd know that if you'd read my resume."

"What makes you think I haven't?" she asked.

"Never mind—it doesn't matter."

"Oh?" *What happened to the man who wanted to work for me?* Leslie wondered.

"Have you changed your mind about applying for the job?"

"It's still the greatest new program that's come down the pike since the Space Shuttle. But I didn't ask you out to talk about work."

*Why did you ask me out, then?* It would have been a natural question, but Leslie knew she shouldn't broach it.

"You never finished answering my question," she said instead.

"Which one?"

"About where you go when you leave town."

He gestured broadly with his hands. "Just about everywhere and anywhere. To Florida to see my folks, to Washington or L.A. or Houston on consulting jobs. Nothing exciting."

"Oh," Leslie said, somewhat deflated and annoyed. *What did you expect him to say?* she asked herself. He had told her what he wanted her to hear, but she doubted he'd told her the whole story. "I suppose nothing on earth could ever be as exciting as being an astronaut," she said.

Hampton glanced at Leslie, then pointed to the heavens, where a few stars shone above the city lights. "Exciting isn't the word," he said, then stopped as if trying to frame his words. "Have you ever experienced the feeling of weightlessness?" he asked.

"Not really. But I have done some scuba diving. Does that come close?"

"Yes, pretty much. In fact, astronauts train in the neutral buoyancy tank out at Marshall Space Flight Center—the first time I visited Huntsville, that was the reason. But there you always know that you're really in water." He pointed to the sky. "Up there, it's an entirely different sensation."

"The view must not be too shabby, either," Leslie said.

Hampton nodded enthusiastically. "You've seen pictures of our planet taken in orbit? Well, the stars are even more spectacular away from earth's atmosphere. Do you know the eighth psalm?"

"The only psalm I know by number is the twenty-third," Leslie admitted. "I didn't know any had to do with space."

"Actually, several do, more or less. The eighth talks about how God set His glory in the heavens, and then the psalmist says, 'When I consider thy heavens, the work of thy fingers, the moon and the stars, which thou has ordained; what is man, that thou are mindful of him, and the son of man, that thou visitest him?' That's exactly the way I felt up there."

"I'm afraid I don't know much about the Bible." Even as she spoke, Leslie knew she sounded defensive.

"Neither did I, until that first ride on the Shuttle. I can tell you, it made a believer of someone who'd seldom thought about God before."

In the darkness, Leslie couldn't see Hampton's face, but his voice ran with conviction. *If he's making this up, he should be an actor,* she thought. "That doesn't sound like what I'd expect to hear from a fact-and-figures computer genius," she said aloud.

Hampton chuckled. "Then you don't know many astronauts or what you call geniuses. The more we scientists learn about the complexity of the universe, the more respect we have for its Creator."

"Really?" Leslie asked, and Hampton again took her hand and held it loosely. She shivered, not entirely from the increasing night coolness. Hampton stood and helped her down the gazebo steps.

"Don't get me started on that topic," Hampton said. "We ought to go now— the car should be there by the time we get back to the Club."

They talked very little on the drive back to Leslie's apartment. He walked her to the front door. She didn't invite him to come inside, nor did he seem to expect that she would.

"Thank you for another lovely evening," she said.

"Likewise." Hampton brushed Leslie's cheek with the back of his hand, touched his forehead to hers, then pulled her to him and kissed her. Leslie made no effort to pull away, but neither did she allow herself to respond. It was almost as if her heart stopped beating for a moment, then resumed only when Hampton released her.

"You shouldn't have done that," she murmured, her voice so low that she wasn't certain he heard her.

"I'll be in touch," Hampton said. He waited for Leslie to unlock her door and turn on an inside light before he touched his forehead in a farewell salute and walked away.

Sighing, Leslie double-locked the door behind him. Each time she saw Hampton Travis he intrigued her more, even though she felt that she knew even less about him. Whatever Hampton was—a God-fearing man genuinely interested in her or an unscrupulous actor who would do anything to get on the VIRCO project—Leslie knew she ought to declare him off-limits. Yet Leslie wasn't prepared to shut out this man who interested her as no else ever had.

*I shouldn't make a hasty decision about him,* she told herself.

🌺

When she awoke Sunday morning, Leslie's first thoughts were of Hampton Travis and the pleasant time she always seemed to have in his company.

*Does he go to church?* she wondered. She tried to imagine which of the many houses of worship in Huntsville might attract him. For a moment she considered calling Sally and inviting herself to Sally's church, but by the time she had finished breakfast she realized it was too late. Anyway, she had plenty of work to take care of that day.

As Leslie worked on VIRCO material on Sunday afternoon, she realized that she would need more help right away. The current Arrow staff had done a great job on the preliminary work, but they all had other duties, too. With Mr. Meredith gone, Leslie was spreading herself pretty thin.

Whether or not she should work with Hampton Travis was becoming academic; VIRCO needed help, and he was certainly qualified. She'd be remiss in her duty if she let personal feelings interfere with considering hiring him.

Leslie went directly to Personnel as soon as she got to Arrow on Monday.

"I'd like resumes for these people," she said as she handed the desk clerk a brief list of names.

"We're shorthanded today. I don't know when I can get to them."

Leslie tried to sound pleasant but firm. "I really need these as soon as possible."

"So does everyone else," the clerk replied, but Leslie noticed that her request went to the top of the stack—a start, at least.

"Good morning," Sally greeted her a few minutes later. "Did you have a nice weekend?"

It was the sort of perfunctory question asked in all offices, and since Leslie had no intention of telling Sally about her date with Hampton Travis, she merely nodded.

"I took the roses to Mr. Meredith on Saturday. I didn't think he looked at all well."

"That's too bad. The work is piling up around here."

"I wish I had his clout in staffing," Leslie said. "Personnel's supposed to send up some resumes later—bring them to me right away, okay?"

Sally nodded and turned away to answer the telephone. Leslie went to her office, where the faint aroma of roses still clung. She called down to Finance to check on the preliminary budget and had worked with the figures for a couple of hours when Sally brought in the requested folders.

"Here they are," she said, putting them on Leslie's desk. "Mr. Meredith's housekeeper just called to tell us he'll be out all this week, maybe longer. She's trying to convince him to go back to the doctor."

"He seemed to think he'd be all right in a few days. I hope this isn't anything serious."

"So do I, of course, but it doesn't sound good."

Sally left and Leslie rifled through the folders in search of Hampton's resume. Twice she went through the stack, but it just wasn't there. With a sigh she dialed Personnel and told the clerk that at least one resume she'd requested was missing.

"I'm sorry, Miss Christopher, but it's quite possible that some of them might be in another office. There are others hiring, you know," she added in a tone clearly meant to make Leslie feel that her request had been out of line. Leslie ignored the comment and asked the clerk to check and let her know who might have the folders.

"It won't do any good. Only one office works a resume file at a time. If anyone else is considering the applicant, you'll just have to wait your turn."

"I see," Leslie said, forcing herself to sound more agreeable than she felt. "Can you let me know when the other resumes come back?"

"We don't usually do that."

"Is Mr. Birch in? I would like to speak with him about this."

"I'll transfer the call," the clerk said stiffly, and Leslie could imagine that her popularity was about to hit the basement. She didn't care, though; she had a job to do, and Lowell Birch ought to know that his people were hindering it.

"Mr. Birch isn't in his office at the moment," his secretary told Leslie.

Leslie left her extension number and hung up, feeling frustrated. *A male programmer wouldn't get this kind of runaround,* she thought. She wished she could ask Mr. Meredith if Personnel were telling her the truth. She knew she had to play by the rules. But first she wanted to make sure that they were using the same guidelines—and she was suspicious that they weren't.

"I'm sorry you're having problems, Miss Christopher," Lowell Birch said when he returned her call a few minutes later. He sounded at least a little sympathetic, which she took as a hopeful sign.

"So am I. I tried to find out who had the other resumes I need, but I was told that they had to be returned by the office who had them, presumably after they'd decided not to hire the people in question."

"Yes, that is the usual practice," Mr. Birch said, but something in the emphasis he put on the word "usual" gave her hope that he might be willing to bend the rules.

"Look, you know our situation with VIRCO," Leslie said earnestly. "If I

178

can't get some people on board here pretty soon, there's a strong possibility that Arrow could miss the RFP deadline. Landing VIRCO would help Arrow's entire operation. I don't know what sort of priorities the other offices have, but it seems to me that at the least you can tell me now if anyone on my list is going to be hired for anther project."

"Fair enough," Mr. Birch agreed. "I'll make a few calls and get back to you."

"Thanks—I really appreciate your help. And by the way, what's happening with the lead computer scientist slot? Have you heard anything else from the home office?"

"They've advertised the position. That's all I know."

"If there have been any responses, I'd like to have them right away," Leslie said.

There was a brief silence before Mr. Birch spoke again. "I understand that Mr. Meredith is on sick leave. The chief usually authorizes such activity. But you could prepare a fax to be ready to go when Mr. Meredith signs the request."

"I'll do that right away. And in the meantime, I'd really like to get those missing resumes."

Leslie accepted Mr. Birch's assurances of cooperation, then thanked him and hung up, feeling somewhat better. Maybe just as well that Mr. Meredith hadn't been available, Leslie thought. He'd encouraged her to act on her own, and now that she was, Leslie was rather enjoying it.

Leslie's first victory turned out to be a small one, however. By the end of the morning Mr. Birch had located three of the four missing folders, but Hampton Travis's wasn't among them. No one seemed to be able to locate it, and of the others, two of the people had already been hired for Arrow projects, and the other lacked the necessary experience.

"Sometimes I think everyone at Arrow is in a conspiracy against me," Leslie told Sally over lunch. "What did I do to deserve such hostility?"

"Some people around here are hostile to their own mothers. You just have to go on and do your best in spite of them."

"I know I wasn't Mr. Meredith's choice for this job. Maybe someone who wanted it resents me enough to make sure things are going wrong for me."

"My, aren't we paranoid today!" Sally exclaimed. "To begin with, I doubt if anyone could mess things up more than Arrow's bureaucracy already does. That's really what you're up against just now. Anyway, the man who was most upset about not getting the job quit before you got here."

"Were all the other applicants men?"

"I have no idea, and we shouldn't even be talking about it. You're doing all right—I'll tell you if you happen to get off course."

Leslie smiled at Sally's declaration, but the information hadn't made Leslie feel any better. And when the rest of the day brought a breakdown in the mainframe computer and a temporary loss of data, Leslie felt even worse by the time she and Sally walked to the parking lot after work.

"This hasn't been one of my better days," Leslie said.

"What can you expect of Mondays? You need to take your mind off your troubles, and I know just the place. Come and ride with me—I'll bring you back to pick up your car later."

"You're not planning on taking me to a singles bar, I hope," Leslie said.

Sally laughed. "No, that's not my scene. This is much better."

"I ought to do some work on the budget tonight," Leslie said.

"The budget can wait," Sally said firmly. "Your assistant says you need a break. Quit making excuses and come on."

"I hope there's food where you're taking me," Leslie said as Sally guided her car into heavy traffic leaving the research park area. "That lunch salad didn't have much staying power."

"Oh sure," Sally said. "Everywhere you look around here there's food. You ought to get your rose-giver to take you to some of them."

Leslie wanted to tell Sally that he had, but instead she shook her head. "I'm afraid I don't have the time or energy to worry about dating just now."

"More's the pity. But you know, a great social life isn't necessarily limited to one man. I called you Saturday to invite you to church with me on Sunday, but you were out. You really ought to try it, Leslie. Everyone needs a firm anchor—and working at Arrow has a way of making everyone need something to hold onto."

"I'm all right, thank you," Leslie said defensively. She wasn't sure what Sally meant about a firm anchor, but she wasn't interested in pursuing it. Then another thought came to her, and she looked at Sally, feeling vaguely alarmed. "We're not going to your church now, are we?"

Sally laughed. "No, although some would probably say that this place is the most popular temple of worship in town."

Sally turned into the perimeter road around the mammoth shopping center that Leslie had noticed on her arrival to Huntsville, but which she hadn't visited.

"Don't tell me that your idea of fun is going shopping!" Leslie said accusingly when she realized that Sally was parking the car.

"Haven't you ever heard that when the going gets tough, the tough go shopping?" she teased. 'No, of course I didn't bring you here to shop. Come on, you'll see," she added as Leslie still looked doubtful.

Leslie followed Sally into the main entrance of a mall that had a floor plan she'd seen a dozen times before. On two levels, the giant building was laid out like spokes in a wheel, so that from any point, one could see only a few of the more than two hundred stores. This particular evening, the first floor of the mall featured lavish displays from the area's many travel agents. Bright posters of faraway places vied for attention with hula-skirted girls and costumed couples performing national dances. A banner over the auditorium door announced that travel films were being shown continuously.

"This is a Travel Fair," Sally explained as they walked through the exhibits. "Maybe you read about it in the Sunday paper?"

"No, I didn't," Leslie replied.

"Well, this is your chance to get away from it all without taking leave or spending money," Sally said. "We can dine on Hawaiian or Mexican food, sample fresh pineapple, guava, and kiwifruit, watch the dancers, and see all kinds of films. I come every year and enjoy it very much."

In spite of herself, Leslie found the Travel Fair to be entertaining enough to take her mind off her troubles for a few hours, and when they had seen all there was to see, she thanked Sally for bringing her.

"I told you you'd like it," Sally replied. "I have to make a quick stop at the Stocking Shop before we leave. Want to go with me?"

Leslie shook her head. "No, I'll wait here for you." She sat on a cushioned bench and looked around, content to watch the passing people and listen to snippets of conversation. A couple passed, arms around each other's waists, the woman's head resting on the man's shoulder. He bent down and said something that made her smile, and Leslie felt a small stirring of envy. A blue-eyed baby in a stroller stared at Leslie, then smiled and held out a balloon that bobbed in his chubby hand as he passed her. Leslie smiled back and waved at the child, who laughed in delight.

She was still smiling when she saw the red-faced FBI agent walking toward her. He surely must have seen her—he looked directly at her—but Andrew Miller passed her without any sign of recognition. The same chill that Leslie had felt before in his presence prickled her skin. He hadn't contacted her since the night he'd asked her to help find security leaks at Arrow. She had half hoped that he'd forgotten about her and wouldn't ask her to do anything after all. But now that she had seen him again and he'd so pointedly ignored her, Leslie had an uneasy feeling that she might hear from him soon.

"Mission accomplished." Sally's voice startled Leslie. "Let's go—I still have one more surprise."

"I'm not sure I can stand anything else after all the excitement I've had tonight," Leslie said dryly. Sally laughed so heartily that several people turned to look at her.

"Oh, Leslie, maybe the Travel Fair wasn't all that thrilling, but at least it got you out of yourself for a little while, didn't it?"

"Yes, and I enjoyed it, but we should call it a day now."

"Almost. One more stop and we're done."

Sally was an aggressive driver, and Leslie didn't try to talk as she threaded the six-lane maze of traffic on University Drive and turned into the parking lot of an ice cream parlor.

"Here's the best-tasting treat in town," Sally said. "Let's see what the featured flavor is."

"I can't believe I'm doing this," Leslie said a few minutes later as they sat in Sally's car, holding double-dip cones of rocky road ice cream.

"Brings back my childhood," Sally said.

"Me, too. Dad used to take me for ice cream as a special treat," Leslie said. "I don't think we ever had a refrigerator good enough to keep ice cream."

Sally launched into a rambling tale about her father, and as Leslie listened with amusement she idly glanced around and saw Hampton Travis enter the ice cream shop. Apparently he hadn't noticed her, and when he left the shop carrying two cones, Leslie turned her head back toward Sally and hoped he wouldn't look their way. From the corner of her eye she saw him walk past a car to his Thunderbird. She turned around in time to see him hand one of the cones to a passenger in the front seat. In the brief light made when Hampton opened his door, Leslie saw a dark-haired woman, but the distance between them was too great to make out the woman's features.

"What are you looking at?" Sally asked after she finished her story.

"I thought I recognized someone, but I was mistaken." Leslie glanced back in time to see the Thunderbird pull into the road and meld into traffic. "This has been fun," she said, wiping her sticky fingers with the thin paper napkin that had come with the cone. "Thanks for bringing me along."

"Hey, you're good company. And you'll still make it home by the ten o'clock news."

❧

"Do you think she saw you?" Barbara asked as Hampton pulled away from the ice cream shop.

"Maybe." Hampton glanced at his rearview mirror several times, but the car in which Leslie had sat didn't appear. "I assumed they were going back to Arrow when they left the mall."

"I told you we shouldn't be out together."

Hampton grinned but didn't divert his attention from driving. "Maybe Miss Christopher will be a little jealous."

"Don't joke about it, Hampton. This isn't very fair to her, you know."

"Let me be the judge of that. I have an idea that something will break soon."

"Don't you think she'll wonder what happened to your resume?" Barbara asked, all business again. "The girl may be somewhat naïve, but she isn't stupid."

"No, but she could be duped. The precautions I took earlier will come in handy. In the meantime, you know what you're to do."

Barbara nodded.

"I'll check with you at the usual time," Hampton added as he stopped the car in front of Barbara's condominium.

He didn't offer to walk her to her door, and as the car pulled away from the curb, Barbara sighed. She and Hampton Travis had worked together before, and she knew he was very good at what he did. But never had she known him to become personally involved in a case. It was dangerous to allow feelings to interfere with work.

*Men can be such blind idiots, even when they have a string of advanced degrees,* she thought. She just hoped that Leslie Christopher appreciated him.

# Chapter 6

Have you heard? Mr. Meredith is in the hospital," Sally greeted Leslie the next morning.

"No, I didn't know," Leslie replied. "Is it serious?"

Sally shrugged. "His housekeeper says he's gone in for tests and exploratory surgery, so maybe they'll find out what's wrong with him."

"I hope so," Leslie murmured.

"In the meantime, headquarters sent a fax after we left yesterday about some applicants for the VIRCO positions, and there's also a lot of paperwork that needs Mr. Meredith's signature."

"I'll take them to him at the hospital—I need to talk to him anyway," Leslie said.

Because of the two-hour time difference, it was too early for Leslie to call Arrow/West about the job applicants they'd located, but she added the fax to the sheaf of papers in her briefcase. On her drive to the hospital, Leslie felt an unwelcome edge of frustration. The VIRCO project was supposed to be hers, yet everyone seemed to assume that she'd ask for Mr. Meredith's approval on all major decisions.

*I really can do this on my own,* Leslie tried to tell herself, but she was beginning to wonder.

Leslie finally located Mr. Meredith's private room in the maze of the hospital's corridors and was shocked to see how much worse Mr. Meredith looked than the last time she'd seen him.

"Well, this is a surprise!" he exclaimed when she entered the room. "I suppose my housekeeper must have called Arrow—I didn't want her to do that."

"You know how it is—we couldn't let you have a rest now, could we?" Leslie said lightly.

"I take it there's some business that can't wait," he said.

Leslie nodded. "Mostly just routine, but I also need your advice about staffing."

She opened her briefcase and handed Mr. Meredith the papers needing his signature. Despite his obvious discomfort, he scanned each one to make sure of its contents before signing it. Then Leslie gave him the fax from headquarters. "Mr. Birch said you needed to approve hiring any of these people."

Mr. Meredith looked at the names and nodded. "Pat Wentworth would be a valuable asset to this proposal—get him if you can. And Bob McLaren's a top-notch engineer, so you should make him an offer, too."

"Without a personal interview?" Leslie asked.

"I know the men, and they know what they'll have to do. Call them both today and ask if they can start right away. We're already too far behind in staffing."

Although his tone hadn't accused her, Leslie felt her cheeks warm. "I had a little trouble with some of the Personnel people, but they're cooperating with me now. I think I can wind up the other staffing quickly."

Mr. Meredith nodded. "Good." He gestured toward the hallway. "Close the door, please," he said.

When Leslie returned to his bed, Mr. Meredith handed her the sheaf of papers and waited for her to replace them in her briefcase before he spoke again. "If you hadn't come, I was going to call you later today and remind you of the need for tight security at all points—files, trash, phone calls—the works."

"I hadn't forgotten," Leslie said.

"I hope not. You know that VIRCO is a prime target for all sorts of espionage."

"Yes, you told me that." *Something else must have happened*, she thought and wondered if Andrew Miller had contacted Mr. Meredith.

"It's true. Internal security believes that a move will soon be made to obtain information on our proposal. In case anything suspicious comes up, there's an unlisted number that will directly connect you to the agent in charge of the case."

"Case," Leslie repeated, obviously surprised.

"Apparently someone is under suspicion, but the person who spoke to me couldn't—or wouldn't—tell me anything more. Of course, nothing may come of it," he added unconvincingly. "Give me a piece of paper."

Leslie opened her briefcase and detached one of her new business cards. With her pen, he scrawled a number she didn't recognize. It wasn't the same number Andrew Miller had given her—his was local, while this was an 800 number.

*I wish I could tell Mr. Meredith that I already know about the investigation*, Leslie thought, but Andrew Miller had been quite specific that she was not to tell anyone, including him. There was no doubt in her mind that Mr. Meredith wasn't involved in any way, but she had given the FBI agent her word, and there was no point in further upsetting a sick man, anyway.

Leslie talked briefly of other matters relating to the office. Then seeing that Mr. Meredith was tiring, she rose to leave. "Let us know what the doctors find out," she said.

"I'm almost certain they're planning to carve me up like a Halloween pumpkin—they just haven't told me yet," he said.

Although he smiled, Leslie knew that Mr. Meredith couldn't be looking forward to the impending surgery.

"We'll take care of everything," Leslie said with slightly more confidence than she felt. "Try not to worry about Arrow."

"I won't. But in the meantime, you must promise to call me right away if you run into any trouble."

"Agreed," Leslie said, although she resolved it would take a major catastrophe before she would burden the ill man any further.

Back at Arrow, Leslie reported on Mr. Meredith, gave Sally the signed papers, then returned to her office with the folders that Personnel had just delivered. Quickly she looked through them, searching for Hampton Travis's. The file was suspiciously slender, and when Leslie opened it she saw why. The only thing it held was a note that the resume had been withdrawn at the applicant's request.

Leslie closed her eyes and recalled how she had felt in his arms, and how much she had wanted to return his kiss. Instead, she had told him they couldn't see each other if they worked together. She had been right; just thinking about working with him made her heart race.

Opening her eyes, Leslie put the folder aside and tried to concentrate on the next one, but Hampton's blue eyes seemed to be mocking her as she did so.

*Did he withdraw his application because of me?* she wondered. Or, more likely, she told herself, one of the consulting jobs he was always taking might be growing into a long-term assignment. *But why didn't he tell me he was doing this?*

"I'll just ask him," she said aloud, and rang his number before she could lose her nerve.

Once more a female voice answered, and in response to her query told Leslie that Dr. Travis had asked for his calls to be held until further notice.

"Did he go out of town again?" Leslie asked.

"I can't say," was the reply, and from her tone Leslie guessed that the answering service woman thought Leslie was probably some love-struck female, chasing a handsome man.

"Please have him call Leslie Christopher at Arrow when he checks in," she said, and hung up.

Leslie's hand was still on the receiver when her phone rang, and she took a deep, steadying breath before she answered it.

"I hope you plan to be at home this evening, Miss Christopher," a male voice said.

Although she had only spoken with him one other time, Leslie recognized Andrew Miller's voice and immediately tensed.

"Yes, I'll be home." Leslie wasn't surprised when he hung up without saying more.

*What could he possibly want me to do?* she wondered uneasily. *Something must have happened that I don't know about.*

Then the phone rang again, and for the rest of the day, Leslie had little time to speculate about anything other than her immediate duties. At least that way she didn't have time to worry about either Hampton Travis or the FBI agent—each disturbing in their own way.

❀

After Leslie had spent several restless hours wondering whether Andrew Miller would appear at all, he arrived just after nine o'clock.

"How is Mr. Meredith?" he asked when she admitted him.

"He's probably going to have surgery soon," she said.

"He'll be out of the office for some weeks, then I expect." Andrew Miller began walking around her living room as if inspecting it for clues to some hidden crime, then he sat in a chair and motioned for Leslie to be seated, as well.

"The time has come for you to help us, Miss Christopher," he said. He was almost smiling, an expression that Leslie found even more sinister than his usual stern look. He leaned forward and dropped his voice as he had done before. "Here's what you do..."

Later, when Leslie tried to reconstruct every detail of his visit, she recalled the way he has used the word "must." Not "Here is what we would like you to do...." Not "Here is what you can do to help us..." But "Here is what you must do."

He had told her she might be asked to do things that made no sense, and what Andrew Miller asked her to do certainly seemed to fit that category.

"Is that all?" she asked when he finished, and Andrew Miller permitted himself half a smile.

"For now. Just carry out my instructions and I'll be in touch later."

*But how much later?*

After the agent left, Leslie found herself recalling the warnings that both Hampton and Mr. Meredith had given her. "Be careful," each had said. To her knowledge, no one had appeared to be trying to steal information, but apparently someone might. And Leslie had been chosen to thwart it. It was a dubious honor, at best.

❀

Leslie barely spoke to Sally when she walked past her desk the next morning and made an excuse not to go to lunch with her as they usually did. Never before had she violated even a single security procedure, much less walked out of a secure building with a briefcase full of confidential material. *I'll probably look so guilty I'll be stopped on general principles,* she thought.

But why should she worry if she were? After all, a breach of security would be handled by the FBI, and for all his lack of charm, Special Agent Miller would certainly vouch for her should the need arise. Still, as the day wore on, Leslie found herself dreading the time when she would have to carry out her orders.

"We got a lot done today," Sally said just before five o'clock. "I think we've

187

earned an evening out—dinner and a movie, maybe. How about it?"

"It sounds tempting," Leslie replied truthfully. "But I still have some work to do."

"I'll stay and help. Many hands make light work, as they say."

"Thanks, Sally. I appreciate the offer. But this is something I must do myself."

"Are you sure?" Doubt was written on Sally's face. "I'll wait for you if I can't help. . ."

"No, no," Leslie cut in, too abruptly, she realized. The last thing she wanted was to make Sally suspicious. "It may take awhile. I'll take a rain check, all right?"

"Sure, but remember—Arrow's managers don't get a dime of overtime."

Leslie stayed at her computer terminal for at least fifteen minutes after the last employee departed, then she tried to print out the data she had on VIRCO. When the printer refused to respond, Leslie realized that the sensitive documents couldn't be printed. And the instructions for those procedures were locked in the vault adjacent to Mr. Meredith's office.

Leslie moved cautiously into the corridor, acutely aware of the clicking sound of her heels on the polished tiles. She had made sure that no one was around to see her enter his office or go to the safe-like door that guarded many Arrow secrets. Leslie closed and locked the office door behind her and approached the vault on tiptoe, even though the carpeted floor muffled her steps. She swallowed hard, then put a tentative hand on the dial. Mr. Meredith had told her the combination as soon as she had her clearance and made sure that she could open the vault, close it, and then open it again. He hadn't had to tell her not to write down the combination; she already knew that. But she hadn't worked it since, and Leslie feared that she might not be able to open it on her first try.

"This vault is like an automated bank teller," Mr. Meredith had told her then. "It'll allow you to try to open it twice. The third time, if you still don't have the right numbers, an alarm goes off in Security. They don't like for that to happen."

*Neither would I,* Leslie thought as she twisted the fat metal dial. There were five numbers in the sequence, reset periodically. She didn't think the combination had been changed since Mr. Meredith had gone on sick leave. She would have been told if it had been.

Or would she? Leslie felt perspiration gathering around her forehead and beading on her upper lip as she put in the last number, pulled the handle—nothing happened. She thought she recalled the numbers, which she had memorized by using the first part of the street number of her Los Angeles apartment. Maybe she had just gone past one or more of them.

Once more Leslie tried, so deliberately that she was certain she had hit each number exactly. But as before, the handle didn't yield. Leslie closed her eyes and tried to visualize Mr. Meredith as he had opened the combination. She was almost positive she had the right numbers; maybe she hadn't cleared the combination properly.

Taking a deep breath, Leslie whirled the dial to the left to clear the combination, then to the right for the first number; further right for the next one; past zero to the left for the third; back to the right for the fourth; and to zero once again as the last number. She thought she'd done it perfectly, but at first it seemed the vault wouldn't open that time, either. Leslie was trying to think of a good reason to be found trying to open the vault after hours, anticipating the alarm that was about to sound in Security, when she heard a soft *click* and the handle turned. Quickly she opened the door and began to search for the manual she would need to override her computer.

"Of course it would be in the last place I look," she muttered. Not daring to remove the manual from the vault, Leslie scanned its pages until she found what she needed, then carefully replaced the book in the file, closed the vault door, and twisted the dial one last time.

Again the corridors were empty as Leslie returned to her office and fed the required information to her computer. A few beeps later, the printer responded to her command, and page after page of flow charts and drawings began to print out. At one point she had to stop the process to add more paper, but finally all the information was printed, and with a last double beep, the printer turned itself off. Leslie gathered up the sheets, without bothering to remove the edges. A glance at her watch showed that it was already seven o'clock. Hurriedly she stuffed the printout into her briefcase, only to find she had to remove the other papers before it would fit. Then she locked the briefcase. Leslie knew that Arrow Security guards sometimes asked workers to open their briefcases, but often waved them on if the cases were locked. It didn't make a great deal of sense to Leslie, but then, many things at Arrow seemed illogical.

Leslie looked around her office one last time to make sure she hadn't left anything incriminating. She walked out of the elevator, intensely aware of the rapid beating of her heart. As the elevator descended smoothly to the ground floor, she decided she must lack some character trait that would allow her to enjoy subterfuge and intrigue. *Some people must like it,* she thought as she walked toward the Security station near the front entrance. *Otherwise, where would all the spies come from?*

"Good night," Leslie said to the guard. An older man who looked as if his feet hurt nodded curtly and held the door open for her. Then she was outside, walking down the familiar path in the fall twilight, feeling exactly as she had when she was twelve years old and some kid she had wanted to make friends with had dared her to take something from the corner convenience store. As long as she lived, Leslie would remember how she felt walking out of that store, a candy bar she hadn't paid for heavy in her coat pocket. She hadn't been caught, but the next day she went back and paid for the candy bar, and never again had she tried to make friends that way. She and her parents had moved on soon after, and Leslie had almost forgotten the incident.

Leslie put the briefcase in her trunk, something she rarely did, and drove home carefully, trying not to call attention to herself by breaking any traffic laws. She remembered cases in which a criminal had successfully eluded the police, only to be stopped for some minor driving infraction and thus been captured. She pictured herself in jail, then scolded herself for allowing such thoughts. After all, she was working on the right side of the law, even though appearances might indicate the opposite.

As Leslie retrieved her briefcase, a couple who lived near her in the same building pulled up beside her car, and they exchanged greetings.

"Don't you know better than to bring work home?" the man said.

"This may look like a briefcase, but it's really my lunch box," Leslie said.

"It certainly beats brown bagging," the woman said with a chuckle.

Leslie's smile faded rapidly as she let herself into her apartment. She wanted to sit in the dark and not answer the door or telephone. She wanted to be in Los Angeles, among people she knew and trusted. She wanted to be anywhere else, doing anything other than sitting here in her apartment, waiting for an FBI agent.

Leslie changed into jeans and a soft sweater. Feeling a faint stirring of hunger, she cooked a frozen entrée in her microwave, As she ate, she thought of the contrast between this, her usual evening meal, and the sumptuous feasts Hampton Travis had lavished upon her.

*I shouldn't be thinking of him at a time like this,* Leslie told herself. *Or, for that matter, at any time.* He obviously didn't want to work with her, after all. Or maybe he had gotten a permanent assignment elsewhere and hadn't bothered to tell her. He certainly hadn't bothered to tell her about the brunette—why would he tell her about a change in career plans? The man was illusive, that much she knew. At least Leslie had her work to divert her thoughts.

Leslie sighed and reluctantly turned her attention to her assignment. She unlocked her briefcase and removed the papers she's smuggled out of Arrow. Laying them out on the sofa, she began separating the printout by categories— the time lines, organization charts, preliminary sketches, technical drawings, budget figures—a dozen parts of the preliminary RFP gathered in one place for the first time in its short history. *Gathered legally,* Leslie thought sourly, but then she reminded herself that anything for the FBI couldn't be illegal.

Leslie was still separating the pages when the doorbell rang. Making no effort to conceal the papers, Leslie opened the door without looking through the peephole first.

"Hello—I was hoping I'd catch you at home. Do you have a minute?"

Leslie's mouth flew open in astonishment as Hampton Travis, apparently taking her silence as a consent, walked into her apartment—and headed straight for the sofa and the VIRCO papers.

# Chapter 7

*T*his isn't happening, Leslie tried to tell herself, but she knew quite well that it was.

"What do you think you're doing?" she asked when she could speak again, although it was obvious that he was looking at the VIRCO papers.

"I'm wondering the same thing about you," Hampton said, strangely formal. "I think we need to have a talk."

"Not now, I'm expecting someone." Leslie walked to the sofa and stood in front of it as if to bar him from seeing any more.

"This won't take long. In fact—"

Hampton broke off as the doorbell rang.

*Andrew Miller,* Leslie thought immediately. *He mustn't find Hampton here or know that he saw the papers.*

"I presume that is your guest?"

"Yes." Leslie glanced nervously at the door. "It would be best if he didn't see you here."

"Oh?"

Leslie felt her cheeks warm as Hampton raised his eyebrows in a knowing look. Helpless to correct his impression, Leslie steered Hampton into the kitchen. "You can go out the back door," she said as the doorbell rang again.

"Why do I get the feeling that I'm being thrown out?" he asked as Leslie opened the door and all but pushed him through it.

"Probably because you are. I'm really sorry."

"Maybe I should come back when you're not so busy," he said, but Leslie had already closed the door.

Feeling as if she had weights on her feet, Leslie crossed the living room and admitted Andrew Miller. His sharp glance swept around the apartment before he spoke.

"Are you alone?" he asked. Leslie nodded and vaguely wondered what the penalties for failure to make a full disclosure to a federal agent were.

"It took you long enough to come to the door. Is this all the VIRCO material?" he added when Leslie offered no excuse for her delay in admitting him.

"Yes, all we have so far." Leslie watched as he rifled through the printout.

"No one saw you take them out?" At her nod, he added a muttered, "Good work."

"I still don't know why I had to do this," Leslie said, but the agent was seized with a sudden fit of coughing and did not reply. She watched as he began to examine each of the pages. "Wouldn't it be easier to take the whole printout? I certainly can't keep it around here."

Taking another coughing fit, Miller couldn't speak for a while. Finally he said, "Your computer system knows that classified information has been printed out, and it must be accounted for. Log the printout into the vault until it's time for the next step."

"What next step?" Leslie asked, alarmed that he intended to ask her to do more.

In reply, Miller bent in a convulsion of coughing that made his face even ruddier.

"Are you all right?" Leslie asked as the paroxysm showed no sign of ending.

He pulled out a handkerchief and wiped his brow. "A sip of water might help," he managed to say between more coughs.

"I'll get it right away," Leslie said.

When she returned, Mr. Miller drank the offered glass of water at a single gulp.

"Thank you, Miss Christopher. That helped."

"I believe you were saying something about a next step?"

"Yes. You know our purpose is to find the person responsible for Arrow's security leaks. So far you have very little that would be of value to another company. When will you have more technical figures?"

"I'm not sure," Leslie replied, although she had asked the engineers to submit their preliminary work no later than the following Friday. "Our lead scientists aren't in place yet."

"Then you really are behind," Mr. Miller said.

Once more Leslie tried not to sound defensive. "A little but we'll move much faster when the whole group gets together."

Mr. Miller looked pleased. "Then we'll see who takes the bait."

"What bait?" Leslie asked, not liking the sound of it.

"Just a manner of speaking, Miss Christopher. Your cooperation today indicates that you can be trusted, and for that we thank you. I'll be in touch."

Andrew Miller hadn't been in her apartment for more than a few minutes, but as Leslie closed her door behind him, she'd aged at least a year. Now that he was out of the way, she returned her attention to Hampton Travis. *He'll think I am carrying on a hot romance, shoving him out like that,* she thought with a hint of a smile. Then she wondered why he'd showed up, at night and unannounced, in the first place. Why hadn't he returned her phone call? Furthermore, he'd seen the VIRCO material—certainly not enough to get any detailed information, but close enough to know what it was.

Leslie had just started to put the papers back together when an insistent knock sounded at the back door. Leaving the papers as they were, she let Hampton in.

"Is the coast clear now?" he asked.

"My visitor is gone, as I'm sure you know. What did you do, hide in the shrubs and watch us through your binoculars?"

"That wasn't necessary," he replied. "I don't know why you're so upset—I'm the one who got thrown out."

"I'm sorry. Come in." Deliberately Leslie stacked the VIRCO papers on the end of the sofa, face down. "If I was rude, I'm sorry. This hasn't been a very good day."

"Apology accepted. Now let's start over, shall we?"

"At what point?" Feeling the need to put more distance between them, Leslie took a step backward.

"At the point where I told you you shouldn't have brought those papers home," he said.

"You shouldn't have looked," she said.

Hampton reached for the top page, a staffing flow chart, and the whole stack slid to the floor.

"Wonderful," Leslie muttered. She lunged at the pages, which were quickly scattering over the floor, and made an effort to pick up as many as she could. The papers were now completely out of order, but she didn't care.

"I asked who your visitor was," Hampton said as he bent to retrieve more pages. "If you don't want to tell me, that's your business. But I don't want to see you get hurt."

Leslie felt her face warming again at the implied criticism in Hampton's tone. "I don't intend to. Believe me, this has nothing to do with you. And while we're asking questions, you might tell me why you withdrew your resume."

It was Hampton's turn to look surprised. "You mean you finally got around to considering me for a job?"

"You said you were qualified," Leslie said somewhat stiffly. "I would have considered you for the lead computer robotics slot."

Hampton's eyes twinkled. "That's mighty generous of you, Miss Christopher. Maybe I should've kept myself in the running, after all."

Leslie dared to look him in the eye. "Why didn't you?"

His expression now serious, Hampton returned her gaze. "Be honest—would you really have hired me?"

"I don't know. I suppose it would depend on whether your resume showed that you were qualified."

"Oh, I'm qualified, all right. In fact—well, never mind that. The question is, would you continue seeing me if we were working together?"

Leslie looked away, afraid of what her eyes might tell him. "If we worked together, I'd see you every day, like it or not."

"You know that's not what I mean." Lifting her face with a hand under her chin, Hampton forced her to look at him. "Would you go out with one of your employees socially?"

Leslie shook her head. "No."

Hampton put his arms around Leslie and drew her to him so quickly that, even if she'd wanted to, she had no chance to protest.

"You hardly know me—and I know even less about you," Leslie said.

Hampton pulled back to look at her, then embraced her again. "I know this much," he said just before his lips met hers.

"Oh, Hampton—" Leslie began, but before she could finish, he kissed her again. This time she responded willingly.

"Maybe I should have taken a job to keep an eye on you," Hampton said when he finally released her. "You don't seem to have any idea that you might be in danger."

Leslie's look of surprise was genuine. "I certainly don't," she agreed.

"Then it's time you did. If you ever need help, I hope you'll let me know."

Seeking to lighten the atmosphere between them, Leslie smiled. "If I have to wait for your answering service to find you, I'd probably already be done in," she said somewhat tartly.

Hampton continued holding Leslie, but now he released her and removed a slip of paper from the breast pocket of his jacket. "This is a private number where I can be reached. Use it if the need arises. I have to go now."

Leslie put the paper in her jeans pocket without looking at it and followed Hampton to the front door. "Does that mean you're going to stay in town for a while?" she asked.

Hampton put out his hand to touch her cheek, then traced the line of her eyebrows with his thumb and touched the tip of her nose. "I'd like nothing better, but the people I did my last consult for want a few changes in the final design and it can't be done long distance. I may be around here a few more days, then you can be sure I'll get back as soon as I can."

"I hope so," Leslie found herself admitting as he pulled her into his arms for a kiss that left her breathless.

"Don't forget to use your deadbolt lock," Hampton said. Then he was gone.

*Hampton seems obsessed about my safety,* she thought as she double-locked the door. Compared to Los Angeles, Huntsville was a relatively crime-free haven. However, she was beginning to realize that there might be other hazards here that she hadn't even considered.

*It's nothing to worry about,* Leslie told herself. With one last look at the VIRCO papers, she turned off the living room lights and left the room.

❧

The next morning Leslie felt a little ridiculous as she walked past the security guard, the VIRCO printout safely locked in her briefcase. She chided herself for having been so paranoid the night before. In the light of day, the whole business seemed absurd, much ado about what had turned out to be very little—and she hoped it would stay that way.

When Leslie reached her office, she dumped the printout on her desk and began to put the pages back in order. Now that she had it, she thought she might as well use it, especially since, as Mr. Miller had pointed out, the internal security system would alert Security that it had been printed.

"Hi," Sally said from the doorway. "You're up and at 'em pretty early this morning, aren't you?"

"Or maybe you're late. I'm trying to see the big picture—this is a printout of our work so far," she added as Sally cast a quizzical look at the pile of papers on Leslie's desk.

"It looks like a good jigsaw puzzle. Did you log it in with Security? I'm not sure anyone told you that you needed to do that."

"They didn't," Leslie said, and wondered what else an ill Mr. Meredith might have overlooked telling her or assumed she already knew.

"Then I predict you'll hear from Security shortly. If they complain, you can always plead ignorance."

Leslie smiled. "I could plead that to a lot of things," she replied.

"Don't forget that Pat Wentworth and Bob McLaren are processing in today," Sally added from the door.

"Great—I'll feel much better when I know they're working on this."

But as soon as Sally left, Leslie returned to sorting the papers, wondering why Mr. Miller hadn't warned her to notify Security in the first place. Surely he knew Arrow's procedures. And why did she have to bring it home? Nothing about the whole thing made any sense to her.

Then another problem presented itself as she completed sorting and counting the papers—she was one short.

*I must have missed a page somewhere,* she thought, and counted again. But this time there was no question about it—the page that held the only really critical data she had gathered so far just wasn't there anymore.

Leslie looked in her briefcase and under her desk. She even lifted her desk blotter, but to no avail—the budget page was missing. She thought back to the night before, when both the FBI agent and Hampton had seen the printout. Only Mr. Miller had handled the pages—except, she recalled, when Hampton helped her pick them up after she dropped them. Could he have taken the budget page at that time? Leslie thought it wasn't likely.

*It's probably under the sofa,* she told herself and wished she could go back to her apartment and look for it that very moment. Since she couldn't, Leslie bundled up the printout and locked it in her filing cabinet, awaiting the arrival of Pat Wentworth, who would need to see part of it. She had just slipped her key ring into her purse when Sally rang for her.

"A visitor from Internal Security is on the way to your office now," she warned.

"Thanks," Leslie replied, replacing the receiver as someone rapped lightly on her door. "Come in," she invited, and a young woman in a very red dress entered the office. Leslie noted that her visitor was tall, attractive, brunette—and familiar.

And every single time she had seen her, the woman had been with Hampton Travis.

"Miss Christopher?" she was saying pleasantly, her hand extended for a firm handshake. "I'm Barbara Redmond, from Internal Security."

"Is there a problem?" Leslie asked, deciding that ignorance would be her best defense.

"In a way. It seems that you printed out some sensitive material without first notifying us."

"I didn't know I should," Leslie replied, honestly enough.

"Well, now you do. Here are the proper forms to use the next time you want a printout from the Arrow mainframe. And here's the one to sign today."

Leslie glanced at the heading on the second page and frowned. "This is a Report of Security Violation. Can't I just postdate one of these other forms?"

"I'm afraid that's against the rules. Don't let the title bother you, though—it's really pretty routine."

"Security violations are routine?" Although the woman had made every effort not to appear intimidating or sound threatening, Leslie felt that Security had taken her measure and found her short of the mark.

"Of course not. I can also assure you that this won't affect your job performance rating, Miss Christopher. You're new, and no one explained our procedures. You certainly can't be blamed for not following them."

"It won't happen again. What else should I know that I don't?"

Barbara Redmond looked directly at Leslie. "Most of our security rules are common sense—probably the same ones you had in Los Angeles, except for our extra computer precautions. And you don't, of course, ever leave the building with classified information."

Barbara Redmond's words made Leslie flush guiltily. Her instincts had been correct—she shouldn't have removed the documents. And she wouldn't have, if the FBI agent hadn't practically ordered her to do so. But Leslie couldn't say so without breaking her vow to remain silent. *Maybe this is part of my test,* she thought.

"I've heard that Arrow has some problems with industrial espionage. Do these rules have anything to do with that?" Leslie asked.

"Our security regulations are standard with the aerospace industry," Barbara replied, pointedly evading Leslie's question.

Leslie's intercom buzzed, and Sally announced that Dr. Wentworth had arrived.

"Thank you. Tell him to wait, will you?"

Barbara Redmond stood. "I won't take any more of your time, Miss Christopher. Don't forget to sign that form and send it to me as soon as you can."

She already had her hand on the door when Leslie asked her to wait.

"One more thing—I believe you know a man named Hampton Travis. He had applied to work on VIRCO, but apparently he's changed his mind."

Barbara's expression didn't change, but the way she looked away made Leslie believe there could have been—and might still be—something personal between them. "I haven't seen Dr. Travis lately. I didn't know he'd given up on VIRCO," she said.

*I'm sure you didn't,* Leslie thought, not believing a word. Maybe Leslie hadn't figured out exactly what was going on, but there was a lot more about Hampton Travis than she was about to tell her.

"Good luck with your project," Barbara said in parting.

"And the same to you with security," Leslie rejoined, letting Barbara make of it what she would.

Leslie knew that even though she could try to put them all—Barbara Redmond and Hampton Travis and Andrew Miller—out of her thoughts, they'd soon be back.

One thing was certain—Leslie devoutly hoped that Andrew Miller wouldn't expect her to violate security again.

❦

Back in her first floor office, Barbara Redmond reached for the telephone and leaned forward, speaking quietly when Hampton answered.

"We must talk," she said without any preliminaries.

"How soon?"

"After work today will do—about six o'clock, my place?"

Barbara hung up the telephone and deliberated whether she should cook for him. It'd be safer than going out to eat, she told herself. Already too many people had seen them together.

And it was always pleasant to spend time with Dr. Hampton Travis.

❦

Leslie quickly briefed Pat Wentworth and Bob McLaren, who arrived at almost the same time. She was immensely relieved when they both seemed to know what needed to be done. While she was talking to them, Lowell Birch called to tell her about a retired military officer with many years of experience dealing with complicated systems. VIRCO would need someone with both experience and maturity as they raced to complete their preliminary proposal, and Leslie told him to ask the man to come in to see her as soon as possible.

"I can't believe that Dr. Wentworth is such a hunk," Sally told Leslie when the men left to check in with Personnel. "I was expecting a real computer nerd."

"So much for stereotypes." Leslie smiled, thinking that Hampton Travis was another good example of the folly of pre-judging people—by their occupations or anything else. "For your information, he's also a widower, no children. . ."

"Be still, my heart!" Sally exclaimed dramatically.

"Try not to distract the man too much, at least not before we get this proposal finished."

Sally put on an exaggerated look of one wrongly accused. "You know nothing will keep me from helping you get VIRCO ready. But after hours, he's fair game."

Leslie chuckled, but as she walked back to her office she wondered why she hadn't found Pat Wentworth as attractive as Sally had—in fact, she'd hardly taken notice of his looks at all. Perhaps it was because she'd been more concerned with his academic and scientific credentials to notice. Or maybe it was because something—or someone—else had kept Leslie from thinking of him personally, knowing they'd be working closely together.

*I won't make the same mistake twice*, she told herself, although she still wasn't sure how she could have done anything differently with Hampton.

Hastily eating a sandwich at her desk, Leslie tried to call Mr. Meredith to tell him she had filled all the key positions, only to be told that he'd been taken from his room to be prepped for surgery.

"I just found out that Mr. Meredith's going to be operated on this afternoon. I know he's been concerned about the VIRCO staffing, and maybe knowing it's going well will make him feel better," Leslie told Sally a few minutes later.

Sally looked concerned. "I thought he'd let us know when the surgery was scheduled. I'm glad you're going. Tell him I'm saying a prayer for him."

On her way down in the elevator, Leslie thought of Sally's words. She would pray for him, Sally had said, and Leslie had no reason to doubt it. There was a bond between all people who shared a belief in the power of prayer, and for a moment Leslie felt a sense of loss that she wasn't a part of that close fellowship.

*I suppose I can pray for him in my own way.* On the drive to the hospital, Leslie did just that, and hoped that her awkward efforts had been heard.

The information desk clerk directed Leslie to the surgical waiting room, where she was told that she was too late to see Mr. Meredith. "He's already in surgery. You're welcome to wait with those people over there if you like."

Leslie looked in the direction the clerk indicated and saw half a dozen people sitting off to one corner of the large waiting area, including a young woman she supposed to be Mr. Meredith's daughter and a middle-aged woman whom she guessed was his housekeeper.

Thanking the clerk, Leslie joined the group. "I'm Leslie Christopher—I work for Mr. Meredith at Arrow. We didn't know he was going to be operated on so soon."

"Hello, Miss Chistopher—I'm Alicia Meredith—I'm Mary Gardiner, Mr. Meredith's housekeeper. He's been real worried about y'all at work."

"I know," Leslie said. "I thought it might make him feel better to know that things are going really well now.".

A tall man with silvery white hair smiled and extended his hand to Leslie. "I'm Paul Carew, his pastor. It's good of you to come to the hospital, as busy as I know you must be."

"I wanted to offer what support I could," Leslie said.

Paster Carew introduced Leslie to his wife and another couple from the church. "We were just about to have prayer. Will you join us?" he asked.

Leslie nodded. Everyone stood, forming a loose circle. Alicia Meredith on her right and the pastor's wife on her left reached out to hold Leslie's hands. All bowed their heads and Pastor Carew began to pray, speaking softly and earnestly.

*Why, he's talking to God as if He were right her with us,* Leslie thought with wonder, expecting the pastor's prayer to be more flowery. She'd seldom seen people praying outside of a church, although she'd once had a friend whose family always joined hands around the table for grace before meals.

"Amen," the pastor concluded, and some of the others added their own "amens."

"Will you wait with us, Miss Christopher?" Alicia Meredith asked.

"How long will the surgery take?" Leslie asked.

"The doctor didn't say—just that it depends on what they find when they get started. It could take several hours."

"I'm afraid I have to get back to work," Leslie said regretfully. To her surprise, she found herself wishing that she could stay there and get to know Mr. Meredith's attractive young daughter and experience more of the calming effect the small group seemed to have on her.

"We understand you're new in town, Miss Christopher," Paul Carew said. "We'd be glad to have you visit our church, if you haven't found one here yet."

"Thank you—I'm afraid I've been too busy to do much on weekends," Leslie said.

"Don't put it off—you're missing a great blessing," the pastor's wife said in parting.

On her way back to Arrow, Leslie wondered what it'd be like to be a part of a close-knit group like those church members who had gathered to pray for Mr. Meredith. *Maybe I should have taken Sally up on her invitation,* she thought.

But for the time being, Leslie had other things on her mind—like the whereabouts of the missing printout page. Even the news, several hours later, that Mr. Meredith had come through complicated stomach surgery in good condition only lifted her spirits temporarily.

"I suppose your prayers worked," Leslie said to Sally after hearing the news.

"Prayer always does," Sally replied.

*Maybe I should ask for divine assistance in finding that pesky missing page,* Leslie thought, but she was sure that God didn't care about petty problems like hers.

# Chapter 8

When she reached her apartment in the semidarkness of the early November evening, Leslie pulled the drapes, turned on every light in the living room, and began to search for the missing budget page. She got down on her hands and knees to look under the sofa. Then she moved the drapes aside, picked up every chair and sofa cushion, and emptied the wastebasket—although she knew the missing page wasn't likely to be there. Nowhere did she find it. What she sought simply wasn't in the apartment. And it wasn't at Arrow, either.

Leslie collapsed on the sofa and tried to decide what she should do. It would be no problem to print out the missing page, now that she knew what hoops she must jump through to do so. But if the page could have been taken by someone intent on selling the information to a competing company, she had a duty to report its loss.

*I suppose I have to tell Andrew Miller,* she acknowledged—she really had no other choice. But before she did, Leslie resolved to confront Hampton directly about the matter. If she could see his eyes when she asked him about it, she'd know if he'd taken the page or not.

Past that point, Leslie refused to think.

❦

"I didn't know that cooking was one of your talents, Miss Redmond," Hampton Travis said that evening as Barbara Redmond set plates of lasagna and salad before him.

"I always heard that the way to a man's heart was through his stomach," Barbara replied with light sarcasm.

"No, really, what's the inspiration for this sudden burst of culinary activity? I thought you were strictly a dine-out or take-out cook."

Barbara's tone was all business. "We shouldn't be seen together again."

"Oh? What happened?"

"I saw Leslie Christoper today about a security violation and she asked me if I knew you. She must have seen us together at the restaurant or the other night at the ice cream parlor."

"What security violation?"

Barbara told Hampton about the printout, and he nodded. "I saw it last night. She brought it home with her."

"And?" Barbara prompted, nettled that Hampton never seemed willing to share all he knew with her, even though they were supposed to be working together.

"And probably showed it to somebody."

"Just somebody? You don't know who?" Barbara sounded incredulous.

"No, I'd just gotten to her apartment last night when someone she didn't want me to see rang the doorbell and she pushed me out the back door. I tried to trail him when he came out, but the Willows' security guard had other ideas."

"How awful!" Barbara said, although her smile showed a certain amount of amusement at Hampton's discomfort. "You didn't get anything on him at all?"

"I could tell he was a large man, but it was too dark to see his face. I'd think it might have been her boss, if he weren't in the hospital—he was about the same height as Richard Meredith."

"What are we going to do now?"

"Wait and see what Les—Miss Christopher does. The material she had there last night wouldn't be important enough for anyone to risk passing on. When she can come up with something that is, they'll make their move."

"What do you want me to do?"

"Watch the printout requests and call me immediately when she does another run. And let me know who she's hired for the head scientist slot."

"It'd be a lot simpler if it could have been you. I still don't see why you pulled back from it."

"You know how often I've been called away lately—those absences would be hard to justify."

"Maybe, but I think you had other reasons as well. What about the man who was at her apartment last night?"

"I have a hunch he's either our man or that he'll lead us to the one who is. I think it's time to let the feds in on what's happening."

❀

While Leslie ate her solitary supper, she considered what she'd say to Hampton when she called him. She didn't dare ask him to come to her apartment; it'd be better to meet him in public, broad daylight, so he couldn't construe it as an invitation for him to kiss her again. As much as she had enjoyed it, Leslie knew there was no place in her life for that kind of relationship now—especially with a man who could be more interested in VIRCO's secrets than in her.

Leslie called the number she had always used for Hampton and, as usual, got his answering service. Hanging up without leaving a message, she found the "private" number he'd given her in the pocket of her jeans she'd worn the night before. Leslie let the phone ring many times, but there was no answer.

*Typical,* Leslie thought as she replaced the receiver. Hampton had said he wanted to help her, then he disappeared. *Well, I can always try later,* she thought—but it was a good thing she wasn't depending on him for immediate help.

❦

It was nearly ten o'clock by the time Hampton returned to his apartment. He hadn't intended to stay at Barbara's so long, but they had seemed to have an unusual number of things to discuss, and the time had passed very quickly. The food had been surprisingly good, too—a pleasant change for Hampton, accustomed to quick bachelor meals eaten out or made in the apartment with the aid of his major staples—a microwave oven and can opener.

*A man could grow to like that,* he thought, but it wasn't Barbara Redmond he envisioned in his kitchen. Could Leslie cook? Hampton didn't know—nor did he care. Staying away from her for the next few days wouldn't be easy.

The telephone rang, and Hampton sighed, took a deep breath, and answered it in his usual way. "Travis speaking."

"Hampton, this is Leslie. I know it's late, but I called earlier and got no answer."

"Leslie! I just got in. Are you all right?"

"Yes, but I need to talk to you. Can you meet me in the Arrow cafeteria tomorrow around eleven?"

"I suppose so," he said, quickly thinking of ways to rearrange his schedule. "What's this about?"

There was a pause, then she said, "I can't tell you now."

"All right. I'll be there."

Leslie thanked him and hung up, leaving Hmpton to wonder what she wanted. Whatever it was, he was glad he'd see her again so soon.

❦

In the lull between the coffee break and lunch hour, the Arrow cafeteria was usually deserted. When Leslie arrived the next morning, Hampton was already seated at a small table near the rear, the only occupant of the vast room.

"Am I late?" she asked as he stood and pulled out her chair.

"No. I was so eager to see you I got here early. Can I get you a coffee?"

"Yes, please." While Hampton was gone Leslie moved her chair slightly so she'd be seated exactly opposite him. She wanted to see the look in his eyes when she confronted him.

"Here you are," he said, setting an old-fashioned white china mug before her. "But be careful—Arrow's brew packs quite a jolt."

"In Los Angeles they claimed that the first rocket fuel was the scientists' coffee," Leslie said, smiling at the memory.

"Do you ever wish you were still in Los Angeles?"

"No, I've been so busy here I really haven't had any time for regrets."

"I'm glad you feel that way. You certainly seem to be doing a good job."

Leslie looked down at her coffee in an effort to stifle the emotions that the look in Hampton's eyes were stirring in her. "That's part of why I wanted to see you today. I need to ask you something related to my job."

"Fire away," Hampton said pleasantly.

Leslie raised her head and stared into his blue eyes. "A page is missing from my VIRCO printout. Did you take it?"

For a moment Hampton resembled a statue frozen in time, his coffee cup suspended near his mouth, his eyes staring back into hers with shocked surprise. Then he looked away as he set his cup down on the table without drinking from it. "What makes you ask?"

"You were there. You handled it."

"Therefore I must be guilty."

"You haven't answered me," Leslie said, her cheeks warming. "A simple yes or no will do."

"I don't suppose pleading the Fifth Amendment would help, would it?"

"Not if you've aready incriminated yourself."

"Have I done that?" Hampton's eyes locked on hers, his message clear. "No, Miss Christopher, I didn't take anything from your printout."

Leslie looked at him closely and sighed, wondering how much her wanting to believe him inclined her to accept his denial. "Are you positive? Maybe a page fell into your coat pocket when you helped me pick them up?"

Hampton patted his pockets. "Nope, there's nothing here but an old parking ticket," he said, opening his pockets for her inspection.

"All right, I believe you. But I don't see how it could have just disappeared into thin air."

"Was the page so important? Surely you must have some kind of backup."

"It's not that," Leslie began, then stopped. If she said more, she would be getting into sensitive areas she couldn't discuss.

"I don't have it, but I have a good idea who might."

Leslie looked at Hampton closely. "Who?"

"I wasn't your only visitor the other night. You might ask that other person about your missing page."

Leslie glanced at her wristwatch and stood. "I must get back to the office. I'm sorry if I was rude."

Hampton chuckled. "I'm not sure that 'rude' covers being accused of larceny. But I hope you find whatever it is that you lost."

At the cafeteria entrance, Leslie offered her hand. "Thanks for coming here," she said formally.

"The pleasure was mine, Miss Christopher," Hampton said. He took her hand in both of his instead of shaking it. "If you need me, you know how to reach me."

Leslie watched Hampton turn in his visitor's badge, and with a last wave in her direction, he left the building. She was almost positive that he hadn't taken the page, but it hadn't reappeared, nor was it likely to. Leslie supposed she had no choice but to report the loss to the FBI.

The number that Agent Miller had given her and warned her not to write down rang so many times that Leslie almost hung up when she heard the click of the connection. "Hello."

"This is Leslie Christopher. I think there might be a problem."

"I'll see you at six," he said and hung up.

※

Andrew Miller was punctual as usual, and as usual he appeared to search the apartment before he spoke.

"What's this all about, Miss Christopher?"

"A page of my VIRCO printout is missing."

Miller frowned his displeasure. "Missing! How could you be so careless?"

"I wasn't careless," Leslie said, unexpectedly put on the defense. "I had it the night you were here, and the next morning it was gone. I've looked here and at the office, and it's definitely not in either place."

"Who else saw it?"

"Some of my office staff—but that was after I took it back."

"There was no one else?" he asked, and Leslie lowered her eyes under his searching gaze.

"There was one other person—a man saw the printout from across the room, but I don't think he took anything."

"Ah." Miller brought out the now-familiar notebook. He wet his lips as he asked for the visitor's name.

"Hampton Travis," she forced herself to say.

"Travis!" he exclaimed, frowning. "I should have known."

"What will you do now?" Leslie asked, not liking Miller's expression.

"For now nothing. He won't be able to make much of the budget's figures yet. But in a little while, after more comes in, we'll make our move. And this time, we'll catch him."

"Surely you can't think that Hampton Travis is the Arrow leak—he hasn't worked there in ages."

Miller frowned and shook his head. "Let us worry about that, young lady."

"I want nothing to do with entrapment," Leslie said firmly.

"I'm afraid you have no choice—you can't quit now. I'm sure you wouldn't want to wind up with a reprimand on your record for violating security, would you?"

"No, but I don't like this. I'm not suited for intrigue."

Miller chuckled as if she'd told him an especially good joke. "You have no idea just how ideally suited you are for this job. I'll be in touch."

Leslie closed the door behind him and leaned against it, a feeling of dread knotting in her stomach. What damage had she already done to Hampton—and what more did Miller expect her do?

Then with almost physical force, Leslie recalled the agent's comment about the budget figures. *I didn't tell him what page was missing,* she realized. *Did he know, or was it just a lucky guess?*

Leslie sat down hard in the nearest chair and put her head in her hands. Something was not right about this whole business, but she couldn't put her finger on exactly what. *I need Mr. Meredith's advice,* she thought, and wished that his surgery could have been postponed until after the VIRCO proposal had been safely submitted.

Leslie glanced at her watch and noted she still had time to get to the hospital before the end of visiting hours. *It won't hurt anything for me to go see him,* she told herself as she slung her purse over her shoulder and started out the door. At the least, she had good news to report about VIRCO staffing. At the most, if her boss seemed up to it, she would tell him about Andrew Miller.

Leslie found Richard Meredith sitting up in bed in his flower-filled room, watching a television documentary about a recent Space Shuttle launch. His daughter immediately rose to offer Leslie her chair.

"I was just about to leave anyway," Alicia said.

"How is the patient?" Leslie asked.

His pallor and pinched look indicated that he was still in considerable pain, but Mr. Meredith made an effort to smile. 'Patient' is a good word for it, I suppose. I'm ready to start feeling better any minute now, starting yesterday."

"The doctor says he really needed the surgery, Miss Christopher," his daughter said. "Dad just doesn't know how to be sick."

"Does anyone ever know how?" he asked wryly.

"When do you have to go back to school?" Leslie asked, aware that Alicia Meredith must already have missed quite a few of her college classes.

"In a few days," Alicia replied. "My profs have been quite understanding, but I don't dare push their generosity much further." She turned to her father and smiled, touching his hand. "I really do need to say good night, Dad. I'll be back tomorrow."

"It's nice to see you again," Leslie said. "Good luck on making up your work."

"I don't believe in luck," Mr. Meredith said as his daughter left the room. "Or rather, I suppose I should say I believe we make our own luck by working hard."

"Quite true," Leslie agreed, "and everyone in Special Projects has been doing just that on VIRCO." Briefly, Leslie sketched the progress she'd made in staffing, and Mr. Meredith nodded, looking pleased.

"I'm sorry I haven't been able to help, but it sounds as if you have everything under control," he said.

"Well, almost everything." Leslie paused, unsure how to broach what might be a very painful subject.

"Now what?" he asked, and Leslie searched for the best way to tell him what had happened.

"I think the FBI is about to ask me to help catch a possible security leak in the company," she said. "I'm not looking forward to it."

Mr. Meredith closed his eyes for a moment, and Leslie feared that she had upset him. But when he opened them, his whole appearance seemed more alert. "Don't worry about it. These people know what they're doing, and we've needed to catch whoever has been betraying Arrow's confidences. I'm just sorry I can't be there to help."

"Then I should do whatever they ask me to do, even if I don't understand why?"

A half-smile crossed his face, then Richard Meredith sighed. "Ours is not to reason why," he quoted. "Who knows, you might even get a promotion if this works out."

*I don't want a promotion,* Leslie thought, *I just want to be out of the counter-espionage business and for Hampton Travis to be cleared.*

"I can see you're tired," she said aloud. "I won't bother you any further with business."

"It's no bother," Mr. Meredith said. "By the way, Alicia told me that you were here during my surgery. I really appreciate that."

"If we'd known when it was going to be, more of us would have come. When I left Arrow, Sally wanted me to tell you she was praying for you."

Mr. Meredith nodded. "A lot of people were. Thank Sally and tell her I still need all the prayers I can get. I'm afraid I'm not out of the woods yet."

On her way out, Leslie stopped at the nurses' station and asked when Mr. Meredith would be discharged.

"That depends on how well he does," was the noncommittal answer.

"A few days, a few weeks, what is usual?" Leslie persisted.

"Probably no less than a week, providing all goes well. Mr. Meredith's doctor will make that decision."

Put in her place by the nurse's tone, Leslie thanked her and left, feeling no better about her relationship with the FBI than she had before.

❀

Leslie glanced at the timeline she had taped to her office wall, knowing all too well that her time was running out. It would take many workers' expertise and energy—and Leslie's wise management—to put the pieces together by the NASA deadline. She only hoped that she could work without any more distractions—from Andrew Miller or Hampton Travis or anyone else—and accomplish what everyone expected of her.

At the weekly staff meeting Leslie looked around the room and wondered how many of the VIRCO team doubted her ability to manage Arrow's bid, particularly in the absence of the Special Projects chief. But if they had any doubts, they kept them unvoiced. The newest members of the team seemed to be working well with the others. Without telling them that someone in the Arrow organization might possibly be selling information to others, she stressed the need for continuing tight security.

"I learned the hard way that we can't even print out documents without the security system finding out," she said, using her own case to let them know how seriously security breaches, even innocent ones, were taken.

Everyone seemed to accept the need for the tightened security, and Leslie was satisfied that her VIRCO team was completely loyal. If someone was selling information—and Leslie still wasn't convinced that was the case—it certainly wasn't anyone on her staff.

Leslie concluded the meeting punctually on the hour, and as the others filed out, she felt as tired as if she had been doing hard physical labor all morning.

"How about a cup of coffee?" Sally asked. "You look beat."

"I feel that way, too, but I need more than coffee at this point. I think I'll just sit here awhile and try to collect my wits."

"All right. Shall I hold your calls?"

"Yes, unless it's an emergency."

After Sally left, Leslie kicked off her high heels, leaned back in her swivel chair, propped her feet on the table, and closed her eyes. She had rested that way only a short while when Sally came back into the conference room.

"I'm sorry, but you have a caller that won't take no for an answer."

"Who is it?" Leslie eyes flew open, and her heart began to beat faster as she imagined that Andrew Miller was about to ask her to do something more for the FBI.

"I don't know, but he insisted that you'd want to talk to him. Shall I transfer the call here?"

"No. I have to go back to my office sooner or later," Leslie said. "I'll take it there."

A short time later Leslie picked up her desk phone, steeling herself for Andrew Miller's voice. "Leslie Christopher," she said crisply.

"Sorry to bother you at work, but I wondered if you'd found that lost item."

Surprised that Hampton Travis would call her at Arrow, Leslie tried not to show it. "Why do you ask?"

"I knew you were worried about it. I thought perhaps you'd taken my advice."

"What about?" Leslie asked.

"Asking the other party about the missing item."

"It's really none of your business, Dr. Travis," Leslie said. On the other end of the line, Hampton chuckled, but his tone was serious when he spoke again.

"So you say." He paused for a moment. "I'm going to be tied up here for a while longer, and there's a telephone number I want to give you."

"What kind of number?" Leslie asked. In the background she could hear the hum of machinery, and she realized Hampton must be calling from wherever he was working.

"It's a private emergency line to the local FBI office. Do you have something to write with?"

Leslie nodded and reached for a pen, then realized that Hampton couldn't see the gesture. "Yes. But I don't understand—"

"Never mind," he said brusquely. "This is a toll-free call, so it's got a lot of digits." He read out the number, then made her repeat it. As she did so, Leslie heard someone calling Hampton's name.

"I've got to run," he said. "I'll contact you the minute I get back. Try to stay out of trouble until then, will you?"

Without waiting for her to reply, he hung up. Leslie imagined him working on someone's else's problems and sighed. *I wish Hampton had stayed here,* she thought. The number he had given her was familiar, Leslie thought as she tucked it into her skirt pocket. Then she remembered—it was the same number Mr. Meredith had given her.

*Every man I meet seems obsessed with giving me a telephone number,* she thought. And it was certainly ironic that both Mr. Meredith and Hampton had given her the same telephone for the FBI, when she was already working for one of their agents.

After sitting for a moment thinking about the look in Hampton's blue eyes the last time she had seen him, Leslie buzzed Sally.

"I ought to report you," she said accusingly.

"Whatever for?" Sally asked with offended innocence. "He said he was a personal friend, and I thought maybe he'd ask you out. You've been pretty down all week, you know."

"He can't—he's working out of town."

"Oh," Sally said, obviously disappointed. "He has a great phone voice, though. Since he's not available, how about coming to my house tomorrow night for a potluck supper?"

Leslie almost immediately said no automatically, but something told her not to miss this one. *I need to keep busy,* she thought. And if she wasn't at home, Andrew Miller couldn't contact her.

"All right, but what's potluck, and when do you want me there?" she asked.

Sally laughed. "They don't have dinners in California where everyone brings something to share? Sometimes it's called a 'covered-dish'—but you don't have to bring anything—just be at my house about six thirty."

*It sounds awful,* Leslie thought, but after she had agreed to go, she found that she was almost looking forward to it.

# Chapter 9

Told to dress casually, Leslie chose black stirrup slacks, worn with flats and a long blue cotton sweater top. Despite Sally's admonition not to bring anything, she had stopped at a bakery for whole wheat rolls. It was fully dark by the time Leslie finally found Sally's address in the maze of a subdivision. To her surprise, more than a dozen cars were already there, and Leslie had to park three houses down.

*I probably shouldn't be doing this,* she thought as she rang the bell. But when Sally appeared, wearing an old-fashioned, bib-topped apron, her welcome smile made Leslie feel more at ease.

"Oh, thank you for bringing the rolls—one of the gals that was bringing bread couldn't come at the last minute, so this is just what we needed. Dale, Harriet—come here and meet Leslie Christopher, from Arrow."

Dale turned out to be a director at Marshall Space Flight Center, the NASA facility in Huntsville. Harriet was about Leslie's age with the kind of face that seemed plain until she smiled, lighting up the entire room.

"I've heard a lot about you, Leslie," Harriet said. "We've been trying to get Sally to bring you to our class."

"Class?" Leslie repeated.

"The singles Bible study group at Glenview," Dale said.

"Of course you'd have to listen to me, but that part doesn't last too long."

"Don't let him fool you—he's the best Bible teacher I ever met."

*Bible teacher—Glenview.* Now understanding what Sally had gotten her into, Leslie looked around, prepared to glare at her, but she'd disappeared.

"Come and meet the others," Harriet said, taking Leslie's hand. In short order she met two teachers, three engineers, a real estate agent, a couple of women who identified themselves as homemakers, a reference librarian, and a doctor.

"Someone who can really fix what ails you, not a scientist," Dale added as he made the final introduction.

Despite her initial misgivings, Leslie soon felt almost as if she had known these people forever. And when they joined hands as Dale said a prayer of thanks for the food, Leslie felt a strange warmth that she'd seldom known before.

"Aren't you glad you came tonight?" Sally asked when, after helping clean up in the kitchen, Leslie prepared to leave.

"Yes," Leslie admitted. "Although you did sort of get me here on false pretenses."

"I didn't mean to," Sally said. "I just thought if you knew some of our group you'd feel more comfortable about coming to Glenview on Sunday morning."

"Oh, I'm going to do that, too, am I?" Leslie asked.

"I hope so." Sally put a hand lightly on Leslie's arm. "You've done very well in your job, but I know something's been troubling you lately. Maybe you can't tell me about it, but whatever it is, God is always there to anchor you. I think you'll feel that at Glenview."

"We all have our bad days," Leslie murmured. More than once she had wished she could confide in Sally, but she had never seriously considered doing so. Even if she hadn't promised to keep silent, it wouldn't have been fair to burden anyone else with her worries.

Sally laughed ruefully and shook her head. "Bad day! I had bad weeks and bad months, until I realized that all my crying and blaming God for Jeff's death wouldn't bring him back. The people at Glenview almost literally dragged me to the singles class—but connecting with it is the best thing that's happened to me since I lost Jeff."

"They do seem to be a caring group," Leslie said.

Sally nodded. "Yes, and you'll meet even more of the class Sunday morning. The ones here tonight are in my interest group—there are many others. Some are younger and some are older, widowed, divorced, or never married—we've got them all."

"I'm not looking for a husband," Leslie reminded Sally.

"Neither are most of the Glenview singles, including me," Sally said. "Of course, there've been several weddings, but that's not what it's about."

"I'm not looking for a church, either."

"No obligation," Sally assured her. "We meet at nine thirty every Sunday."

"Glenview's that big round church over in the valley, isn't it?"

Sally nodded. "The same. Be ready at nine fifteen—I'll come by for you."

"That sounds like an order," Leslie said.

Sally smiled. "At Arrow, you're always my boss. On the weekends—"

"I still do what I like," Leslie said. "Thanks, Sally. I'll see you Sunday, then."

Leslie worked all day on Saturday, cleaning her apartment and doing her laundry. She hoped that Hampton would call and feared that Andrew Miller might instead, but the telephone never rang all day. After she had washed her hair and gotten ready for bed, Leslie wished she hadn't been so quick to say that she'd go to Sally's church. It had been years since she'd attended a regular church service, and the memories she had of them were not pleasant.

But Leslie had agreed to go, and she wouldn't go back on her word.

❧

Whatever Leslie might have thought about Glenview, its reality far surpassed her imagination. The church was huge, yet everyone seemed to know everyone else, or greeted them as if they did, anyway. The singles class members wore ID badges—"Just like at work," Sally joked as she pinned Leslie's to her suit lapel. And while she recognized a few faces from Friday night, most there were new to her.

After a brief fellowship time with coffee, Dale came forward to lead the group in prayer, after which he opened his Bible and began to read Psalm 121. Leslie hadn't thought to bring her own Bible—which she'd moved from California and put away in her bookcase—so she looked on with Sally.

" 'I will lift up mine eyes unto the hills, from whence cometh my help. My help cometh from the Lord, which made heaven and earth. He will not suffer thy foot to be moved; he that keepeth Israel shall neither slumber nor sleep. The Lord is thy keeper: the Lord is thy shade upon they right hand. The sun shall not smite thee by day, nor they moon by night.

" 'The Lord shall preserve thee from all evil: he shall preserve thy soul. The Lord shall preserve thy going out and thy coming in from this time forth, and even for evermore.' "

Leslie recalled Hampton's comment that people had always thought that God lived on mountaintops. Certainly the beauty of the mountains that formed the backdrop for the city was proof of the magnificence of God's creation.

Keeping the book open on his knees, Dale began talking about the historical background of the psalm and the trust the verses expressed. He told them about some times in his life when had had to learn to rely on God's protection and asked those in the group who had similar experiences to share theirs as well. Soon nearly everyone had joined in a lively discussion of the psalm's application to modern life.

Intellectually, Leslie understood what they were saying, but in her heart she had doubts. How could the Lord preserve anyone from evil when they still had to live in an evil world? *Things must have been different in those long-ago times,* Leslie concluded.

The Bible study hour ended, and Sally ushered Leslie into the huge circular sanctuary. "I always sit here—force of habit, I suppose," Sally said when they were settled in a pew near the front of the church.

"It's so big," Leslie said, watching as a robed choir filed into a loft behind the raised pulpit platform.

"Wait until you hear the acoustics—they're first-rate."

Then the minister entered, and with a shock Leslie realized it was the man who'd prayed for Mr. Meredith in the hospital. "I didn't know Mr. Meredith was a member of this church," she whispered to Sally, who merely nodded in reply.

The music—provided by choir, piano, organ, and a small orchestra—soared to the round dome of the sanctuary, and when a young couple sang a duet to a taped accompaniment, Leslie felt chills march up and down her spine. For the sermon, coincidently or not, the pastor also chose a text from Psalms. As he read it, Leslie was reminded of the time she heard Hampton quote some of the same words.

" 'O Lord, our Lord, how excellent is thy name in all the earth! who hast set thy glory above the heavens. Out of the mouth of babes and sucklings thou hast ordained strength because of thine enemies, that thou mightest still the enemy and the avenger. When I consider thy heavens, the work of thy fingers, the moon and the stars, which thou hast ordained; what is man that thou art mindful of him? and the son of man, that thou visitest him?' "

A tide of emotion washed over Leslie, and fervently she wished that Hampton could be there with her to hear the very words he had once quoted to her. In this place, it almost seemed that she could sense the presence of God near her.

*Help me, God,* she began. Past that, Leslie hardly knew what to say. She tried to follow the pastor's words but often found her mind wandering, anticipating with dread what lay in store for her in the days ahead.

*Perhaps there's some measure of comfort to be found in a church, but these people have nothing to do with me,* she told herself, and deliberately Leslie resolved not to give in to the strange new emotion she felt while the choir sang softly during the altar call.

Outside in the bright, cold November sunshine, Leslie blinked as if she were awakening from a dream and assured Sally she had enjoyed the services.

"Next Sunday you can come on your own, now that you know where it is," Sally said when she let her out at the Willows.

"Yes," Leslie agreed, although she had already decided not to make a habit of churchgoing—at least not until the VIRCO business was straightened out.

*Then maybe I can have a real life,* she told herself.

❧

A large portion of the VIRCO proposal came together in the next week as Leslie worked nonstop coordinating, delegating, and checking all the details.

Leslie has menacing dreams about the FBI agent. And as the days passed, she wished he would go ahead and assign her final task and have done with it. She found herself startling nervously when the telephone rang, expecting each time that Andrew Miller was calling to say it was time to set the trap.

The most critical period would be the week before the proposals were sent to NASA, when there was still time to alter them before the pages and pages of documents were finally printed and bound in the manner prescribed by the Request for Proposal. At last the end was in sight. Except for a few of the more complicated engineering studies and graphics, the proposal was basically finished. And still she hadn't been contacted by Andrew Miller. But just after lunch the next Friday Sally buzzed her on the intercom.

"An FBI agent is on his way to your office. Quick, hide the evidence!"

"I hope he can't hear you," Leslie said, aware that Sally would never say such a thing if the agent hadn't been well out of earshot.

Leslie was surprised that Andrew Miller would come to her office, since he had made such a point to stay away from it before. But she had an even bigger surprise when she opened her office door.

"Miss Christopher? I'm Jack Taylor," he said, displaying his badge. "We met when I ran your security check."

"Yes, I remember. Please have a seat." Leslie sat behind her desk and waited for him to state his business.

"I've been asked to check out a possible security leak here at Arrow, and I think you can help."

"Security leak?" Leslie hoped she didn't sound as dazed as she felt.

"Yes. Mr. Meredith may have mentioned it—I discussed it with him earlier and neither of us thought there was enough evidence to take more drastic measures—until now."

Mr. Taylor stopped talking and regarded Leslie as if he expected some response to what he had told her.

"What sort of security leak?"

"We're not sure, and that's where you come in. We know that you printed out a preliminary report on the VIRCO proposal and took it to your apartment. We believe that someone asked you to do it, and that a part of the material you brought home turned up missing. Is that correct?"

*He doesn't need to ask,* Leslie thought, certain that her face betrayed her consternation. She nodded.

"Would you like to tell me about it?" he asked, sounding like a counselor trying to soothe a troubled patient.

"I didn't want to do it—I always felt something wasn't right about it. But the FBI asked me, and the agent made it clear I was expected to help."

"The FBI? I can assure you that you weren't dealing with any of our agents."

Leslie felt as if she had been physically struck. *How could I have been so stupid?* She forced herself to speak. "He had a badge just like yours. I had no way of knowing—"

"What name did he use?"

"Andrew Miller. I suppose that's probably as phony as his badge."

"What does he look like?" he asked, making notes as she spoke.

"He's a short and stocky man with a ruddy complexion—maybe five-eight, around two hundred pounds, I'd say—middle-aged. His hair is light brown, and thinning on top."

"That's an unusually good description. Do you know where he lives?"

"No, but he gave me a phone number where I could call him. I used it once."

"Do you remember it" he asked, and Leslie repeated it.

"Excellent! When did you last see this man?"

"The night after I brought home the printout. When I couldn't find the other page I called Mr. Miller to tell him it was missing, and he came over."

"Has he contacted you since then?"

"No, but he said he'd be in touch before our proposal went out. He said I'd have to do one last thing so the FBI could catch whoever was leaking information."

"Do you know what he'll ask you to do?"

Leslie shook her head. "I assume it would have to do with printing out some of the key parts of our proposal. He said something about using it as bait."

"Bait, indeed!" Jack Taylor slapped the notebook against his hand as he closed it.

"Will you arrest him now?"

Jack Taylor shook his head. "No. All he could be charged with now is impersonating a federal agent, and that's not enough. We want to catch him accepting Arrow documents."

"How will you do that?"

"With your help, I hope, Miss Christopher."

"That's what Mr. Miller said, and I was stupid enough to be taken in by it. Why would I make the same mistake twice?"

"You thought you were doing the right thing then—that doesn't matter. Now you have the chance to help your company and put away a criminal at the same time."

"What do I have to do?" Leslie asked, feeling suddenly chilled.

"When he contacts you, go along with whatever he suggests. All you have to do is meet with him. We'll take care of the rest."

"It seems that I've heard that before, too. What if something goes wrong and he passes our material to someone else before you can arrest him? We could very well lose the right to compete for this contract."

"Make up some of the material—real enough so that he won't be suspicious, yet fake enough so that Arrow's real proposal wouldn't be affected if it should fall into the wrong hands—which of course won't happen, anyway. Will you do this for us?"

Leslie was silent for a moment, then she sighed and shrugged. "Yes, but I must tell you that I don't look forward to it at all."

For the first time, the agent smiled. "I'd be worried about your sanity if you did. Here, take this," he added as he stood. He handed her a standard business card bearing two phone numbers. "If I'm out of the office, the second one is my beeper number."

"I just hope he contacts me soon. I want this business to be finished."

"Of course you do," he said sympathetically. "And one other thing," Jack Taylor added from the doorway. "No one else is to know about this."

In spite of herself, Leslie laughed. "You FBI agents are all alike," she said, surprised that she could salvage any glimmer of humor from the situtation. "That's exactly what Andrew Miller—or whoever he is—told me."

"I'm glad you can still smile. It won't be much longer now—try not to worry. And call me the moment you hear from him, day or night."

"I will," Leslie promised.

As she closed the door after Jack Taylor, Leslie leaned against it for a moment, her anger growing stronger as she thought of the way she had let the man who called himself Andrew Miller take her in.

Then another thought came to her mind. How did Jack Taylor find out about it? Only one person could have pieced together what had happened—*Hampton Travis.*

She should have asked Jack Taylor about him, she thought as she sat back down at her desk. Hampton must be involved in some way, but how?

Leslie found it hard to focus her attention on the figures she was supposed to be reviewing. They swam before her eyes, then cleared as another name came to her mind. Barbara Redmond! She seen the Arrow security worker with Hampton several times, and Barbara knew that Leslie had made the printout. Hampton no doubt had told Barbara he'd seen it, and she must have passed the information to Jack Taylor.

Where Hampton fit into the whole business Leslie didn't know, but she dismissed any idea that he might be the security leak that Arrow had asked the FBI to find.

Who was Andrew Miller, really? Leslie thought that Jack Taylor should have no trouble identifying him from the information she had furnished—and she dearly hoped that he would get what he deserved.

*If I knew how to, I'd pray that this whole business would end soon,* Leslie thought.

🌼

Later that day, Leslie had just finished proofreading the first portion of the proposal when she finally received the call she had both hoped for and dreaded.

"Will you be at home about nine this evening?" the man who called himself Andrew Miller asked.

"Yes," Leslie replied, trying very hard to sound normal.

He hung up without saying anything further, and Leslie immediately called Jack Taylor's office number.

"This is Leslie Christopher. Andrew Miller is coming to my apartment at nine o'clock tonight."

"Did he ask you to bring anything home?"

"No. He'll probably tell what he wants tonight. Have you found out who he is really is?"

"Not yet, but we're working on it."

"I hope I can pull this off without telling that slug what I think of him."

"I'm sure you can. The less you say to him, the better. We'll be in the vicinity, watching. When he leaves, I'll knock four times on your apartment door. And by the way, don't use your home phone to call us—it might be bugged."

"Surely you're not serious!"

"We haven't had a chance to check it out yet, but as slick as this operator is, it's a distinct possibility."

"Just like in the spy novels," Leslie said without enthusiasm.

Jack Taylor chuckled. "Almost. Remember that this will soon be over."

After he hung up, Leslie remembered that she hadn't asked him about Hampton. It was just as well, she thought. There was no point in dragging his name into the situation—it might cause needless trouble.

Leslie ate an early supper and tried to watch television while waiting for the man she knew as Andrew Miller to arrive, but she couldn't concentrate and soon switched off the set. She had just started to work a crossword puzzle when the doorbell rang, just before seven thirty.

"You're early," Leslie said when she opened the door.

Ignoring her remark, Andrew Miller once more looked carefully around the apartment. "Your proposal should be ready to go by now."

"All except the final proofreading. It's been a real struggle to finish on time."

"Yes, I'm sure it has, and the last thing you need now is for someone to give all that hard-earned information to a competitor, right?"

"Do you still think someone will?" Leslie forced herself to say.

"That's why I'm here. We believe that with your help we can now catch the guilty party."

"What do you want me to do?"

"Are you familiar with invisible dye?"

"No. Is that like invisible ink?"

"It's used to mark money—invisible until it rubs off on the hands of anyone who touches it, then it turns a dark purple that doesn't wash off."

"I don't understand."

"You don't have to," he said impatiently. "Just bring the engineering abstract and the cost figures. I'll treat them, then you take them back to Arrow and leave the proposal in plain sight in the staff room. That purple dye will lead directly to the security leak—and we'll have the proof to put him—or her—away."

*He must think I am really stupid to fall for such a crazy scheme,* Leslie thought.

Then she remembered how she'd so easily been duped into thinking Miller was an FBI agent and realized he would naturally think she would continue to go along with anything he said.

"Do you think it will work?" Leslie said aloud.

"It'll do the job," he replied, looking self-satisfied. "I wouldn't be surprised if you wind up with a promotion as a result of your cooperation."

"I just want this to be over," Leslie said honestly.

"Quite so. Now here is what you must do—"

Again it was what she *must* do.

"You're quite specific about the information I should bring you," she said. "Are you certain that you need that much?"

"There has to be enough information to make the risk worthwhile," he said, again looking pained at having to explain to her. "It shouldn't take you long to get those pages together."

"I'll have to unbind a copy. Documentation will wonder why one is missing."

"Not if you copy the pages first," he said, again speaking as if she were an extremely slow learner and he the patient teacher. "Do you understand what you are to do?"

Leslie nodded.

"Good," he said, all but patting her on the head as a stupid girl who'd finally recited her lesson correctly. "I'll see you tomorrow evening, then."

Andrew Miller hadn't been gone more than five minutes when four knocks sounded on her door in rapid succession. Leslie looked through the peephole to make sure it was Jack Taylor before she let him in.

"He was early," he greeted her. "How did it go?"

"From your standpoint, very well, I suppose. I've agreed to bring home several summary documents—the heart of the proposal—tomorrow night."

"Great! I presume you'll be able to doctor the material."

"Yes, but I'll have to be careful with it—they'd think I'd lost my mind."

"At least you have one to lose," Jack Taylor said with a rare smile. "In my business, we sometimes struggle to hang onto ours."

"I can imagine," Leslie said, wondering how anyone could survive on a steady diet of tension and intrigue. But to them, her career and the problems that came with it were obviously not ordinary.

"We'll assume that he'll come back here tomorrow night. I'll need a key to your apartment. Unless he changes the plan—call me immediately if he does— we'll be hiding in the apartment when you get home. As soon as he takes the papers, we'll grab him. Then you can go back to being a full-time private citizen."

"That can't happen soon enough to suit me," Leslie said.

She had never spoken more sincerely in her life.

# Chapter 10

As soon as she got to work the next day, Leslie disassembled one of the preliminary proposals and selected a few of the pages. She didn't have to worry about changing all of them, since Andrew Miller—or whoever he was—wouldn't have time to look at them before he was arrested. But the top few pages ought to look good, and with these she took special pains.

Leslie finished her task well before noon, replaced the original sheets, and sent the proposal back to word processing, which was still working on last-minute changes. The copied sheets she put into her briefcase, then locked and stowed it in her file cabinet, which she also locked. Satisfied that the pages were secure, Leslie turned her attention to last-minute proposal details.

"We're not in sync on some of the figures," Pat Wentworth told her at lunch. "I don't know how it happened, but a few of the engineering calculations just don't match up."

"Recheck them," Leslie suggested. "Let's hope it's just some kind of small error in arithmetic."

"There are no small errors in space," said Bob McLaren as he joined them. "It's a very unforgiving environment."

"I'd like you to take a look at the figures," Pat told Bob. "I don't know how they got so haywire, but we can't submit the proposal if the math doesn't work."

"We're running out of time, gentlemen," Leslie reminded them. Such a glitch at this stage would've usually upset her, but compared to what she faced that night, this problem seemed almost minor.

"We know. I tried to get Hampton Travis for a consult, but I haven't been able to locate him."

At the mention of Hampton's name, Leslie's head came up and she looked questioningly at Pat. "He's out of town," she said.

Bob McLaren nodded. "Yeah, we know—we tried to call the outfit he went to work for and the stupid robot that answers his phone said Mr. Travis was unavailable. When I tried to leave a message for him, it bleeped at me and hung up. I don't think that electronic pile of junk works."

"Yeah," Pat agreed, "just like everyone says—'How come we can send a man to the moon, but we can't make a decent answering machine?'"

Leslie laughed with them, but the mention of Hampton's name reminded her that she missed him very much.

A last-minute flap in another project on which Leslie was filling in for Mr. Meredith kept her from her own desk until after five o'clock. Since no messages awaited her, Leslie presumed that the plans for the evening hadn't changed. By the time Leslie left the building, most of the other employees were gone. Walking to the parking lot, her head down against the biting wind, Leslie recalled a bit of a poem she had once read that described, "No sun, No warmth, November." On these cold days, Leslie really missed the Southern California weather. Yet, despite all that had happened to her in Huntsville, she had no desire to return there.

Leslie put her briefcase in the trunk, unlocked her car, and slid behind the wheel, and then she closed the door. She had just fitted her key into the ignition when, suddenly aware that someone was standing beside her car, she turned her head and saw Andrew Miller.

More surprised than frightened, Leslie rolled down her window. "Is something wrong?"

"No. Did you get the material?"

Leslie's mind raced as she tried to decide how to handle this new development. *Play it cool, Leslie,* she told herself. "I thought you were coming to my apartment."

"This dye is rather messy. It would be better to have the papers treated elsewhere."

"Where?" Leslie asked, now faintly alarmed.

"A place I know. Move over—I'll drive us there. It's a little hard to find." Andrew Miller opened the car door and would have sat on her lap if Leslie hadn't quickly moved out of his way. The gear shift lever stabbed her legs as she slid across the passenger seat.

Leslie weighed her options. If she tried to run away from him now, he would have the papers and her car and could probably escape arrest. If she went along with him, he would undoubtedly let her go as soon as he had the material he wanted. In any case, Leslie didn't want to make him suspicious of her.

"I'd prefer to drive. You can give me directions," she said.

"No. It'll be much better if I drive."

"I hadn't counted on this," she said as he left the parking lot and drove east. He hadn't bothered to adjust the seat, and his knees stuck up grotesquely. Thinking that he looked like a grown man trying to ride a child's bicycle, Leslie stifled an urge to giggle. *How can I laugh at a time like this?* Aware that she might be on the verge of hysteria, Leslie forced herself to take deep, calming breaths. She couldn't afford to lose control now.

Mr. Miller remained silent, concentrating on driving through the heavy Friday evening traffic. He didn't handle her car's manual transmission well, and Leslie winced as the gears protested each time he shifted. After several turns they reached a road that soon began to wind around the side of the mountain.

"Is this Monte Sano?" Leslie asked. "It doesn't look familiar."

"We're on the Bankhead Parkway. It goes up the back side of the mountain."

"Oh, I see. Do you live up here?"

"No," he said, and fell silent again.

Leslie glanced at the lighted dials on her dash, trying to see the fuel gauge. She knew she couldn't have much gas left; she usually filled her car as part of her regular Saturday chores. She didn't know which would be worse, to run out of gas and be stuck on the side of this lonely road with Andrew Miller, or to get wherever he was taking her. And why had he insisted on using her car? Leslie decided it was a reasonable question.

"Is something wrong with your car?"

"My car?" he repeated, as if he hadn't understood her question.

"I'd think you'd prefer to drive your own car up here. Mine seems to be giving you some trouble."

He ignored her. When they reached the top of the mountain he turned into a narrow gravel road. Leslie tried to watch for landmarks, but in the darkness it was hard to make out the few signs they came across.

"It isn't very far now," he said after they had jolted over a particularly bad rut in the road. Leslie winced as her transmission groaned at his attempt to force it into a lower gear. "Perhaps you understand now why I wanted to drive," he said as he pulled into another, narrower lane, almost overgrown on both sides with underbrush and now-scarlet sumac.

*At least I know how to shift gears,* Leslie thought, but stayed quiet. The last thing she would do would be to antagonize this strange man. She would hand over the papers and let him do whatever he would with them, then she'd get home as fast as she could—that was her revised agenda for the evening. Jack Taylor and the FBI would just have to catch Andrew Miller without any further help from her.

"Here we are," he said a few minutes later. He stopped beside a weather-beaten cabin perched on the edge of a mountain. Except for a motorcycle parked to one side there was little evidence that anyone had been there in years. Far below, the lights of the city twinkled in a panorama that under ordinary circumstances Leslie would have found breathtaking. Tonight she barely glanced at the view as Andrew Miller fumbled with the lock on the cabin door.

"Stay where you are until I can light the lantern," he directed when he finally opened the door. He struck a match to the wick, his sinister face in the shadowy light. The lamp smoked a little, then the flame took hold and burned brightly as he replaced the chimney and set the lamp down on the table.

"Is this where the FBI usually hangs out?" Leslie couldn't resist asking.

The man gave her a sharp glance and did not answer. Looking around, Leslie noted that the room contained a makeshift table and two ramshackle chairs that looked as if they might collapse if anyone tried to sit on them. Against one wall stood an army cot, neatly made up with a blanket and pillow. There was a closed door to the rear of the cabin that could lead to another room or outside.

"This is a strange place to transact business," Leslie said. She tried to overcome the feeling of dread that had followed her up the mountain, but the dismal place to which she had been led only made her more apprehensive. Why had she ever agreed to this wild scheme in the first place? And she must have been insane to allow him to bring her here.

"But it's very private. The papers, Miss Christopher?"

Leslie put her briefcase beside the lamp on the rickety table and reached into her purse for the key. Mr. Miller watched closely as she opened the lock and withdrew the papers. Handing them over, Leslie was grateful that the dim lantern wouldn't allow him to make a very thorough inspection. She had fabricated several pages that could pass as the genuine article, but the others wouldn't fool anyone who had ever seen an engineering proposal.

"Is this all?" he asked, rifling through the slender stack.

"It's what you asked for," she replied steadily. "Now if you'll just go ahead and use the dye, I'd like to go home."

"Oh? Perhaps someone is waiting for you there?" His tone chilled her to the bone, and instinctively Leslie shuddered.

"What do you mean?"

"I mean I know about Hampton Travis," he said smoothly. "He thought he could fool both of us, but it didn't work."

"I don't know what you're talking about," Leslie said. She devoutly wished that she had never challenged him. The lamplight made the glint in the man's eyes look even more evil.

"I believe you," he said with a faint half-smile. "In fact, Miss Christopher, there are a great many things that you don't know. That's why it's so totally unacceptable that you were put in charge of the VIRCO project."

"What?"

"You're a woman and you're much too young. I don't care how many hotshot things you did for Arrow in California, VIRCO should have gone to a man with experience and maturity, who knows Arrow/South inside and out."

"Someone like you, perhaps?" Leslie said as the last piece of the puzzle fell into place. She recalled how both Mr. Meredith and Sally had implied that she had won the job over local applicants. And Sally had mentioned that one of the men who had been passed over had left Arrow—

"Of course! It's really too bad that Arrow made the mistake of hiring a clumsy young woman with little enough sense in her pretty head to try to sell the company's secrets."

"What are you saying!" Leslie exclaimed, now genuinely alarmed.

"I'm saying that anyone with little enough sense to do what you've done could quite easily fall off the side of this mountain. Of course it could be a very long time before anyone thinks to look up here for you. They might not even bother to look at all, since they'll be sure you sold out to the highest bidder and took the money and ran. You might never be found," he finished, smiling as if the thought gave him a great deal of pleasure.

"You must be insane," Leslie said, her helplessness causing her to abandon caution. He made her fate very plain. She had to see to it that he wouldn't be able to carry out his plans for her. But how?

He laughed without humor. "No one ever accused good old Jim Roberts of insanity. 'Good old Jim will do it,' Arrow always said when they wanted a job done right. And good old Jim always did what they wanted. But do you know what, Miss Christopher? After a while good old Jim wanted more than a pat on the back. It's hard to work for a company for half your life and wind up with nothing to show for it."

"You deserved to be promoted, even before the VIRCO project, didn't you?" Leslie questioned. She believed that as long as he was talking about himself, he wouldn't be likely to make a move against her. And maybe if he talked long enough, Leslie could figure a way to escape.

"Of course I deserved it!" he exclaimed.

"And when Arrow wouldn't pay you what you were worth, you started going to other companies with information about its projects."

He allowed himself a small chuckle. "Even a stupid young woman like you can see that clear as day, right? All a man has is his work. No one—and certainly no *woman*—ought to be allowed to take that from him."

"Oh, I agree," Leslie said, slowly edging toward the table. If she could get near enough to push her briefcase, she could knock the lantern off the table and distract him long enough to get away. He had pocketed her car keys after he'd taken the briefcase out of the trunk, but that didn't matter. She would gladly walk all the way back down the mountain to escape this madman.

"Anyone but the fools at Arrow can see it wasn't fair," he began, looking at Leslie's face instead of her hands. Quickly she lunged toward the table and pushed the briefcase as hard as she could. It didn't slide well enough on the rough table top to knock the lamp to the floor; instead, the lamp merely teetered back and forth for a moment, then steadied, its flame barely disturbed.

His face contorted with rage, Jim Roberts grabbed Leslie's left wrist with such force that she cried out in pain.

"Oh, you think you're so smart, don't you? Let's see how smart you really are, Miss Christopher."

Still gripping her arm quite tightly, Roberts pushed open the back door and dragged her outside. The cold night air hit her face like a slap, clearing her head. Leslie remembered a move she'd learned in a self-defense course she'd taken. If done correctly she could throw a man twice her weight. She thought she could still do it, but first she had to make her captor grip her more closely. If she struggled the right way, perhaps he would.

"You know you can't get away with this," she said, trying to dig her high-heeled shoes in the soft earth.

"I already have," he said, jerking her after him. "Your FBI friends are sitting around your apartment, waiting to spring their stupid trap. Won't they be surprised to find that their little decoy has flown the coop?"

"How did you know that?" Leslie asked.

He chuckled evilly. "Surveillance can work both ways, you know."

"You mentioned Hampton Travis," Leslie said. "What do you know about him?"

"I said I fooled him and I did," Roberts replied. "He's probably right there with old Jack Taylor and the others at this very minute."

"Hampton Travis works for the FBI?" Leslie asked. His evil laugh, her reply.

"He fooled you good, didn't he? He and that stuck-up girlfriend of his that works in Security."

"Barbara Redmond," Leslie said, not surprised. *So they do work together,* she thought. If Hampton was in love with someone else, surely he wouldn't have kissed her the way he had—

With a sudden sense of panic, Leslie saw that they were almost to the edge of the mountain, and she reached out and hooked her right arm around a slender tree. She hung on to it with all her might as Roberts continued to pull at her other arm, at first unaware of what she had done.

"You're just making it harder on yourself," he said, twisting her left arm until tears came into her eyes. "Let go of that tree."

As she did, Leslie bent double, made a fist with her right hand, and swung as hard as she could. His surprised cry of pain told her she had hit her target, and as he reflexively relaxed his hold on her arm, she wrenched away from him.

Leslie ran around the side of the cabin and down the lane that led to the road. If he pursued her, she'd go into the woods and try to lose him in the thick undergrowth. Aware that her high heels slowed her progress, she kicked them off. She felt pain as sticks and rocks poked through her stockings, but she kept running anyway.

She thought she had gone as far as she possibly could without resting when a motorcycle roared to life. At the sound, Leslie crashed into the dark woods, trying to avoid the motorcycle's probing headlight. She half-ran, half-walked until a stitch in her side bent her double and forced her to stop. Her lungs felt as if they would burst, every breath bringing new agony. She crouched behind a fallen log and tried to recover her breath.

The sound of the motorcycle was never far away. Sometimes it grew fainter, but she could always hear it. It would only be a matter of time until he found her; he knew she hadn't left the area. Her only chance of escape was to press on and hope to find a safe hiding place before his motorcycle headlight could pinpoint her.

After a few minutes, Leslie left her hiding place and continued walking. She decided not to run unless she was in immediate danger—there was too much risk of falling in the darkness. If she sprained an ankle—or worse—it would be all over. She shivered, not entirely from the cold. Leslie had no doubt that Jim Roberts was deranged enough to be capable of tossing her off the mountain without a second thought.

But first he would have to find her. Ironically enough, in all the turmoil of her thoughts, a snatch of a psalm came into Leslie's mind. *I will lift up mine eyes unto the hills, from whence cometh my help.*

Well, tonight this mountain was the site of her destruction, not her deliverance. Leslie walked on for several minutes, each seeming an eternity. She'd thought she was bearing away from the cabin, but suddenly she saw it through the trees on her left hand and realized she'd been walking in a circle.

"Lost people bear to the left," Hampton had said that golden day when they had gone hiking on this very mountain.

Thinking of him gave Leslie a temporary lift. Whoever he was, an FBI agent as Roberts had implied, or just a man who had given up a job at Arrow for her sake, Leslie knew that Hampton Travis meant a great deal to her.

*What would Hampton do if he were in my place?* she asked herself. Almost immediately, recalling the quiet strength of his faith, Leslie knew that Hampton would probably have started praying a long time ago. And while she wasn't accustomed to it, Leslie shut her eyes and spoke earnestly, almost whispering.

*Lord, I'm not very good at this prayer business, but I do believe that You can help me, and You certainly know I need help.* As an afterthought, Leslie added "Amen" and opened her eyes just as the sound of the motorcycle grew increasingly louder.

A feeling of the most intense peace she had ever experienced flooded over Leslie like a benediction, but she didn't have time to consider its source or what it meant. Over her shoulder Leslie saw the headlight beaming through the trees, heading straight toward her. Summoning a final burst of energy, Leslie ran toward the cabin, lurched inside, closed and leaned against the door, panting for breath.

She heard the motorcycle engine cut off and footsteps on the cabin porch. Quickly she grabbed one of the chairs and raised it high as a dark shape entered the cabin. Leslie brought the chair down as hard as she could on the side of Jim

Roberts' head, and he fell forward with a muffled groan. Quickly she bent to search his pockets for her car keys. She had them in hand and had turned to leave when a new set of headlights appeared in the narrow lane.

*What next!* she thought. Casting a wary eye on Roberts, who seemed to be out of it for the time being, Leslie went out the rear door and crouched behind the cabin as an automobile pulled up behind hers and stopped. She heard car doors opening and closing, followed by footsteps on the cabin porch, then a loud exclamation.

"Here's Roberts, but I don't see the girl."

Then Leslie's eyes widened and her breath caught in her throat as a voice she instantly recognized called her name. She made her way to the back door of the cabin and sagged against the door frame, feeling suddenly faint.

"Here I am," she said weakly.

Hampton turned, and Leslie knew she would always remember how he looked, silhouetted in the lantern light as he reached out to her and held her as if he never intended to let her go.

"I've never been so glad to see anyone in my life," Leslie said when she could speak again. "I won't even ask what you're doing here."

"I'm rescuing you, of course," Hampton said. He continued to hold Leslie tightly until she winced and pulled away from him.

"My arm seems to be a bit skinned," she said apologetically.

"Thank heaven we got here in time," the first voice she had heard said, and Leslie looked past Hampton to see Jack Taylor handcuffing the awakening figure on the floor.

"God heard me—I haven't prayed that hard since that shuttle flight when we had to make an emergency landing."

"He told me you work for the FBI," Leslie said to Hampton. "Why didn't you tell me?"

"I couldn't." Hampton led Leslie closer to the lamp and inspected her arm. "Jack, look at her arm—we need to get Leslie to the hospital right away."

Jack Taylor walked over to inspect her arm and nodded in agreement. "I'm afraid that'll take some stitching."

"I'm not hurt all that much," Leslie protested, but she allowed Hampton to pick her up and carry her to the car as Jack Taylor brought Roberts out and put him in the other car.

Using his cellular phone, Jack Taylor made a call. "Barbara? You can leave the apartment now. The suspect is in custody and Miss Christopher is safe."

"Barbara?" Leslie repeated, looking quizzically at Hampton. "She's in my apartment?"

"We all were there for a while," Hampton replied with his best smile. "It was quite a party."

"Nobody invited me," Leslie said.

"It's not our fault you ran out on us."

"Or mine, either. That man had other plans for me."

Hampton put his arms around Leslie and kissed her tenderly. "Thank God he didn't get to carry them out."

Leslie glanced at her captor. He sat in the backseat of Taylor's car, his head down. Despite all he had put her through, Leslie felt stirred by a strange sense of pity.

"What will happen to him now?" she asked.

"That's up to the federal courts, but he'll likely be charged with abduction and assault, in addition to whatever Arrow slaps him with."

Leslie sighed. "Poor man. He wanted my job."

"And your life," Hampton reminded her.

As they followed Jack Taylor's car down the mountain, Hampton kept glancing over at Leslie as if he couldn't bear to have her out of his sight, even for a moment. Despite the throbbing pain in her arm, Leslie felt content just to be with Hampton again and to know how he felt about her.

"You gave us quite a scare, young lady." He reached out and brushed a twig from her hair with his free hand.

"I was pretty scared there for a while myself," she admitted. "But a strange thing happened when I realized that I might not be able to get away from him." She stopped, suddenly shy talking about how she had felt when she had prayed for deliverance.

"I think I can guess what it was," Hampton said. "I can see that in all of this you've been touched by the Lord."

"Can you?" Leslie pulled down the sun visor and looked at her scratched face. "It looks more like I was touched by a porcupine."

"I'm right, though?" he persisted, and Leslie nodded.

"I can't describe it—I was so tired and I didn't think I could take another step, and he was coming after me—and I knew he meant to throw me over the side of the mountain—then I just asked God to help me, and He did. The next thing I knew, I was able to sprint to the cabin."

Hampton nodded as if he understood exactly what had happened. "It's a little scary, isn't it?"

"Not as scary as what almost happened. He was going to let everyone think I'd been selling information from Arrow."

"I know," Hampton said. "I prayed that we'd reach you in time, but you and God were obviously doing pretty well on your own."

"I guess the secret of good management is knowing who to get the job done," Leslie said, attempting a weak smile. "But seriously, I didn't know you were back in Huntsville—and how did you know where to find me? I didn't even know where I was myself."

"I came back because my work in California was finished, and I knew whoever was trying to get the VIRCO information would act soon. My plane got in about four thirty and I went directly to your apartment, where Jack and Barbara were waiting. They filled me in on what was happening to you and Jim Roberts. When you hadn't shown up by six o'clock, they knew something had gone wrong."

"But I still don't know how you knew I was up here."

"I put a tail on your car before I went to California, a gizmo that sends a message to a satellite, which is then beamed back to earth at an assigned frequency. It led us straight to you."

Leslie shivered. "He drove my car up here, even though I tried to talk him out of it."

"It's a good thing he didn't listen to you."

"What made you think that I might need protection?"

"We knew that whoever was selling secrets would probably try to get them on VIRCO."

Still confused, Leslie frowned. "Is that why you wanted to be assigned to VIRCO?"

"That was the original plan. But for several reasons—including a very personal one—I decided to let Barbara keep an eye out for you instead."

"I always hoped that you were on the right side all along," Leslie said despondently, "but I've been so stupid—"

"Here, here, there'll be none of that!" Hampton stopped for a traffic signal and leaned over to kiss her cheek lightly. "You don't have the corner on stupidity. I should have suspected Roberts from the start, but we thought he'd left town."

"Oh, Hampton," Leslie began, but he touched her lips gently with his free hand.

"Hush."

"But—" Leslie began again.

"Later. Here's the hospital. They'll probably think I've been battering you," he said as one of the emergency attendants came out with a wheelchair.

"What happened to you, honey?" the admitting clerk asked. "You look like you fell off the mountain."

"Almost," Leslie replied. She shuddered again, thinking how close she had come to disaster. "I seem to have a few scratches and bruises."

"Abrasions and contusions," the nurse said. Leslie and Hampton exchanged smiles.

"Wait here," the nurse instructed Hampton as Leslie was wheeled away for treatment.

He'd barely had time to drink a cup of cool vending machine coffee before

Leslie returned, sporting several stitches in her right arm and bandages on the worst of her leg wounds.

"She'll live," the young emergency room doctor told Hampton. "I'd keep her off the mountain for a spell, though."

"I'll try, but you know how flighty these females can get sometimes."

"If I felt better, I'd hit you," Leslie said as Hampton helped her into the car.

"I don't think you're going to be hitting anything for a while. You really do look awful."

"Thanks a lot," Leslie said.

When they reached her apartment, Leslie lay on the sofa and Hampton sat cross-legged on the floor facing her. "I should go now and let you get some sleep," he said, but she shook her head.

"Stay a little while. Anyway, I haven't seen you in so long, I'd almost forgotten what you looked like."

Aware that she was teasing him, Hampton smiled and took one of her hands in his. "I've been doing some serious thinking lately," he told her.

"About what?" Leslie asked. With her hand in his, Leslie felt at ease for the first time in almost as long as she could remember.

"A lot of things, but mostly about you. My work has always been important to me and I never backed out of an assignment in my life. But as soon as I met you, I knew that if I had to choose between seeing you and infiltrating Arrow, it was no choice at all."

"Why didn't you tell me what you were up to from the start?"

"I couldn't. It would have endangered the whole operation and especially you."

Leslie sighed. "I must be the most lied-to person in this town. How can I ever believe anyone again after this?"

Hampton sat beside her on the sofa and brushed her lips lightly with his. "Do you believe this?"

Leslie reached her hand out to touch his face, allowing her fingers to caress the cleft in his chin and explore the corners of his mouth. "I'm not sure I can," she whispered before his lips closed on hers once more, and he kissed her gently but passionately.

"You can trust me forever and ever," he said as he pulled back and looked into her eyes.

"That's a long time," she said, and he kissed her again.

"A lifetime, as a matter of fact. The important thing is that I love you, my dearest Leslie, and I think you just might feel the same way about me."

Tears came to Leslie's eyes, and she nodded, unable to speak.

"Then you will start thinking about marrying me, I hope."

Leslie smiled. "But I've just found a wonderful singles group at Glenveiw—"

"Really? I understand they have wonderful couples classes too."

"We would be a couple, wouldn't we?" Leslie said with wonder. "Will you stay in Huntsville permanently, then?"

Hampton kissed her lightly on the nose. "You're tired. We'll talk about all of that later."

"How wonderful it is to have a 'later,'" Leslie murmured against his cheek.

"All the laters in our lifetime," he assured her.

As Hampton's arms tightened around her once more, Leslie knew that she had found what she had been searching for all her life, without even knowing what she sought. At last she had the promise of the security she had been missing.

"It's all a matter of security," she murmured.

Hampton looked at her and smiled. "What is?"

"Us," Leslie replied, knowing she made no sense but unable to express the feelings that crowded her heart.

In reply, Hampton gathered her to him again and Leslie sighed in contentment.

Having the security of her and Hampton's love throughout their life would be wonderful; but God had also offered Leslie another, more important security.

She had glimpsed it briefly at Glenview and then fully realized it in her desperate prayer in the woods. Leslie also had the promise of God's security, which far surpasses any human love and would last for all eternity.

# *Epilogue*

I don't think this chapel is big enough to hold everyone who wants to see you and Hampton get married," Sally said minutes before the organist was scheduled to play Mendelsohn's "Wedding March." Sally had just looked through the peephole in the Glenview Chapel bride's room, and when she turned to Leslie, her face glowed with excitement.

"I hope the security people we hired keep out the TV cameras," Leslie said.

"That's the price you have to pay for being a celebrity," Sally replied, only half teasing. In the six months since Leslie's abduction, the tabloid press had had a field day with the story of an ex-astronaut who had come to the rescue of a beautiful young woman bravely working as an undercover agent to help the FBI apprehend a spy.

"Hampton once told me he'd had his fill of being in the spotlight—now I know what he meant."

"But at least some good came of it. What a great testimony you and Hampton gave to the millions of people who heard you praise God for helping you through it!"

"Right now I'm only concerned about one person," Leslie said. "Despite that old superstition about brides and grooms not seeing each other on the day of the wedding, I'd feel a lot better if I could have talked to Hampton today."

"Well, for the record, I did see him. Other than saying he's more nervous today than he was on his first trip into space, Dr. Travis seems to be holding up well."

"What about Pat? How is he holding up?" Leslie asked, unable to resist teasing her matron of honor about the man that had become an increasingly important part of her life.

"Your wedding has set us both to thinking that maybe our getting married wouldn't be such a bad idea."

"I can hear Dale now, complaining that he's losing all his singles class to matrimony," Leslie said with a smile. "What's happening out there now?" she added, hearing a different tune from the organ.

Sally turned back to the keyhole. "Hampton's mother is being seated. You can tell she lives in Florida—she has a great tan. Now here come Pastor Carew and Hampton and his father. Hampton looks a little pale."

"Where's my bouquet?" Leslie asked, temporarily losing her fine edge of organization and order.

"Right here," Sally said. She handed it to Leslie as a light rap sounded on the door, and Richard Meredith, looking splendid in his morning coat, beckoned to them.

"I think I'm supposed to walk you down the aisle for some reason or the other," he said lightly. Gratefully Leslie took his arm.

"You look very nice, sir," Leslie said.

"So do you," he returned.

In her simple white satin gown, adorned only by a string of pearls from Hampton, Leslie didn't know if she was beautiful, but the joy that she felt sure made her feel radiant.

The first strains of the wedding march swept through the Glenview chapel. Sally gave a thumbs-up sign to Leslie and turned to walk slowly down the aisle, where groomsman Pat Wentworth watched her with obvious admiration.

"Shall we?" Mr. Meredith asked.

Forcing herself to walk slowly, Leslie began to move down the aisle, her eyes fixed on Hampton.

As soon as he saw her, Hampton broke into a broad grin. Leslie smiled, overwhelmed by her feelings of gratitude. With a full heart she acknowledged that the things that had happened to her since her arrival in Huntsville—capturing Jim Roberts, her successful management of Arrow's VIRCO proposal, her love for Hampton Travis, and, most especially, the security of her salvation—had all been a part of God's plan for her life.

At last she reached the altar and Mr. Meredith handed her over to Hampton. He gripped her hand tightly and looked down at her with such a look of love that Leslie almost wept from the emotion enveloping her.

"Let us pray," Pastor Carew said. Gratefully Leslie bowed her head. *Thank You, Lord,* she said silently, and knew that Hampton was probably breathing the same prayer. *Help us to always remember this day and the feelings we share.*

As Leslie and Hampton exchanged their vows in voices that never wavered, she somehow knew that the God who had brought Hampton to her would help them stay together as they looked to Him for their security.

KAY CORNELIUS

Kay grew up in Winchester, Tennessee, met the love of her life, Don Cornelius, in 1950, and they married in 1951 while attending George Peabody College of Vanderbilt University. They came to Huntsville, Alabama, in 1958. Kay taught English for twenty-five years and earned her Masters degree in education while Don worked on contracts, first for Army missiles and then for NASA's Space Shuttle program. After his civil service retirement, he became contracts manager for Lockheed-Martin Space and Missiles. Kay and Don have two grown children, a granddaughter who is a mortgage loan officer and rescues miniature pinschers, and three grandsons. Their eldest grandson has a BA in English and wants to teach literature at a university. His first cousin, a senior English education major at the University of Alabama, started his student teaching in Queensland, Australia, in January 2009. Their youngest grandson, Kyle, a high school senior, builds and launches model rockets that break the sound barrier and wants to become an astrophysicist

# THE BRIDE WORE COVERALLS

## COVERALLS

by Debra Ullrick

# *Dedication*

In memory of my beloved sister-in-law, Linda Elaine Suppes (1951–2006). I love you and miss you terribly.

Joe, Amanda, Jaydon, Brent, Chrissie, Leah, and Beau Suppes, I love you all very much.

A ginormous thanks to my extraordinary friend/mentor/tutor, Staci Stallings—you and Jesus helped make this happen. Jeanne Leach and Michelle Sutton, thanks for believing in me. Terri Smith in Alabama, Joe Docheff, and ACFW members—thanks for all your help. Sharmane Wikberg, look what you started. Mom loves you, kiddo. Rick Ullrick, I love you more than words can say. Thanks for believing in me and supporting me. You're *my* hero.

# Chapter 1

A s much as I hate to say it, their chauvinistic remarks are starting to get me down," Camara Cole admitted to her best friend, Lolly Morrison.

"Ca-mare-ah Che-velle Cole," Lolly said in an exaggerated pronunciation of her name, "don't you dare let them pull you down." Lolly shook her well-manicured finger at her. "Stan teases you, too, and he's proud of your accomplishments."

Camara searched her friend's eyes to see if she was just trying to make her feel better. "Is he really?"

"Yes. He tells me that all the time. In fact. . ." Lolly's red curls bounced as she glanced around Tooties Gourmet Coffee Shop. Camara followed her gaze, wondering what she was looking for. "Yesterday Stan told me he wished he was as good at building and racing mud bog trucks as you are."

Shock rippled through her. "Stan?" She dipped her head sideways. "We're talking about your husband Stan, right?"

Lolly laughed. "Yes. I'm talking about my Stan. What other Stan do you know?"

Camara shook her head. "He really said that?"

Lolly put her coffee cup down and laid her hand on top of Camara's. "How long have you known me, Cam? Would I lie to you?"

"No. But it's just hard to believe. Stan teases me almost as much as the rest of the guys."

Lolly flipped her wrist. "Oh, you know how guys are. They stick together. By the way," she said as she shook her finger at Camara, "don't you go telling Stan I told you what he said. He'll never tell me anything again."

"I won't." Camara smiled. She picked up her drink and took a sip. "It's all Chase Lamar's fault. Ever since *I*"—Camara tapped her chest—"a mere female, started beating his times, Chase has said women have no business racing in a *man's sport*." Camara rolled her eyes. "The frustrating part about this whole thing is now he has the rest of the guys teasin' me, too. I get so angry anymore. I've prayed about my temper, and I'm trying to get it under control, but man, those guys sure know how to goad me." She tucked her shoulder-length blond hair behind her ears. "Honestly, Loll. . .I don't know what to do. Last Saturday at Pete's Mud-n-Track, they were horrible. Especially Bobby-Rae."

"What did Bobby-Rae do?"

"Well, when I finished checking under the hood of The Black Beast, Bobby-Rae came up and started saying all sorts of cruel things."

"Like what?"

Camara pursed her face to imitate Bobby-Rae's macho attitude and quoted him. " 'You're a disgrace to Southern women. Women don't race, and women don't build trucks. When ya gonna quit playin' mechanic and act like a real lady?'" Camara shook her head. "I refuse to live in a time warp. Besides, I know Bobby-Rae's just mad because I refused to go out with him. I—"

"Bobby-Rae asked you out?" Lolly's blue eyes widened. When Camara didn't deny it, Lolly raised her eyebrows. "Well, shoot a monkey and kiss a pig. I can't believe it. When?"

"After work one night a few weeks ago."

"What did you say?"

"I told him no. That it was nothing personal, but I'd made it a rule a long time ago never to date coworkers because too many times it causes problems on the job. And, boy, has it."

"Well, that explains his attitude toward you. Is that all he said?"

"After I turned him down, he went on and on about how greasy my finger-nails and hair were." Camara held her hands out. Studying her rough-looking hands and chipped nails, she inwardly cringed. "I know my nails are a mess. But what'd he expect? I'm a mechanic. Besides, he didn't have to say it the way he did. It really hurt."

"So that's why you changed your hairstyle?"

Camara self-consciously touched her hair. "Yeah, I thought maybe if I looked more feminine, the guys would leave me alone. I've never worn bangs before. Does it look okay?"

"I love it. It makes your eyes look bigger. I wish I had pretty brown eyes like yours." She popped a bite of raspberry-swirl cake into her mouth. "But enough of that. Did he say anything else?"

"No, not that night. But he started ripping on me again at Pete's Mud-n-Track last Saturday. He repeated everything he'd said the night I turned him down. Plus he said"—she pulled her face into a manly pose to imitate Bobby-Rae again—" 'No man in his right mind would ever go out with a Miss Know-It-All like you.'" Camara chuckled.

Lolly's brows rose. "What's funny about that?"

"Nothing. That's not why I'm laughing. You won't believe what happened next." Camara snitched a small piece of Lolly's cake and tossed it in her mouth. "Guess who came to my rescue?"

"Who?"

"Take a guess."

"Your brother, Erik?"

"Nope. Chase Lamar, that's who."

Lolly's mouth dropped open so fast Camara giggled.

"Well, I'll be. You're kidding, right?" Lolly blinked several times.

"Nope. I about passed out from shock."

Lolly slowly shook her head. "That's a hard one to believe."

"I know. Ironic, isn't it?"

"Y'all have been rivals for as long as I can remember," Lolly said. "He's teased you unmercifully for years." Lolly moved her coffee out of the way and leaned toward Camara. "I want to know everything. And don't leave anything out."

"Not a whole lot to tell. Chase told him, 'Leave her alone, Bobby-Rae. And apologize to the lady.' Bobby-Rae opened his mouth, but Erik showed up and Bobby-Rae hustled to his truck and hightailed it out of Pete's Mud-n-Track like his backside was on fire."

"And?"

"And nothing. Erik and Chase started talking, and I went back to work on my bog truck." Camara took a long drink of her coffee. "I still can't believe Chase and Erik are good friends now. Maybe Erik felt sorry for Chase because the first couple of times Chase came to singles night at church he looked pretty uncomfortable. Erik always does gravitate toward those in need of help. And Chase *definitely* needs plenty of help." She snickered then turned serious. "Ya know, Loll, ever since John started bringing Chase to singles night at church, he doesn't act like the same obnoxious bully. He's. . .well, he's almost sweet."

"That *has* to be God."

They both laughed.

While finishing their coffee, they chatted about some of the drastic changes in Chase.

For years Camara and Chase had been Chevy/Ford rivals. Just like their parents. Except his dad used family money to purchase Ford dealerships, and her dad, through hard work and perseverance, bought Chevrolet dealerships. But the real rivalry began when they both started mud bog racing four years ago. Chase had become downright ornery and sometimes cruel. And now he was. . .what was he? Camara decided she didn't know or care. She didn't want to think about Chase Lamar.

As much as Camara hated to leave her friend's company, she picked up the keys to her Hummer and stuck them in the pocket of her faded jeans. "Well, Loll, I'd better go. I have a few vehicles at the shop I need to work on the next couple of days, plus I want to finish getting The Black Beast ready for Saturday's mud bog race."

Outside, Camara shielded her eyes against April's warm sun and glanced at the row of historical buildings lining the streets of Swamper City, Alabama. They reminded her of the men she raced with. . .out-of-date and antiquated. In the past when she raced at several other places in the Heart of Dixie, none of the men were offended that she raced bog trucks and was a mechanic. In fact, they were just as friendly and hospitable as the rest of the people in Alabama. Camara heaved a sigh, jumped in her Hummer, and drove toward Cole's Chevrolet. Maybe it was something in Swamper City's water that made the men here act the way they did. Camara laughed at that thought. It was a possibility.

❀

At four thirty the next morning, Camara pulled into Cole's Chevrolet and parked. She loved getting to work early. That way she got all her work done during the week so she could race on Saturdays. She hustled into the auto shop and headed straight to her work stall.

Awed by the 1958 Corvette parked in front of her, Camara lovingly ran her fingers over the baby blue classic. She hurried into her yellow grease-stained coveralls and opened the hood. Goose bumps rose on her arms. What a privilege to work on Mr. Banks's pride and joy. She still couldn't believe he trusted its care to her only. Well, she wouldn't let him down. She'd have it fixed in no time.

Three hours later the Corvette roared to life. Satisfied with a job well done, Camara leaned over to pick up her tools. Footsteps sounded behind her. Smiling, she stood and turned. Her smile dropped at the sight of a big burly man. He may have been handsome, but his hairy body and tattoos reminded her of a rebel biker. Good thing she'd made the no-dating-coworkers rule a long time ago. He was definitely not her type. "What are you doing here so early?"

Bobby-Rae's gray eyes darkened. "I came to see if I could work on Mr. Banks's car. But, as usual, the boss's daughter gets to."

Camara frowned. "What does me being the boss's daughter have to do with anything?"

He snorted. "Well, it definitely ain't because you're a better mechanic than the rest of us here, that's for sure. No man in his right mind would ask a *woman*"—he spat out the term as if it were a dirty word—"to work on a vehicle of this quality unless he was insane or, in this case, a friend of the family."

Camara shook her head. It wasn't just Mr. Banks who requested her. Several people did, and each time it angered the men she worked with. So what was she supposed to do? Not do a good job so their egos were pacified? No way. She had worked hard to get where she was. If the men she worked with couldn't handle that people requested her, then that was their problem. Not wanting to defend herself for the millionth time, she tossed out the only word she could think of. "Jealous." She brushed past him and headed toward the restroom.

❀

Saturday proved to be a nice sunny day. Camara stood at the front of the mud pit at the east end of Swamper Speedway's oval racetrack. The foamy water on top of the mire reminded her of froth on a root beer float—or a black cow, as her mamaw would call it. She glanced at the empty wooden grandstands that covered one side of the racetrack, knowing that in a couple of hours they would be full of spectators.

The sound of loud glasspack mufflers drew her attention. Two pickups pulling trailers entered the contestant's area. Pretty snazzy—and pricey. Camara looked around at the few other rigs that were there. She recognized several of them and marveled at what she saw. Knowing what some of them did for a living, they surely must have gone into hock to own those rigs. Camara gave a short snort. Typical of most people who love vehicles and racing—they would rather have a garage full of cars, pickups, and monster trucks than eat. Well, okay, maybe not eat, but close. Camara wasn't any different. Except that hers were paid for. However, if she had had enough room in her garage, she'd own a variety of classic cars and trucks with big tires and lift kits. As it stood now, she had a Hummer, which she bought at cost through her dad's dealership, a '68 Camaro that her dad gave her on her eighteenth birthday—he was the original owner—and her '74 Chevy bog truck that she picked up at a junkyard for a hundred dollars and completely modified.

Looking up, Camara did a double take at the bog vehicle pulling in. Sitting high on a trailer, the bogger resembled a giant outer space bug. She wondered what it sounded like and how it ran. From the looks of the other contestants' vehicles, she might have some stiff competition today. She turned her attention to the 3½-foot-deep, 150-foot-long mud pits to see if today was one of those days when they added more mud to the usual twenty inches. Sometimes they did that, and it made a real difference to anyone who wanted to win.

"Don't fret your pretty little head off." Chase's deep Southern drawl boomed from behind her. "With any luck, your poor Chevy will make it through."

Startled, Camara sucked in a sharp breath and spun around. Her foot slipped on the clay mud. One leg headed directly toward the mud pit, which was exactly where the rest of her would have followed if not for Chase's strong arm encircling her, hauling her upright.

The rain-fresh scent of his aftershave wafted up her nose, reminding her of a spring shower. As he steadied her, she gazed into his dark green eyes, mere inches from her face. She knew she should exercise her manners and thank him, but she didn't. It was his fault in the first place that she'd been nearly dipped in mud.

She moved away from him so he was between her and the pits. "Do you always sneak up on people?" she asked frostily, her heart rapping at two thousand rpms. Planting her hands on her hips, she sent him an icy stare.

Chase chuckled. "By the way, *Camaro*, you're welcome."

"It's *Ca-mare-ah*, thank you very much. And I'm welcome for what?" She tipped her head sideways and hiked a brow.

"For saving ya from an unwanted mud bath." He grinned.

She clenched her jaw. That man could be so infuriating. She was in no humor to play his game—whatever it was. Instead she wanted to wipe that smug grin right off his face. Strutting close to him, she shook her finger under his nose. "What do ya mean you rescued me? *You're* the reason I almost fell in the first place, sneaking up on me like that."

"I didn't sneak up on you. You were just concentrating too hard." Squinting, he rubbed his chin. "Afraid your truck won't make it through, huh?"

Camara glared up at him from shoulder level.

Chase's eyes twinkled. "Anyway, ya owe me."

"What do you mean, I owe you? Owe you for what?"

A deep chuckle rumbled from Chase's throat.

Camara pursed her mouth and frowned. Was he laughing at her—again? Her anger started boiling over like an overheated radiator. She jutted her chin and spun the bill of her yellow Chevy cap around. *One, two, three. Help me to control my anger, Lord. Four. . .*

"Ya owe me because as tiny as you are, if you'd have fallen in that pit, no one would be able to find ya."

*Five, six. . .I'm trying, Lord.*

"So, see, I just saved ya from a muddy grave." His snide grin did it.

"Ack! You!" She shoved him hard.

Eyes widening, Chase backpedaled and his arms flailed as he futilely tried to avoid falling into the trench. Camara couldn't hold down the laughter bubbling from within as he landed with a *smack* in the thick mud.

Quick as a flash Chase jumped to his feet, but he lost his balance. Struggling to stay upright in the knee-high mud, he staggered before falling forward. He shot his arms in front of him to break his fall but plunged face-first deeply into the mud. When he finally stood again, his body was coated with muck, and a shock-filled gaze peered out from under his mud-masked face. His normally spiked dark brown hair lay limp from the heavy mire.

"That'll teach ya," she declared, pivoting in triumph.

She'd barely taken a step when muddy arms wrapped around her waist, tugging her backward. Her Chevy cap flipped off her head and landed on the ground.

"Noo!" Camara screamed, but it was too late.

Chase pulled her down next to him in the pit. She gasped at the gooey mud. Using Chase for leverage, she stood. Her mouth fell open. Even in the shallowest part of the mud pit she couldn't see her knees. She shook her hands, trying to rid them of the gelatinous mud that was starting to seep through her shoes and clothes.

"That'll teach me what?" Chase snorted with a mixture of indignation and humor.

*Insufferable man!* Camara scooped up a big glob of mud, her mouth curved in a vengeful smile. Twisting without warning, she slung it at him, hitting him square in the mouth. Chase sputtered and spat.

Now was her chance to escape. In hopes that her tennis shoes remained on her feet, Camara gripped them with her toes and leaned forward toward the embankment. Using her arms to balance herself, she forced one leg forward and then the next. One more step and she'd be able to climb out.

Suddenly she felt solid arms wrap around her, pulling her backward.

"Oh no, ya don't. You're not getting away that easy, *Ca-mare-O.*" Pulling her back tight against his chest, Chase pinned her arms to her body and scooped up a handful of mud with his free hand.

"Don't you dare!" She fought to twist sideways, rearing her head and staring up defiantly at him.

"Or what?"

His hand headed toward her face. She jerked her head back and forth, but Chase managed to smear her cheeks and chin with mud. Camara strained to free herself from his strong but strangely gentle grasp. However, Chase held her even closer to his chest.

"Ya know, Cammy,"—he waggled his eyebrows—"in Hollywood they pay a fortune for this stuff. So, see, I'm doing your skin a huge favor, and it didn't cost ya one red cent." He tossed back his head and roared with laughter.

Camara dipped a handful of mud, flung her hand behind her, and slapped it against his neck.

"So, that's how ya wanna play, huh?" His voice sounded mischievous.

In one fluid motion he gathered a large handful of mud, held it over Camara's head, and shot her a wicked grin.

As much as she hated to admit even to herself, she was enjoying this playful side of Chase. She ducked when a few clumps landed in her hair.

"You play dirty." She tried wiggling out of his grasp. "No fair. You're stronger than me."

Chase drew her closer and waved the mud mere inches from her face. "Do you concede defeat then, matey?" he asked in a pirate accent.

"Never, vermin! I shall go down with the ship first," she imitated him. The mud was a whisper away from her mouth. She arched her head backward. "Let me put it to you this way. If you do, I'll just have to pay you back." She smirked and then smiled sweetly.

He leaned his head down. His breath brushed across her face when he spoke, "Oh yeah, and just *how* will you pay me back?" His eyes twinkled and then turned serious when he glanced at her lips.

Camara swallowed hard. She didn't like the look on his face. Was he going to try and kiss her? Well, there was no way she'd let Chase Lamar kiss her, no matter how good-looking he was. She jerked herself free and scrambled out of the pit.

Snatching up her cap, she stoically made her way toward her vehicle. The muddy clothes clung to her, making it difficult to walk.

Chase strolled up beside her. "If your Chevy moved half as fast as you did just now in that pit, ya just might have a chance of winning today. But don't count on it. It's a Chevy." He chuckled.

Camara stopped dead in her tracks. She turned sideways, facing him.

"My Chevy moves just fine, thank you very much. It's that Ford of yours ya need to be concerned with." Placing her finger over her lips, she squinted. "Hmm. Now let's see. . .what does Ford stand for again?" She snapped her muddy fingers. "Oh yeah, I remember: Fix Or Repair Daily. Or, Found On the Road Dead. Too bad there aren't any initials for 'Can't run worth diddly-squat.'" She sent him a smug grin.

Truth be known, she liked Fords, Dodges, and just about any other make of vehicle. She liked their power and the intense challenges they presented. But she'd keep that information tucked away from Chase or anyone else.

"No, Ford stands for: First On Race Day." He grinned. "Remember last week? It was *my* Ford that beat *your* Chevy."

"And do you remember the week before that? It was *my* Chevy that won the *big* trophy and the *big* moneys at Jenson's Speedway," Camara stated proudly. "And I seem to recall you telling me that me and my Chevy had zero chance of winning." She smiled smugly.

"You still don't."

Her smile dropped.

"Aw, Cammy, c'mon. You and I both know that if the Mud Boss hadn't broken an axle, you wouldn't have beaten me."

Camara frowned.

"So why don't you stop playing trucks with us big boys and go home and play with your dolls?"

Her old defense mechanism kicked in, and his twinkling eyes did nothing to soothe the anger rising in her. She spun the bill of her cap around, closed her eyes, and started counting. *One, two, three, four, five. . .*

Her eyes darted open. Even though he was teasing, Camara couldn't take it anymore. If looks could burn, he'd be a crispy critter with the fiery flames she shot his way. "Let me tell you something, mister. I didn't graduate at the top of my class from the best auto mechanic college in the world to play with dolls. I plan to keep on racing and to keep on winning. And there is nothing that you or any other chauvinistic male will say or do to stop me." Camara crossed her arms and glared at him, challenging him to refute her claim. She hated that she'd allowed him to rile her again. Attacking him made her feel about as slimy as the mud dripping from her body.

Chase took a step forward and flicked a piece of mud off her shoulder.

"What are you doing?"

"Knocking that chip off your shoulder."

*One, two. . .* So much for feeling slimy.

"Listen, bucko, the only chip on my shoulder is the one you put there with all your hateful, mean-spirited remarks and your constant put-downs. I've worked hard to get where I am. Y'all are just jealous because I can build and drive a truck as good as any man. I've proved it, too." She looked toward The Black Beast and then back at him. "I paid a hundred dollars at the junkyard for a rusted-out bucket of bolts and turned it into a clean, mean running machine. But no matter what I do or how hard I try, because I happen to be the wrong gender, y'all constantly put me and my truck down."

His macho, cool-as-chilled-watermelon expression melted.

"Well, just wait and see. My new modifications will speak for me." She twisted the bill on her cap forward. Not giving him a chance to retort, she whirled around. "See ya at the pits." She strutted toward her mud bog truck.

❈

"Lord, that woman drives me crazy," Chase muttered. "I know I deserved what I got. I'm the one who started it. Why can't she see I was just having fun?"

In spite of her getting his goat, he chuckled. He had to admit just how fun it was watching her get all fired up. It tickled him that every time she got angry, she'd spin her cap around backward and close her eyes.

Those big brown eyes of hers, framed with thick eyelashes, glowed every time she talked about trucks and racing. She was as passionate about them as he was. His attraction for her had grown, along with his respect. "Lord, Ya gotta help me not to antagonize her anymore. Please."

He remembered her words about being cruel and felt instant remorse. She might appear tough on the outside, but he saw the hurt in her eyes when she mentioned how they'd all put her down. Even though he was just teasing her now, before he became a Christian he'd been as mean as a rabid dog, constantly putting her and her truck down—a fact he was now ashamed of. From now on, he'd watch his teasing of her. Plus, he needed to ask her to forgive him for being such a jerk.

First, Chase needed to get out of his muddy clothes. He looked over where Camara's truck and trailer were. Erik was using their water tank to hose the mud off her. Good thing he wasn't using the power sprayer. As tiny as she was, the pressure would send her flying. An idea struck him. He grabbed a towel and headed toward them.

"I'm next," Chase said, grinning.

Erik glanced at Chase and back at Camara. A smile of understanding spread across Erik's face. "So, y'all couldn't wait for the race, huh? Next time don't forget to take your trucks."

"Very funny, Erik. Ha, ha. Someday remind me to laugh." Camara narrowed her gaze at him menacingly.

Erik turned off the nozzle at the base of the tank and shook Chase's hand. "Good to see you again." He eyed Chase up and down. "From the looks of things, I'd say she bested ya."

Chase glanced at Camara, who quickly looked away. She snatched up a large towel and headed toward her Hummer.

"I have to admit, she did."

"Toss your towel over there." Erik jerked his head once toward the trailer. "I'll hose ya down."

While Erik sprayed him off, Chase watched Camara storm toward the bathroom.

She was an enigma for sure. Feminine and sweet. Rustic and gutsy. And feisty as all get-out when someone teased her about being a female mechanic—or about her Chevy losing—or about her short stature. That's when the feminine side of her evaporated like water drops on hot asphalt. Make no mistake about it, Camara Cole could hold her own against any man in any race—including him. Many times she'd given him a run for his money. And anytime he had beaten her, it had been by a mere one-hundredth of a second.

Camara was one of Alabama's best mechanics. She knew her stuff, and Chase knew she could teach him a thing or two about building and repairing engines. He just wasn't ready to admit that to her or anyone else yet. He chuckled.

"What's so funny?" Erik asked.

"I was just thinking about your sister."

"Oh yeah?" Erik's eyebrows waggled.

"Not like that." Chase rolled his eyes. "I was just thinking that she's not afraid of a little mud or grease. And she sure doesn't back down from a challenge."

"That's for sure."

Both had a hearty laugh.

Then Chase remembered her comment about her modifications. Just what *did* she have under that hood? He'd soon find out. And he could hardly wait.

# Chapter 2

Fed up with Chase's constant Chevy-bashing, short jokes, blond jokes, and female-mechanic slamming, Camara stormed off. Even though he was only teasing, she had heard enough to last her a lifetime. "You just wait and see, Chase," she grumbled under her breath. "My Chevy's gonna surprise you today." She grabbed a set of extra clothes from her Hummer and headed toward the women's restroom. Her body shook from the cold hosing down.

Inside the bathroom stall, Camara changed quickly. While tucking in her yellow T-shirt, she noticed her grease-stained nails and sighed at the futility of making them look nice. By the time she finished checking things under the hood today, they'd look a whole lot worse than they did now. She had to make sure everything ran in tip-top shape.

Usually Swamper Speedway only held mud bog races twice a month. But because mud slinging had become so popular, the owner decided to make it a weekly event. He had announced that the winner of this season's mud bog racing would receive the honor of having a replica of their bogging vehicle, along with its name, sported on all of next year's trophies, so it was even more important to win this year.

Not only would she be the first female to win, but she would finally prove that she could build and drive a truck as good as any man. Maybe then the harassment would stop.

She stuffed her clothes in her bag and smiled. After losing precious seconds at the start-up line, she had finally figured out how to gain a second or two—a stall converter. Today she'd see if her efforts paid off. She could ramp up the rpms until the torque converter engaged and then her truck wouldn't stall anymore.

It was the best four hundred dollars she'd ever spent. And if that didn't work, she knew what she'd found in a popular off-road magazine would.

She put on her jean jacket and hugged it tight, relishing its warmth. If Chase hadn't thrown her into the mud pit, she wouldn't be this cold. What had come over him anyway?

He sure had been acting different lately. She wasn't at all sure she liked the new Chase. At least with the old one, she knew how to act around him: barb for barb, jab for jab. When he'd slam her Chevy, she'd slam his Ford. Truth be known, she loved his '34 Ford Coupe. Camara pictured how macho and handsome Chase looked sitting in it.

Her thoughts drifted to earlier. She couldn't believe Chase had almost kissed her. She wiped her lips off with her shirtsleeve and scrunched her face. She would have decked him if he had.

Camara gathered the rest of her things and stuffed them in her duffel bag. After dropping it at her Hummer, she headed toward the entry booth.

"Good morning, Sam."

"Morning." Sam's bronzed tan made his bright smile appear even whiter, and his white hair made him look much older than forty-three. Camara smiled at his familiar face. If Sam wasn't making sure the contestants completed their entry forms, signed their insurance waivers, paid their entry moneys, and received their contestant numbers, he was out flagging or doing any other volunteer job that needed doing.

She took the proffered clipboard with the attached entry form and a rules pamphlet. Holding up the pamphlet, she sent Sam a questioning look.

"Something new this year," Sam replied to her unspoken question. "You might want to go over it before you enter, Camara."

Camara walked over to a picnic bench and sat down. Tapping the pen against her lips, she pondered whether she should mention the changes she'd made to her bog truck. Places she usually raced had Modified, Super Modified, Stock, and Super Stock classes, but because Swamper Speedway only ran an 8-cylinder Open class where anything was permissible and tire size didn't matter, she decided against mentioning the nitrous oxide system.

Finished filling out the form, Camara handed her entry fee and form to Sam. "Thanks, Sam."

"Good luck today, Camara."

❧

Camara removed her favorite yellow Chevy emblem cap, tossed it on the front seat of her Hummer, and sprinted over to The Black Beast. Once inside her 1974 Chevy bog truck, she fastened her harness and watched as Erik moved her step stool out of the way.

Giving her a thumbs-up sign, he said, "Go show 'em how it's done, girl."

Thankful that her brother believed in her and had always been there for her, Camara smiled.

Admiration for her six-foot-tall, athletically built brother made her sigh. Being the youngest and only girl in her family, Camara had always followed in her closest sibling's footsteps. Everything Erik did, she did—including building and racing mud bog trucks. In fact, Erik had raced boggers for years until he decided driving a monster truck sounded more interesting. Perhaps someday she'd build and race a monster truck, too.

Looking at the instrument panel, she flipped two toggle switches and simultaneously pressed the starter button and racing gas pedal. The engine roared to life. Shivers of delight raced up and down Camara's spine. Strapping on her helmet, she put the truck in gear and drove toward the mud pits.

Chase pulled up to the pit next to her. She smiled. *Good.*

Even though it was a timed event, her wish of running side by side with him came true. Excitement bubbled inside her, knowing the men who belittled her would be watching as she blew off Chase's doors.

*Pride goes before a fall.* Guilt tugged at her soul, but the desire to prove to everyone that she was a proficient competitor drove her harder. A hint of sadness dabbled over Camara. If only they would accept her.

Over the PA system, a voice announced: "Lining up at pit number one is contestant number 23, Chase Lamar, driving the Mud Boss, a 1934 Ford Coupe with 39.5 boggers. Powered with a 351 Cleveland small block."

Camara watched as they hooked up the pull cable to Chase's receiver hitch. Her gaze followed the other end of the cable where a backhoe sat ready to pull them out if need be. Without it, if any of them got stuck in the middle of the mud pit, they'd have no way of getting out. Camara was grateful to whoever thought up the idea. She might like mud racing, but she didn't want to get out in the middle of the pit.

She watched the flagman motion Chase forward. When he reached the start-up line, the flagger jerked his fist shut. Chase stopped and revved his engine. Expectant faces peered out from behind the protective chain-link fence. Men, women, and children of all ages clapped when Chase's name was announced.

She hoped they would be as excited to see her as they were to see Chase.

"At pit number two, we have contestant number 24, Camara Cole, driving a 1974 modified Chevy pickup, The Black Beast. Camara's running 38-inch Super Swamper TSL tires with a 400 small block engine."

Camara glanced at the crowd and grinned. More than half the crowd stood clapping.

"C'mon, Cammy! You can do it!" she heard Erik yelling above the noise. She glanced toward the nearby contestant's pit. Erik stood at the end of the orange fence blockade along with her dad, mom, and brothers Tony and Slick. All of them gave her a thumbs-up. *Thank You, Lord, for a family who supports me.* She looked to see if anyone was there for Chase. The only person she noticed was his friend John.

Turning her attention back to the task at hand, she quickly perused the deep ruts made by the other drivers. At the end of the mud pit was a thick muddy wall that the other drivers hadn't penetrated. It seemed to mock her. Strong determination rose up inside her. She'd show that mud pit she could break its barrier.

She studied the ruts. If she went to the left of the deepest one, she'd end up out of control and perhaps over the side, disqualifying herself. She looked toward the right. Noting a fresh spot where no one had gone, she decided to try it.

That wall would not best her. She'd show it who was boss.

The flagman motioned Camara forward. She inched her way until he signaled her to stop.

Goose bumps rose on Camara's flesh. Her adrenaline kicked into overdrive. She tugged on her leather gloves and clutched the steering wheel. Her right leg started shaking.

Chase revved his engine again.

Not about to be outdone, Camara pressed the pedal to the floor. *Rrrruuun rrrruuun.* She let up, allowing the engine to idle. *Crr crr crr crr.*

She pressed it again.

Over the loud rumbling inside the cab of her truck, she heard the crowd roaring.

Chase tapped his pedal fast two times. She looked over at him. He waved a pointed finger, smiled, and gave her a thumbs-up.

*What's that all about? Humpft.* She liked it better when he was an arrogant jerk.

The flagman raised the green flag.

Camara flipped the master switch. Every nerve stood on end. She fidgeted against the harness.

With her left foot on the brake, Camara pressed the gas, ramping up the rpms.

The flag dropped.

She slipped her left foot off the brake and floored the gas pedal. The Black Beast lurched forward then dropped into the pit, dipping her stomach right along with it.

The front tires pulled to the right. Arms tensed, she clutched the steering wheel tighter. With all her might, Camara jerked the wheel left. The rear stayed to the right, and she had to correct back to the right.

Her tires gripped their way through the deep mud, slinging the muck a good twenty-five feet into the air and onto her windshield.

Using all her bodybuilding strength, she tightened her grip to keep The Black Beast headed down the center of the pit. She darted a quick side glance toward Chase but couldn't see him because of all the mud flying.

Nearing the end of the pit and that mocking mud wall, she mashed the secret weapon button on the steering wheel with her thumb. Surging with power, The Black Beast shot forward. Quickly, she broke through the mud wall, raised her thumb, and up and out of the pit she flew.

Realizing she beat Chase, she pumped her fist and whooped and hollered, "Yes! Yes! Yes!"

She stuck her head out the window so she could see where she was going as she drove to the contestant's pit and revved the engine before shutting it off. She jerked her helmet off and shook her hair loose.

Erik slung the door open, yanked her out of her truck, and swung her around. "Way to go, Cam!"

When he put her down, she held her breath, waiting to hear her and Chase's times.

"Well, folks, each contestant runs twice, and we combine their total times. For this run, Camara's time is 9.26, and Chase Lamar's time is 11.83. . . ." The announcer's voice faded as several people came up to congratulate Camara on a great run. She thanked them, keeping her eye out for Chase. Her heart did a funny flip-flop when she saw him heading toward her.

"Congratulations, Camara. Nice run." Chase grabbed her hand and shook it, holding it longer than necessary. Vibration ran up her arm from his touch. Uncomfortable, she snatched it back. What was wrong with her? That had never happened before.

She blew away the unwanted feelings.

"Thanks," she said. Then she turned around and talked to Lolly.

❦

Chase stepped back. Whatever she had under that hood had worked. He walked back to his Coupe and started hosing it down. When he saw his father heading toward him with a scowl on his face, Chase cringed.

"What are you doing letting that Cole woman beat you?" his father spit out.

"Hi, Dad."

"No son of mine is going to let a girl, let alone one of them Coles, get the best of him. What happened out there?"

"I didn't let her win, if that's what you're thinking. She beat me fair and square." Chase chuckled. "Whatever modifications she did to her truck worked." As soon as his gaze met his dad's disapproving glare, Chase's smile faded.

"Well, we'll just have to find out now, won't we? You took care of it in the past; you can do it again."

*That was in the past*, Chase wanted to tell him. But as angry as his dad was right now, Chase knew better than to say anything.

At one time, Chase had wanted to make Camara look bad, too. More to please his father than anything. But secretly he was jealous of her. She could outbuild and outdrive most men, and she was an amazing mechanic. He'd heard her praised by lots of people. However, since accepting Christ as his Savior, he no longer cared about showing her up. Mud slinging was a sport he loved and nothing else. Well, almost. Sure, he wanted to win. What man wouldn't? It was tough losing to anyone, much less a woman.

"Chase, did you hear me?" His father's raucous voice broke through his musings.

Chase hated how his dad could make him feel five years old again.

"What are you going to do about it?" The hatred in his eyes made Chase's skin crawl.

Even though he knew why his dad was so bitter toward the Coles, he no longer wanted to take on his dad's offense as his own. Sure, at one time he had. Especially after Camara had become his biggest competitor. Rather than face his dad's displeasure at a Cole beating him, Chase had started messing with her bog truck. At first it was exciting, thinking of different ways to make The Black Beast run badly. Each time he'd beat Camara's time, his dad had praised him. Approval from his dad was something Chase sought. But after giving his life to Christ, his desire switched from wanting to please his earthly father to wanting to please his heavenly Father. And the difference was huge.

Chase drew in a deep breath. It was time he started standing up to his father. And there was no time like the present.

"Not a thing, Dad." Chase refused to flinch under his dad's evil stare.

"Well, somebody should." His father stormed off.

Something about the way his dad said it caused a deep, sinking feeling in the pit of his stomach. Hard telling what his father was capable of these days. Whatever it was, Chase knew it was bound to be bad. He shuddered. From now on, Chase would have to keep an eye on his dad—especially around Camara.

# Chapter 3

Camara and Chase had just made their final run of the day. She pulled next to her trailer, shut off The Black Beast, and held her breath waiting for her final time. She glanced at the dashboard and flipped off the master switch and all her toggle switches.

Hickory smoke from a nearby barbecue wafted up her nose, making her stomach growl. She patted her abdomen. Until she heard her time, her empty belly would have to wait.

"Are you ready for this, folks?" The announcer's voice echoed through the loudspeaker. "We have a new record here at Swamper Speedway. Camara Cole's time is. . ." He paused.

Camara's heart froze. "C'mon."

"8.78! Congratulations, Camara." The announcer's voice faded as she slung open the truck door and jumped out.

Her dad, mom, and three brothers gathered around her, hugging and congratulating her.

"I'm proud of you, baby girl," Daddy whispered in her ear. Her family stepped back, making room for other well-wishers.

"It's my turn," Lolly singsonged. She spun Camara around and gave her a big hug. "I wish it were Stan breaking the speedway's record, but. . ." She looked around. "If it had to be someone else, I'm so glad it was you. All those men will be eating barbecued crow tonight, won't they?" Lolly hugged Camara again. "Oh, here comes Chase. I'll talk to you later." With that, Lolly darted off.

Camara turned just as Chase neared her.

"Congratulati—"

"Told ya I'd blow your doors off today," Camara cut Chase off and sent him a playful but prideful grin. "Now what was that you said again about beating me?" She placed her finger on her lips and squinted. "Better get rid of that hunk-o-junk Ford and invest in a Chevy," she teased. "I know where there's a great Chevrolet dealership who'd give ya an awesome deal."

Chase shook his head, sighing. "When are you gonna grow up, Cammy? It's not about winning but about how you play the game."

Her eyes widened then narrowed as the memory of catching him under the hood of The Black Beast the previous year streaked through her mind. "The only thing *you* know about playing the game is messing with my bog truck and playing mind games before a race. Well, it didn't work today, did it?" She smiled again smugly, grateful she had shown up him and all the other guys.

Taking a step backward, Chase gazed at her. "Look, I know I've tinkered with your truck before and that I tried to psych you out before a race. I also know I've played a big part in you being defensive." He glanced at the ground then back at her. "I'm sorry. For all of it."

Stunned by his humility, her mouth fell open and her pride siphoned from her, leaving her feeling foolish.

Chase tilted his head sideways and sniffed the air. "Nitrous. You're running NOS? So that's your power booster."

Camara flipped her eyebrows upward. "Among other things." She smirked, feeling arrogant and rather pleased with herself.

Chase shook his head. He glanced at her truck. "Hope that pride of yours doesn't destroy you. Enjoy your victory, Camara."

He turned and strode off, stopping at the announcer's stand briefly before heading toward his bogger. Pride deflated from Camara. Chase's words stung. Hadn't her father said over and over again that her pride would be the ruin of her and true winners never boast? Her victory lost its sweetness. She'd been so busy worrying about winning and proving to the guys that she was just as good as them that she forgot all about building inner character and walking in love.

Staring at the ground, she scuffed her toe in the dirt as she thought about how she and Chase had constantly teased and bantered back and forth over the years about winning and who would beat whom. But this time, she'd gone too far. She could kick herself. Would she ever learn to shut her mouth and feel confident enough in her own abilities without trying to prove herself all the time?

🌺

Chase felt sorry for Camara. Didn't she know what a desirable woman she was until she opened her mouth? All that boasting turned his stomach, but unfortunately not his heart. His heart had changed toward her when he saw how she treated other people at church. She always made it a point to talk to the elderly and offered to help them. Whenever there was something going on to help another in need, Camara was first in line to volunteer. Oftentimes he wondered how she found time to work at her dad's dealership all day, keep her bogger in top running condition, and help those in need. He guessed she'd always been that way, but he was so busy trying to please his dad and trying to oust her that he'd never taken the time to see the goodness in her, nor did he care to at the time. But now he wanted to know her better.

Chase grabbed the sprayer and turned on the generator. Bent at the waist, he sprayed under the fender wells, tossing an idea back and forth in his mind. Maybe he would let Camara win this year. After all, he couldn't care less about winning anymore. His dad was the one who pushed him to succeed, saying it would be great advertising for his companies.

Realization hit him like a Mack truck. Chase straightened. Like everyone else in his dad's life, Chase had been a pawn to further his father's empire.

His dad never cared about him. His only concern was Chase's winning because it benefited him.

He remembered when his father had discovered his only son had "gotten religion."

"Someday you'll take over for me, son." Arrogance oozed from his voice. "But to succeed, you'll have to get rid of that religious nonsense. All of them Christians are brainwashed, poor folks. What's really important in this life is money and power. And I've got both."

Thanks to the millions Granddad had left him.

Chase wished he could get his dad to understand that money wasn't the answer. And what Chase had found wasn't religion—it was relationship. His relationship with the Lord was his number-one priority now.

"Will Camara Cole, Chase Lamar, Bobby-Rae Wallers, and Trey Daum come to the announcer's stand, please?"

The announcer's voice broke through Chase's reverie. He turned to his friend John. "Hey, buddy, will ya finish washing the mud off my Coupe for me?"

"Sure. No problem."

Chase handed the sprayer to John and walked away. "I owe ya one."

"You owe me two now," John hollered at him, chuckling.

He sure did owe John. He was the one who never gave up inviting him to church. He chuckled as he thought about how they'd met. Chase had just finished running and was heading toward the contestant's pit. His windshield was covered with mud, so he had hung his head out the window to see where he was going. He was concentrating so hard watching his side that he failed to watch the other side. When he heard a thump, he slammed on his brake and jumped out. John, a muscle-bound, hulking African-American man the size of a sycamore tree, lay on the ground in front of his Coupe.

"I'm sorry, man, I didn't see you. Are you okay?"

"I'm fine." John had started to rise. Chase reached out his hand to help him up. As John rose, Chase slowly leaned his head back, looking up at him. He guessed John weighed in around 240 pounds, mostly muscle, and was about six-foot-five. He normally would have found someone that tall intimidating, but the kindness in John's eyes and his large smile put him at ease. "I should have been watching where I was going. I know y'all can't see where you're going after running. It was my fault."

Chase had been so stunned that John didn't cuss or yell or anything. With all of his family's money, most people looked for an excuse to sue them. Not this guy. He took the blame. That was the beginning of their friendship.

*Thank You, Lord, for John.* He smiled as he approached the announcer's booth and stood next to Camara.

"Camara," Dan, the owner of Swamper Speedway, said. "It's come to our attention that you ran nitrous in your truck."

"Yes, sir." She shot a dirty look Chase's way and focused her attention back on Dan.

"Do you have a fire extinguisher in your bog truck?"

"No, sir." She frowned. "Why?"

"Did you read the pamphlet Sam handed out to every driver?"

Camara turned pale and shook her head.

"It states in there that anyone running nitrous oxide is required to have a fire extinguisher. And that anyone caught without one would not be allowed to race. Had we known about the NOS before you ran, we wouldn't have let you. I'm sorry, Camara. Because you didn't have an extinguisher, we have to disqualify you from the race today, and your time will be stripped from the records. First place will now go to Chase. Second to Trey, and third to Bobby-Rae."

Camara stepped back as if in shock. She blinked several times as she darted glances at the other male contestants. "But. . .but you can't. . . I didn't know. I worked so hard. I. . ." Her blinking increased. She turned her face away from their view.

Chase scanned the men's faces, trying to see them from her point of view. What he saw made his heart wrench. Poor Camara. Judging by the smirks on several of their faces, he got a glimpse of what she'd been up against, and what he, too, had put her through.

When he looked back at her, she whirled and ran, but not before he noticed a tear slide down her cheek. Chase's heart broke for her. Erik had mentioned to him that Camara hated for anyone to see her cry because she wanted to fit in and be one of the guys. One of these days he would get her to see that it was okay to let people see her vulnerable side. Then maybe she wouldn't run off. But who knew. Some habits are hard to break.

He looked at Dan. "I don't mind, Dan, if you let Camara have my points and trophy. She didn't know the new rules."

"Chase, I know you're trying to do what you think is right here, but just because she didn't read the pamphlet doesn't mean she can get away with breaking the rules. I would have had to do the same thing no matter who it was. Trust me. I hate having to do this. Camara deserved it. She flew through that pit."

Camara's shocked, hurt-filled face raced through Chase's mind. She'd obviously worked hard setting her truck up to run nitrous. She had outraced them all. He couldn't stand it that he was the one to take the trophy from her. It meant everything to her and nothing to him.

He had to find her and see if there was something he could say or do to comfort her. "Congratulations, y'all," he said, shaking Bobby-Rae's and Trey's hands. He hurried to find Camara. But the only thing he saw was Camara leaving in her Hummer, pulling The Black Beast behind.

❦

For the twentieth time, Camara reprimanded herself. She had a feeling she should have mentioned the nitrous. But no, pride wouldn't let her. She didn't want anyone to know. She just wanted to show all of them she could do it. Well, she did it all right. She blew it big time. Camara slammed her hand on the steering wheel. "I knew I should have read that stupid pamphlet."

With darkness settling over the long stretch of empty road, the abandoned cotton fields with some of the old cotton still clinging to them held a certain eeriness. Normally she loved this area. Because it hadn't been farmed in years, nobody ever came out this way, so it was her escape from the hubbub of the city and a place to be alone when the pressure of having to prove herself became too much. But with darkness falling fast, the shadows from the massive oak trees loomed like big monsters reaching their strangling arms toward her.

Never in her life had she felt more humiliated than she did now. Tears blurred her eyes. Camara struggled to see the road. She leaned toward the glove compartment and popped it open. Glancing back at the road and then back again at the box of Kleenex, she tugged a couple out. When she looked back at the road, her eyes widened and she jerked the steering wheel, fighting to avoid hitting a deer.

The deer survived; however, her Hummer rammed head-long into a deep ditch, bashing Camara's head against the steering wheel then whipping her backward. Spots twinkled before her eyes. Camara struggled to stay conscious, but everything turned dark.

❦

Camara squinted as she opened her eyes. The interior of her vehicle was pitch-black. Her head throbbed. She placed her hand on the back of her neck and rolled it slowly. It hurt to move.

How long had she been here? She pushed the clock button on the dash. 9:58 p.m. Peering up at the sky, she focused on the Big Dipper, and it all came back to her. She was out near the abandoned fields. Groaning, she laid her head back against the headrest for a moment and then leaned forward.

A chorus of howling coyotes caused the hair on the back of her neck to rise. Were they nearby? She shuddered.

Her hands shook as she put the Hummer in reverse and pressed the gas. It didn't move an inch. She put it in drive and hit the gas. Nothing but spinning tires. Knowing the trailer must be jackknifed, Camara flipped the overhead light on, opened the center console, and groaned. Once more, she'd forgotten to grab her cell phone.

257

Her head started reeling, and she felt nauseous. "Lord, please send someone to help me." She laid her head back against the headrest and closed her heavy eyelids.

She awoke to the sound of a vehicle. Even in the midst of her grogginess, she recognized that sound. "Oh no, not him. Lord, please don't let it be him."

The door on her Hummer opened.

"Cammy, thank God I found you."

Camara groaned. *Is this some kind of joke, Lord? You sent the enemy to help me?*

# Chapter 4

What Chase saw when he opened the door to Camara's Hummer turned his stomach. Her cheek and neck were caked with dried blood from the nasty gash on her forehead.

"Are you hurt anywhere?" Chase fought to keep his voice steady as he drew near and scanned her body. "Besides your head."

"What are you doing here?" she asked then winced.

"I was worried about you."

She raised her brows and shivered. Chase removed his light jacket and draped it over her shoulders.

"I called your house. When I kept getting your answering machine, I finally called Erik. He said not to worry about you. But every time I prayed for you, I couldn't shake the feeling something was wrong." Chase removed his cap and ran his hand over his spiked hair. "Every time I asked God if He wanted me to do something, I felt like I should go look for you. So I did." He shrugged. "That was hours ago. I almost gave up until I spotted your rig."

Her face softened then quickly turned into a frown. "Why were you trying to call me?"

"It's a long story. I'll explain it on the way to the hospital."

Before he had a chance to help her out, she swung her legs around and hopped down. His jacket fell from her shoulders as she slumped to the ground. Chase grabbed her arms and eased her up. "You okay?"

Camara closed her eyes and opened them slowly. "I twisted my ankle," she whimpered, "and my head is spinning."

Not asking her permission, he scooped her into his arms and carried her up the steep embankment toward his pickup. When she didn't argue, his concern grew.

The driver's side door stood open. Balancing Camara, Chase stepped on the sideboard and gently sat her in the middle of the seat. Making sure she was secure, he ran back to her Hummer, snatched up his coat, and slipped and slid his way up the steep ditch. He hopped in his truck and shut the door.

"Wait!" Camara clutched his arm. "I can't leave my Hummer and bog truck out here."

Chase flipped the interior light on. "Look, Cam, I'm not worried about that right now. I need to get ya to the hospital. That gouge in your head is pretty deep." He engaged the clutch and put it in first gear. "I'll call someone to take care of them."

"No!" Camara's voice filled with desperation.

He stopped the truck and faced her.

"Please?" The pleading look in her eyes unsettled Chase. He struggled with the need to get her to the hospital and the desire to succumb to Camara's plea to take care of her vehicles first.

Camara glanced at his belt where his cell phone was clasped. "May I use your phone to call Erik? He can get the shop's tow truck and haul them for me."

Knowing how much she prized The Black Beast, Chase relented. Nodding, he unclipped his cell phone and handed it to her. He put the truck in neutral and set the emergency brake.

Glancing over, he watched Camara punch in some numbers then put the phone to her ear. Each movement looked as if it pained her to make it.

"No, it's me, Camara. I'm using Chase's cell phone." She sighed heavily. "Yes, Chase's phone. Erik," her voice sounded strained and annoyed, "forget that for now. I need a favor. Could you and Tony grab Daddy's tow truck and come out to the abandoned fields and—" She closed her eyes. Frustration etched her forehead. "I know I shouldn't have come out here, but I did. Please, Erik." Her voice softened, breaking Chase's heart. She looked so vulnerable.

"I know it's late, but will you *please* come and get my vehicles? I don't wanna leave them here." She paused. Chase felt funny eavesdropping, but where was he supposed to go? He tried focusing on the chirping katydids outside and the million stars filling the inky night, but his ears kept tuning to Camara's voice.

"No, I swerved to miss a deer, and it high-centered in a ditch." She pulled the phone away. "Erik, please don't yell. I have a splitting headache." Tears slipped down her cheeks.

Chase wanted to pull her into his arms and comfort her, but he knew better.

"Yes, I'm fine." Her voice quavered. "Please, will ya take care of them?" More tears. "Thank you, Erik. I'm really sorry to bother you." She slowly nodded. "Okay. Just a minute." She handed the phone to Chase. "Erik wants to talk to you." She faced forward and stared out his windshield.

"Hey."

"Is Camara really okay?" The concern in Erik's voice for his little sister touched Chase. The only people who cared about him like that were his twenty-year-old sister, Heather, and his mother. But they had moved closer to Heather's college about a hundred miles from Chase's house. He sighed inwardly. If only his dad hadn't forced Heather and his mom to give up Christ or get out, they would still be living at his dad's house and he'd get to spend time with them. Chase often thanked God he had his own place, or his father would have booted him out, too, when he chose to follow Christ.

"Chase." The panic in Erik's voice snapped Chase from his musings.

"Sorry. She has a nasty cut on her forehead and a twisted ankle, but other than that, she seems okay." He glanced at Camara, who wiped her eyes and rubbed her nose. Again he fought the urge to console her, but not knowing how she would react, he thought it best if he didn't.

"Are you going to take her to the hospital?"

"Yeah."

"Then tell her I'll call Mom and Dad, and I'll be there as soon as I get The Black Beast for her." There was a short pause. "That truck means everything to her."

"Don't I know it." Chase heaved a dry chuckle.

"Let me know as soon as you find out anything."

"Will do. Talk to ya later." He flipped his phone off and attached it to his belt.

He looked over at Camara and was about to let her know what Erik said, but he stopped. Her chin touched her chest, and her shoulders shook. When he heard her sob, Chase didn't care what she thought. He carefully pulled her into his arms. She made no attempt to push him away, so he rocked her soothingly.

"It's okay, Cammy. You don't have to be tough all the time, ya know."

Her only response was the shaking of her shoulders. When she stopped crying, she whispered against his shirt, "Were you trying to call me earlier so you could gloat because I blew it big time today?" Her timid voice held no bitterness, only a heartbreaking vulnerability.

"No. I called to see how you were. When you drove off like you did, I was worried about you." He gently grasped Camara's chin and turned her to face him. Torment and tears glimmered in her big brown eyes, crushing his heart. Trying to gain control of the fresh, unexplained emotions he was experiencing toward her, Chase cleared his throat. "I tried talking them into letting you keep the trophy. After all, you deserved it. But Dan said he couldn't."

She blinked, and her wide eyes stared at him. "Why would you do that?"

"Because you beat me, and I care—," Chase caught himself. He didn't want her to know how much she affected him. "Look, I need to get you to the hospital." He pointed to her forehead. "That cut looks pretty nasty. How long have you been out here anyway?"

"Since about nine thirty."

Chase groaned. "That was. . ." He twisted his wrist and checked his watch: 12:47. "More than three hours ago."

His heart ached knowing she'd been stranded that long. Releasing her from his arms, he started to leave.

"Can't we wait till Erik gets here?"

"Look, no one's been by here in over three hours." He nodded toward her vehicles. "I think they'll be safe."

"Could you at least lock them up for me?" Chase knew what it cost her to ask him, her enemy, for help.

He sighed in surrender. "Does Erik have a set of keys?"

"Yes."

He nodded and quickly took care of it. When he got back in the truck, he flipped the interior light off and headed toward Swamper City.

❀

The pounding in Camara's head reminded her of an African ritual drumbeat. With each throb came sharp pain. She desperately wanted to rest her head and go to sleep, but first she needed to ask Chase something. She looked at him. "Chase?"

"Yeah." He glanced at her then back at the road.

Her gaze slipped to her fingers in the darkness. "After you smelled the NOS, I saw you stop by the announcer's stand. Are you the one who reported it?"

In the dark interior, Camara saw the white of Chase's wide eyes. "No, I didn't. I can understand how you might have thought it was me, especially considering what I've done to you in the past. But I stopped by the stand and told Dan that with the way you just ran I had my job cut out for me this summer." The lights on the dashboard cast shadows on his face when he glanced at her. "You did a great job with that truck." He turned his gaze back toward the road.

Camara's brows rose. She must have hit her head harder than she'd thought. Did Chase just say she'd done a great job on her truck?

"But," he said as he glanced at her with a teasing smile, "ya still need to get a Ford."

"Oh, you." She slapped him on the arm then instantly regretted the action. The quick movement caused searing pain. Camara clutched her head.

"What's wrong?"

"My head's killing me."

Chase accelerated the engine.

❀

Camara opened her eyes. Her head rested against Chase's shoulder, and she was snuggled up against him as if. . . Camara tossed the unwelcome thought aside and quickly scooted over. The quick movement caused shooting pain through her ankle and head.

Embarrassed, she mumbled, "Sorry."

Chase glanced at her and back at the road. "For what?"

What could she say? *For resting my head on your shoulder and sitting so close to you that I was practically on your lap?* She glanced at the clock on his dash: 1:33. Instant remorse smacked her as she realized the hospital was at least another fifteen minutes away. *Poor Chase.* "For making you stay up so late."

He reached over, wrapped his hand around hers, and gazed at her. "You didn't make me do anything. I came of my own free will." He smiled and turned his attention toward the road. "I'm just glad I followed the Holy Spirit's leading and came looking for you. You might have been out there for days before anyone found you."

"Nah, my parents or Erik would have come looking for me eventually."

"I don't think so. When I called Erik, he told me not to worry about you because you do this a lot and you'd show up at work on Monday morning."

The enormity of Camara's situation bulldozed over her. She drew in a shaky breath. "You're right." She lowered her lids and spoke softly, "Thank you, Chase."

He reached over and squeezed her hand again. His calloused hand felt warm, and a strange tingling sensation powered up her arm even as he let go to put his hand back on the steering wheel.

"Thank the Lord, Cammy. He's the One who laid you on my heart." His tone had a strange huskiness to it.

It occurred to Camara that ever since Chase had accepted Jesus as his Savior, he'd actually become a nice guy. At singles night at church, he and Erik had become close friends. And Erik was a great judge of character. Maybe she should cut Chase some slack and give him the benefit of the doubt.

From the corner of her eye, she watched him. A sensation that could only be described as tickling feathers tingled her stomach.

To think she'd been frustrated at God for sending Chase. Now she didn't mind at all. In fact, she was almost grateful. Subconsciously she touched her forehead. She really must have hit her head harder than she'd thought. She was getting soft where Chase Lamar was concerned, and she wasn't sure that was such a safe thing to do.

# Chapter 5

Camara gazed out her kitchen window and watched the sun rise. Taking the last bite of her grits, she marveled at how the raindrops slid off the yellow bell bushes and yet remained stationary on the red daylilies, purple impatiens, pink and white lantanas, and black-eyed Susans. The beautiful blooming flowers, along with the hot pink blooms on the crepe myrtle trees, brightened Camara's yard and her gloomy mood. After being stuck inside for six days, she couldn't wait to get out of the house. "Erik, where are you?"

The doorbell rang.

She tucked her crutches under her arms and hobbled into the living room. Erik popped his head inside. "Hey, Cam. Ya ready?"

"Sure am, bubba. Just waiting for you."

"You need help with anything?"

"Just my backpack." She pointed toward the floor.

Erik opened her door, and Camara stepped out. Dampness, mingled with honeysuckle and fresh-cut grass, wafted up her nose.

The sight of The Black Beast caused a thrill to race up her spine. One thing was for certain: She was a mud-boggin' fanatic. As she hobbled her way across the wet grass, moisture from last night's rain clung to the toe of the tennis shoe on her good foot, soaking it. She stopped for a moment and allowed the sun's morning rays to penetrate her pores, warming her through.

"Come on, Cam."

"Spoilsport. Give me a break. I've been indoors all week. I forgot how nice the sun feels."

"You sure you're up for this?" His brown eyes held concern.

"I'm fine." She hobbled to her Hummer. "It was a minor concussion, that's all."

Erik laid her crutches against her vehicle and lifted her up as if she weighed no more than a hummingbird. Making sure she was situated, he placed the crutches alongside her and closed the door.

Erik hopped in the driver's side and slid the key in the ignition.

"Now don't forget to. . ."

Erik pointed a stern finger at her. "Cammy." The impatience in his voice was evident. "I know what you're fixin' to say."

"Sorry. It just seems so strange having someone else driving my vehicle. It'll be even weirder watching you run The Black Beast today." She shifted her weight toward Erik. "You brought a fire extinguisher, right?"

"For the fiftieth time, yes."

"Whatever you do," she said, pointing her finger at him, "don't forget to make sure the nitrous switch is off and that the hose isn't kinked before you fire the Beast up. And when you go to take off into the pit—"

"Camara! You act like I've never driven your truck before, or any other truck for that matter."

"Sorry. It's just that you've never run NOS before, and I didn't want you to forget."

"How could I? We've been over this a million times already." At his frustrated look, Camara knew she'd gone too far.

"Sorry. I'm just nervous." She giggled. "I have drilled you all wcck, haven't I?"

"Nah." Erik started the Hummer, looked over his shoulder, and steered the vehicle onto the road. "Only six days." He sent her a teasing smile. "You're one day shy of a week."

What would she do without Erik? He was the best brother a girl could have. "Erik."

"Yeah." He glanced at her then back at the road.

"Thanks."

"For what?"

"For being you. And for always being there for me."

He leaned over and ruffled her hair. "That's what big brothers are for. Besides, someone has to keep ya out of trouble."

"That's for sure." They both laughed.

❋

Chase removed the nylon straps from the Mud Boss even as he watched for Camara's vehicle to pull in. She probably wondered why he hadn't called her. There was no way he could explain to her why he hadn't. When his dad found out he'd helped Camara, he came unglued.

"If I ever hear you talking to that. . .that Cole girl again, I'll disown you," his dad sneered.

"Dad. That's ridiculous. I see her every weekend at the mud bogs. I can't just ignore her."

"You can, and you will."

Knowing it was a no-win situation, Chase decided rather than argue with his dad he would instead make an appointment with Pastor Stephans to find out just how far a person was supposed to go in honoring their parents. Were children supposed to do whatever their parents said, even if they were twenty-three years old and living on their own? Chase loved the Lord and wanted to obey Him, but his dad's obsessive hatred toward the Cole family was driving Chase crazy.

Jumping inside the Mud Boss, Chase backed it off the trailer and pulled alongside his Ford pickup. After revving the engine a couple of times, he shut it off. He caught sight of Camara's yellow Hummer. His heart switched to high gear. Not sure what to do, he sat and watched.

❀

Camara scanned the contestants' pit looking for Chase. She thought surely he would have called or dropped by this past week to see how she was doing, but he hadn't. Not that she wanted him to, but after his attentiveness toward her, she thought he might. Spotting his rig, her pulse shifted into overdrive.

Erik opened her door and helped her gain her footing on the uneven ground. Camara gimped back to her trailer and tried manipulating her crutches around so she could unlatch one of the straps attached to The Black Beast.

"Camara Chevelle Cole! What do you think you're doing?" Erik picked her up and moved her aside. "You're gonna hurt yourself. I'll take care of this." He unclamped one of the straps. "Why don't ya go enter me?" His frustrated look said he wasn't in the mood to brook any argument from her.

"Fine. I was only trying to help."

"Listen, sis. I've got it handled, okay?" He grasped her upper arms and looked her square in the eye. "Trust me."

"Thanks, bubba." She gripped her crutches and made her way toward the entry booth.

Between the high humidity and the exertion of using crutches on the loose gravel, Camara was panting by the time she reached the booth.

"Good morning," Camara greeted Sam's back.

He turned, and his eyes widened. "What happened to you?"

"I tore the ligaments in my foot." She hoped he wouldn't probe further.

"How'd you get that nasty cut?" He leaned forward and studied it.

Too embarrassed to tell him, Camara changed the subject. "Listen, Sam. I won't be driving my truck today. Erik will."

Sam nodded and handed her the forms. Camara took a quick look behind her. "Do you mind if I stand here and fill this out? I promise if someone comes I'll move out of the way."

"No problem."

Camara hustled to fill out the form.

"Did you bring a fire extinguisher today?" Sam asked.

Camara looked up from the form. The hopeful look in his eyes made her smile. "Oh yeah," she said, drawing out the words.

She reached in the back pocket of her jeans and pulled out the ready-made check and handed it, along with the entry form, to Sam. Without looking, Camara swung her crutches around and smacked into something, throwing her off balance. Her hair flew across her face. Someone grasped her upper arm and steadied her.

She tossed her head back and looked upward into familiar dark green eyes. "Chase." She smiled with uncertainty. His rain-fresh scent swirled around her.

He lifted his cap off his head and tugged it back on. "How's the foot?" he asked, glancing around.

Camara panned the area to see what he was looking for and wondered what had him so jittery. Not seeing anything out of the ordinary, she responded, "Fine. I'm getting around much better."

"You driving today?" His brows rose.

"No. Erik is."

"Oh."

She waited for him to say something else. When he didn't, she couldn't stand it any longer. Eyes downcast, she asked, "Chase, can we talk?" Camara peeked around. Two of the other drivers headed toward the booth. "Privately, please?"

He rubbed his forehead and eyes, saying nothing.

"Sorry." She shifted her crutches sideways, hopping on her left foot. "I know you need to register." As fast as she could, she scooted off. She recognized the sound of The Black Beast and figured Erik must be taking it off the trailer.

Chase fell in step beside her. Camara kept moving until Chase touched her arm. She stopped and looked up at him. Gazing into his emotionless eyes, Camara wanted to slink away. Where was the sweet man who had helped her so tenderly last Saturday? She must have been delusional and only imagined Chase being so thoughtful and caring.

"Cammy?" The deep softness in his voice didn't match his eyes. "I'm sorry. You said you wanted to talk. Let's go over there." He pointed to a wooden bench shaded by a large oak.

Camara maneuvered her way to the seat. Placing her crutches to the side, she stuck her foot out carefully. As she lowered herself down, Chase grabbed her arm and steadied her. She shifted her weight forward and cringed.

"You okay?"

*No.* But there was no way she was going to tell him she'd just taken a splinter in her backside. "Fine." She waved him off then glanced at her fidgety hands in her lap. "Look, I just wanted to tell you how much I appreciated everything you did for me."

"I'm glad I was able to help." With only his foot on the bench, Chase perused the area as if he were looking for something—or someone.

She grabbed her crutches and rose, placing them securely under her arms. "Well, I know you need to go get ready, so I won't keep you. Thank you." Hating feeling so vulnerable, Camara put her head down. "I don't know what I would have done if you hadn't come along." She peered up at him.

His green eyes softened, and his face finally showed some emotion. He laid his warm calloused hand on her arm. "The thought of you being out there all alone—" His chest expanded, and he blew out a long breath. "Well, I'm glad you're okay." With that, and the barest of smiles, Chase stepped past her and walked away.

Camara didn't know what to think. One minute, Chase acted like he didn't want to be near her; then in the next, he acted like he truly cared about what happened to her.

The day and a half she had spent at the hospital nursing a concussion, Erik had told Camara repeatedly that Chase had changed since accepting Christ, but Camara still had a hard time believing it. She couldn't even trust her own assessment the night of the accident. Sure, it was true that Chase went with Erik to a men's fellowship breakfast every Thursday morning and to Wednesday's singles night and that they had become great friends. . .but Camara still couldn't bring herself to trust Chase. It was just too impossible to believe anybody could change that much.

# Chapter 6

Chase leaned against the Mud Boss, which was parked about fifteen feet away from the orange fence barricade situated in front of the mud pits. He watched Erik get ready for a run.

"At pit number one is Tim Rosser, driving the Mud Hog, a '47 Willys Jeep with 38-inch Super Swampers, powered by a 350 engine.

"At pit number two, driving for Camara Cole, we have Erik Cole driving The Black Beast. . . ." The announcer's voice continued over the loudspeaker, but Chase's thoughts trailed to Cammy's beautiful face and those big brown eyes.

His heart had done funny things earlier when he'd run into her at the entry booth and she'd told him she didn't know what she would have done if he hadn't come along and helped her that night. That rare, vulnerable look on her face had almost caused him to pull her into his arms and kiss it away. That would have been a huge mistake. At that moment, he knew he had to get a grip on his growing feelings toward her. In the past, whenever Chase had dated a woman of whom his dad didn't approve, his father had made both their lives miserable. Chase couldn't let that happen to Camara. He'd just have to keep his distance from her. A heaviness settled into his stomach. *Lord, help me not to care for Camara.*

As soon as the prayer left his thoughts, he knew that was going to be impossible. Instead he had to figure out a way to break the control his dad had on his life—which wasn't going to be easy. Ever since he was a kid, his dad had controlled him. Whenever his father wanted his way, he made Chase's life miserable until he could no longer stand the pressure. Chase caved in to his father's demands every time. When he moved out of his parents' house, he thought the control and the need to win his dad's approval would vanish. But it hadn't. What constantly baffled Chase was that, even though he couldn't stand his dad's torturous treatment, he still loved him. Loved him enough to date the spoiled, highfalutin Brittany van Buran, with whom he had nothing in common. Dad approved of her because of her father's position—mayor of Swamper City. A long time ago Chase realized what he wanted and how he felt didn't matter to his dad. But at least he'd managed to untangle himself from Brittany. . .for now.

The loud roar of the trucks taking off in the mud pit drew his attention. Erik and Tim were even in the pit. At the sound of someone's screaming, Chase's gaze followed the noise until it landed on Camara. What a sight! Camara jumped up and down on her good leg while her crutches swung precariously outward at her sides. His heart leaped to his throat. Chase dropped his socket wrench and ran toward her.

Just as Erik pulled out of the mud pit barely ahead of Tim, she completely lost her balance. Thankfully, Chase caught her from behind. With his hands under her arms, she looked up at him and caught his gaze.

He steadied her as every emotion he tried to deny swept through him. Surprise bombarded him when she pivoted on her good foot then threw her arms around him.

"Did you see that? What a run!" Camara abruptly pulled away, glancing everywhere but at him. Her fingers dug into his arm as she struggled to keep her balance. "Where are my crutches?"

With one arm supporting her, he leaned over, picked up her crutches, and handed them to her.

Her gaze plummeted to the ground. "Thanks. Sorry I got carried away." She smiled sheepishly.

"I hadn't noticed." He started laughing. She shot him a mock sneer. It made him laugh harder. The sound of her beautiful laughter sang in his ears.

Erik pulled up in The Black Beast, and the fun moment dissipated. Her brother hopped out.

"Great job, bubba!" She gave him a high five.

"Thanks," he replied then glanced at Chase.

"How's it going?" Erik clasped Chase's hand.

"Pretty good," Chase answered. "Great run. Did you hear your time yet?"

"No, I missed it." Erik looked at Camara. "Did you hear it?"

"Um, no." She glanced at Chase and giggled.

Erik looked back and forth between them. "Did I miss something?"

"You mean you didn't see your sister? She started a new dance fad called the crutch swing."

Cammy wrinkled her pert nose at him.

"It's not safe to leave her alone, Erik. Well, gotta run. I'm up after these two." He glanced over at the Chevy Blazer and '79 Ford lined up at the pits.

"Talk to y'all later." He spun around but in the next heartbeat stopped dead in his tracks. Twenty feet away stood his dad with his arms crossed over his chest, glaring at him. Chase cringed. *Might as well get it over with*, he thought as he strode toward his dad.

❀

Camara glanced past Chase to see why he'd stopped so suddenly. His dad scowled in their direction.

Camara licked her lips. Her mouth felt as dry as sand. She trudged her way toward the ice chest only a few yards from where Chase and his dad were. Shifting her crutches, she opened the lid.

"I'd better never see you talking to them Coles again, or I'll disown you. Not only that, I'll make sure the Coles regret the day they ever came near you. I told you before: Whatever you can do to destroy them Coles, do it. Is that understood?" Camara heard Chase's dad growl.

She didn't hear Chase's reply. Camara quickly snatched a Coke and quietly shut the lid. She moved away as fast as she could hobble. How sad that Chase's dad hated her family so much. And what did his dad mean that they'd be sorry? Whatever he meant, she didn't want to find out.

She rounded the corner of The Black Beast and met Chase's dad coming from the other direction. He glowered at her and hissed, "Stay away from my son." Her insides quivered at his toxic words and the evil in his eyes. "Or you'll be sorry," he spat. Then he stormed off.

Camara glanced at Chase, whose mouth was fixed in a straight line. His face was flushed, and the pained expression broke her heart. Now she understood why she hadn't heard from Chase and why he, too, had treated her so badly the last four years. It was because of his father's hatred toward her family. With a helpless shake of her head, she turned and started back to where Erik was hosing off The Black Beast.

❧

Chase hated when his dad showed up at the mud bog races. He wished he would leave. He had never been so humiliated in his life. He wanted to dive into the mud and bury himself there. What must Camara think of him? Knowing his dad would stop at nothing to keep him away from her, Chase knew he needed to avoid her as much as possible and stop thinking about her.

After asking John what Erik's time was, Chase pulled himself up into his Ford Coupe, put on his helmet, and headed toward the pit. The rumbling in the cab pounded against his aching head. Normally he loved the powerful sound, but today the stress of his dad being there and the way he talked to Camara made his head throb.

Knowing he had to beat Erik's time or his dad would ream him, the pressure in his head intensified. He glanced at the other pit. Dave Marks's '78 Chevy Blazer, Time Bomb, rumbled. And although Chase knew his Coupe had enough power to beat Dave's, with the state of mind he was in, he wasn't sure he could beat anyone. He had to force himself to concentrate.

The flag dropped. Chase slammed the gas pedal to the floorboard. He dropped into the pit and took off, driving like a crazy man. It was as if he were pushing through his problems and burying them in his wake. He lunged up and out of the pit and glanced behind him. Dave's Blazer sat halfway through the pit. Chase drove to the contestants' pit, shut off his engine, and waited to see if he beat Erik's 11.7. He hated competing against his best friend. Erik had been nothing but good to him over the years. Even before he was a Christian, Erik made it a point to talk to him. In a way, he wanted Erik to win. But knowing what his dad's response would be, Chase prayed that this time he'd win.

"Chase Lamar's time is 11.7. So far, we have a tie for first place between Erik Cole and Chase Lamar." Chase ignored the rest of the announcer's message and jumped out of his Coupe.

John gave him a high five. "Great job, buddy."

"Great job, my eyeball," his dad's gruff voice ground out. "You could have done better than that and showed up them Coles. Quit messing around and get out there and win."

Chase looked over his shoulder. John pointed toward the Mud Boss and the power sprayer and left.

Chase's heart nearly stopped. *Oh no!* Erik was heading his way with a big smile on his face. *God, please don't let Erik come over here. Please.*

"Hey, Chase. Great run. What'd ya do? Put wings under your hood? You flew through that pit." Erik clasped Chase's shoulder.

*God, please don't let Dad say anything to humiliate me.*

To his surprise and relief, his dad simply scowled and walked off to the side. Chase let out the breath he didn't know he'd been holding. "You had a good run, too."

"Oh, man. I forgot how much fun this was. I should build me another bogger." They both chuckled.

"Between running one of your dad's dealerships and building and racing monster trucks, when will you find the time to build a bogger?" Chase asked.

"Well, a guy can always dream, can't he? Besides, it would be odd competing against my baby sister. I could just hear her now."

Chase stuck his index finger in his ear and shook it. "Me, too. And it ain't a pretty sound."

They both burst out laughing.

It had been a long time since he'd had a good belly laugh.

"There's Stan," Erik said. "I'd love to chat, but I need to talk to him. I just came by to congratulate you and wish ya luck on your last run."

"You, too."

Erik turned and strode away. Over his shoulder he hollered, "May the best man win!"

"The best man will win," Chase's dad groused with a smirk on his face.

Something about the way his dad said those words caused a lump to settle in Chase's stomach. *Lord, I don't know what Dad meant by that, but please, keep Erik and Camara safe.*

# Chapter 7

Camara popped the last french fry into her mouth. She maneuvered her crutches on the loose gravel as she headed toward Erik, who had just hopped into The Black Beast. Up next was the tiebreaker between Chase and Erik.

"Don't forget, bubba. Flip the NOS switch this time—right before the flag drops and—"

"Sis!" Erik cut her off and shot her a "That's enough!" look.

"Okay, okay. But your last run, you forgot to turn it on. You would have beat Chase's time by a good couple of seconds if you would have run the NOS."

"You wanna drive?"

Camara dropped her head. "No. Sorry."

"Look, I'm sorry I forgot to turn on the nitrous. I know how much winning this race means to you. I won't forget this time."

"Thanks, bubba." She backed away and worked her way to the guardrail.

"Hey, sis."

Camara turned. "Tony! Where ya been?"

"Workin'. What else?"

Camara eyed him warily.

"Okay, okay. After Dad had me putting in sixty-plus-hour weeks for the last seven months, I took a minivacation and went fishin'. Another bass tournament." A grin stretched across his face. "Caught a four-pounder. And I got my barbecue all ready and waiting for ya at my house. I told the wife I was certain I could talk ya into grilling it for me."

Wrinkling her nose, Camara narrowed her brows. "Yeah, right. In your dreams. I wouldn't touch the slimy thing."

"You blow me away. You play in the mud in them there trucks, but you won't touch a fish?" He chuckled at her expression. "You know I'm teasing you, sis. Besides, the fish is being mounted." He hiked his foot on the guardrail. "So, what'd I miss?"

"C'mon. You're just in time to watch the tiebreaker between Chase and Erik." Over the loudspeaker, Camara heard The Black Beast and the Mud Boss lining up at the pits. Camara's finely tuned ear honed in to the sound of her engine. It wasn't running right. "Oh no. Not now."

"What's wrong?" Tony asked.

"Can't you hear it?"

"Hear what? It's so loud you can't hear anything but the trucks."

"The engine's missing—the spark plugs aren't firing right. I don't understand. It was running great awhile ago."

Unfortunately it was too late to do anything about her engine now. The flagger dropped the red flag. The Black Beast dove into the mud pit before the Mud Boss.

Camara held her breath. Halfway through the pit, The Black Beast bogged down. The more rpms Erik poured into it, the more the engine sputtered.

Chase leaped out of the pit.

The crowd roared.

The announcer's voice reverberated throughout the area. "Chase Lamar's time is 10.99." The announcer continued talking, but Camara tuned him out.

She couldn't wait until Erik brought her truck back so she could check it out. Crutches or no crutches, she'd figure out a way.

Tony beat her to her truck. By the time she hobbled to it, Erik had the hood raised and was leaning over the engine.

Camara hobbled next to them. "Tony, would you get my stand, please?"

"You'll get all muddy."

"I don't care. Please?"

Tony quickly retrieved her stepladder.

"Find anything, Erik?" Waiting impatiently on the ground caused her insides to jiggle.

"I'm just taking off the filter now so I can check the carburetor out. I don't get it. It ran fine earlier."

"Let me up there. I wanna check something. I think I know what's wrong."

Tony placed the stepladder in front of her. Camara crooked her bad ankle upward and leaned her crutches against the truck. Tony clutched her waist and hoisted her onto the top step, making sure she had her balance before letting go. "Tony, would you mind grabbing a plastic cup out of my Hummer, please?"

Tony headed toward her vehicle. Her brothers knew that once she got something on her mind, she went for it. No crutches would stop her. Camara unplugged the hose from the carburetor and manually pumped some fuel into the cup.

Several minutes later, the fuel settled. "I knew it."

"You knew what?" Tony and Erik asked.

"There's water in the fuel." She'd seen this enough times; she knew before she ever got under the hood what was wrong.

Erik's forehead creased. "How'd water get in the fuel cell? I filled it this morning myself. And I know the racing fuel was good then."

"Tony, will you help me down, please?"

Tony lowered her to the ground and handed her the crutches.

When she looked over at Chase and his dad, she thought they both looked rather pleased. Surely Chase wasn't so desperate to win that he would stoop so low as to sabotage her truck?

Earlier, when Erik had gone over to congratulate Chase and then talk to Stan, she'd gone to the restroom. Camara decided to see if Lolly noticed anyone hanging around the Beast.

"I need to drain the tank."

"I'll do it," Erik said.

"Thanks, bubba. I'll be right back."

"Where ya going?"

"To check on something."

She hobbled across the contestant's pit. "Hey, Stanley. I'd high-five ya, but with these crutches, I'd fall," she teased the lithe, six-foot-two man.

"Please don't. I don't wanna catch ya. Ya ain't big as a minute. I'd have to stoop too low for such a shrimp like you that I might hurt myself." He chortled, his blue eyes sparkling with mischief.

Camara feigned a scowl. "Oh, go play in traffic. Just cuz you're a corn-king giant." She wrinkled her nose at him.

"Well, it's better than being a baby-pea-pod. Or Little Miss Shrimput who sat on her truckut." His lips twitched with mirth.

"That was *so* bad, Stan."

He raised a palm upward. "Hey, what can I say? I tried."

Camara glanced around. "Where's Lolly? I need to talk to her."

"What?" He held his hand over his heart. "You mean you didn't come over here to see me and declare your undying love for me?"

She giggled. "You nut. I'm sure Lolly would appreciate that."

Lolly stepped from behind their blue Ford. With her finger on her lips as a *shush* sign, she walked stealthily and stood behind her husband. Camara suppressed the urge to laugh.

"She wouldn't have to know." He waggled his brows.

"Oh yes, I would." Lolly pinched his arm and walked around to face him.

"Ouch." Stan wrinkled his face and rubbed his arm. "She pinches like a goose."

Lolly scrunched her nose at him. "Well, if you'd behave, I wouldn't pinch you at all."

Lolly gave Camara an awkward hug around the crutches. "Long time no see. Sorry I wasn't there to help you this past week."

"You were where you needed to be. Your sister Jenny needed your help with her new baby. How are they doing?"

"Really good. Little Tyler is so cute. After being around him, I want one now."

She looked at Stan and winked.

"That can be arranged." Stan gave Lolly a loving look.

"Okay, you two lovebirds."

"Sorry, I got carried away." Lolly's voice held no apology. Her face turned serious. "I'm so glad you didn't get hurt worse than you did. I don't know what I would do without my best friend." Lolly leaned closer and examined Camara's stitched-up, jagged wound just below the brim of her cap. "Will you have a scar? How you doing? And what have you been doing besides playing in the ditches?"

"First things first." Camara leaned on her crutches and held up a finger. "One, I'm supposed to tell you that I came over here to declare my undying love for your husband."

"For this big burly guy? Consider it declared. You can have him." She winked at Stan.

"Nah. I think I'll pass. He's too tall for me, and besides, he doesn't like us shorties. But thanks anyway."

Stan rolled his eyes while Camara and Lolly giggled.

Camara held up another finger. "Two, I'm doing really well." She popped up a third finger. "Three, the doctor doesn't think it will scar too badly." Camara jerked up a fourth finger. "And four, what I've been up to is only 5 feet 2½ inches."

"Shrimp," Stan muttered.

Camara wrinkled her nose at him. "Jealous?"

His brows arched.

"Excuse us, Stan, I need to borrow your wife a second." Camara looped her arm in Lolly's. Looking at her crutches, she shrugged and let go.

"I'll be back in a second, sweetie," Lolly said.

Stan nodded and headed toward his bogger.

Camara panned the area. Keeping her voice down, she asked, "Did you notice anyone hanging around The Black Beast?"

"You mean besides the millions of spectators who had their noses under that hood of yours or the scads of people taking pictures?"

"Smart aleck." Camara tapped Lolly's arm and leaned closer. "I mean, did you see anything unusual?"

"Well, I'd call that bunch you work with unusual," Lolly teased. "But Bobby-Rae, Lem, and Tim are always hanging around your and everyone else's trucks."

"Would you be serious, please? Someone put water in The Black Beast's fuel cell."

"What?"

Camara's gaze jerked around. Stan peeked at her from under One Bad Mudder's hood.

"Shh."

"Sorry. Is that why it ran so poor today?"

Camara nodded.

"Wow. I'm sorry." Lolly's forehead wrinkled. "Let's see. The only other people I noticed were Dave Marks. . ."

One of her competitors.

". . .some kids. . ."

There were always kids hanging around.

". . .and Chase and his dad. But again, that isn't unusual. They hang around everyone's boggers." She eyed Camara. "You don't think one of them did it, do you?"

"I'm not sure."

"You know, it rained for about an hour during the night. Maybe the cap wasn't on, and it rained in it."

Camara shook her head. "No. Erik said he had it in the shop all night."

"Loll." Stan's voice broke through their conversation. "You ready to get something to eat? I'm hungry."

"I'd better go. But if I hear anything, I'll let you know."

"Thanks." They shared a quick hug.

"Bye, Stanley."

"Ya know, Camara, the way that Chevy of yours missed today, you might consider getting rid of that thing." He chuckled. "And leave the auto mechanics to us men."

"Stan! Stop it!" Lolly rebuked him.

He winked at Camara. "She knows I'm just teasing." He grabbed Lolly's hand and tugged her away. "Bye, shrimp."

Lolly looked over her shoulder and mouthed, "Sorry."

It was like being sucker punched. Although Stan was teasing her, it still hurt. Anytime one little thing went wrong, he'd tell her to get rid of her Chevy and leave the auto mechanics to the men. It seemed like no matter how hard she tried, it was never good enough. Guys still teased her and sometimes got downright cruel.

Dejected, Camara hobbled toward her truck.

Dave Marks stepped out from the side of his Chevy Blazer right in her path. Camara jerked to a stop, nearly falling. After gaining her balance, she looked at him and inwardly groaned. Dave stood almost eye level to her with his chest puffed out and his arms akimbo. He reminded her of a bantam rooster. She sighed heavily. Just what she needed—another harassing moron. Well, she refused to let him intimidate her. Camara looked him square in the eye.

His brown eyes dimmed. "I keep tryin' to tell ya to get rid of that piece of junk ya race. And," he added with a disgusting macho attitude and a spit of tobacco, "it's obvious by the way that Chevy of yours ran t'day that ya don't know what you're doin'." His snide, egotistical smile made her skin crawl.

Camara spun the bill of her cap around. *One. . .two. . .*

Dave raised his hands. "Hey, don't go blowin' a gasket on me. I'm only tryin' to help."

*Yeah, right. And donkeys fly. And pigs swim. Three. . .four. . .five. . . Help me to control my anger, Jesus.*

Besides, the only reason her truck ran so poorly today was because someone had sabotaged the fuel. But she didn't need to justify herself to him—or anyone else. If it took forever, she'd find out who did it. And she'd start with Chase Lamar and his father.

Camara tried hobbling around Dave, but he kept getting in her way.

"Ya need a man's help fixin' that thing."

*Six. . .seven. . . Give me grace, Lord.*

"Someone like me," he said, pointing to himself, "who knows what he's doin'."

He clutched her shoulders. Flames shot out from Camara's eyes. He was pushing it. She glared at him then flicked his hands off her shoulders. Dave grasped them again, sending pain racing down her arms. With his face mere inches from hers, his garlic and tobacco breath about bowled her over. Normally she liked the smell of grease and fuel, but the combination of them, the garlic, the tobacco, and the sweat turned her stomach. She tried pulling back, but he clenched her more firmly. *Eight. . .nine.* She reined in the urge to bop him with her crutch.

"I think we'd make a pretty good team." He looked at her mouth and licked his dry, chapped, tobacco-stained lips.

*Ew, gross. Put those disgusting things anywhere near me, buster, and I'll belt ya one. Ten!* "Oh, go play in traffic. You'd be the last person on earth I'd ever team up with. Now, let me go, ya big bully!" She squirmed, trying to free herself from his strong grasp.

"I love a feisty woman." His hands gripped her even tighter, hurting her.

"Leave me alone!" Camara flipped her arm upward, trying to hit him with her crutch.

"You heard the lady. Let her go."

Camara jerked around as Chase came and stood next to her.

"I said, get your hands off her. . . . Now!" Chase's voice brooked no argument. He stood a good eight inches taller than Dave.

Dave's hands fell from her arms. "Cool your jets. I was just havin' some fun with her."

Camara leaned on her crutches and rubbed her aching arms.

With his fists clenched at his sides and the veins in his arms bulging, Chase got right in Dave's face. "You *ever* so much as even look at her again, you'll answer to me."

Dave backed away. "So, that's how it is," he drawled. "The two rivals are now lovers." He spun around. As he strutted away, he yelled over his shoulder, "You kin have her. I want a *real* lady."

Chase took a step toward Dave. Camara grabbed his arm and shook her head. Although Dave's words stung, she didn't want Chase getting in a fight because of her.

She studied Chase's profile as he stared in the direction Dave headed. What kind of game was Chase playing anyway? Rescuing her one moment and possibly plotting with his dad to sabotage her truck the next. Was he messing with her mind or what? Why didn't he just do what his dad told him to do and leave her alone?

# Chapter 8

Two weeks had passed since Chase's bitter victory. The trophy on the glass shelf mocked him. He was convinced if someone hadn't messed with The Black Beast, Erik would have won. Chase just hoped it wasn't who he thought had deliberately messed with it. Slinging himself from his mahogany leather couch, he hustled over to the trophy and snatched it up. In seven strides, he stormed into the kitchen and tossed it in the trash can.

He stomped back to the couch and plopped down. Dejected, he leaned forward, placed his elbows on his knees, and clasped his hands. "Lord, what am I gonna do? You command us to honor our father and mother, but Dad is so obsessed with beating the Coles, I think he's losing it. And, Lord, I really like Cammy, and I'd love to get to know her better. I wanna ask her out after the mud races next Saturday, but what if Dad finds out?" Chase pressed his hand over his face. "I hate feeling like I'm five years old again, needing permission to go play at a friend's house. But it's hard telling what Dad might do to me and to Camara if he found out. Since he booted Mom and Heather out, he's gotten worse.

"Father, please give me wisdom on how to handle this whole thing. It shouldn't even be an issue. I don't live at home, and yet Dad still controls my life. All I want to do is own a mechanic's shop and work on vehicles. But Dad insists I learn the business so I can take it over one day. Heather's begged Dad to let her run his companies after she graduates. She has a great head for business, but he refuses because she's female." He glanced skyward. "I know, I used to act that way, too. If only Dad would become a Christian, he would be happy." Chase paused. "Come to think of it, Lord, I don't think I've ever seen my dad happy." Chase released a long breath. "Lord, give me the grace to handle this. In Jesus' name, amen."

The heavy burden lifted. He was grateful John had been persistent and that he'd found Jesus. Now, if only God could get ahold of his dad.

Chase glanced at his watch: seven thirty p.m. Maybe Pastor Stephans was home. He'd been so busy the last two weeks he hadn't had a chance to call and make an appointment. Chase picked up his phone and dialed the number.

After making a lunch appointment for the following afternoon, Chase looked around his lavish house. The circular mahogany couch with the matching love seat and recliner barely made a dent in the space of the large room. Chase hated the abstract pictures on the walls. He preferred a more rustic look.

The only part of this house that represented him was the den that sported his trophies and collector model cars. His father had insisted on hiring a famous decorator to furnish the place. His mother had offered to help, but his father refused. Chase wondered if he'd ever get up enough guts to break free from his father's domineering personality.

His dad believed money bought happiness. Well, the plantation-style mansion with its lavish furnishings hadn't made his dad happy. The old adage about money can't buy happiness...his dad was living proof of that. And so was Chase until a few months ago when he'd given his life to the Lord and found the true source of happiness. If only his dad understood that true fulfillment comes from a relationship with Jesus Christ.

Chase ran his hand over his spiked hair. He needed answers from Pastor Stephans on how to break free from his dad's controlling powers and yet still honor him as the Bible commanded. Plus, he needed wisdom on how to deal with his dad's destructive attitude, and he needed them before his dad did something everyone would regret. Especially him.

❧

After showering, Chase pulled on a pair of neatly pressed jeans, brown suede loafers, and a light pink shirt. He checked himself in the mirror and decided he would be presentable for his luncheon engagement with Pastor Stephans after church this morning. Chase gathered his keys and headed toward church.

Spotting a couple of empty parking places, he parked his truck and got out. Several maple, pine, and Bradford pear trees shaded the back of the parking lot. But because the Alabama sun was so hot, the shade didn't help ward off the heat. Chase wiped the sweat off his forehead and glanced at the large A-frame church. Prisms of light danced off the three stained-glass windows. Camellia, the reddish-pink Alabama state flower, lined the front of the white building, giving Chase a small glimpse of heaven's brilliance. Camara pulled her Hummer into the spot next to him.

When she stepped out, Chase's breath vanished. She looked amazing in the blue floral summer dress that flowed to her calves. A few strands of her blond hair blew across her cheeks. It took every bit of self-control he possessed to keep his hand from reaching out to move the wayward strands from her face. Her tanned skin made her brown eyes look like creamy hot fudge topping. A pink hue fanned the scar on her forehead.

"Um, uh." Camara cleared her throat.

Chase felt heat start from his stomach and end up in his cheeks. "Good morning." He fought to mask his embarrassment. "What, no crutches?"

"Good morning to you, too. My ankle's doing much better." Her bright reply surprised and delighted him. He wasn't sure how she would act toward him after the way his dad had spoken to her.

"It's late. We'd better hurry. Race ya." She sent him an ornery look and took off running.

Chase stared after her. Her sandals slapped against the asphalt. He noticed she favored her sore foot. Not about to be outdone, he darted after her. Only two feet separated them. Chase changed his mind and deliberately slowed his pace so Camara would win.

Camara stopped at the steps and swirled around. "Told ya," she said breathlessly. Giving him a smug look, she threw her shoulders back, clutched her compact Bible to her chest, and strode up the steps still limping generously on her hurt ankle. Nothing seemed to stop Camara. Chase smiled and shook his head. She was some kind of woman. His kind, to be exact.

On his way up the steps, he overheard an elderly woman speaking to the gray-haired gentleman whose arm she clutched. "Oh, Donald. Don't they make the cutest couple? He must love her dearly. When we were young, you used to let me win, too."

Chase swallowed back his embarrassment at the lady's remark. He quickly glanced to see if Camara had heard. If she did, she didn't let on. She just kept walking toward the door. That lady didn't know what she was talking about. He didn't love Camara. He liked her a lot, and she consumed his every thought lately, but love? Shaking the absurd thought from his brain, Chase made his way toward the double doors.

❧

Camara had felt pretty smug about winning until she heard an elderly lady say something about Chase letting her win because he loved her. Obviously that lady didn't know what she was talking about. Chase had never *let* anyone beat him at anything, especially Camara. They'd been rivals too long. Rivals who loved goading each other. Sure, things were different between them since her accident. She now noticed his good looks, handsome smile, and physique that even a bodybuilder would envy.

When she reached for the church door handle, Chase's hand landed on top of hers. She peered up at him. His warm, rough hand melted her insides. Moving ceased to be important. Someone behind them cleared their throat. Camara blinked. Her cheeks flamed.

"Let me get that." A slow, knowing smile spread across Chase's face.

She jerked her hand out from under his and looked away. "Thanks."

Chase opened the door and motioned her ahead of him.

Peppy praise music greeted her. Not wanting to walk down the long aisle late, she spotted a seat in the back row clear against the far wall.

She limped over and politely asked the middle-aged man if he would move over a bit. He smiled and scooted down the pew. Setting her Bible on the seat, she started clapping and singing.

A slight nudge on her shoulder made her look sideways. Chase motioned for her to scoot over.

Her eyebrows shot upward. There really wasn't enough room for him. She glanced at the man next to her, and as if he knew, he scooted over as far as she thought he could.

Chase's presence filled the end of the row. There wasn't any extra room between her and the man next to her. Not wanting to be rude by crowding the gentleman, she had no choice but to allow Chase's arm to press tightly against hers.

The touch sent a foreign, tingling sensation throughout her arm.

She darted a quick glance at him and wondered if he felt it, too. By his stunned expression, he must have.

Their gazes locked, and the air evaporated from the room. The next song started, and Chase broke the connection. Camara swallowed. What had come over her? This was Chase. Chase Lamar. . .her longtime rival. *Get a grip, Cam.*

Chase's deep baritone voice disrupted her thoughts. Forgetting everything for a moment, Camara focused on the two men standing on either side of her who were praising God in perfect harmony. The bass voice of the man next to her mingling with Chase's baritone sent chills all over her body. She closed her eyes and let the wonderful presence of God wash over her. *Oh, Lord, I love You. I'm so grateful to know You as my Lord and Savior. Thank You for the privilege of being in Your house. You're so wonderful, Lord.*

Several songs later, she glanced at Chase. Eyes closed, face tilted heavenward, light seemed to radiate around him. She'd never witnessed a more beautiful sight. Mesmerized, Camara stared at him.

Was this the same man she'd been rivals with? The same man who had mercilessly tormented her for being a Chevy lover, a mud bog racer, and the forbidden female mechanic? This Chase loved God and wasn't afraid to show it. This man glowed from within. And this man, if she wasn't careful, could easily capture her heart.

❧

As Chase sang, unchecked tears trickled down his face. He silently praised God for His loving-kindness, His mercy, His grace, His peace, but most of all for allowing a man such as himself to find God's forgiveness through Jesus Christ. What an amazing, loving heavenly Father Chase served.

Chase thought about his own father. Heaviness shrouded his heart.

*Oh, Jesus, if only Dad knew how wonderful You really are. Then he would understand why I love You so much and why I won't give You up.* Chase swiped away his tears. *Since Mom became a Christian and no longer cares about worldly things, I think it makes Dad feel like he isn't needed anymore. He sure has changed since he drove out Mom and Heather. In fact, he's become so mean he's starting to do things that border on being dangerously illegal.*

Camara stirred next to him. The smell of her sweet gardenia perfume permeated the air.

*Lord, I'm afraid for Camara. I have this feeling that my father will follow through with his threat toward her.*

Feeling a need to connect with her, keeping his eyes closed, Chase clasped Camara's hand. *Keep her safe, Lord. And help my father to know You.*

When the music had stopped, Chase wasn't certain. He opened his eyes and found Camara staring at him. Then she looked down at their clasped hands and hiked both brows. Chase smiled and reluctantly let go. He opened his mouth to say something, but Pastor Stephans walked up to the podium, asked them to be seated, and started his sermon.

Chase didn't hear a word he said. His mind stayed on Camara. Why had he never seen how truly lovely she was. . .inside and out?

# Chapter 9

Camara leaned against her Hummer and watched the entrance to Swamper Speedway, waiting for Chase to arrive. Ever since church last Sunday, she viewed Chase in a whole new light.

During worship when Chase had held her hand, she was completely taken aback. When she looked over at him and noticed the tears trailing down his cheeks and his face glowing with peacefulness, her heart had softened instantly toward him.

The familiar sound of his diesel pickup drew her attention. Chase pulled his pickup and trailer alongside hers.

Camara couldn't control her rapid-firing pulse.

Chase stepped out of his pickup, walked over to her, and gave her a quick hug. She eyed him suspiciously. She wanted to know who this man was and what he did with the old Chase.

He laid his hand on her arm, causing a tremor to shimmy up her arm. Not used to her new feelings toward him, she didn't know how to act.

He smiled, and her breath caught in her throat. Why hadn't she appreciated how truly handsome he was before?

Chase looked over her head, and his smile vanished. Camara turned around to see what had wiped the smile off his face.

Chase's dad was driving toward them. Remembering his threat, Camara said, "I gotta go get ready." Never one to back away from a challenge, for Chase's sake, Camara turned and sprinted around the back of her trailer. Because of Mr. Lamar's hatred toward her family, she knew there could never be anything between her and Chase. Not even friendship. His dad would see to that. Besides, she didn't want anything coming between Chase and his dad—especially her. All things considered, Camara decided it would be best to just stay clear of Chase.

Unsnapping the straps from The Black Beast, she felt someone tap her shoulder. Camara spun around.

"Ya need some help?"

"What do you want?" Camara asked, narrowing her gaze at the grease-stained mountain sporting a red T-shirt minus the sleeves.

"Well now, I figured I'd been so awful to you that I'd make it up to ya by seeing if ya needed any help." Bobby-Rae's smile didn't quite reach his eyes.

Camara scrunched her face. Why would he offer to help her when he barely talked to her lately, and the last time he had, he'd insulted her so badly? She had a feeling he was up to no good.

"Hey, what's up?" Camara heard Chase's voice behind her. She watched Chase step forward, relieved that he'd interrupted them.

"That offer stands," Bobby-Rae said to Camara. Looking at Chase, he turned and stalked off.

Judging from his hasty departure, Camara assumed Bobby-Rae didn't want to tangle with Chase. Not that she blamed him. Chase was a stout man whose quickness and skill during fights had earned him a reputation as someone not to mess with. Now she had another Chase-saving-her-skin story to tell Lolly. If she wasn't careful, she might end up with a whole bunch of them, the way this was going. Stifling the thought and a giggle, she turned to him.

"Did you want something?"

"I was just passing by and thought I'd say hi." He sent her a look she couldn't quite decipher.

Disappointed, she plastered on a fake smile. "Okay," she said, forcing a light-heartedness into her voice. One she didn't feel. "See ya at the pit."

When Chase made no effort to leave, she sent him a questioning look.

"Actually"—he raised his Ford cap and tugged it back on his head—"I came by to see if you would have lunch with me today."

Camara tilted her head, studying Chase's face to see if he was serious. Unable to discern if he was or not, she said, "You and me"—pointing between herself and him—"have lunch together?" She chuckled nervously. "That's funny, Chase."

Chase's features went from chipper to crushed. "I'm serious. Would you like to have lunch with me?"

She started to say yes until she caught a glimpse of his dad standing several yards away from them, scowling at her.

"Maybe some other time, okay? I can't today."

"Some other time then." He tipped his cap, turned, and left.

She watched Chase meander toward his father. The two of them talked then looked toward her. Something about that whole scene made Camara uneasy.

Erik pulled up next to Camara in his semitractor trailer loaded with his monster truck. With his elbow resting against the door, he leaned his head out the window. "Hey, sis," Erik said over the loud *crr crr crr crr* of his diesel engine. "I'll park this thing and then come help ya."

While they unloaded The Black Beast from the trailer, Camara told Erik about Bobby-Rae's offer to help.

"I thought he was mad at you."

"Me, too." She shrugged. "Oh well. It's Bobby-Rae. Who ever knows what he's thinking."

A deep voice came over the loudspeaker announcing it was time to start signing up for the day's events. Camara headed that way.

Chase walked in step beside her. "Mind if I walk with you?"

She darted a glance at him. "Won't your dad mind?"

He laid his hand on her arm and stopped her. "Listen, Cammy. I know what Dad said to you. But that's how he feels. It's not how I feel. I'll deal with my dad."

"Chase." She gently removed his hand. "I don't think it's wise if we talk. Your dad hates us, and I don't want there to be any more problems between us. We've just started becoming friends. Let's keep it that way." She looked up at him and caught his gaze. Willing him to understand, she added, "Better make that distant friends." Camara quickly trotted toward the entry booth.

While Camara stood in line, Chase walked up next to her and whispered in her ear, "No. Not distant friends. I want more," he said then moved into the other line.

Camara's heart revved up. She didn't know what to think of Chase's new-found interest in her.

❦

After they attached the cable to the rear receiver hitch of her truck, Camara lined up at the pit. Next to her was Ben Sands, driving his silver Chevy Cameo pickup, the Mud Slinger. This was the last race of the day. In order to win today's race, she had to beat Chase's time of 10.72.

The flagman raised the flag.

With shaky hands, Camara pushed the master switch, turning on her NOS. She put her left foot on the brake and pressed her right foot on the gas.

The flag dropped.

Camara jerked her left foot off the brake and floored the gas pedal. The Black Beast lunged forward ahead of Ben. Halfway through the pit, right before she was ready to engage the NOS, her truck started sputtering, slowing her pace. Camara watched Ben pass her and lunge up and out of the mud pit. Turning her wheels to the right, then to the left, The Black Beast bogged down in the thick mire with her engine not running right. "Oh, man!" Camara slammed her hands against the steering wheel. What had gone wrong? Everything was running fine when she checked it before leaving the shop this morning.

Camara flipped the NOS switch off. She wanted to hide her face while they pulled her out of the pit. Despair and anger wrapped around her as she realized Chase had won again. Now he was ahead of her by two races.

Camara's truck jerked and sputtered as she made her way toward the contestants' pit.

Erik met her and swung open her door. "What went wrong? It sounds terrible."

"I don't know." She flipped all the toggle switches off, shutting off the pickup.

She hopped out, ran around to the passenger side, and grabbed her stepladder.

Camara placed the ladder near the front fender of the truck and stepped up.

"What happened out there?"

With a close of her eyes to rein in her anger, she groaned at the sound of Chase's voice. Opening her eyes, she studied his face to see if there was any sign of gloating. However, what she saw was worse. Pity. Well, she didn't need or want his sympathy. Right now she only wanted to find out why her truck ran so rough. "I don't know, but I'm fixin' to find out. Now if you'll excuse me."

Doing her best to ignore him and everything else, she popped the hood open. From the corner of her eye, she noticed him turn to leave. *Good.*

Her brother leaned over the hood as she checked through the system. Everything seemed to be fine. She stepped down and walked to the back of the truck. In one instant, she saw the problem—fuel dripping from the fuel cell exit line.

A sick thudding feeling pitted Camara's stomach.

"Erik, look at this." The hose clamp was loosened enough on the fuel line that it had caused it to suck in air.

Erik examined the clamp. "How'd that happen?"

She had her suspicions but didn't voice them. The only time her truck had been unattended was when she and Erik had gone to grab a barbecue sandwich. Maybe the fiend did it then. Surely he wasn't so desperate to win that he would do such a thing to her. Would he?

❀

During the next two weeks, Camara and Erik watched The Black Beast at every conceivable moment. She'd won both races since then, and now she and Chase were tied in points. Not wanting to risk losing, she vowed to continue watching The Black Beast like a hawk.

"Hi, Cammy." Chase's deep drawl broke through her thoughts. "Erik." Chase reached for Erik's hand and shook it.

She'd been avoiding Chase like a bad virus. She glanced up to find both Erik and Chase staring at her. Did she have food on her face or something? She self-consciously wiped at her mouth. "What?" she asked them. "What are y'all looking at me like that for?"

It was clear neither one wanted to be the one to start. With a glance at Chase, Erik took the dive. "Well, sis. Chase and I've been talking."

*Uh-oh.* She raised her brows. "About what?" she asked, not really wanting to know. She took a sip of her sweetened tea.

"About you."

She hiked a brow. "What about me?"

"Well. . ." Erik shifted his weight back and forth. A sure sign he was up to something she wouldn't like. She knew that look in his eyes. He was pleading with her to understand. "The church needs a new roof. And, well. . ." Erik glanced at Chase and then back at her. "Chase and I thought about a fund-raiser."

Camara frowned. Not really wanting to ask but wanting to know what the two of them were up to, she drew in a deep breath and asked, "What kind of fund-raiser?"

"We've already talked to Pete, and he said we could use Pete's Mud-n-Track to have a mud bog race."

Camara let out the breath she'd been holding. "Oh. . .is that all?"

"No, there's more," Chase chimed in. "Erik was so sure you'd win that I challenged him."

"That challenge includes you," Erik added sheepishly.

"Me?" She tilted her head. "What's this challenge involve, anyway?" She darted a quick glare her brother's way.

"If you win, I have to wear a Chevy-lover jacket the rest of the mud bog racing season."

"You?" Camara hooted.

Nodding, Chase grimaced. "But if I win, you have to agree to spend a whole day with me."

"What?" Camara's mouth dropped open. She whirled her gaze toward her brother. "Are you crazy? Me and *him*? On a date?" she shrieked and shook her head furiously. "Y'all have been smelling too many gas fumes." She sent Erik a how-could-you? look.

"What? You afraid of losing?" Chase challenged.

Camara scrunched her face and stared hard at him. "Lose to *you*?" She tucked her hair behind her ears. "I have only one thing to say. . . . Name the day and time, and I'll be there."

# Chapter 10

What had Camara gotten herself into? How was she supposed to know Chase had installed nitrous oxide in his '34 Ford Coupe prior to the fund-raiser? She'd been so certain she'd win that she really hadn't thought about the ramifications of accepting the challenge. Camara sighed heavily. If only he'd lost. She giggled just thinking about him having to wear a Chevy-lover jacket at the mud bog races. That would have been one for the history books.

Camara pulled on white shorts with her favorite flower, yellow daisies, on the bottom left side. Her blouse had the same print on the right side near her shoulder. She slipped on her white sandals with tiny yellow daisies across the strap and buckled them. Checking herself in the mirror one last time, she shook her head. Never before had she worn so many cute outfits and dresses as she had this summer. Today, for some odd reason, she wanted to look her best for her date with Chase. Who would have ever thought she, Camara Cole, would be going on a date with Chase Lamar? Stranger things had happened, she supposed.

She started wondering about where he might take her. She'd always wanted to go to Noccalula Falls Park in Gadsden to see the statue of the legendary Indian chief's daughter, Noccalula, who chose to jump off the falls rather than marry the man she didn't love. That was where Slick took his last date, and it sounded romantic. And last summer Lolly couldn't stop talking about the Gilliland-Reese Covered Bridge at Noccalula. That sounded romantic, too. Then again, Lolly had a way of romanticizing anything she and Stan did together. Camara readjusted her top. Well, maybe Chase would take her to the botanical gardens there or on the nature trails. She glanced at her sandals. If he did that, she'd have to change shoes. For a split second she considered changing them but decided that was a dumb idea, since she didn't even know where they were going.

In fact, knowing her luck, Chase would probably be ornery enough to take her coon hunting. Or even worse, drive hours to Tuscumbia to the Key Underwood Coon Dog Memorial Graveyard or take her bass fishing. Camara shuddered as the options got worse. She hated fishing and hunting of any kind. That's where her girlie side kicked in. What the local guys got out of killing animals was beyond her comprehension. Many more even less intriguing possibilities spiraled through her mind. She stared in the mirror and wondered what had possessed her to go ahead with this date in the first place. Because she trusted

Erik's judgment, that's why. Camara found herself actually looking forward to today, providing there were no coons, fish, or dead deer in sight.

The doorbell rang. Camara's stomach fluttered. She skipped down the steps.

❧

Chase rang Camara's doorbell, drew in several long breaths, and exhaled slowly. Uncertain of the reception he'd receive, he fumbled for a breath mint and popped it into his mouth. He couldn't believe how jittery his insides were. It wasn't like this was his first date. He'd dated plenty. But this date was different. Camara had been hoodwinked into it.

It seemed like he'd waited a lifetime to spend a day alone with Camara. He wanted to get to know the real her—the other part of her, aside from the competitive, maniacal, racer-mechanic he'd butted heads with the last four years.

The door opened. His eyes widened as he drank in the sight of her. Standing in front of him was a very feminine, beautiful woman. Each time he saw her dressed like a lady instead of a grease monkey, he wanted to ask why she didn't let the world see her like this more often. But each time, he held his tongue, not wanting to rile her.

"Hi, Chase, come on in. I'll just be a minute." She moved out of the way and let him enter. When he walked past her, he caught a whiff of soap and spring flowers.

"Is there anything I need to bring?" She tilted her head. The way her hair fell across her eye did strange things to his insides. He wanted to reach out and move it away then run his finger over her soft cheek. His gaze went to her mouth.

"Chase? Did you hear me?"

Heat rose to his cheeks. He couldn't believe he was blushing. His buddies would never believe it, and he wasn't going to be the one to tell them.

The amused look on her face made him want to run out the door. But no way would he miss his chance to finally go out with her.

He pulled himself together. "You'll need to bring a light jacket and a swimsuit."

"Oh? Where are we going?"

"You'll just have to wait and see." He smirked.

She looked adorable the way she wrinkled her pert nose at him. He couldn't wait to get to know the real Cammy—the feminine Camara standing in front of him. He also hoped they could put their differences aside and get to know each other for who they really were—not just competitors at the pits.

"I'll grab my things." She turned and sashayed toward the stairs.

Chase glanced around her bright living room. On his left was a fireplace with a round oak table between two overstuffed couches. A sycamore table sat in front of the wall-to-wall sliding glass windows. He could see out into her yard, where he noticed a large rock fountain in the center of a well-manicured lawn lined with yellow daisies. When he heard a door shut upstairs, his gaze drifted that way. Along one wall near the stairs was a floor-to-ceiling glass and brass bookshelf with trophies and classic model cars. Plus several replicas of famous monster trucks. The shelf reminded him of his.

"Okay." She grabbed a lined Windbreaker and keys and shoved them in her yellow duffel bag. "I'm ready."

She might be ready, but was he?

❀

To protect her shorts-clad legs from the hot leather seat, Camara spread a beach towel over one of the front bench seats on the pontoon boat. She couldn't take her gaze off Chase sitting behind the wheel. While he paid close attention to navigating the boat, she imagined the deep concentration in those dark green eyes hidden behind those black sunglasses. Eyes that earlier had stared at her when he'd first arrived at her house. She stifled a giggle.

He'd looked so cute standing there speechless and blushing. That was another side of Chase she'd never seen before. And one she found extremely attractive. Her heart did a funny little dance.

Her gaze shifted to the bronze skin of his arms. She glanced at her lightly tanned legs and was envious of him. Reaching inside her duffel bag, she grabbed the suntan lotion with bug protection and started rubbing it on her legs, arms, and face; then she tossed it back in her bag. Perfumed coconut lingered in the air. Mosquitoes buzzed around her but didn't land. The cool, refreshing spray of the water was a reprieve from the ninety-degree weather.

As they traveled across Lake Guntersville, the beautiful lake nestled in the Appalachian Mountain foothills, Camara marveled at how many tiny islands there were. Lush trees lined the shore in some areas, while others were dotted with tall, spindly trees and geese. Several mansions spread along the winding shoreline. Camara sniffed the air. The sweet smell of coral honeysuckle and magnolias wafted around her.

Along the way, Camara returned the friendly waves of people on their houseboats near the bank.

Leaning back on her hands, she closed her eyes and enjoyed the hot sun on her body and face. She was so glad Chase brought her to this fantastic place.

"Dollar for your thoughts?"

Camara's eyes opened. She turned her face toward him.

"I was thinking about you."

He dipped his head, lowered his sunglasses on his nose, and peered over the dark rims. "Oh yeah?"

"Yeah." She paused, wondering how much she should tell him. "I was thinking about how much you've changed."

"Oh." He sounded disappointed as he pushed his sunglasses back in place. "In what way?"

"Well"—she swiped a tiny bug off her leg—"I was thinking about the day Erik told me you'd accepted the Lord. I didn't believe it." She glanced at a sailboat passing by and returned the passengers' wave then looked back at Chase. "When I saw you in church several weeks ago"—she placed her bare feet on the carpeted boat floor, facing him—"you had tears flowing down your face, and you glowed. I knew your conversion was real because the Chase I knew was so busy being Mr. Macho that he wouldn't have let anyone see him cry."

She wished he'd take off his sunglasses. It had been said the eyes were the mirror of the soul, and she'd love to get a good glimpse into his soul right now

"I can see why you didn't believe him. I was pretty mean...especially to you." He slowed the boat down and turned sideways in his seat. Even though he had sunglasses on, his head was bowed so she knew he was looking at the seat rather than her. "Look, I want you to know I'm sorry for the things I've said and done to you. If you wanna know the truth...I was..." He removed his sunglasses and caught her gaze. "I was jealous of you." He quickly replaced his sunglasses, but not before Camara glimpsed the sincerity in his eyes.

"Why would you be jealous of me?"

"Because of your family's close relationship."

"Oh," she said, keeping the disappointment out of her voice. She secretly hoped it was because of her racing and mechanical abilities.

Chase looked forward and then turned the steering wheel left. "I've always wanted a close relationship with my father, but he's too busy trying to make money and thinking of new ways to outsell your dad." He killed the engine and looked at her. "Dad believes that whenever he takes business away from your father, he's somehow getting revenge for what happened in the past. For years, my mom told him what your dad did was an accident and that he needed to let it go because it was eating him alive. But her words only led to a massive fight. He said it would be over his dead body before he forgave that—" Chase suddenly stopped and smiled sheepishly. "It's still hard to believe they were best friends from sixth grade until their senior year in college."

Camara pursed her lips and nodded.

A shadow covered the boat. A strong wind whipped her hair across her face. She glanced up at the sky. Chase followed her gaze. They'd been so intent on their conversation, they hadn't noticed the dark clouds rolling in.

Chase started the boat and shoved a lever forward. The boat picked up speed as they headed toward the shore.

"Where are we going?"

"To my family's vacation house."

Camara's eyes darted open. How could he take her to his family's vacation house? What if his dad showed up there? After all, the man seemed to show up everywhere else.... She knew she shouldn't have trusted Chase. She never should have accepted that stupid challenge in the first place. But then again, if she hadn't, Chase would have believed it was because she thought he would win. *Ack!* She could boot herself in the backside for reneging on her vow not to trust him. If nothing else, she should have at least gotten involved in planning this date.

"Don't panic." His smile did nothing to reassure her. "My dad is out of town on business until Tuesday. Or otherwise I wouldn't risk taking you there."

Camara's mouth slackened. Had he just read her mind?

Lightning cracked across the sky like a jagged scar. A loud boom immediately followed, raising the hair on her arms. Camara squealed. She quickly gathered her things and moved to the seat directly behind Chase so she could be under the canopy.

"Grab a couple of life jackets from under that seat," Chase ordered.

Against the rocking movement of the boat, Camara struggled to balance herself while she retrieved a couple of jackets from the storage unit under the seat. She let the lid slam shut. After handing Chase a jacket, she quickly slid into hers and fastened the three straps. Plopping herself down, she grabbed hold of the railing and hung on for dear life.

Water sprayed her face as small waves splashed over the boat. Camara scanned the area. Black, threatening clouds loomed over the rolling landscape as far as she could see. In a breath, heavy sideways rain started pelting her skin. She picked up her duffel bag, grabbed her Windbreaker from it, and tried putting it on, but it was too small to fit over the life jacket. She hurried to remove the jacket; then she put on her Windbreaker and the life jacket over it.

When she looked ahead, she saw a large plantation-style house not too far away. "Is that it?"

"Yes."

"God, please help us make it there," she whispered, knowing how vicious these Appalachian storms could be. Her heart slammed against her ribs as fast as the waves were beating against the boat. Was it her imagination, or was the boat no longer moving forward?

"Chase? Are we gonna make it?" She couldn't keep the quiver from her voice.

"We need to get this boat docked as soon as possible and get inside before..." He looked toward the sky. "Before the hail hits."

Camara watched Chase struggling to keep the boat heading toward the house. Camara relaxed a bit. They were only feet from the dock.

"Hold on, Camara. The way the waves are, it might be pretty rough." Chase's voice boomed over the loud thunder.

Lightning pierced the sky again. Camara closed her eyes. *Lord, please help Chase get the boat docked. And keep us safe.* She opened her eyes.

As Chase maneuvered the vessel alongside the private dock, a large wave pushed the pontoon boat, slamming it against the dock. Camara hoped the padded sides would keep the boat from getting dented.

"Wait here." Chase anchored both ends of the boat and ran back to her. "C'mon, we've got to hurry and get to the house."

Before Camara had a chance to even respond, Chase grabbed her hand and helped her out of the boat and onto a wooden walkway.

"We'll have to make a run for the house."

The wind whipped her wet hair across her face, making it difficult to see. Hail pelted her skin, sending sharp stinging pains with each hit.

The slippery grass made it difficult for them to keep their footing, but the overhead trees kept some of the hail at bay. They hurried as fast as they could until they reached the sheltered porch. Chase dug in his pocket, pulled out a set of keys, and quickly unlocked the door.

Once inside, they stood in the foyer, dripping and catching their breath.

"That storm sure came out of nowhere." Camara shuddered before removing her life jacket and Windbreaker.

"I should have been paying more attention." Chase removed his life jacket. He took hers from her, laid them both on a bench in the foyer, and then faced her. "I had my mind on other things." He stepped closer. Camara stepped backward until her back pressed against the wall. Placing his arms on each side of her with his hands flat against the wall, he stared down at her. Rain dripped from his hair, and water beaded on his face and lips. Chase dipped his head toward her. Camara's insides shook, not only from being chilled but from knowing what was about to happen.

His mouth touched hers in a questioning kiss. When she responded, he pulled her into his arms and kissed her thoroughly. How could the man she'd been rivals with for so many years make her go weak in the knees with his toe-tingling kiss? More to the point, how could she be kissing a guy she'd vowed not to trust only half an hour before? Nothing was making sense. Pushing him away was a viable option, but right then, as dumb as it was, she didn't want to.

When he pulled back, Camara looked into his eyes, feeling a bit awkward.

"We'd better get dried off." His drawl was low and shaky. He backed up, putting space between them. After that kiss, she needed plenty of space. . .and air.

"Is that you, Chase?"

Camara spun toward the sound of the deep male voice.

"Hello, Roberts." Chase nudged Camara forward toward the handsome man who appeared to be in his mid-forties. With his dark hair, blue eyes, and medium build, he reminded her of Clark Gable.

"This is my friend, Camara. Camara, this is Mr. Daniel Roberts."

She tried not to stare at him as they shook hands.

"He and his wife live in the cottage out back. They've taken care of this place since I was four."

"Oh." She nodded, not knowing what else to say.

"Nice to meet you, miss."

"Chase!" A beautiful, petite blond woman ran toward them and threw her arms around Chase. "When I saw that storm coming in, I was so worried about you." She stepped back and looked at Camara. The lady's large green eyes sparkled when she looked at her.

"This is my friend, Camara. Camara, this is Mrs. Helen Roberts."

"Pleasure to meet you, ma'am." The lady shook her hand.

Helen stepped back. "You're soaked. We need to get you into some dry clothes." She eyed her up and down. "We're about the same size. I have something that'll fit you."

Camara looked at Chase, who smiled sheepishly at her.

"Follow me." Helen smiled.

Relieved to get rid of her wet clothes, Camara gladly followed the woman.

❦

Chase couldn't help admiring her feminine walk. She was a complete enigma to him. She could repair and build trucks and outdo any man, but she could be feminine and sweet with equal ease. She was the most desirable woman he'd ever met. Whenever he'd teased her lately, he did it because it gave him an excuse to be around her. He might have taken on his dad's attitude toward the Coles for a time, but that was long over. He wanted to pursue a relationship with Camara and see where it would lead.

He couldn't believe he'd kissed her. His heart was still racing. He'd waited for her to shove him away, but when she didn't, he pulled her closer and deepened the kiss. And what a kiss. Who would have thought that feisty little mechanic could kiss with such passion? But, he realized, everything Camara did, she did passionately.

"Reliving that kiss?" Roberts asked, nudging him.

Chase felt heat rise from his stomach to his face, even though Roberts and Helen were more like family to him than his father's employees.

"Don't worry. I won't tell Helen. If I did, she'd have the two of you married off next week." He chuckled. "Thanks for giving us plenty of notice. Helen has everything ready, just as you asked. I hope your guest enjoys her meal. Talk to you later."

Chase nodded. Taking the steps two at a time, he went to his room and changed into some dry clothes. He couldn't wait to see Camara's face. With his dad out of town until Tuesday, Chase confidently arranged a surprise luncheon, regardless of his dad's insistence on being informed whenever anyone used the place. Chase had only himself to blame. On his sixteenth birthday, he'd secretly thrown a wild party and his friends had trashed the house.

He hurried back downstairs, grabbed the fireplace remote, and turned it on. Then he rushed into the kitchen, making sure Helen had everything ready. He wanted today to be special. Plus, he wanted to show Camara that he wasn't the same jerk he had been in the past.

"Chase." He heard Camara calling.

"Be right there," he hollered. Seeing everything was ready, he headed back to the living room.

Camara stood in front of the white marble fireplace with her hands extended toward the flames. The homey image sucked the breath out of him. Wearing a white sweat suit with a towel wrapped around her head, she looked as if she belonged there. That idea did funny things to his insides.

He drew in a breath and cleared his throat. "Lunch is ready," he said, walking up behind her. Chase offered her his arm. When she slipped her hand through his elbow, his stomach quivered. Never before had a woman's touch affected him so strongly. What was it about her that made his body tingle and his heart race ninety miles per hour?

❦

The afternoon flew by in a flurry. After an intimate lunch, the two of them had talked and played games with the Robertses. Even though she understood why Chase wanted to get the boat across the lake before dark, the thought of leaving made Camara sad.

When they stepped outside, the thick humidity dampened her clothes. Orange, yellow, and silver danced throughout the lake's ripples as the sun lowered against the horizon. The trip back was quiet and serene until they neared the marina. Camara heard Chase groan.

"What's wrong?" she asked, sitting forward.

Chase jerked his chin once toward the wharf.

Her stomach plunged to her toes.

Chase expertly guided the pontoon boat against the dock. Before Camara rose, his dad hopped on the boat and glared hard at her.

"Get away from my son!"

Camara blinked at his animosity.

In horror, Chase gasped. "Dad!"

"Stay out of this, Chase." Mr. Lamar pinned her with his gaze. "I warned you to stay away from my son. Now do it or else," he ground out.

Stunned, Camara barely heard the protest Chase aimed at his father. Then as quickly as he'd arrived, he left, leaving in his wake a heavy foreboding feeling. Camara glanced at Chase standing with his mouth agape.

Knowing Chase had to secure the boat before he could leave, Camara snatched up her bag and fled. This time his dad's threats had truly frightened her. For Chase's sake as well as her own, she needed to avoid him.

She ran several minutes before ducking into a bait shop. She stayed close to the bathroom door in case she saw Chase; that way she could slip inside so he wouldn't find her. Once the coast was clear, she'd call a cab.

# Chapter 11

C hase pulled his Ford behind Camara's Hummer parked in front of the dilapidated house. The shingles were all but gone from the roof, the steps needed repair, three of the windows were boarded, the paint had peeled, and the railing on the porch was missing in several places. The place was devoid of grass. The only color was a variety of bright wild flowers dotting the yard. Pine trees surrounded the house.

Looking for Camara, Chase scanned the volunteer workers from Living Water Fellowship. When he didn't see her, disappointment shrouded him. He was hoping to get a chance to speak to her alone today because she'd avoided him since their date. He wasn't about to let his dad's negative attitude stop him from getting to know Camara. On Pastor Stephans's advice, Chase had confronted his father and let him know that his vendetta against the Coles was just that—his. And Chase would no longer be a part of it. Nor would he let him control his life any longer.

That hadn't gone over well, but he couldn't worry about it right now.

Chase grabbed a can of paint and a brush from the church van. In hopes of finding her, he headed around the back of the house and spotted her standing by herself stripping old paint from a window.

He quietly walked up beside her. "Can we talk?"

Camara held her scraper in midair. She didn't turn. Chase held his breath and wondered if she would bolt.

After what seemed like an eternity, she faced him. She removed her Chevy cap, tucked her hair behind her ears, and looked him in the eye. "Look, I don't want your dad seeing us together." She put her cap back on her head.

"My dad isn't gonna come clear out here. Besides—"

"The point isn't whether or not your dad will come out here, Chase." She set the scraper on the windowsill. "Your dad hates me." She closed her eyes briefly, picked up the scraper, and started removing the peeled paint again.

Chase grabbed her free hand. "Listen to me, Camara." He turned her face toward his. "I don't care what my dad thinks. I'm a grown man. His problems with your family are just that—*his* problems. Not mine." He searched her eyes. "I care about you, and I want to see where this relationship will go."

"There can be no relationship. Don't you see that?" Her big brown eyes looked sad. Or maybe it was just wishful thinking on his part that she was as bothered about the situation as he was. "Your dad will make both of our lives miserable."

"I won't let him, Camara. I'm not afraid of—"

Camara cut him off. "I don't want a rift coming between you and your father because of me. Family is too important."

Her concern for him touched Chase deeply. It proved she did care.

"Ah, Cammy." He pulled her into his arms. She tried to push away from him, but he held her tighter and whispered against her ear. "I appreciate your considering how our relationship will affect me and my dad's, but. . ." He released her enough to look into her eyes. "I told my father I loved him, but I refused to be a part of his grudge against your family." He gazed intently at her. "And that I wasn't going to stop seeing you, either."

Chase felt her tense. When she backed out of his arms, he didn't stop her. After sharing his heart, he wanted her to be in his arms because she wanted to be, not because he forced her to.

She looked up at him. "What did he say?"

"It doesn't matter what he said, Camara. I won't have my dad controlling and manipulating my life anymore. He's done that my whole life, and I'm tired of it." He cupped her chin. "And I don't want you avoiding me, Cam. I had a great time the other day, and I'd like to spend more time with you." Uncertainty danced in her eyes. If only there was something he could say to reassure her. "How about if after church on Sunday, we go to Swamper's together and watch Erik run his monster truck?"

She didn't answer him. Instead she turned and started scraping the old paint chips off the windowsill.

Happy voices rose above the noise of the electric saws. Symphonic hammering echoed through the woods. Several buzzing bees landed on nearby azalea blooms. And yet the silence was killing him.

"Will your dad be there?" she asked softly without looking at him.

"Nope. He's leaving Saturday evening after the mud bog races and won't be back till Monday night."

She scraped more paint off then looked at him. "Okay." She smiled shyly. "I'd like that. But"—she tilted her head sideways—"I'll ride with Erik and meet you there."

"That'll work." Chase held up the can of paint he had in his hand. "I guess I'd better get busy."

His heart felt light and carefree again. But as soon as he thought about his dad's threats, uneasiness settled over him. He wasn't sure if his dad would follow through with them or not. As much as Chase didn't want to fight with his dad, he refused to let his father's unforgiveness ruin his chance at a happy future. And Chase had a feeling his happy future included Camara.

❧

Removing the straps from The Black Beast, Camara kept glancing toward the entrance into Swamper Speedway. The thought of seeing Chase sent a fluttering feeling through her. How would her nervous stomach survive until their date tomorrow evening?

She still couldn't believe that she, Camara Cole, had gone out with Chase Lamar. What had equally surprised her was she'd had an amazing time, and his kiss had weakened her knees. Who would have thought Chase Lamar could kiss like that? He certainly wasn't the same awful person she'd known all those years. This new Chase seemed to be a sweetheart.

She struggled to get the latch loose on a strap. Too bad Erik wasn't here today. But there was a problem at Daddy's dealership, and Erik had to take care of it. Tugging at the latch with all her might, Camara finally got it unsnapped.

At the familiar sound of Chase's Ford diesel, Camara's heart sped up and matched the timing of his truck engine. *Crr crr crr crr. . .thump thump thump thump.* In between the row of rich green dogwood trees she spotted it. Not wanting to get caught looking for him, she quickly dropped the ramps, climbed into her bog truck, fired it up, and put it in reverse. Making sure her tires lined up on the ramps, she eased her truck off the trailer. She pulled The Black Beast next to her trailer and shut it off.

From the corner of her eye, she watched to see where Chase parked. Her stomach dipped. Chase parked close to the registration stand on the opposite end of the contestants' pit from her. She wondered why until she noticed his dad climbing out of the passenger's side.

Camara grabbed her stepladder, popped the hood of her truck, and started her usual routine, checking everything out.

"Hey, beautiful."

Camara jerked upward, banging her head on the hood.

"Ouch. Bet that hurt. You all right?" Chase asked.

She hopped down and rubbed the back of her head. "I'm fine."

"I thought I'd come over and say hi before both of us got too busy." Chase looked at the truck with its hood raised. "Is something wrong?"

"Nope, just making sure everything's running okay."

"It's a Chevy. How can it be okay?" His dark green eyes twinkled with mirth.

Camara tilted her head and scrunched her face.

Chase held up his hands. "Sorry, I couldn't resist."

"Well, it's better than a For—" Camara's jibe stopped on her lips when she noticed Mr. Lamar glaring their way.

Chase followed her gaze. "Don't pay any attention to him. It's his problem, not ours."

His dad yanked on the nylon straps holding the Mud Boss. "I'd better go before Dad breaks a strap." His look was apologetic.

Camara fought back her disappointment. "Yeah, probably so. Talk to ya later." She gathered her tools and put them in her yellow toolbox.

She watched Chase and his dad leave the Mud Boss and stand in a long line at a faraway concession stand. With only a handful of people in the contestants' pit this early in the morning, Camara realized this was her chance to leave her truck unattended and go register. Knowing she'd be back in a flash, she sprinted toward the registration booth.

By the time she reached the line, four people had gotten in ahead of her. Anxious and nervous about not being able to see The Black Beast from where she stood, Camara shifted her weight back and forth. If only this blasted entry booth didn't obstruct her view, then she could relax. When her turn came, Camara quickly grabbed the clipboard and furiously filled out the forms then handed them to Sam. When she stepped around the corner, she saw Chase standing by The Black Beast, looking around.

"Camara!" Sam hollered.

"Yeah." She ducked her head back around the corner of the booth.

"You forgot to give me your entry fee."

*Ack!* Camara jerked it out of her pocket and handed it to him. By the time she got to the end of the booth again, Chase and his dad were nowhere to be seen. She scanned the area again just to make sure. When she couldn't find them, a mixture of relief and anxiety filled her stomach. At least she could avoid another horrible encounter with Mr. Lamar when she passed the Mud Boss on the way back to her truck. Now, if she could only calm her nervous stomach. But that wasn't likely to happen anytime soon. She couldn't stop her thoughts from wondering where Chase and his dad were and what they'd been up to.

Camara picked up speed as she walked past Chase's rig.

Mr. Lamar stepped out in front of her.

Camara stopped abruptly, barely missing plowing into him.

"What part of 'Stay away from my son' don't you understand?" Mr. Lamar's nostrils flared, and his eyes narrowed into tiny slits.

Fear raced through Camara.

"What's going on here?" Chase's voice boomed from beside her, causing her to jump.

Wide-eyed, Camara spun her gaze toward Chase, then his dad. The hatred in Mr. Lamar's eyes as he glared at her made her insides rattle like a loose muffler. Not wanting to be in the middle of this war, Camara whirled and sprinted toward her bogger.

❧

"Why can't you accept the fact I like her, Dad? I told you, this is your battle with them. Not mine. I love you. But I'm a grown man. I'm not a child anymore."

His dad snorted derisively. "A grown man who lives off his father's money."

Chase's stomach plummeted. Even though he oversaw one of his dad's Ford dealerships and earned every penny he got, his dad didn't see it that way. As far as he was concerned, it was still Lamar money.

Chase gathered his courage. "I work hard for what you pay me."

"It's still *my* money." His dad stepped closer. "I'm telling you, if you don't quit associating with them people, then you leave me no choice but to fire you and withdraw you from my will. I will not have disloyal employees."

The look of triumph on his father's face sickened Chase. Is that what he was to his dad? An employee? In that instant, Chase decided he would no longer tolerate his dad's controlling personality.

"You won't have to fire me. I quit." In five long strides, Chase hopped in his Coupe.

"Those Coles will pay for stealing my son. I'll personally see to it," Chase heard his dad growl before he stomped in the other direction.

Chase placed his palms against the steering wheel and laid his forehead against his knuckles. "God, protect the Coles from my father. He's so full of bitterness and unforgiveness toward them it's making him act like a lunatic." Chase thought about his dad disinheriting him. If he did, Chase would have to deal with it. He could no longer handle his dad's hatefulness. Chase raised his head and swiped the moistness from his eyes. He fired up the Mud Boss and headed toward the lineup. It was his turn to race.

Trying to draw comfort from the fact that he had made some sound investments and could live quite comfortably without his job, Chase worked through the details of that. But the idea of his dad disowning him broke his heart. Chase might not like what his father was doing, but he still loved him.

*Father, give me the grace and the wisdom I need to handle this whole situation.*

He lined up at the pits, and in spite of being upset, he still made a great run. When he got back to his rig, his dad was nowhere around. Wondering how his dad got home, Chase looked around and noticed that Bobby-Rae's vehicle was no longer parked next to him. Chase found that strange, considering Bobby-Rae never left until the races were over. He thought about how his dad and Bobby-Rae had gotten awful chummy lately—which was odd since the man worked for the Coles. But then again, everything his dad did lately surprised him.

❧

Stan and Tim lined up in front of the pits. Camara was up after them. Her dad and brothers had arrived moments before, after resolving the crisis at the dealership, and Erik held the door open for her. She jumped in and fired up The Black Beast. It missed and shook like an out-of-balance tire. She jammed the emergency brake and jumped out. Popping the hood, she quickly grabbed her stepladder and checked the distributor cap. The screws were loose. Someone had tampered with her truck. . .again. If only she hadn't been so upset earlier by Mr. Lamar's tirade, then she would have thought to recheck The Black Beast after she'd left it unattended. Desperately she wanted to share her encounter with someone, but what good would it do? The only One who could do anything about it was God. *Lord*—

"What's wrong, sis?" Erik asked from behind her.

*Lots*, she wanted to say. But instead she chose to pray about it later. Right now she needed to deal with her truck. "Someone loosened the distributor cap." She jiggled the cap.

"How do you know someone messed with it?"

"Because I made sure it was tight this morning when I got here." She stuck her head out from under the hood. "Will you grab my toolbox from off the floorboard?"

Erik nodded. Camara ducked back under the hood. In seconds he was back. He handed her the distributor wrench. Adrenaline running at full speed, Camara adjusted the distributor until the engine ran smoothly again. After tightening the distributor in place, she grabbed her tools and hopped down.

"Thanks, bubba. I gotta hurry." She slammed the hood and hustled into the cab.

After tugging on her helmet, she pulled on her harness and clamped it; then she slid her hands into her leather gloves. Making sure the coast was clear, she backed out of her spot and rumbled her way toward the pit. Camara drew in a long breath and exhaled slowly, trying to gear down her anger. Whoever did this to her would not get the best of her. She had to get out there and win.

She rolled her window down so she could hang her head out if need be. Her mission—to flash in and out of that pit like lightning. And no mud-covered windshield, no poor sportsmanship, no male chauvinist, or no anything would stop her from accomplishing that feat.

With her eye on the flagman, she inched The Black Beast forward until he clenched his fist, her signal to stop.

She riveted her gaze on the flagman.

He raised the flag.

With shaky hands, Camara flipped the master switch, engaging the nitrous. She held the brake and pressed the gas.

The flag dropped.

Camara jerked her foot off the brake and shoved the gas pedal to the floor. She lunged into the pit ahead of Tom Combs's Ford Bronco, the Aggressive Digger.

Her Chevy flew so fast through the mud pit it felt like The Black Beast was on top of it instead of in it.

Her heart revved as fast as her truck. She lunged up and out of the pit and didn't bother looking back. Instead of heading straight toward the contestants' pit, Camara pulled off to the side, jerked off her helmet and harness, and listened for her time.

The announcer's voice echoed over the loudspeaker. "Well, how about that, folks! We have a new record here today. Camara Cole's time is 8.48!" Camara's mouth fell open. "Let's give her a big round of applause."

Camara pumped her arm in the air. "Yes! Yes! Yes!"

Her truck jerked forward as she headed back toward the pit as fast as safety would allow. The second she put it in park and shut the engine off, the door flew open. Erik jerked her out and swung her around. "Way to go, Cam!"

When her feet touched the ground, Tony and Daddy took turns hugging her and congratulating her. None of them seemed to mind the mud draped over her because Slick grabbed her and lifted her off her feet, as well.

"Guess you showed them, huh, sis," Slick said proudly while setting her down. He glanced at her bog truck. "You're gonna have fun getting all that mud out of the inside of the cab. That'll teach ya to leave the window down." He tapped her chin with his forefinger and stepped back to let other well-wishers in.

Several minutes later when the congratulations died down, Camara set about hosing off The Black Beast. Whoever had messed with her truck must feel sick that their plan didn't work. She wondered who could possibly hate her so much that they would do such a cruel thing. Instantly Mr. Lamar's venomous eyes sparked through her mind. Was he the one sabotaging her truck? She searched her memory in hopes of finding the answer to that question. Suddenly she realized Mr. Lamar wasn't around her truck every time it had been messed with. But Chase was. A nauseous feeling hit her stomach. Everything inside her desperately wanted to believe it wasn't. . .

She envisioned Chase at church—tears flowing down his cheeks. *Oh, God, I'm so confused. I don't know what to think. Did Chase do it, or didn't he? Can I trust him?* The longer she mulled it over, the more convinced she was that Chase had loosened the distributor cap. After all, he'd done the same thing in the past, along with loosening a nut here and a spark plug wire there. And he *was* the only person she'd seen around her truck today. Camara groaned. If only she would have waited until Lolly or one of her family members had arrived before registering, then none of this would have happened. What an idiot she'd been for leaving her truck unattended and allowing herself to get suckered in by Chase's good looks and charm. Camara wanted to slap herself for trusting him. Well, never again.

❧

"Is that what you meant, Dad?" Chase moved his cell phone to the opposite ear. "Did you do something to Camara's truck?" Chase fought the urge to run over and congratulate Camara. Instead he had to find out if his father was behind her truck running so poorly. After all, he did say he'd make the Coles pay. And what better way than to mess with Camara's truck and keep her from winning?

"What do you mean?" His dad's voice sounded phony.

Chase removed his hat, wiped the sweat off his forehead, and replaced his cap. The hot sun grilled him, and the humidity clung to his body, making him drip with sweat. "You know what I mean, Dad. Camara's truck wasn't running right."

"Did she have trouble?" Chase knew his dad's concern wasn't real.

"Yeah, she had trouble."

"Oh, that's too bad."

"Well, it doesn't matter now." Chase paused, waiting to see if his dad would ask him why. When he didn't, Chase continued. "Camara broke the track record."

"She *what*?" The question was more of a shriek. "How can that be?"

"How can what be, Dad?" Chase asked innocently. He just knew his dad had done something. He wanted to let him know his plan didn't work.

"Nothing. You just said that something was wrong with it, and now she's gone and broke the track record. Your record." The hate inside his father came through loud and clear.

"She got it fixed before she ran. Guess whoever did it feels pretty rotten about now. It only made her more determined than ever to win. So their plan backfired."

"What makes you think someone did this? As far as I can see, she's just a lousy mechanic."

Chase shook his head and glanced heavenward. "She's not a lousy mechanic, Dad. She's one of Alabama's best."

"I don't have time for this," his dad barked and hung up on him.

With a click, he shut off his cell phone and headed toward Camara. He couldn't wait to congratulate her.

"Hey, beautiful. Congratulations on—"

"Don't you ever come near me again, Chase Lamar!" Camara snapped then turned the sprayer off.

Stunned, Chase stopped in his tracks and stared at her. "What's wrong?" He stepped closer and laid his hand on hers. She jerked her arm away.

"As if you don't know," she ground out. "Did you really think I was that stupid?" Her big brown eyes shot flaming arrows his way. "You thought you could befriend me, get me to like you, and even take me out on a date so you could win my trust. I should have known better than to trust you. Well, your plan didn't work, did it?" The smug look on her face felt like a slap to his.

"What plan are you ranting about?"

Camara spun the bill of her Chevy cap around.

*Oops. Wrong choice of words.* That meant only one thing: She was madder than an angry bull.

"As if you don't know," she bit out. "Stay away from my truck and from me."

"Camara?" Chase grabbed her hands. She tried getting free from his grasp, but Chase clutched her tighter. His stomach lodged in his throat.

"Leave me alone!" She squirmed.

"What's going on here?" Erik asked, looking at Camara then at Chase.

Chase dropped her hands. "That's what I'd like to know."

"Chase sabotaged my truck. That's what's going on."

Chase's eyes widened along with Erik's. "What?" Chase blurted. "You think *I* messed with your truck?"

"Cam, you don't mean that," Erik said incredulously.

"Oh yes, I do. I checked everything out when I got here today." She glared at Chase.

"What's that got to do with anything?" her brother asked.

Camara faced Erik and planted her hands on her hips. "You're taking *his* side?"

"No. I'm just trying to get to the bottom of this thing."

"Well, look no further, bubba." She pointed at Chase. "He did it." The disdainful look she sent Chase made him inwardly cringe. He still wasn't over the shock of her thinking he'd messed with her truck. "When I was busy registering, he"—she jerked her thumb Chase's way—"loosened the distributor cap."

"What makes you think that?"

Chase wanted to hear the answer to Erik's question, too.

"Because I saw *him*"—Camara pointed toward Chase—"hanging around my truck. He knows I'm his biggest competition, and he can't stand the thought of me, a mere female, beating him."

Chase couldn't believe what he was hearing. He may have stooped that low in the past, but didn't she believe he'd changed now? From the accusing look on her face, she didn't. *Lord, show me what to do.*

"Listen, Cammy," Chase said.

"Don't call me that. It's *Camara* to you," she snapped.

"Camara." He paused and gathered his composure. "I'd hoped by now you would have noticed Christ has changed me." He searched her eyes looking for any sign she believed him. He saw a spark of softness, so he continued. "I know I used to sabotage your truck just to win. But please believe me when I say I'm not now. I promise you, I will find out who is, though." He nodded toward Erik then looked back at Camara. "Good luck on your next run. And congratulations for breaking the track record. I'm proud of you." With that, he turned and headed toward his Coupe.

As he walked, he shook his head slowly. *Lord, show me if my father really is behind this. If not him, then please help me find out who is.* A knot lodged in his gut. It broke his heart to think Camara thought he'd messed with her truck. The old Chase might have allowed her to believe it was him and even found pleasure in it. But now that he loved her, he couldn't stand the thought of her not liking him or thinking badly of him. Chase stopped and removed his cap. The realization that he loved her yanked the air from his lungs. He ran his hand over his short hair and replaced his cap. Until he proved his innocence, he knew Camara wouldn't have anything to do with him. Well, he would find out who the culprit was. And whoever it was would pay. He'd see to it personally.

❧

"Camara, how many times do I have to tell you your stubborn pride is going to ruin you?" Camara's father's voice came from behind her.

Camara spun around. "What do you mean?"

"I heard you accuse Chase of messing with your truck. When are you going to get it through your head that Chase has changed since giving his life to Christ?"

"But, Daddy. . ." Camara set her socket wrench down. "He was the only one hanging around my truck, looking all suspicious-like. And someone *did* mess with it." She looked at the ground and kicked some gravel with her toe. "What if he's just using me to gain my trust?"

Her father's brows rose. "You don't really believe that, do you?"

She shrugged.

"Camara, sweetheart. You need to be careful accusing people. 'Judge not, that you be not judged. For with what judgment you judge, you will be judged; and with the measure you use, it will be measured back to you.'" Her father's eyes held only compassion. "You need to pray and ask God to reveal the truth to you." He laid his hand on her shoulder and squeezed. "In the meantime, you owe that man an apology."

"But I don't know that he *didn't* do it."

"That may be true. But you don't know that he did, either." He grew quiet for a minute. Camara knew he was thinking. "What if the situation were reversed and Chase had accused you?"

"Me?" she squeaked. "I wouldn't stoop that low. Besides, my Chevy could beat his Ford any day."

"Baby girl." He pushed himself off her vehicle and stood to his full six foot two inches. "You have judged, convicted, and sentenced that poor man without any proof. Do you really want that judgment to come back on you? And what kind of mercy would you want in a case like this?"

Although Camara felt Chase might still be guilty, she knew she had sinned against the Lord by judging him too quickly.

"Listen to me." He clutched her face in his large hands. "Don't let your pride cost you the love of a good man."

Love of a good man? Chase didn't love her. And she definitely didn't love him.

Camara needed time to think. She glanced at her watch. It would be an hour before her second run. "I'll be back." She hugged him. "Thanks, Daddy." She headed toward the thicket of dogwood trees behind the speedway.

❧

"Chase?"

Chase wiggled himself out from under his Coupe. Camara stood over him, tucking her hair nervously behind her ears and looking at the ground.

He stood and dusted the dirt off his shirt. "Hi." He suddenly felt shy and uncertain about what to say. Deciding to let her do the talking, he just watched her.

"Look, I'm sorry for accusing you of sabotaging my truck. It was wrong, and I apologize." She looked up at him.

"What made you realize I didn't do it?"

Camara frowned. "Nothing. I'm still not sure that you did or didn't."

Chase felt like he'd been sucker punched. She still believed he was guilty.

"I just wanted to let you know that I accused you without having proof. My father showed me how wrong I was to do that."

"Cam, thank you for apologizing. But I had nothing to do with messing up your truck."

Chase reached for her hands, but she jerked them behind her back. "Daddy always says that the truth has a way of speaking. And until I find out the truth, I'm canceling our date." She looked him square in the eye. "I won't be made a fool of." She whirled and sprinted off.

Chase fought to breathe. *God, You've got to help me find out who did this. I don't wanna lose her.*

# Chapter 12

Chase missed Camara. When she hadn't shown up for church the next day, the word *disappointment* hardly did justice to the feeling. And he hadn't seen or heard from her all week. He stared out his office window at the mechanic shop below. Someday, Lord willing, he'd own his auto shop. He arched his back to get the kinks out. Two and a half hours of paperwork and he was caught up. He glanced at the clock: 6:45 a.m. Time to go. He made a quick phone call to John, telling him he'd be by in a few minutes to pick him up.

He couldn't wait to get to Swamper's and see Camara. There was no way she'd miss a mud bog race. Especially now that the two of them were tied in points.

In some ways he wanted Camara to win, but his old fleshly nature, the competitor side of him, hadn't been crucified yet. He'd even thought about switching from nitrous to alcohol. But knowing how hard it was on engines, he decided not to. He'd just have to leave the race results in God's hands. If it was God's will that Camara won, so be it.

He pulled into Swamper's and looked for Camara's rig. Disappointment draped over him. This was the first time he had arrived before Camara. She had remained true to her word by keeping her distance from him. *Lord, please show me what to do to make things right with her. Expose whoever is doing this.*

He turned to John. "Don't forget, John. We have to keep an eye on Camara's vehicle. While I'm running, you watch it close, okay?" He parked his rig.

"Gotcha, boss."

"And stop with the boss thing already. We're friends first." John had been Chase's employee for four years now. No matter how mean Chase had been to him and no matter how much he'd made fun of John's God, John had never retaliated. Instead he always had a peace about him that Chase envied. One day he had vowed to find out what John had that he didn't.

Chase's life had never been the same since then. In fact, it was because of John that he could face his job every day. And after his father had paid him a surprise visit last Saturday night asking Chase if he would reconsider working for him again, Chase had wanted to honor his father, so he went back. If he could be half the light to his dad that John was to him, he would be happy.

They got out of Chase's pickup and removed the straps on the Coupe.

Chase hopped in the Coupe, drove it off the trailer, and parked it.

The sound of tires crunching on gravel grabbed Chase's attention. His heart skipped a beat. Camara's Hummer and Erik's semi rounded the corner. Chase had parked close to where Camara normally parked. The closer she got, the faster his heart beat. However, when she drove right by him without even looking his way and parked clear down on the far end, he groaned.

John laid his hand on Chase's arm. "Trust God, Chase. He's the only One who can take care of this whole mess."

Chase forced his eyes away from Camara and onto John. "Thanks, John. Keep praying, will ya?"

"I haven't stopped since you told me what happened." John smiled.

Chase had never had a friend he trusted enough to confide in until John. After watching his integrity for years, Chase knew John was a man to be trusted.

Erik headed toward him. He was another person Chase knew he could trust.

"Good morning." Erik shook John's hand and then Chase's. "I want you to know that no matter what happens between you and my sister, you'll always be my friend." Erik glanced toward Camara, then back at Chase. "Don't let it get to ya." Erik squeezed his shoulder. "She'll come around. And for what it's worth, I know you didn't mess with her truck."

Bobby-Rae pulled up alongside them in his Chevy and said something. Chase couldn't make out his words because of his loud exhaust.

"Excuse me." Chase walked around to the driver's side. "I didn't hear that. What'd ya say?"

"I said. . .good luck today." Bobby-Rae looked around and lowered his voice. "I'm sure glad you installed NOS. Us guys have to show Camara how it's done." He gave a derisive snort and drove off. Chase stood there, frowning. How did Bobby-Rae know he'd installed NOS? The only ones who knew were Erik, Camara, John, and his dad.

"What'd he want?" Erik asked from beside Chase.

Chase repeated what Bobby-Rae had said.

"He's been downright belligerent to Camara lately."

"Why?" John asked.

*Good question*, Chase thought. And he planned on finding out the answer.

❧

Camara was up next. For her second run, she was side by side with Chase. Even though she had forgiven him, she still didn't trust him. Trust was something you learned as a child and earned as an adult. He hadn't earned hers yet. And she wasn't certain he ever would.

Chase revved his engine. Camara refused to look at him. Instead she focused on the flagman. Her heart thumped wildly against her ribs, and her trembling body matched the vibration of her bog truck.

The flag rose.

Camara flipped the master switch, pressed the brake, and then the gas pedal. The engine roared. The exhaust rumbled.

The flag dropped.

Camara jerked her foot off the brake, shoved the gas pedal to the floor, and drove like a woman on a mission through the pit. She did a quick glance sideways. Chase was nowhere in view. She lunged up and out of the pit. Without a backward glance, Camara headed toward the contestants' area.

Erik jerked open her door. "Wow. Whatever you were trying to prove certainly worked."

"Good," she said with no emotion.

Shutting off The Black Beast, she removed her helmet, gloves, and harness and jumped out. Before her first run, someone had let the air out of both tires on the passenger side. Thank the good Lord she'd had a compressor. As much as she hated where her thoughts were taking her, she couldn't shake the feeling that Chase was somehow behind it. It couldn't have been Mr. Lamar. He wasn't even at the track today. Daddy said not to judge, but all the evidence was stacked against Chase. It broke her heart because she'd really had a good time with him. But Camara knew from experience that even so-called Christians hurt and used other people to get what they wanted. And besides, she really didn't know Chase all that well.

Absentmindedly, Camara dug the mud out of the tire grooves. The announcer's voice came over the loudspeaker. "Camara's on a roll today, folks. Her time is 8.9. Chase Lamar's time is 9.22." Camara heard what she'd wanted to hear. But she was too numb to enjoy it.

"Congratulations, Camara." Chase's voice sounded from behind her.

She turned and faced him. "Thanks," she said glumly. She turned and walked to the front of her pickup. From the corner of her eye, she watched him leave. It ripped the air from her lungs.

"Don't let it go to your head. It won't happen again."

Camara whirled to find Bobby-Rae glaring at her. "What's your problem, Bobby-Rae? You jealous?"

"Of you?" he scoffed. "Not hardly."

"Well, I don't see you winning."

"That's cuz I don't have a rich daddy giving me everything I want."

"Neither do I. I work hard for my money."

"Yeah, right." Bobby-Rae snickered snidely.

Camara turned her cap around.

"Just you wait. By the end of this season, I'll have enough money to build a better bogger and to afford NOS, too." He jerked his head forward and snorted. "It'll make yours look like a puddle jumper."

"We'll see."

"Yeah, we will."

Having had enough of him, Camara shoved her way past him, started the pressure washer, and began hosing off The Black Beast.

What was his problem anyway? Was he still angry with her for turning him down? She huffed out a breath. If his lousy attitude continued, she'd talk to Erik about transferring him to a different shop. For months now, the guy had treated her like dirt. She had enough stress in her life without having to put up with the likes of him.

Camara's gaze drifted toward Chase's rig. Her biggest stress came not from her desire to win but from her dilemma where Chase was concerned. She really liked him, but as hard as she tried to believe in him and trust him, she just couldn't. The thought of never spending another day with Chase like she had at his family's lake house caused a wave of sadness to gush over her. She sucked in big gulps of air. She had to get away from here—and fast.

# Chapter 13

C amara couldn't believe it was Friday, the Fourth of July, already. Where had the time gone? She'd had so much to do at work that the week had flown by.

After filling all her bird feeders with birdseed, she walked to her patio and sat on a lounge chair. She closed her eyes, tilted her face toward the morning sun, and soaked up the warmth spreading across her face. A symphony of birds caused her body to relax.

She drew in a deep breath. For a month now there had been no more incidents with The Black Beast. Whoever had been sabotaging her truck must have finally given up. Or they realized they had no chance of messing with it since someone stayed near it all the time.

Once again, she and Chase were tied in points. Since he had installed NOS, one week she'd win and the next he did. It saddened her a bit to think there were only six more races till the end of the racing season.

Camara picked up her coffee, took a long drink, and enjoyed the warm liquid as it slid down her throat. Then she picked up her Bible and let it fall open. As she flipped through the pages, several scriptures about forgiveness and pride seemed to leap off the pages, convicting her about her attitude. Flipping the pages again, her gaze landed on a scripture about the accuser of our brethren. She thought about how she'd been accusing Chase and wondered if Satan had used her to falsely accuse him.

"Camara."

At the sound of Chase's voice, Camara jumped and nearly sent her Bible toppling. She caught it before it slid off her lap. She swung her legs off her lounge chair and planted her feet on the cool concrete.

"What are you doing here?" She wanted to be angry at him for showing up unannounced, but noting the look of uncertainty on his face, she couldn't. In spite of what she believed he'd done to her truck, she had missed him.

"I know it's only eight thirty, and I'm sorry to barge in on you like this, but I was hoping you were up and about."

"Why?"

"Well, I wondered if we could talk." His eyes held such hope that she found she couldn't refuse him.

"Okay." She laid her Bible on a patio end table and motioned to an empty chair across from her, as a soft breeze rustled the azalea bushes in her yard. "Please have a seat."

Chase took the seat across from her. Camara held her breath in anticipation of what he had to say.

"Listen. I want you to know I talked to Stan last night, and he told me how Lolly saw me near your truck again the day you had the flat tires. I was, but I didn't mess with it." She looked for any kind of deception in his eyes but saw none. "I was waiting for you. You can ask John. He was there with me."

Camara didn't know what to think. She rose, put her back to him, and crossed her arms. Had she misjudged him, or were these more mind games?

Chase placed his warm hands on her shoulders. "Cam. I know you think I wanna win at any cost, and the old me would have, but now I would never. . .I repeat, *never* mess with your truck. Please believe me. You can even ask the Lord to show you the truth." His breath felt warm against her ear, sending her body into a shiver spasm.

"You cold?"

Unable to speak past the lump in her throat, she shook her head.

Chase turned her until she faced him. Camara refused to look at him. Instead she focused on a dead bug lying on the concrete patio.

He tilted her chin up. "Please, look at me."

Camara raised her eyes.

"I want you to see the truth in my eyes when I tell you that I did not sabotage your truck. I care too much for you to do something that despicable."

The soft sincerity in Chase's green eyes made her realize that he was telling her the truth. She closed her eyes and released a sigh.

"I'm sorry, Chase. I really don't know what to think anymore." She tucked her hair behind her ears. She owed it to him to be honest. "I'm not used to this new Chase. The old Chase would have done anything to win."

Pain etched his features. "When are you gonna realize that I'm a new creature in Christ? That 'old things have passed away; behold, all things have become new'? Jesus is changing me." He released her chin and turned away from her. "Do you have to keep reminding me of my past mistakes and sins?"

Camara's heart sank. Who was she to hold the past against him? She herself was still dealing with pride. She laid her hand on his arm. His muscle twitched under her palm.

"I'm sorry, Chase. Forgive me." He looked at her with sad eyes. "Please be patient with me. I'm having a hard time getting used to the new you." She tried lightening the mood with a bright smile.

"So is my dad." His voice sounded wistful.

"Your dad?" She tilted her head.

"Forget I said that. How about a truce?" He flashed her a 100-watt smile.

"A truce?" She pinched her lips shut and placed her finger over them. "Hmm. I don't know. That sounds pretty boring."

Chase's brows rose. "Boring?" He dipped his head sideways.

"Yeah. If we call a truce between us, then I won't be able to remind ya how that Ford of yours is full of cobwebs. You know. . .gutless," she said, winking, unable to resist teasing him.

"Hey, all's fair in love and war. At Swamper's, it's war." He pulled her into his arms and captured her gaze. "Here, it's love."

Love? Staring up at him wide-eyed, she watched his face lower, and his lips softly touched hers for a brief moment. Chase's words replayed in Camara's mind. Surely he didn't mean he loved her. And surely he was just using that old cliché. Wasn't he? She wasn't so sure she wanted to find out.

☙

No doubt about it, Chase was in love with Camara. Now all he had to do was win her love. He studied Camara, who still hadn't uttered a word. With dreamy eyes, Miss Tough-As-Nails looked softer than he'd ever seen her before.

Chase cleared his throat. Camara blinked and looked at him. Her face turned pink. Seeing her discomfort, Chase decided to rescue her. "Have you eaten yet? I'm starving. How about we go get some breakfast?"

Camara's stomach chose that moment to growl. She giggled. Her sweet laughter sounded like chimes floating on a gentle breeze.

"You're on. I'll go change."

Chase opened her sliding glass door and allowed her to pass. He slid the door closed and clicked the lock.

Camara raced up the stairs, quickly changed, then slid sidesaddle down the banister. "I'm ready," she announced when her feet hit the floor.

Chase chuckled. "Do you always come down the stairs like that?"

"Only when I'm in a hurry."

With a smile on his face, he headed out the door, and they strolled to his vehicle.

Camara laid her hand on the passenger side door handle.

"Oh no, you don't."

She looked up, surprised. He grabbed her hand and led her to the driver's side and opened it. "I want you sitting next to me." He smiled before placing his hands around her small waist and lifting her up. She weighed no more than a kitten.

She slid over, and he hopped in. Chase placed his arm around her and tucked her tight against his side.

"Chase."

He moved his arm from around her and started the truck. After checking for traffic, he headed down the street. "Yeah?"

"Thanks for coming today and setting things straight."

He glanced at her and noted her shyness.

"I've really missed you," she added softly.

Chase glanced at her. "I've missed you, too." He looked back at the road. Hesitating a moment, he continued. "I don't want anything like this happening again. If we're gonna have any kind of a relationship, we're gonna have to learn to trust each other."

❈

Sitting next to Chase, Camara pondered his words. Did she want a relationship with him? The idea was both frightening and appealing.

"Where are we going anyway?"

"You'll see." He glanced at her. "You don't have any plans for today, do you?" He looked back at the road.

"Only this evening."

"Oh."

Was that disappointment she heard in his voice? "Why?"

"Well, I was wondering if you'd like to spend the day with me."

"Only if you take me to Swamper Speedway this evening. Erik's running his monster truck in a freestyle event tonight. Then they're gonna have a fireworks display afterward."

"Sounds great."

"I should warn you, though. My whole family will be there."

"You mean I don't get you all to myself?" He winked.

"Nope. Take it or leave it."

"I'll take it."

❈

The all-day Fourth of July festivities were well on their way at Civitan Park. Many people greeted them as they scanned the concession stands. Once they got their bacon, eggs, grits, and orange juice, they headed toward the covered picnic area.

Stone and cement pillars holding the suspended A-frame roof provided some relief from the sweltering sun. Chase scanned the shelter for an empty picnic table.

"Excuse me." A bald-headed gentleman snagged Chase's attention. "If y'all are lookin' for a place to sit, there's an empty picnic table over there." He pointed to one under a canopy of tall trees.

"Thank you, sir." Chase smiled. "That was right nice of ya."

The man smiled and turned back to his food.

"Man, it's hot, and it's not even nine thirty yet. Today will be another scorcher." Arriving at the table, Chase set their plates down and then sat down across from her so he could see her beautiful face.

316

He hadn't taken two bites when suddenly someone covered his eyes. "Guess who?" Chase's heart sank at the sickeningly sweet tone of Brittany van Buran's voice. When would she get the hint that things were over between them? "Brittany," he said none too happily.

"Hi, sweetie. Miss me?" she purred. Wrapping her hands around his neck, she planted a kiss on his mouth.

He pulled her arms from around him and moved her away from him. Chase glanced at Camara, who stared at him wide-eyed. She looked back and forth between him and Brittany. Her brows rose questioningly.

"Now, Chase, sweetie." Brittany ran her hand down his cheek and over his chin. "Is that any way to treat your future wife?"

# Chapter 14

The words hit like a punch. Camara slung her legs around the bench, leaped up, and darted off. Once again, he'd made a fool of her. Once again, she'd trusted him and he had smashed her heart to smithereens. How many times would she buy into his lies, fall for his charm, put herself on the chopping block?

"Camara, wait!" She ignored Chase and ran as fast as her short legs would carry her. Not bothering to look back, she headed in the opposite direction of where Chase had parked and lost herself in the throng of people. Making sure she was out of sight, she leaned against a large maple tree. She clutched her aching sides as she gasped to pull air into her starving lungs. The humidity wasn't helping, and neither was the heat. Even the sweet smell of gardenias was enough to turn her stomach.

What was all that garbage about a relationship and trust? How could she have been so stupid? He had a fiancée, for pity's sake. Boy, did he play her for a fool. She swiped at the unwanted tears. Tears over someone she should never have trusted in the first place.

"Camara."

She hunched her shoulders toward the tree, not wanting Chase to see her crying. "Go back to your fiancée."

"Fiancée?" He tried to turn her around, but she brushed his hands off and kept her back to him. "Brittany isn't my fiancée."

Camara blinked away more tears and sniffed. "She asked if that was any way for you to treat your future wife, and she kissed you."

"Ah, Cammy." He laid his hands on her shoulders. "I only dated Brittany for a few weeks last summer. My father wanted us to marry. But he only cared about her father's position as mayor and how good it would make him look. He didn't care that I didn't love her. I overheard him telling Brittany I was just playing hard to get and to keep trying. She hasn't stopped since."

Gently Chase turned Camara around. His gaze softened when he looked at her. She was certain it was pity because of her tear-filled eyes. Chase pulled her into his arms and pressed her cheek against his chest. "I'm not in love with her, Cam. And she is not my future wife."

Camara sniffed again. In her wildest imagination, Camara never figured that one day she would feel such relief hearing that Chase was a free man. She wasn't sure, but if the way her heart ached when she saw the gorgeous brunette kiss him was any indication of loving someone, then she suspected she might be in love with Chase. The thought terrified her.

Chase tilted her head up and rubbed his thumb under her eyes. "You believe me, don't you?"

"I'm sorr—"

Chase placed his fingers over her lips. "Don't apologize."

"I should have trusted you, Chase. This was my first test in trusting you, and I failed." She pulled back a bit and looked into his eyes. "I'm so sorry. Bear with me."

"Listen, Cam. I understand. After the way I treated you for so many years, I know it's gonna take time to earn your trust." He cupped her face and leaned his face toward hers. "But I have all the time in the world. If you do."

"I do." Her voice sounded husky.

Chase wrapped his arms around her and lowered his head.

"Oh, honey, isn't young love sweet?"

Camara jerked her head back and turned toward the voice.

"Reminds me of you and me forty years ago." An older couple holding hands stood watching them.

Camara felt her face, neck, and ears heat up.

"Whaddya mean, forty years ago?" The gray-haired gentleman dipped the older lady and kissed her. When he let her go, they laughed and continued on the path.

Camara pictured her and Chase acting like that couple in forty years. Giving herself a mental shake, she wondered why she had even thought that.

She and Chase married? Not likely.

☙

"I'm famished. Let's go get something else to eat. I tossed the other in the trash before I came looking for you," Chase said, looping her hand through his arm. They headed back toward the concession stands in Civitan Park.

"I'm sorry I ruined breakfast."

"You didn't ruin anything. We'll just get something else."

Chase noticed a sign at a nearby concession stand in the park. Funnel cakes, pecan cake, waffles, pancakes, sweet potato biscuits, fresh fruit, boiled peanuts. His stomach growled just reading the list. "Do you like funnel cakes?" He pointed toward the concession stand.

"Like them? I love 'em. Race ya there." She dropped his hand and sprinted off.

She might be wearing a dress, but she was all tomboy. But what a beautiful tomboy she made. He dashed after her, arriving at the same time she did.

Finding a shaded picnic bench, Chase grabbed Camara's hand and lowered his head. "Father, thank You for Your provision. May we never take Your grace for granted. And thank You for mending the fence between me and Camara and for allowing me to spend time with her. In Christ's name, amen."

Camara echoed his amen.

He was so grateful he'd found Camara and was able to explain about Brittany. By the horrified look on Camara's face, he thought he'd never get another chance to be with her. He found the more he was around her, the more he was falling for her. Who would have ever thought even six months ago that he and Camara would be dating?

Chase took a sip of his sweetened tea. "There's a patriotic-decorated boat parade and a classic auto show today. Would you like to go?" He popped a bite of funnel cake into his mouth.

"Do trucks require fuel to run? Is mud bog racing fun? Do Fords die early deaths?"

If he hadn't noticed her cheeky grin and the teasing glint in her eyes, he might have retaliated. But instead, he pointed his finger at her in warning. "Don't get me started, Ca-mare-oh."

"Okay, okay." She held her hands up. "I surrender." She wiped her mouth with her napkin. "Actually, I never turn down a car show, and a patriotic boat parade sounds great." She broke off a piece of funnel cake and stuffed it into her mouth.

They talked for more than an hour after they finished their funnel cakes and then headed to Civitan Park's parking lot. As they neared, Chase's breath caught in his throat. Classic cars were lined up all over the place. Some of them were jacked up over mirrors, revealing their chrome undercarriage.

A silver 1971 Mach 1 with two black stripes on the hood snatched his attention. He grabbed Camara's hand and headed straight for it. "I've always wanted one of these." The hood was up, and a sign on the hood latch read PLEASE DO NOT TOUCH. Chase longed to hear the Ford's 429 engine come to life.

He noticed a rotund man in his fifties sitting in a chair behind it. How he envied him. Chase had searched for years trying to find a car like this one in good restoration condition. But he'd always called too late. Maybe someday.

Feeling guilty for neglecting Cam, he turned to talk to her. She was gone. He scanned the large area looking for her and spotted her pale yellow dress, so he headed that way.

"Sorry I got carried away back there."

Camara turned and flashed him a dashing smile. "No problem. Sorry I left, but I had to see this."

Chase looked at a purple metal fleck 1934 Ford Coupe all chromed out. This one had Mountain Crusher rims with white raised lettering. After examining it for a few minutes, he turned to Camara. "I knew you had good taste. I wondered how long it would be before you couldn't resist a Ford."

She smiled. "I admit. It's gorgeous. Are you happy now?" Camara walked away and said, "But this one's better." She stopped in front of a baby blue mother-of-pearl and jeweled 1968 Chevrolet Camaro. The opened hood showed off a chromed-out 396 with three deuces on top.

Chase noticed the sign in the window. OWNER: CAMARA CHEVELLE COLE.

Stunned, his gaze flew to Camara. Her face glowed with pride. "This is yours?" He couldn't keep the shock out of his voice.

Camara nodded and smiled. "I customized and restored it all by myself." Her statement didn't sound prideful.

"You?" he asked, still dumbfounded. "Customized this by yourself?" He knew he sounded like a bumbling idiot, but he had never seen a more incredible car. For a Chevy, that is. He couldn't help but think he had no idea of the depth of her capabilities. He was even more impressed with her and even more in love with her than before. Not wanting his mind to go there, he ducked his head inside the driver's side door and checked out the car's interior. Chase let out a long whistle. He was impressed. It had dark blue diamond tuck upholstery, bucket seats, B&M custom speed shifter, and a full set of street racing instruments. Chase stood and stared in awe before asking, "Don't you have to be here with your car?"

"Normally, yes. But"—she looked bashful—"I wanted to spend time with you today, so when I changed clothes, I asked Daddy if he would come down here. I knew he wanted to anyway. After all, this was his baby before he gave it to me on my eighteenth birthday four years ago. He loves it."

"I love what, honey?" Mr. Cole's voice sounded from behind them.

Chase and Camara spun around.

"Hi, Daddy. Hi, Mom." Camara's parents stood next to them, each one holding a beverage and a cardboard bowl containing fried catfish and hush puppies.

"Hi, honey."

Camara kissed her mother's cheek.

"Hi, Chase," her mother greeted Chase cheerfully. "It's right nice to see you again."

"It sure is," Mr. Cole agreed. He set his drink down then shook Chase's hand.

Chase envied Camara's loving family. The times he'd been around them, they made him feel like family…as if they genuinely cared about him. He looked at Camara chatting amiably with her mother. If he had anything to say about it, he would soon be part of this loving family. But first things first. He had to win Camara's heart—which wasn't going to be an easy task.

🌺

Later that afternoon, Camara changed into her white capris, blue knit tunic sailor shirt, and her matching blue and white canvas sneakers for the second half of their date. Camara chuckled as she thought about how she looked like a sailor in this outfit. Too bad she hadn't worn it on their first date. She would have fit right in on Chase's pontoon boat. Camara couldn't recall when she'd ever been happier. Spending the whole day with Chase had been like a dream. One from which she didn't want to awaken.

When she heard the doorbell, Camara trotted down the steps and swung the door open. Chase looked handsome in his jeans, green polo shirt, and brown leather loafers.

"Ya ready?" he asked.

"Ready as I'll ever be." She grabbed a light jacket from the coat rack, turned the lock on the door, and shut it behind them.

His hand felt warm against her back as he led her toward his Pantera. "What, no Ford? Are you slipping?"

"Hey, I like other cars, too."

When Chase opened her door, it flipped open upward. "Nice."

"I like it." He winked at her.

On the way to the speedway, they reminisced over the cars they'd seen at the auto show. Chase shared with her how he'd always wanted a Mach 1 but that every time he'd gotten wind of one for sale he'd always been too late. When they neared the speedway, Chase asked, "Do we park in the contestants' pit or near the grandstands?"

"I asked Erik if he needed any help, and he said no. I think it would be fun to sit in the stands for a change."

"Sounds good." Chase parked the car. "Wait there." He hurried out and ran around to her side, then opened the door for her. Such a gentleman. This guy was full of surprises.

Chase intertwined her fingers with his. Her hand felt small in his larger one. "You hungry?"

"Starved."

"What do ya want?"

"Golden Flake chips and a hot dog sounds good."

Chase held his hand over his heart. "Ah, a lady after my own heart."

They stopped at a concession to get their food. Then they carefully made their way up the wooden steps and sat in the front row.

An hour later, Chase and Camara stood rooting and hollering as Erik flew his monster truck over several dirt mounds and a row of cars. Then he went into a cyclone, spinning around and around. The crowd roared, nearly deafening Camara. She wondered if the people rooted this much for the mud bog racers. With about thirty seconds left of his two minutes, Erik spun around and leaped over an RV, crushing it into shattered pieces. Then he headed toward a semi-trailer and flew up over the partially mashed trailer. The Mad Masher landed on its front wheels then flipped over on its top. He'd made the full two minutes.

Camara and Chase rose, clapping and hollering. When the freestyle was over, Erik had won third place. On the way down to the contestants' pit, Chase told Camara he wanted to take her someplace special to watch the fireworks.

"But for the last five years, I've watched the fireworks here."

"Well, not this year." He flashed his best smile.

Down at the contestants' pit, they congratulated Erik and said their good-byes to her family.

Later they pulled up to the same dock where Chase had taken her on their first date. Camara sent him a questioning look.

"Don't worry. I promise you Dad won't show up tonight." His shining eyes and bright smile reassured her. Chase came around, opened her door, and grabbed a bag from behind the seat. With his other hand, he grabbed their jackets.

"C'mon." He shuffled his possessions; then he took her hand and led her to the dock. He stopped in front of a sunburst orange metal-flecked speedboat.

"Wow. Is this yours?"

"Yeah."

"How many boats do you own anyway?"

"Three."

"Only three?" Camara giggled.

"Yeah, this one, the pontoon boat, and. . ." He smiled as he situated the cache he'd brought into the boat. "A twenty-eight-foot cabin cruiser." Chase frowned. "Actually, I bought all these"—he made quote marks with his fingers—" 'toys' when I was looking for happiness. But the joy of having them didn't last as long as I thought it would. That's why there are three. Took me awhile to figure out boats and cars didn't fill what I was trying to fill." He was still fussing with the supplies, not seeming to really be listening to his own words. "I didn't find true fulfillment until I found Christ."

Chase climbed aboard and offered her his hand. He helped her climb on board and motioned to a captain's chair next to the driver's seat. Then he hopped down and untied the dock lines before climbing aboard again.

Chase sat in front of the wheel. "If you get cold, there are blankets under the backseat." Chase fired up the boat. The 327 inboard motor crackled louder than her bogger, sending chills racing through her veins. She gave him a thumbs-up. Chase smiled and backed it away from the dock.

Chase joined the cluster of boats gathering around the barge on Lake Guntersville and dropped the anchor. He helped Camara up, and they walked to the back of the boat.

"Would you like something to drink?"

"Not now, thank you."

Chase sat on the white leather bench and pulled Camara next to him. She snuggled into him and scanned the area. A million twinkling stars sprinkled the sky. Light from the many boats danced along the rippling water. The smell of sulfur smoke mingled with fish filled the air.

Camara glanced at him, but before she had a chance to look away, their gazes locked. The attraction between them sizzled. Chase lowered his head and lightly touched her lips. He pulled back and looked at her as if seeking her permission. Camara closed her eyes and tilted her face upward. Chase's lips found hers in a sweet, tender kiss. A loud boom caused them both to jump. Over a loudspeaker, a deep voice announced, "If I could have your attention please... Would everyone please stand and face the barge?"

Camara and Chase stood.

The announcer continued. "We take this time to remember all the men and women who have laid down their lives so that we might enjoy this glorious freedom we're celebrating today. And don't forget to thank God for this blessed nation we live in."

Camara's mouth dropped as they lit a huge fireworks display of the United States flag. Red, white, and blue blazed as "The Star-Spangled Banner" played. Tears pooled in Camara's eyes as overwhelming gratitude washed over her. She thanked God for not only the men and women who gave up their lives, but for those who were still fighting to give her the freedom she sometimes took for granted. And for the freedom she now enjoyed. Eyes closed, she tilted her face toward heaven and thanked God for His grace and mercy and prayed for protection over all those defending this wonderful country she lived in.

When she heard Chase sniff, she opened her eyes and looked into his. Sadness filled them. Before she had a chance to ask him what was wrong, he said on a choked whisper, "My best friend and cousin, James, died in the service a little over a year ago." He swiped his eyes.

Camara remembered how Swamper City had honored his heroic death. Her heart wrenched for Chase. . .and for his loss. "Oh, Chase. I'm so sorry." She pulled him into her arms and held him.

Loud booming caused them both to jerk but, not letting him go, she looked skyward. Colored confetti fell from the sky and reflected in the dark water. Chase wiped his eyes and smiled. Camara had never seen anything so beautiful: Chase's tender heart. His bright smile. And the huge gold, red, white, and blue fireworks drizzling from the sky and fizzling out. "Ooo," she drew out.

Chase sat down and pulled her next to him. She rested her head on his shoulder and stared above them as more fireworks dispelled the Alabama darkness.

Thirty minutes later when the sky lit up with the grand finale, Camara was a bit saddened, knowing her evening was about to come to an end. She loved being cradled in Chase's arms, and she didn't know when she'd had a better time. Who would have ever thought one of her best memories would be made with

Chase Lamar? When the fireworks display ended, she whispered, "Beautiful." She glanced up at Chase, who was staring at her.

"Yeah, she is."

Camara's eyes widened. He was talking about her, not the fireworks. As he leaned down to kiss her, her heart tripped over itself. What was happening to her? Was she falling in love with him?

# Chapter 15

Oh, Lolly, my date with Chase yesterday was so romantic." Camara took a bite of her pecan pie and chewed slowly as she contemplated just how much she should reveal to her friend. She didn't want her to tell Stan, who in turn might say something to Chase. Although no other man's kisses had affected her the way Chase's had, and no one else occupied her every thought like Chase did, she was still uncertain of her feelings toward him. Yes, she wanted to trust him. She wanted him to be the man he was on the boat and at the lake house, but was he really that person? The question would not leave her alone.

"What was so romantic?" Lolly tucked her unruly red curls behind her ears.

Camara looked at her friend. "All day long we talked about anything and everything. Then he took me out on his fancy speedboat." She gazed at her coffee. "We snuggled while we watched the fireworks."

Lolly sighed. "Then what happened?" She scooted forward.

Camara looked around the room, then at her friend. Lowering her voice, she added, "Good thing I was sitting when he kissed me because I wouldn't have been able to stand." Camara took a long drink of coffee.

"Sounds like a woman in love." Lolly's eyes looked dreamy.

Camara coughed and sputtered, patting her chest.

Lolly jumped up and started pounding her back. Camara shook her head and waved her off.

"Are you okay?"

"Fine, fine," she rasped, coughing some more.

Lolly handed Camara a glass of water. Camara sipped on it till her throat cleared. "Are you crazy? I am *not* in love with Chase Lamar."

Lolly stared at her. "Uh-huh. If you say so." Her friend's blue eyes twinkled. Lolly peeled off a piece of her honey bun, stuck it in her mouth, and smiled while she chewed.

Camara glanced at her watch. "Will ya look at the time? I'd better get out to Swamper's. I don't wanna be late. Besides, Stan will wonder where you are."

Lolly grabbed Camara's arm. "Just cool your jets, lady. You're always the first one to arrive. Besides"—Lolly glanced at the clock behind the counter at Tooties Gourmet Coffee Shop—"it's only 6:23. You still have plenty of time. And Stan knows exactly where I am. He also knows I'll be home in time to ride with him to Swamper's. Now quit stalling and spill."

"Spill what?"

Lolly sighed heavily. "Are you in love with Chase or what?"

"No. I am not in love with Chase. I told you that. A great kiss doesn't constitute love." Now if only she could convince her heart of that.

"Okay, I'll drop it. For now. But only if you tell me about the rest of your date."

Camara laughed as her friend shoved her plate with her partially eaten honey bun to the side and leaned forward. No wonder Lolly stayed so skinny; she ate like a newborn baby.

Camara finished the last bite of her pie, shoved the plate to the side, and leaned closer to Lolly. She motioned her to come closer with her finger. "No." She stood up, grabbed her yellow cap with the black Chevy emblem, plopped it on her head, and headed out the door.

"Meanie!" Lolly hollered at her.

Camara stepped out to the cloud-covered sky. It looked and smelled like rain. She wished she had grabbed her jacket. Lolly walked up beside her. "You know I'm gonna bug you until you tell me."

Camara smiled at her friend. "Yeah, I know. Tell Stan hello for me." Her brows furrowed. "Lolly." She laid her hand on her arm. "Please don't say anything to Stan." Her gaze fell to the concrete. "About Chase and me. I do have feelings for him, but I don't want Stan to say something to him or anyone else for that matter. This is all really new to me, and we don't need everyone asking questions. Please, promise me you won't say a word."

"I promise." She crossed her fingers over her heart. They hugged. "But remember, it's okay to love him, Cam." With that, her friend walked off to her car and got in. What was that all about? Shrugging the question off, Camara turned to her own vehicle as lightning zigged across the sky, followed by loud thunder. Camara jumped into her Hummer and drove off.

Thirty minutes later, Camara pulled into Swamper Speedway much later than normal. Her heart sped up at the sight of Chase's rig. In a weird way, her feelings for him frightened her. Camara hated that she couldn't seem to gain control over her emotions where Chase was concerned.

Chase stepped out from behind his trailer and glanced her way, motioning for her to park next to him. She sighed. He sure looked good. His blue denim jacket bulged where his biceps were. Those same biceps that held her yesterday.

Camara parked next to him and had barely shut off the engine before Chase opened her door and tugged her out and into his arms. She melted into his embrace.

"What do you think you're doing?" The voice snapped them apart.

Camara spun, nearly losing her balance, and found herself looking into Mr. Lamar's scowling face. *Oh, great.* Camara wanted to hop back into her vehicle and go as far away from his dad as possible. She took a step backward.

Chase draped his arm around her shoulder and tucked her close. "Morning, Dad."

"I told you to stay away from them Coles." He glared at her.

If venomous words had striking power, Camara knew she'd be dead.

"Listen, Chase," Camara said. "I need to unload my truck anyway. I'll talk to you later."

He let her go. She hated being in the middle of family squabbles. Especially this one.

Last night they'd had a deep conversation about how his dad felt about her family. Chase reassured her he refused to be a part of his dad's hatred toward her family. Still, it made her uncomfortable. A part of her never wanted to go near Chase again, but she enjoyed his company way too much to stay away forever. Even the *thought* of staying away from him forever drove fear through the middle of her. Seeing no other option, she did what she always did. "Father, please show me what to do," she whispered as she leaned over to remove a nylon strap from The Black Beast. "Please heal the rift between Chase's dad and my family. Thank You."

From the corners of her eyes, she watched Mr. Lamar get in his vehicle and head toward her. He stopped next to her and rolled down his window. "Stay away from my son, or you'll be sorry. This is the last time I'm gonna warn you." With that, he spun gravel and left. Lightning streaked across the sky and thunder bellowed, making her shiver.

"What did he say to you?" Chase asked from behind her.

Camara spun around. Chase's green eyes held concern. He put his arms around her and hugged her. "Please tell me."

She pulled back. "Can we talk about this later, Chase? I haven't even registered yet, and I have a few things to do." She fought to keep her tone light, but the aggravation she felt came through anyway.

He let her go. "I know a brush-off when I hear one."

Making sure his dad wasn't anywhere around, she laid her hand on his arm. "Look, I'm not giving you the brush-off." He didn't look convinced.

"Don't forget, Cam. In order for us to have a relationship, we have to trust each other. Communication is a part of trusting." He grabbed her hands. Electrical currents shot up her arms, and it wasn't from the lightning flashing around them, either.

"You still wanna be with me, don't you?" The uncertainty in his eyes broke her heart.

She stood on her tiptoes and planted a kiss on his cheek. "Does that answer your question?"

He frowned petulantly. "No."

She pulled his mouth down to hers and kissed him soundly. "Does that answer your question?"

"No," he answered, his eyes sparkling. "Still not clear."

"Oh, you." She shoved him away.

Chase pulled her back into his arms. Raindrops spotted her cheeks.

She wanted to stay in Chase's embrace, but his father's threat played over and over in her mind. Slowly she pulled away from him so as not to tip him off to her thoughts. "We'd better get our vehicles unloaded."

At that moment, the heavens opened. In the next second, sheets of rain poured on them. Chase grabbed Camara's hand, and they rushed toward his pickup and hopped in.

They sat inside his truck talking for about twenty minutes, his arm around her and she enjoying the safety it provided as they waited for the rain to subside. It took another ten minutes for the sun to peek through the clouds. When the last of the raindrops receded, they both hopped out. "We'd better get unloaded and then go register."

Camara nodded. She quickly unloaded the Beast, and the two of them headed toward the entry booth. By the time they reached the booth, the sun had retaken control of the sky. The thick humid air invaded Camara's lungs.

Chase finished filling out the forms before Camara. "I'll get us some coffee while you finish."

Camara glanced up from the clipboard. "Thanks." She went back to work on filling out the form. Ten minutes later, she finished. She handed the forms along with her fee to Sam, then perused the area looking for Chase. It sure was taking him a long time to get two cups of coffee. Where was he?

A few minutes later, Chase walked around the entry booth. "Sorry it took so long. They had to make more." He handed her a cup.

Warmth seeped into her hands. "I'm so glad you waited." She picked off the lid and blew into her coffee before taking a sip.

Camara and Chase laughed and joked all the way back to their vehicles. "I'll talk to ya later, Chase. I'm gonna check a few things on The Black Beast."

"Yeah, I have a few things to check, too."

"Bet you have more than a few things." She wrinkled her nose at him. "After all, it is a Ford."

Chase sent her a warning look. Camara winked at him.

When she got back and fired up the Beast, her heart sank at the sound. She put on the emergency brake, grabbed her stepladder, and popped the hood open.

Camara knew from the sound there were loose spark plug wires. She started checking them. Sure enough, three of them were loose. Someone had messed with her truck. . .again. But when? She looked around. Her gaze landed on Chase. She hated where her thoughts were going, but Chase had finished filling out the forms long before she had. And when he'd gone for coffee, it had taken an awfully long time. But then again, she needed to be careful not to judge him. *If we're gonna have a relationship, we have to trust each other.* Chase's words echoed through her mind. Desperately she wanted to.

"Lord, I'm asking You to please, please show me the truth. Expose whoever is doing this." She swallowed hard. "Even if it is Chase."

# Chapter 16

"Welcome to Swamper Speedway." The announcer's voice over the loud-speaker grabbed Chase's attention.

He'd drawn number one, so he was up first today. Lined up next to him was Bobby-Rae in his beat-up '36 Chevy pickup, Left Behind.

Chase glanced at the contestants' pit and noticed Camara still under the hood of her truck. He knew she'd drawn number three. Whatever she was doing, she needed to hurry up and get it done.

He tried to focus on the flagman, but every time he looked over and saw Camara with the hood still up, his concern increased. His belly sank. Had someone messed with it again?

Two bangs on his Coupe drew his attention. The flagman backed up and guided Chase as he inched his way to the starting line. His heart wasn't in this race. It was with Camara. "Lord, whatever is wrong with The Black Beast, let her get it fixed in time for her run."

It amazed Chase that he no longer cared about beating Camara. He still wanted to do his best, but secretly he wanted her to win. However, knowing how she felt, he'd drive his best and let her earn first place. If he let her win and she found out, she'd be furious with him.

The flag dropped.

Chase flew through the pit. He knew his lightning-fast run stemmed from sheer willpower to go see what was up with Camara's truck.

Without waiting to hear his time, he drove back to his trailer and hopped out. "John, would ya wash this off for me? I'm gonna go see if Camara needs help."

"Sure thing."

"Thanks." Chase sprinted toward Camara. "What's wrong?"

Camara ducked her head out from under the hood and looked at him. Her friendly demeanor and smile were nonexistent. He watched as she studied his face. "Someone messed with my truck again. The spark plug wires are loose, and there's a slit in the vacuum advance hose."

"What?" Chase stood on the tire and peered at her engine. "What can I do to help you get ready? You're up next."

"I don't have a spare hose, so I'll have to tape it for now. If you'll tighten the spark plug wires while I get some duct tape, that would be great."

He looked around. "Where's Erik? And the rest of your family?"

"There was a problem at the shop. Erik couldn't come." She grabbed the duct tape out of her toolbox. "Tony and Slick had to work, too." She climbed her ladder. "And Mom and Dad are at Civitan Park at the auto show with my car."

"Oh." Chase started tightening the wires.

They worked quickly together and finished just in time to hear the announcer's voice. "Last call for Camara Cole."

Chase gathered the tools and slammed the hood while Camara jumped inside and put on her helmet and gloves. She released the emergency brake. Chase motioned to her that all was clear. She backed up and headed toward the mud pits.

Chase watched her zip her way through the pit. Mud was slung twenty feet or more in the air. Her engine roared, giving him goose bumps. He still loved Fords and always would. But he had to admit The Black Beast was one mean running machine. For a Chevy.

He wondered who had messed with it again. His stomach wrenched as reality struck him. The reason Camara had acted differently toward him was because she probably thought he'd done it again. He knew he should have waited until she was finished before going for coffee. It wouldn't have taken so long if the young girl hadn't tipped over the huge coffeepot. She was lucky it didn't have much in it, or she would have been burned. He'd waited while she made another pot. Camara would probably never believe him. Would she ever learn to trust him? At this point, would he trust him if he were in her position? The only way to prove his innocence was to find out who was behind this.

🌼

Camara didn't know what to think. Why would Chase help her if he'd done it in the first place? Or was he just trying to throw her off? No, that didn't make sense. Whoever it was wanted to make her look bad and wanted her to lose. Well, their plan didn't work. Thanks to Chase's help, she didn't miss her run.

On her right, Camara watched as the flagman motioned Stan Morrison forward in One Bad Mudder. Lolly leaned around Stan and waved at Camara.

Camara revved her engine and waved back. It felt strange racing against her best friend's husband. Well, best friend or not, she had to do her best. She had to show whoever was behind this, making her look bad, that she wasn't a quitter. Her hands shook so badly she could barely grip the steering wheel, and her insides shook equally as bad. *I just have to win. I'll show you, whoever you are. You won't get the best of me. Oh, Lord. Why don't they just leave me alone? All I ever wanted to do was race and fix and build trucks. But no, they have to use my gender against me.* She snorted. *Like I can help that.*

The flag dropped.

Camara jerked her foot off the brake, floored the gas pedal, and dove into the pit. Mud covered her windshield as The Black Beast flew through the pit. She hung her head out the window and watched the side of the pit until she felt her truck leap out of the pit and land with a light thud. "What a rush!" Mud dripped from her arm.

Back at the contestants' pit, she ripped off her helmet, gloves, and harness. Chase yanked her door open and pulled her into a hug.

"What a run! You've heard of Jesus walking on water? Well, girl, you just walked on mud." He swung her around and planted a kiss on her muddy lips.

As his lips molded over hers, all doubts vanished. There was no way Chase had messed with her truck.

❀

When Chase raised his head, Camara giggled.

"What's so funny?"

"Now your lips are muddy, too." She reached up and ran her finger over his lip. Amid the grit, her fingers felt soft and warm. She stood on her tiptoes and kissed him, making his lips tingle.

They didn't hear the boots on the gravel. The voice was the first indication either of them had that they had an audience. "What would your father say if he could see you now?"

Camara jerked back. Bobby-Rae stood glaring at her.

"My father would tell me to do it again," she replied curtly.

"Not you. Him." He nodded toward Chase.

"What does it matter to you? And how do you know what my dad would think?" Who did this guy think he was anyway?

Big burly Bobby-Rae's cheeks flushed. "I. . ." He shifted his weight. "I heard him tell Camara that she'd better stay away from you, or she'd be sorry."

Chase looked at Camara as concern twisted through him. "Is that true?"

She nodded then glared at Bobby-Rae. "Don't you have anything better to do? Like go play in traffic or something?"

His smirk turned to a frown. He opened his mouth as if to say something, looked at Chase, then whirled and stormed off.

Camara shook her head. "He sure has changed. It's kinda sad. Before people started requesting me to fix their vehicles at work, Bobby-Rae and I used to have a lot of fun and were even friends. Now he's downright hateful since I turned him down." She jerked her head toward Bobby-Rae and looked at Chase.

"Turned him down for what?"

"Never mind."

The reality of what she wasn't saying crashed over Chase. Bobby-Rae must have asked her out, and she had turned him down. That explained why he was making her life miserable.

"Is it true what Bobby-Rae said? Did my dad threaten you again?"

She took three steps away from him to the power washer, but she didn't pick it up. "Yeah."

Chase stepped over to her and gathered Camara's hands in his. "Don't let my dad bother you, Cam. His bark is worse than his bite." As the words left Chase's mouth, a pit settled in his stomach. He no longer knew what his dad was capable of. Lately his father's obsession to ruin the Coles looked more and more dangerous. An awful thought slid through him. Certain his dad was somehow involved with Camara's truck incidents, he knew he had to figure out a way to prove his suspicions.

"I won't," Camara said softly. "I just feel bad that he hates us so much."

Chase was more than surprised when she wrapped her arms around him and laid her head against his chest. He drew her close and kissed the top of her head. Love for this woman compelled him to protect her. Even against his own father.

❧

"I'm hungry. How about you?" Camara asked, moving out of his arms.

"Do you think it's safe to leave The Black Beast?"

"I'll ask Lolly to keep an eye on it."

Camara grabbed her cell phone from her Hummer and called her friend. A minute later, she disconnected the call. "Okay, let's go."

At the concession stand, they each ordered fried chicken, nachos, and sweetened tea.

Camara set her food down and straddled the picnic bench. Chase lowered himself beside her, grabbed her hand, and bowed his head. "Father, we thank You for this food, and we ask You to bless it. And, Lord, please expose the person who's sabotaging Camara's truck. In Christ's name, amen."

Camara's heart chirped a happy tune. She truly believed if Chase was guilty, he would not have prayed about it.

"What are you smiling about?"

Returning his smile, she answered, "Nothing. Nothing at all." She leaned over and boldly kissed him.

# Chapter 17

The last day of the season's mud bog race dawned more perfect than if Camara had ordered it herself. Only one small cloud dotted the blue sky arching over the grandstand, which sported the white flag with the red Saint Andrew's cross. Just like her home state, it was simple yet etched in dignity. Over it flew the American flag, which brought goose bumps to her arms with the memory of Chase standing on a boat, his hand over his heart and tears in his eyes. Strange how even the smallest of things could make her think about him. Several people were already seated in the grandstands. More than forty mud bog trucks had showed up today for the final runs of the season.

Not threatened by any of them, Camara smiled. She knew she still had to deal with her prideful attitude and the need to prove herself, but if she beat Chase's time today, she'd be Swamper Speedway's mud bog champion. If not, they would most likely tie for first.

Wanting everything to be in tip-top shape, she popped open the hood, grabbed her stepladder, and bent over the engine.

❀

Weeks had passed since Camara and Chase had started seeing each other regularly. Chase discovered they had more in common than just their love of building and racing bog trucks, fixing and restoring vehicles, and God. They openly shared their thoughts, their feelings, and their dreams, which happened to crisscross each other very nicely. Greatest of all, though, was that Camara now trusted him.

Numerous times Chase had fought the urge to tell Camara he loved her. By her response to their conversations and his kisses, and by the way she looked at him, he thought she loved him, too. But until he knew for sure how she felt about him, he'd wait to voice his feelings.

Chase leaned across the seat of his '34 Ford Coupe feeling around on the floorboard for the fuse he'd dropped. Hearing his father's lowered voice, he froze, listening.

"Did you take care of it this time?"

"I sure did." The voice sounded familiar, but Chase couldn't quite place it.

"Did anybody see you?"

"Not a soul. This time should do the trick."

Chase heard a vile laugh that made his blood turn cold.

"Miss Hoity-Toity will finally be knocked off her high horse. And I'm gonna be right there when she is."

Chase strained to hear above the vehicles revving their engines around him.

"No one will get hurt, will they?" his father asked.

"What do you care? You paid me to do a job, and I did it."

"I paid you to make sure Chase won."

*What?* Chase couldn't believe what he'd just heard. How could his dad do that to him? Chase swallowed hard against the bitter bile rising up his esophagus. The urge to hop out and say something overwhelmed him, but he wanted to hear the whole conversation.

"He will. I made sure of that. In fact, I should pay you." The man's chuckle sounded demonic. "I've waited a long time to watch her fall flat on her face. Every time someone came into the shop, they'd always ask for Camara as if she were the only one good enough—"

Chase had heard enough. He flew out of the Mud Boss, infuriated at the very thought of anyone hurting Camara. His dad and Bobby-Rae stood a foot from his Coupe gawking at him. Chase seized the front of Bobby-Rae's shirt with his fists. "What did you do to Camara's truck?"

"Wouldn't you like to know?" he sneered.

"Tell me now, or I'll—"

"You'll what?" Bobby-Rae challenged. "Besides, it's too late to do anything about it now." The contemptuous way Bobby-Rae said it made Chase's stomach clench.

Before Chase could respond, his father asked, "What did you do to it, Bobby-Rae?" A frown marred his face.

"Let's just say she won't be doing any racing or anything else for quite some time."

His dad moved closer to Chase. "I didn't hire you to hurt her, only to make sure she didn't win."

His suspicions had been confirmed. But the very idea of his dad hiring someone to sabotage The Black Beast caused Chase's mind to nearly blow a gasket. His thoughts whirled with the ramifications of what Bobby-Rae could have done to Camara's truck.

"What did you do?" His father's commanding voice demanded an answer.

Chase fought the urge to run to Camara right then, but he figured it was best if he found out just exactly what Bobby-Rae had done.

A look of pride and a snide grin filled Bobby-Rae's face. "You told me to keep a close eye on what they do. Well, I learned one very important detail. Before starting the truck, Erik never checks the nitrous oxide switch cuz it ain't never turned on until Camara's lined up at the pit. So about an hour ago, I flipped it on."

"You what?" Chase's gaze darted toward the far end of the contestants' pit. His heart stopped beating. The hood was raised on The Black Beast, and all Chase could see was Camara's short legs and backside. His stomach lodged in his throat. "Lord, no!" She was leaning over the engine, and Erik was inside the cab. Why of all days had he been forced to park clear on the opposite end of the pits from her?

Without waiting for more explanation, Chase tossed Bobby-Rae to the side and took off at a dead run. "Camara!" he screamed at the top of his lungs. However, with all the mud bog vehicles revving their engines, the music blaring from the PA system, and people's laughter, she didn't even look his way. Chase slipped on the loose gravel and landed on his hands and knees. Ignoring the pain in his legs, he jumped up and willed his legs to go faster. "Erik, don't start the truck," he yelled. "Erik!"

❁

Standing on her stepladder in front of the fender well, Camara hollered, "Okay, Erik, fire her up."

*Kaboom!* Her head jerked up, slamming against the hood. Pain ricocheted through her hands, her face, and the back of her head. The world spun, and then everything turned black.

❁

It was as if Chase were watching a horror movie playing in slow motion. Metal particles flew from Camara's engine. Camara slumped to the ground next to the fender, limp as a rag doll.

"Caa-m-a-rr-aa!" His heart slammed against his ribs.

Chase and Erik reached her at the same time. She lay crumpled on her side in a heap.

"Cammy?" Erik's voice shook. "Oh no! No! Please no!"

Erik reached for her, but Chase clutched his arms. "Don't move her." His gaze landed on the back of Camara's head. Her beautiful blond hair was soaked with blood. And her arms had blood trailing down them. When his gaze landed on a piece of metal sticking out of her arm, Chase swallowed as he fought the urge to throw up.

*Oh, God, please let her be okay.*

A crowd gathered. Over the loudspeaker, Chase heard the announcer's voice. "We need the medics to the contestants' pit immediately. There's been an accident." A hush rushed through the grandstands.

He looked back at Camara's still form.

Mr. and Mrs. Cole knelt beside Camara and prayed for her. Comforted by their presence and prayers, peace washed over Chase.

The ambulance attendants arrived, and as one, everyone stepped back to let them through.

*God, please don't let anything happen to her. I need her.* Chase drew in a long, shaky breath and slowly exhaled, fighting to keep the fear from overpowering him as he watched them slowly roll her onto the loose gravel. Her face was streaked with oozing crimson streams. *Oh, God, help. I love her.*

In the middle of fear, anger snapped like lightning. None of this would have happened if it wasn't for his father's hatred toward the Coles...and his lack of confidence in Chase. Chase couldn't believe how much that thought hurt. For years he'd tried desperately to win his father's approval, only to fail over and over again.

"I'm sorry, son." Chase felt his father's hand on his shoulder. He looked over to see his father's repentant face. His being sorry wouldn't help Camara. Chase couldn't deal with him right now. As angry as he was, he knew it would be best if he just walked away until he had a chance to calm down. Besides, all he wanted to do was get to the hospital as soon as possible. He spun around. With his father on his heels, he headed toward his pickup and quickly unhitched the trailer.

"Where you going?" his father asked. "You have a race to finish."

Chase shook his head in utter disbelief. He must have imagined the look of repentance on his dad's face. He whirled, facing his father. "Winning is everything to you, isn't it? You don't even have the decency to feel bad that Camara is on her way to the hospital right now because of your obsession with destroying the Coles and winning. I hope you're happy now." He dug in his pockets. "Here are the keys to the Mud Boss. You wanna win so bad, you drive. I've got more important things to do." He started his Ford Power Stroke pickup, ground it into gear, and spun out.

On the way to the hospital, he prayed, "Lord, how can I ever forgive my father for what he's done to Camara? I know I'm to show him the love of Christ, but how do you deal with somebody like him? His obsession could have killed Camara."

He closed his eyes at the thought that he wasn't sure it hadn't. At the sound of a horn honking, his eyelids flew open. He swerved back into his own lane and mouthed an apology to the lady driver shaking her fist at him.

At the hospital, Chase parked his truck and sprinted into the emergency room entrance. Camara's dad and Erik were talking to a staunch-looking nurse.

Chase stopped several yards away from them. Did he have a right to be here, knowing his dad was responsible? They hadn't seen him yet. However, before he had a chance to leave, Erik and Mr. Cole spotted him and walked over to him.

"How's she doing?"

"The doctor's in with her now. Mom said she'd let us know as soon as she knows anything." Erik's eyes glistened, and worry lines etched his forehead. "This is all my fault. I should have checked everything before I started it up."

He couldn't let Erik blame himself, knowing the truth. "I need to tell y'all something." At their nodding assent, Chase motioned for them to follow him. How would Erik and Mr. Cole feel about him once they found out the truth?

They went to the empty waiting area and sat. Event by event, Chase explained everything.

Erik shook his head. "I know your dad hates us, but this has got to stop."

"It will."

Chase's gaze darted toward the sound of his father's voice. "What are you doing here?" Chase ground out. "Haven't you done enough damage for one day?"

Mr. Cole laid his hand on Chase's arm and signaled Chase with a slight shake of his head.

*God, help me here.* For a single second, he thought about Camara's counting-to-ten tactic, but that thought just slammed more anger into him.

However, seeing his father's haggard face—bowed with guilt and remorse—softened him. His father looked at Erik and extended his hand.

Erik stood and accepted his proffered hand.

Next he extended his hand to Mr. Cole. Chase couldn't have been more shocked if a lightning bolt had hit him. If he hadn't seen it with his own eyes, he'd never have believed it. His dad was actually shaking the hand of not just one Cole, but two.

"I know it's too late to say I'm sorry." His dad looked at the floor and released Mr. Cole's hand. "But I am." He looked at Erik and Mr. Cole and then at Chase. "More than y'all will ever know." Mr. Lamar motioned to a nearby seat. "May I?"

Mr. Cole nodded. "Please."

When all three were seated, his dad looked at Chase then at Mr. Cole. "I never meant for Camara to get hurt, Landon. I know that's hard to believe considering how I've done everything in my power to make you pay for what you did to me." He rubbed the back of his neck.

Chase darted a glance in Mr. Cole's direction, scoping out his response. All he saw was love, mercy, and compassion. He no longer wondered how Mr. Cole felt after he heard the news that his dad was behind Camara's accident. Chase forced back the tears stinging his eyes and focused his attention on his dad.

"Ever since that day in our senior year of college"—his dad's gaze looked distant as if he'd slid back in time—"when that pro football scout offered me a job after I graduated from college, I couldn't wait to tell you and Cassandra. But when I found my girlfriend with her arms around my best friend's neck and the two of you kissing, I felt betrayed and angry. All I remember is punching you in the face several times and then being slammed into the ground. When I woke up in the hospital, the doctor informed me I'd suffered a blow to the head and had been in a coma for nearly three days. Like it was no big deal, the doctor said, 'Sorry, young man. But pro football isn't in your future. No one can risk hiring you after a head injury like this.'"

His dad closed his eyes briefly then looked right at Mr. Cole. "Every time I watched a football game and was reminded of what I'd lost, all I wanted was to make you pay for destroying my career. Because you were always big into Chevys and I was always into Fords, when you bought a Chevrolet dealership, I figured the one way to get even with you was to buy a Ford dealership and take business away from you."

He sat, shaking his head, his gaze on the floor. "And every time you bought another dealership, I did. When that didn't work, I tried everything I could think of to make your business and your kids look bad. But nothing worked. So when I overheard Bobby-Rae telling another guy that he'd had it up to his scalp with Camara Cole and he'd do anything to make her look bad, I saw another opportunity to get even with you." He shook his head. "But I never meant for this to happen." Seeing his superior, I'm-in-control father broken melted Chase's anger.

"Barry, I'm so sorry." Mr. Cole exuded compassion. "There's nothing I can say or do to change what's happened. But I'm asking you to hear my side. Please?"

Mr. Lamar gave a quick nod.

"You know how Cassandra was the biggest flirt on campus and kissed any man in a football jersey."

Mr. Lamar briefly closed his eyes and nodded.

"Well, that night she'd had one too many to drink. I told her she needed to go home and sleep it off. She asked if I'd join her. Before I had a chance to respond, she threw her arms around my neck and kissed me." He swiped his lips. "When you grabbed me and started decking me, all I wanted to do was stop you from using my face as a punching bag. I never meant for you to get hurt when I tackled you to the ground." He moved his head from side to side in slow motion. "I never saw that rock." The look in Mr. Cole's eyes when he gazed at his dad begged him to believe he was telling the truth. "I tried so many times to tell you I didn't betray you, but I couldn't get you to really hear what I was saying." Sadness dimmed his eyes. "I've always loved you, Barry. Like a brother. Still do."

His dad's eyes widened. He shook his head. "I should have read the letters you sent me and taken your calls. But I couldn't. I blamed you, and I wanted to hurt you like you hurt me. I was wrong. And now Camara is paying for my bitterness." He ran his hand over his face.

Erik pulled himself to his feet. "Speaking of Camara, I wanna check on her."

"Me, too." Mr. Cole stood.

Chase and his dad rose. "If y'all don't mind, I'd like to go, too."

"Of course." Mr. Cole didn't hesitate to agree, much to Chase's relief.

Chase turned to his dad. He grabbed him and hugged him. "I love you, Dad." Chase pulled back. "Do you wanna come with us?"

"No." Mr. Lamar shook his head. "I'm tired. I need to go home and rest." He shook Erik's and Mr. Cole's hands. "Thanks for understanding, Landon. I'm really sorry about everything."

When his father turned and strode off with his shoulders hunched, Chase wondered if he was really going to be okay. In fact, he wondered if any of them would ever be okay again.

# Chapter 18

Right before closing time, two weeks after her accident, Camara stood outside Mr. Lamar's main Ford dealership office. *Lord, give me the courage to talk to him.* She drew in a deep breath and knocked softly on his door, almost hoping he wouldn't be there.

"Mr. Lamar, may I speak with you, please?" Camara trembled as she pushed the door open. It wasn't from fear of him but fear of him rejecting her.

"Camara." Shock and uncertainty marred the older man's features. He slowly rose. "Come on in." His voice quavered.

She couldn't believe how haggard he looked. In fact, he looked worse than she did with the jagged gash that now made a diagonal across her forehead. Camara walked into his office and closed the door. He stood in front of his chair, facing her. Camara drew in a deep breath.

"Chase told you everything, didn't he?"

Boy, he didn't waste any time. "Yes, he did. But that's not why I'm here." At his puzzled look, Camara continued. "I wanted to let you know that I won't be pressing any charges."

She had wanted to tell Bobby-Rae the same thing, but he'd skipped town. With all her heart, Camara wished she could have convinced Swamper Speedway not to press charges against either man, but they had anyway. The trial was pending. With any luck, Mr. Lamar would only have to pay a hefty fine and do community service.

Mr. Lamar's eyes widened, and relief flooded his features, making him instantly look ten years younger. It was the first time Camara had seen him speechless. He motioned for her to sit down. Camara lowered herself into a mahogany leather chair. It squeaked as she crossed her legs. "I came to let you know I understand why you paid Bobby-Rae to sabotage my truck." The words, though skittish and slow, were coming easier than she had imagined they would.

"It all seems so foolish now." Mr. Lamar's gaze roamed over her singed, scab-streaked arms and then over the gash on her head. "I can't tell you how sorry I am."

Camara's heart went out to him. She'd never seen him look so vulnerable. Most of the time he reminded her of Goliath the giant: in control, prideful, powerful, arrogant, and extremely intimidating. But not now. Not today.

"I understand," Camara said softly. "Winning was everything to me, too. My obsession with proving I was just as good a driver and mechanic as any man drove me to do some foolish things." She looked down at her lap as shame washed over her afresh. "My foolish pride nearly cost me my life. . ." Drawing in a shaky breath, she looked at him. "Twice."

Her arm itched where the stitches had just been removed. She subconsciously rubbed it lightly.

Mr. Lamar's gaze seemed anchored to the table. "I never meant for you to get hurt."

"I know. Chase told me."

He never looked up.

She uncrossed her legs and rose. "Well, I've taken up enough of your time."

Instantly he looked at her and walked around the desk. "Thank you for not pressing charges, Camara. And for being so understanding."

Camara chuckled. "Don't thank me, Mr. Lamar. Thank the Lord. If it wasn't for Him humbling me and showing me three very important lessons, I'd still be a prideful brat."

He smiled and paused. "And what lessons are those?"

Surprised that he asked, Camara responded, "One. . .pride only brings destruction and misery to yourself and to those you love." She darted a quick glance at the ceiling. "I learned that the hard way." He nodded his agreement. "Two. . .I was so obsessed with proving to everyone I could build and race as good as any man that I neglected to work on what was really important: building inner character and walking in love." She stopped and let that sink in. When understanding crossed his face, she went on. "And three. . .it's not about winning. It really is about how you play the game."

He nodded, and a hint of a smile flashed through his eyes.

"Well, thank you for seeing me, Mr. Lamar." She turned and started to walk away.

"Camara?"

She stopped and turned. "Yes?"

The humility on his face showed how hard it was for him to look at her. "You'll never know how much your coming here today means to me. Thank you."

"You're welcome." She smiled. With her heart lighter than it had been in weeks, she nearly floated to her car.

✿

Chase and Camara walked into the sanctuary of the church and sat in the last pew. Everyone came up to Camara and asked how she was doing. Chase knew she still had headaches a lot and that her arms and head were still tender where the burns and gashes were.

He looked up at the enormous royal blue banner hanging on the wall at the opposite end of the pew. In gold letters, he read 1 Corinthians 13:4–8: "Love suffers long and is kind; love does not envy; love does not parade itself, is not puffed up; does not behave rudely, does not seek its own, is not provoked, thinks no evil; does not rejoice in iniquity, but rejoices in the truth; bears all things, believes all things, hopes all things, endures all things. Love never fails."

He looked at Camara and smiled. She slipped her soft hand into his and returned his smile.

Although the sign spoke of God, Camara had suffered long at Chase's hands, his father's hands, and the hands of her fellow workers and racers. She had every right to be angry with all of them, but instead she chose to walk in love. She forgave them all, and she'd even gone to his father's work and shown *him* love. Love for her radiated from the center of Chase's soul.

Camara's eyes widened as she glanced past Chase's shoulder. "Mr. Lamar!"

Chase jerked his head around. "Dad! What are you doing here?"

"I came to see what my family found so fascinating." He extended his hand toward Camara. "Hello, Camara. Good to see you again."

Chase was speechless. All he could do was stare.

With a glint in his eye, his father smiled. "Aren't you going to ask me to sit down?"

Chase had never seen his father like this before. Camara tugged on his hand and moved down. "Oh. . .um. . .yeah."

His father's smile widened as he sat down next to Chase.

During the service, the pastor talked about God's powerful love and forgiveness. And how there was nothing too big or too bad that God would not forgive. Chase glanced at his father. Tears trickled down his cheeks. Chase silently interceded for his father's soul to be saved.

At the end of the service, the pastor asked anyone who wanted to be forgiven of their sins and to accept God's free gift of love and salvation to come forward. Without hesitation, Chase's dad stood and walked down the aisle. Dumbstruck, Chase looked at Camara. Her face was wet with tears. Part of his prayers had just been answered. Now the only unanswered prayers remaining were for his parents to get back together again and for Camara to say yes to his proposal.

☙

Everyone stood around Mr. Lamar congratulating and welcoming him into the family. Camara was the first to hug him.

He whispered next to her ear. "It's all because of you, you know. Your actions yesterday showed me what true Christianity is all about. Love and forgiveness." His gaze caught hers as he gently patted her back. "Thank you."

Camara's heart swelled. A shudder vibrated through her at the thought of what might have happened if she would have been vengeful and pressed charges.

Outside the church, under the hot Alabama sun, Mr. Lamar stopped and faced them. "This stuff is new to me. But will you two pray for me?" He looked at Chase. "I'm going straight to your mother's place and ask her to forgive me for being such a prideful fool." He smiled at Camara then looked back at Chase. "And to see if she'll take me back."

❀

"Where are we going?" Camara asked Chase for the third time.

"You're not very patient, are you?" he asked with a smile in his voice.

"No, I'm not."

Twenty minutes later, Chase turned at the Swamper Speedway entrance. Camara looked at him and frowned. "Why are we coming here? Nothing's scheduled for today."

"You'll see." Chase stopped the vehicle behind the wall of dogwood trees and looked at Camara. "Close your eyes and don't peek until I tell you, okay?"

Camara let out a slow, dramatic breath. Chase chuckled. "Such a drama queen, you are. Just close your eyes."

Camara slapped his arm and closed her eyes. Chase couldn't resist. He leaned toward her and gave her a long, lingering kiss. When he pulled away, Camara slowly opened her eyes with raised brows. "Is that why you wanted my eyes closed?"

"Nope." He smiled. "I just couldn't resist those pouty lips. Now promise me you won't open your eyes again until I say it's okay."

Camara gave him a pretend annoyed look; then she nodded and pinched her eyes shut.

Chase drove down the long lane toward Swamper Speedway and pulled into the center of the oval racetrack. "Don't forget. No matter what, don't open your eyes, okay?"

"I got it already." She giggled.

After shutting the truck off, Chase got out and grabbed her hand and helped her out. "Don't look, okay?"

"I won't." Her voice sounded impatient.

Chase gently led her up the three steps into the white lattice gazebo.

"Don't move or open your eyes yet." He let go of her hand, lit the candle, filled their glasses, and turned on the hidden video camera in the corner; then he went back to her. Making sure he was out of the camera's way, Chase stood off to the side and fixed his gaze on Camara's face. "You can open your eyes now."

❀

Camara opened her eyes and gasped. She was standing inside the most beautiful white lattice gazebo she'd ever seen. Lined along the walls of the gazebo were vases filled with hundreds of yellow daisies. Her favorite flower. For as long as she could remember, her daddy had given her a bunch of yellow daisies every time she was sad or discouraged. He said they would cheer her up. And they did. A smile lifted the corners of her lips.

She continued perusing the gazebo. In the middle was a small round table with a white lacy tablecloth draped over it and two white wicker chairs. In the center of the table sat a ring of yellow daisies wrapped around a tall crystal votive cup with a yellow candle inside. Two silver covered dishes with yellow linen napkins and silverware were set on the table, along with two crystal goblets filled with a clear sparkly beverage.

She looked at him as awe and thankfulness filled her soul. "Oh, Chase. It's beautiful." Her forehead wrinkled. "What's the occasion?"

Chase stood for one more second, cleared his throat, then dropped to one knee in front of her. Her heart leaped out of her chest, and her stomach did the dance of a million butterflies.

"Camara Chevelle Cole, I love you with all my heart, and I hope you love me, too. Will you marry me?" The hopeful look on his face crushed her. Didn't he know she loved him? Of course not. She'd only implied it, not spoken it. But then again, neither had he—until now.

"Oh, Chase, I love you, too." She nodded so fast she thought her neck might snap. "Of course I'll marry you." She tugged his arms until he stood. Carefully she placed her arms around him and kissed him soundly.

When she pulled back, Chase reached inside his pocket and pulled out a model of a Dodge pickup. Camara raised her brows.

He opened the hood. Inside lay a glistening daisy-shaped ring with a large diamond in the center surrounded by yellow diamonds. "Oh, Chase." They were the only two words she could find in her heart. Tears pooled in her eyes as she looked up at him. "I've never seen anything so beautiful in my life."

Chase took the ring out and slid it on her left ring finger. After a kiss that left her weak in the knees, she glanced at the Dodge model still in his hand. "But, what's with the Dodge?"

"Well." He took a step back and looked at her. "I figured you'll always be a Chevy lover. And I'll always be a Ford fan. So, to stop any fighting before it gets started, I thought we should compromise and build a Dodge mud bog truck together and call it. . ." He turned the model sideways until she could see the name on the door.

Camara threw her head back and laughed. "X-Rivals. . ." She drew out the last word in a deep masculine voice. "Domination."

# Epilogue

Camara stepped out of her parents' car and looked around. Of all the fancy places in town where they could have gotten married, they chose Swamper Speedway. Both sets of parents thought they were nuts, but to Chase and Camara, this place was and always would be special.

The early spring day felt hand chosen, as well. The endless blue sky seemed to smile down its approval on them. The dogwood trees on the east end of Swamper Speedway were in full bloom, a symbol of a new beginning, just like her and Chase.

The parking lot was filled to capacity with their guests' vehicles. At the far end of the contestants' pit, she spotted Chase's truck and smiled. Today she would become Mrs. Chase Lamar. Her insides trembled with excitement.

"Come on, dear. You don't want Chase to see you," her mother coaxed. Arm in arm, they sashayed toward the makeshift tent dressing room. Inside, Camara stared in the mirror. Her mother stood behind her, shaking her head.

"Well, one thing's for certain. There's never been another bride anywhere dressed like you." Her mom smiled. "Somehow I imagined my only daughter's wedding differently. I envisioned white lace, long sleeves, a beaded dress with a long train and veil." Her mother chuckled. "Not loose-fitting white coveralls, white steel-toed work boots, and a white lacy cap with a yellow Chevy emblem and a waist-length veil."

Her mother turned Camara around and kissed her cheek. "I can honestly say, though. . .this outfit definitely fits you."

"Cammy, can I come in?" Lolly's voice sang from outside.

"Come in."

"Hurry up, Lolly. Only ten minutes until the ceremony," her mother playfully chastened. When Lolly entered, Camara's mom did a slow inspection of her attire, as well. "I like the coveralls."

Behind her mother's back, Camara winked at Lolly.

Her mother turned back and pulled Camara into a hug. "I love you, sweetheart. See you out there." She turned and left.

Camara and Lolly burst out laughing. "Won't they all be surprised?"

Lolly reached into her satchel and handed Camara a portion of their surprise. Camara tucked them in the pockets of her coveralls and peeked outside through a small slit. She stared at the exact gazebo where Chase had proposed to her. Almost everything was the same. Yellow daisies lined the wall, and a small round table sat in the middle. But instead of the crystal votive cup with the yellow candle in the center, a four-foot-tall trophy, the one she and Chase had won with their tied points, stood in the middle. They had opted to forgo a tiebreaker and had chosen instead to share the title. Chase and Camara had asked Dan if he would agree to have their winning trophy sport The Black Beast on the left, the Mud Boss on the right, and above those two the X-Rivals Domination Dodge truck. Dan thought it was a great idea and gladly obliged.

She gazed at Erik, standing front and center, waiting for Chase and the pastor to make their entrance. As Chase's best man, Erik was the one person who had been there for both of them through even the rough patches. She wondered where she would be without her beloved brother's constant support and his belief in both her and Chase.

"You ready, Camara?" her dad called from outside the small tent.

"Yes, Daddy."

The band started playing the Beach Boys' song "409." "That's your cue, Lolly."

Camara moved out of the way. Lolly pulled the drawstring on the tent opening, lifting it like a swag.

They picked up their daisy bouquets held together with new spark plug wires. Camara watched her guests' mouths fall open as Lolly strolled out of the tent and up the yellow runway. Inwardly she giggled.

When Lolly took her place up front, "The Wedding March" started.

Camara clutched her father's arm tighter. Her knees felt weak.

"You okay, baby girl?"

"I'm fine, Daddy."

"Have I told you lately how proud I am of you?" His eyes registered the love he had for her. "You've grown into a fine young lady."

Camara looked at her coveralls and then up at her daddy. They both chuckled.

When they stepped in view of the guests, gasps rippled through the crowd. She looked at Chase. There was surprise for only a second, then a smile so broad she thought his face would crack from the strain to his lips. She sent him a quick smile and a wink.

Three steps down the aisle, Camara stopped. Her father looked at her with concern.

"Would you hold this, please, Daddy?" She handed him her bouquet.

Camara leaned over. Making sure she didn't mess up her grease-free, French-manicured nails, she removed the steel-toed work boots and exposed her bare, light yellow pedicured toes. She reached into the pockets of her coveralls, pulled out a pair of white strap sandals, and placed them next to her feet. Then she unzipped her coveralls, pulled the sleeves off her shoulders, and stepped out of them. While slipping her feet inside the sandals, she heard her guests gasping again, followed by oohs and aahs.

When she straightened, everyone was smiling, and several were shaking their heads and laughing.

Underneath the coveralls, she had on a white, lacy-sleeved, beaded wedding dress that hugged her tiny waist. The scarf-style hem flowed freely to her knees in the front and hung to her calves in the back. Camara caught her mother's glistening eyes as she dabbed at them with her white linen hankie. Camara smiled at her mother then signaled Lolly to step out of her coveralls. She looked beautiful in her light yellow scarf-style dress.

"Come on, Daddy." She looped her arm in his, satisfied that everything was now perfect. As they headed toward Chase, who looked drop-dead gorgeous in his black-tailed tuxedo and light yellow shirt, she captured his approving gaze and willed her eyes to show him how much she loved him.

After Pastor Stephans had them repeat their vows, he said, "You may now kiss the bride."

Chase's lips melded with hers in a heart-stopping, knee-buckling kiss. His grip tightened as he held her up. When they pulled apart, Pastor Stephans announced, "I'm pleased to present to you Mr. and Mrs. Chase Lamar."

Camara looked at her guests. Her gaze landed on her new father- and mother-in-law and sister-in-law, Heather. Mr. Lamar winked at her and then smiled lovingly at his wife. Camara refused to cry. Mrs. Lamar had profusely told Camara how grateful she was for her part in her husband coming to the Lord. And how happy she was to be living under the same roof again with the man she had never stopped loving. . .or praying for.

Camara squeezed her newly wedded husband's hand and smiled at him. Now he had two loving families. And so did she.

After they cut the cake, Camara grabbed Chase's hand and tugged him outside the huge tent. His steps thumped next to hers, trying to keep up. "Where are we going?"

"You're not very patient, are you?" She winked at him.

Chase snickered. "Already throwing my words back at me, are you? This doesn't bode well."

"Close your eyes, and don't open them until I tell you it's okay."

"Again with my words."

Camara stopped and put her hands over his eyes to force them closed. "Okay, don't open them until I tell you."

"Okay, I get it." Chase imitated her annoyed tone.

Camara pulled the soft car cover off and tossed it on the ground.

"Okay, you can open your eyes now."

Chase's eyes bulged with shock. "What's this?" he asked, gaping at the silver 1971 Mach 1 he'd seen at the car show.

"My wedding present to you."

"What? When? How?" Chase stammered, running his hands over the metal.

"When you said you'd been trying to find one for years, I got the guy's number and offered him a deal he couldn't refuse."

Shaking his head slowly, Chase pulled Camara into his arms. "Thank you, sweetheart." He kissed her.

"You're welcome," she whispered against his lips.

Several hours later, toward evening, Camara slipped back into her coveralls. They said good-bye to their guests and strolled hand in hand toward the Dodge X-Rivals Domination bog truck.

"I get to drive," Camara said.

"No, I'm driving."

"No fair," Camara argued as they continued their way toward the truck and the mud pit. "Why should you go first?"

"Cuz I'm the man." He winked.

"Well, haven't you ever heard of"—she smiled coyly—"ladies first?"

Chase handed her the keys. "Okay, you win."

"I sure did." She kissed him. "I won the best man in the whole world." She handed him the keys and ran around to the passenger's side and hopped in.

They glanced at their guests watching them from a distance and waved. Then each grabbed their harnesses.

With tin cans and streamers hanging all over the Dodge, her husband started the truck and revved the engine. The perfectly running engine sent goose bumps all throughout Camara's body. "Something else we have in common."

Chase looked at her, puzzled. She pointed at his hands and legs. "You shake before a race, too."

Chase smiled at her. "What can I say? Adrenaline rush."

Camara nodded her agreement. She knew the feeling only too well.

John raised the flag and dropped it.

Chase gunned the engine. Excitement coursed through Camara's veins as they dropped into the mud pit. Goose bumps rose on her flesh as Camara watched Chase's biceps bulge under the strain of keeping the truck inside the pit. She smiled as she thought about how many times those strong arms had held her and how many times they would hold her in the years to come. Quick as a flash, up and out of the pit they flew.

Erik rushed to their window and gave them their time: 7.46. Chase's smile matched her own. They had just broken both of their own records at Swamper Speedway. Together their combined skills and expertise had paid off. Their new Dodge truck, X-Rivals Domination, truly dominated in both speed and power.

As fast as her fingers would allow, Camara unlatched her harness; then in two long scoots, she slid over to Chase's side.

In the privacy of their mud-encased truck, they wrapped their arms around each other and sealed their rivalry's end with a long, passionate kiss.

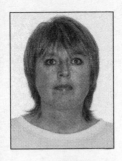

DEBRA ULLRICK

Debra is married to her real-life hero of thirty-four years. She has one grown daughter who is married to a wonderful man. Debra and her husband lived and worked on cow-calf ranches in the Colorado Mountains for over twenty-five years. Recently, they moved to the flatlands. Mud-bog racing, classic cars, monster trucks, writing, reading, drawing western art, watching Jane Austen movies, feeding wild birds, and playing with her Manx cat occupies most of Debra's time. Plus, she loves to hear from her readers. You can email her at christianromancewriter@gmail.com. To check out Debra's other books, visit her Web site at www.DebraUllrick.com.